The Girl Who Fled the Picture

Jane Anderson

HOWE STREET
PUBLISHING

My journey to publication has been a long one and not all my early supporters are still with us.

For Edma, Gill and Sarah
I miss you

About the Author

Jane Anderson is an Edinburgh based writer of historical fiction. Born in Fife, Jane originally studied English Literature at Edinburgh University. She spent most of her working life living in countries as far-flung as Vietnam, Azerbaijan and most recently, Egypt. She has travelled extensively, including frequent visits from Cairo to both Istanbul and Rome, immersing herself in their ancient cultures and histories. Retelling history from the point of view of women is where the fun begins.

This novel was inspired by a Jean-Étienne Liotard painting, sometimes called *The Girl with a Book*. You can see the image and discover the story behind the inspiration on Jane's website:

https://jane-anderson.co.uk/

Chapter One

Buda, Hungary, April 1742

Isabella feigned an innocent smile, as Uncle Richard quoted Mr Collins an exorbitant price for the gold necklace. Collins' Adam's apple bobbed up and down. He coughed and laid the heavy cascade of amethysts back on the table. 'On reflection, I believe my fiancée has a similar piece.'

Brazen liar, she thought.

'Is your heart set on a necklace?' Richard Godfrey asked. 'I have several lovely brooches. Or would you consider a piece made of silver?'

Isabella had already warned Uncle Richard that this one wouldn't go for gold. She'd endured his company touring the sights of Buda for two whole days. Her uncle had struck up a conversation with Collins and pretended that his gout left him unable to take Isabella sightseeing. Mr Collins fell for the trap and requested she join him on excursions with his tour guide. Unfortunately, Collins had talked over their knowledgeable guide, then failed to tip him. Isabella usually felt sorry for the wealthy tourists her uncle fleeced, but Edward Collins was a miserly, pompous idiot.

1

An uncharitable thought; had her heart become hardened by weeks of pretending to be something she was not? She'd agreed to Uncle Richard's scheme reluctantly, charming these Grand Tour travellers with the specific aim of turning them into clients. She thought it a sordid transaction but she'd also discovered that the art of bland conversation was hard work. This man wasn't interested in her, he was travelling through Europe gathering objects and she was merely a temporary acquisition, a pretty accessory.

Mr Collins peered over the array of jewellery, his head so close to Richard's that their wigs collided sending up a puff of starch. Despite this, his whisper was clearly audible.

'Thing is, Mr Godfrey, Isabella's company has so enriched my stay in Buda that I'd like my budget to cover a gift for her too.'

It was amazing how these English gentlemen with their booming voices seemed to think her deaf as well as stupid. Of course stupidity was not an unreasonable conclusion after her simpering performance.

'Take a look at these brooches, Mr Collins. This one is set with splendid aquamarines.'

'And what stone is this?' Collins asked, picking up the paste brooch.

'That, sir, is a strass, a new continental fashion. We've only just started using this special glass and it offers excellent value.'

Uncle Richard looked up and blinked twice, the signal that he wanted her help.

'I so love these strasses.' She picked up the paste brooch. 'Look how they sparkle, why a girl would feel like she was wearing diamonds.'

Isabella turned the brooch to catch the light.

'It's remarkably convincing,' Mr Collins agreed.

'Would you bring us some brandy please, Isabella,' Uncle Richard said.

Isabella left the room, closing the door behind her. Collins would no doubt assume the brandy was in some pantry, or on an elegant sideboard. In fact, it sat with two glasses on a shelf in her bedroom cupboard. Fetching brandy was a ruse to leave while Uncle Richard talked money, and their two small bedrooms were the only other rooms in this apartment. She knew to give them five minutes.

These boarding house rooms suited their needs because of the decent parlour for receiving guests, whilst the meagre bedrooms meant the cost was not too high. Isabella opened her window, the old whorled glass let in light but gave no view. She kicked off her shoes and climbed up onto the deeply recessed window sill, hugging her knees while she looked down on the cobbled street below. The road was empty but for a patient donkey standing motionless in front of a cart. Buda was disappointing after three extraordinary weeks in Vienna, where the streets thronged with people day and night.

Isabella had turned fifteen in February and her uncle had declared it time to put her genteel lessons to use. They'd practised their act through the small towns of France and Switzerland. By the time they'd reached Vienna, Issy was confident of her ability to talk to rich strangers. She walked into the dining rooms of expensive hotels with an easy manner. That they normally lived in three dingy rooms above the jewellery workshop in London, was their secret.

A boy appeared and jumped up behind the donkey, the jingle of the harness faded as they disappeared around the corner. Isabella sighed and climbed down. She had to stretch to relieve the discomfort where her boned stays dug into her stomach. A lady's outfit was most uncomfortable.

· · ·

3

Both men smiled at her when she returned and poured two brandies. Mr Collins raised his in a toast and handed her the velvet box.

'A small token of my esteem, Miss Godfrey. This is the last stop on my European tour and your companionship has made it the highlight.'

She thanked him and curtsied. When their glasses were drained he picked up his hat.

'Will you change your mind about the theatre, Isabella? I've taken a box.'

'Unfortunately we have a commitment tomorrow evening,' Uncle Richard said.

'Then I look forward to seeing you in the afternoon. If it's dry we could walk by the river,' Mr Collins added.

Isabella lit her chamberstick from the candelabra and went to the door.

'I'll see you out, Mr Collins. Be careful on the stairs and remember our landlady is on the lower level, we promised her no noise.'

She held the candle aloft creating a pool of light in the dark passage, then preceded him down the stairs. Just before they reached the front door the man pressed her against the wall, one hand on her breast and the other pulling up her skirts.

'No,' she said, and tried to push him away.

He silenced her with his mouth, no tender kiss but another assault. She struggled and dropped the chamberstick, plunging them into darkness. Panic gave her new strength and she burst out of his grasp. He growled deep in his throat like an animal.

The sound of footsteps above and a flicker of light signalled Uncle Richard's approach. He appeared holding the candelabra at the top of the stairs.

'Is everything all right?' he asked.

'All fine thank you, Mr Godfrey, only Isabella dropped the candle. I'll be on my way now.'

He adjusted his hat and looking her straight in the eye, winked at her. She was about to slap him when their landlady cracked open her door.

'See you tomorrow,' he said, then left.

'Thankfully not,' she muttered under her breath.

'He gave you some trouble?' her uncle asked when they were back in their chambers.

'The rogue thought a paste brooch bought him intimate privileges.'

Her uncle shook his head. 'Precisely why we never let you go to a box. We should have taken him for the aquamarines.'

'The amethyst necklace wouldn't make the swine tolerable.'

Her uncle went to bed and Isabella tidied all the jewellery back into the cabinet. The familiar routine calmed her nerves while she replayed what had happened in her head. She felt sick and her skin crawled with repugnance. In her room she stripped naked and poured water into a basin, she scrubbed herself to banish his touch. Isabella swilled a mouthful of brandy and swallowed it with a shudder. Men had over-stepped the mark before but this time she'd felt in real danger. She wished she'd kicked him.

Issy retrieved the brooch from the pocket in her petti-coat. She ran her fingertip over the fine engraving and felt how each stone was set firmly and in perfect alignment. This was her own work and she'd been proud of it. Now she grimaced, that man had sullied the piece. She'd have to rework it.

. . .

The next morning they were in their carriage leaving Buda just before daybreak. They exited every city in the dark. Uncle Richard swore they were doing nothing illegal, but they always left without a goodbye or any mention of their destination.

'I think I'll look for a boat in the next town. I'm told the Danube is a quicker route south and there seems no point in lingering. There were few enough tourists in Buda and it will only get worse,' Uncle Richard said.

'I'll be glad to escape a coach for a few days. How far can we get by boat?' she asked.

'Almost to Belgrade, I believe.'

He was quiet for a few minutes, then asked: 'Did you remember to pick up your new gown from the dressmaker?'

Isabella grimaced. 'I did and it's in the latest fashion as you suggested, but honestly it's a ridiculous design. Some fool has decreed that the hoops should be even wider at the sides this year. Heaven knows how I'm meant to tackle doorways and stairs.'

'By turning sideways I suppose,' he answered drily. 'If the ambassador agrees to meet us, I'm sure his doors and stair-cases will be plenty wide enough.'

Issy stared at her uncle in astonishment. 'If? You said Sir Everard had invited us. Surely we've not come this distance to be turned away?'

He shrugged. 'He was a good friend of your father. He's bound to be pleased to see you. If we're lucky and you play your part well, there'll be no need to do business with the likes of Edward Collins again.'

Isabella wriggled inside her tight stays. Surely Uncle Richard wasn't going to attempt to use their trickery on an ambassador? The very thought made her feel hot with embar-rassment. She had been working with her uncle since her father died seven years ago. He often reminded her she was lucky she hadn't ended up in the workhouse, since most bachelors wouldn't have taken on an eight-year-old. She was grateful to have avoided that fate, but she knew he needed her too. His eyesight had started to fail and her growing skill in fine work allowed her to take over. She loved working with jewellery, but this new role playing the lady made her uncomfortable. Despite his assurances her conscience was troubled.

The mighty Danube flowed dark and fast beside the road and Isabella looked up for a last glimpse of the castle. Its profile against the pale dawn sky was unmistakeably European. She wondered about the buildings she'd see at the end of their journey. In ten days they'd be in Constantinople.

Chapter Two

Constantinople, Turkey, May 1742

They skirted Constantinople's city walls on a fine May evening. Then crossed the strait in a small boat to the district of Pera, where all the foreigners lived. The porter unloaded their luggage onto the quayside and went to ask for directions to their boarding house. The heat of the day radiated up from the stone jetty beneath Isabella's feet, and now she looked back for her first proper view of the old city. There on top of the hill beyond the stretch of water they called the Golden Horn, was the magnificent Hagia Sophia, its huge dome and minarets dominating the skyline.

This dock was crowded with people and boats. Tall-masted frigates and Arab dhows strained against their anchors in the fast-flowing Bosphorus, and sailors called to each other in a dozen different languages. Her feet were in Asia, and her long journey through Europe was beyond the horizon. This was the furthest edge of the Western world. The place was buzzing with an excitement Isabella felt as a shiver down her spine. Surely this was the kind of place a girl's life might change?

. . .

Four days later they were on their way to take tea at the British Embassy. Her fears of being turned away had been unfounded. The ambassador, Sir Everard Fawkener, had responded to Uncle Richard's note immediately and now he was in a state of high excitement. Her uncle had emphasised the importance of making a good impression so often, that she felt sure she would stumble or drop her teacup. Tea was expensive, not a drink they could afford in London, and the dainty porcelain cups made her nervous.

Isabella gazed out the carriage window to take her mind from her churning stomach. She'd visited so many cities on her way here, but even Vienna couldn't rival Constantinople for fascinating pedestrians. Local men wore long robes and huge turbans which must have used yards of cloth. Some women were completely swathed in black including their faces, but others wore coloured dresses and a veil so diaphanous it emphasised their beauty. There were European women in pastel gowns and matching parasols and the merchants' clothes revealed traders from all over the world.

Their chaise drove up the hill through row upon row of low wooden houses. The British Embassy was at the peak, and the large stone building appeared very grand in comparison. The sight of it set Isabella's heart galloping again.

Uncle Richard helped her out of the coach. 'Shoulders back, head high. I'm told the ambassador is considered both polite and sociable, you've nothing to fear.'

It's your silly fussing that's making me nervous, she thought to herself. How many nibs had she met in her journey? An ambassador was surely just another man in a silk coat.

They mounted the marble steps. Uncle Richard rapped the large iron door knocker twice and the loud echoing sound caused her heart rate to quicken. She heard steps approaching. The huge wooden door swung open and Uncle Richard gave the uniformed footman their names.

'Sir Everard is expecting you,' he said.

They entered a panelled room with high ceilings, a rich Turkish carpet stretched across its width. An ordinary looking middle-aged man jumped to his feet and grasped Uncle Richard's hand. Only the footman's deference revealed this was actually the ambassador.

'Mr Godfrey, you cannot imagine how delighted I was to receive your letter, and this must be Isabella.'

Uncle Richard gave a small bow. Isabella curtsied.

'It is most kind of you to receive us, Sir Everard.'

'The pleasure is all mine, please don't stand on ceremony.'

He indicated a long couch, and they sat down.

'I've missed so much of young Isabella's life. We have a great deal of catching up to do.'

Isabella looked at her uncle in confusion. His smirk told her that he wasn't surprised by the ambassador's words.

A footman entered with a tray of tea things.

'May I offer you some tea and would you like honey? I normally have Turkish coffee at this time of day, but I assume you'd prefer tea.'

'I profess I find the local coffee too strong for my stomach, Your Excellency, but surprisingly Isabella likes it.'

The ambassador gave a loud laugh. 'I should have guessed, it's in her blood, her father adored it. Jenkins, please pour Mr Godfrey some tea. I'll call Ahmed to do us coffee, Jenkins hasn't the knack at all.'

Isabella stared at Sir Everard. His warm tone implied an intimacy with her father. The pang she felt was a mixture of loss and jealousy. She so wished she could remember her father more clearly. The ambassador turned towards her uncle. She hoped he didn't find Richard's ingratiating smile annoying.

'I'm so pleased to make your acquaintance, Richard. I can't believe we never met before,' he said.

'When I joined my brother's business my role was strictly behind the scenes. After James's death, I was forced to get involved in everything.'

A man in local dress arrived with coffee in a swan-necked brass pot. When he poured, the distinctive scent of cardamom-laced coffee made Isabella smile. She loved the idea that her papa had liked it too.

Uncle Richard had only told her this powerful man had known her father and that he hoped his influence might open doors to wealthy customers back in London. Isabella hadn't anticipated the meeting would unlock memories of her happy childhood. She'd trained herself not to think of what she'd lost.

The ambassador passed Isabella a small gilded glass of coffee. 'You're so grown up, Isabella, but I do think I can still see that little girl.'

Should she remember him? His smile was friendly but still she felt wary. Her life had been so isolated and those men she'd met on the journey had taught her caution.

'Excuse me for asking, Ambassador, have we met before?'

'Many times. I knew your father before he married, then I had the honour of being at you parents' wedding.'

'You knew my mother too?'

He nodded. 'I never knew two people more in love. I don't think your father ever got over your mother's death.'

Issy tried to imagine her parents as young and in love. Her mother had died when she was four and Isabella knew no one but Richard who remembered her. She longed to ask him a dozen questions.

'I'm so sorry I don't remember you,' she replied.

'Why would you? You were often in bed when I visited and I guess you were only six or seven the last time. I left London to come here. I only heard of your father's death long after I arrived in Constantinople. I still can't believe it, and I'm so very sorry. When I heard he'd died I tried to track you down. I often worried about what had happened to you.' The ambassador smiled at Uncle Richard. 'I'm delighted to find you have family to care for you.'

Richard Godfrey was her only family. Perhaps he did care for her in his way?

'So what do you make of Constantinople, Isabella?' the ambassador asked.

'I think it's the most beautiful place I ever saw. I do wish I could visit the Stamboul side.'

'Ah, you are your father's daughter, curious and intrepid. You do know you'd have to wear a robe and veil?'

'I wouldn't mind,' she replied.

'Bravo. There are European ladies in Pera who've lived here for years and never ventured over. What would you like to see? The Hagia Sophia? It's rather hard to get admittance for a lady, but I'd do my best.'

'That would be marvellous.'

She glanced at her uncle, who smiled broadly. She decided to risk it.

'Most of all, I'd love to visit the Grand Bazaar. Uncle has been and says the gold market is incredible.'

'Gold, fabrics, carpets, more things than you can possibly imagine,' Sir Everard replied. 'So you take an interest in your father's business?'

She sensed her uncle's glare without looking at him, he took her for an idiot.

'Which girl doesn't love beautiful jewellery?' she replied.

The ambassador laughed. 'Well, a visit to the bazaar is the

easiest thing in the world to organise,' he turned to Uncle Richard, 'if your uncle will allow it.'

'It's most kind of you to offer, Ambassador.'

'Where are you staying, Mr Godfrey? I'll send you a note with the arrangements.'

'We're in a temporary boarding house,' he said, writing down the address, 'although if I can do some business here we might look for a small house to rent.'

'And you still work with jewellery?' the ambassador asked.

'Yes. I've a mind to find some inspiration in Constantinople and perhaps sell some pieces too.'

'Splendid idea. Would you like some advice on houses?'

'If it's not too much trouble, although I must tell you our budget is tight.'

'Let me make some enquiries.'

They parted with an arrangement to go to the bazaar a few days later.

She challenged her uncle, as soon as they got back in the chaise. 'Why didn't you tell me he was a close family friend?'

'I only knew lately and I wasn't sure. Today went even better than I hoped. The warmth of his welcome signals a change in both our lives. We're on the up, Isabella.'

Meanwhile, in Constantinople's harbour, an English gentleman stepped ashore. Sir John Brady raised his chin and puffed out his considerable girth. He liked the look of this place; any number of pleasures might be bought by a man of his wealth. It was the last destination in his Grand Tour and he meant to enjoy himself.

Chapter Three

Their bazaar visit was postponed for a week to allow them to move into a house. Sir Everard called it modest, but compared to their London rooms it was huge. Isabella had only the vaguest memories of the substantial house in Russell Square where she'd spent her early childhood. This wooden villa was over two storeys, had three bedrooms and a lovely little courtyard. Best of all from Uncle Richard's point of view, it had a small domed outdoor oven he could use to melt gold and silver.

'Surely we can't afford this,' she said.

'It costs less than we were paying for our rooms in Vienna. It was rented by some Levant Company manager who had to go home partway through the lease, so we got a good deal. The Levant Company are huge here, they pay for the embassy and the ambassador too,' Uncle Richard replied.

'I'm worried Sir Everard must be covering part of the cost, what with a cook and a maid, as well as a guard.'

Uncle Richard shrugged. 'Labour is cheap here and what does it matter if he is paying part? He can afford it. Anyway, he feels guilty for not helping you before, that's exactly what I was hoping for.'

'But it's an unnecessary extravagance to pay for a cook.'

'The cook is essential. You can't shop here on your own and I'm not about to start. You'll be able to get back to your jewellery making soon, so long as we're discreet. Let's see what ideas we get at the bazaar.'

Isabella pulled on the simple cotton dress that had languished at the bottom of her trunk since they left London. Sir Everard had sent her a black street robe to wear for their trip to Stamboul. Since she'd be fully covered she could dress for comfort underneath. Jamila, her new maid, plaited her hair and pinned it up.

'Thank you,' Isabella said. The girl returned her smile in the mirror.

Jamila was also fifteen but she'd worked as a lady's maid for three years already. Their housemaid in London had been tasked with helping Isabella with her clothes but she'd been clumsy and scornful. That maid knew she worked beside her uncle in the workshop and only put on a ladylike façade to go out. Issy had heard the girl mock her behind her back. In contrast, Jamila was calm and graceful. Issy had felt comfortable with her immediately. The fact that she spoke almost no English, seemed hardly to matter. Jamila helped her into the full-length black robe.

The head covering the ambassador had sent was white. Issy turned it around in her hands but couldn't work out how to put it on. Jamila took it from her and draped it over her hair so it framed her face and fell in folds down to her shoulders. Then she took one loose piece across Isabella's nose and mouth, pinning it under the other side. She looked so ridiculous in the mirror that Issy struggled not to laugh, then she caught Jamila's amused expression. They both succumbed to a fit of the giggles.

'Isabella, Turkish girl now,' Jamila said, once they'd recovered. She pointed to the face covering. 'Yashmak,' she added.

This extraordinary outfit covered everything except Issy's eyes and since they were brown, she would look like all the other women in the market.

'Isabella, what in all earth are you doing up there? Hurry up!'

Her uncle's tone was irritated, no doubt he disapproved of them laughing together. Issy crossed her eyes at Jamila in the reflection and that set them both off giggling again.

Nevertheless, Uncle Richard smiled when she went downstairs.

'I think your dear father would be impressed by your adventurousness, Isabella, but I fear your mother would have been appalled.'

'Surely someone who would sever her family ties to marry the man she loved, must have been adventurous too,' Issy retorted.

They got into a chaise for the short journey to the harbour, where they would meet Sir Everard.

'This is a huge honour, Isabella. The ambassador will not often guide visitors himself. It's evidence of how taken he is with you. But remember not to reveal your knowledge of jewellery. We must keep your ladylike image intact.'

'It seems wrong to deceive Sir Everard if he was a family friend.'

'We're not really deceiving him and I intend to tell him about your financial bad fortune, it might gain you some patronage.'

She turned to him in alarm. 'But surely you won't try to sell him jewellery?'

'Of course not. Do you take me for a fool?'

She shook her head, he was far from a fool. Her uncle was certainly one of the most calculating people she'd ever known.

'Anyway, Fawkener is no idle diplomat, he's a man of commerce and knows the value of things. Besides, I hear he's a confirmed bachelor, he has little need for jewellery.'

Issy felt her shoulders relax at his reassurance. It was the oddest thing to be dressed in this bizarre outfit and feel more at ease than she'd done in months.

Walking into the covered market of the Grand Bazaar felt like entering a dream. The air, which was several degrees cooler than outside, buzzed with the sound of bargains being made. Bearded men in turbans and long robes haggled over their wares below the vaulted ceiling. Light streamed in through high windows, and the architecture reminded Isabella of a cathedral, except this noisy atmosphere was quite unlike a church. Tall arches edged with blue bricks stretched off into the distance. A throng of people came towards them, some bearing baskets and trays balanced on their heads, many donkeys, and even one man on a prancing white horse. They walked past a stretch of stalls selling blue and white ceramics, stacked on shelves almost to the ceiling. Then turning left at the next junction, Issy breathed in the exotic smelling spices. Stallholders called out and offered handfuls from the baskets at their feet. Sir Everard stopped to buy a bag of fragrant cardamom pods and a bundle of cinnamon sticks. Dried chillies hung above the owner's head and high rows of shelves behind him were stacked with large lidded spice jars.

The ambassador had explained the bazaar was too big to see everything in one day, so she'd asked to visit the gold and fabric sections. They headed to the gold market first. Issy soon lost all sense of direction, as they wound their way through the maze of corridors. Finally they turned into a whole alley of shops piled high with glittering gold jewellery. The dazzling profusion made Isabella think of a sultan's treasury, or a pirate's hoard.

'This is amazing,' she said.

'It's impressive, isn't it,' Sir Everard replied.

What might she learn if she could spend a week poring over these riches?

'I saw some pieces that I thought might appeal to the London market when I visited before. However, my lack of the language is an impediment to effective bargaining,' Uncle Richard said.

'I'll take you to a couple of vendors I know and trust. They won't cheat you once they know you're a friend of mine.'

The shopkeeper jumped out of his seat when they entered. He greeted Sir Everard like a very important long lost relative. The shopkeeper insisted they all sit, and brought everyone glasses of mango juice. Isabella left hers untouched. She must ask Jamila how she was meant to drink or eat in the veil. Sir Everard said something to the owner and soon the counter was strewn with jewel-set pieces.

'You speak Turkish?' she asked.

'I do a little, but Faisal was born in Egypt and I'm fluent in Arabic. I lived in Aleppo for nine years. That's where I first met your father.'

'Really? I'd no idea he travelled in this area.'

'Oh yes, Richard is following a family tradition sourcing items from the East.'

Richard smiled, before turning back to the pendants and brooches. Isabella itched to touch them and longed to tell him which pieces to examine more closely. Perhaps the ambassador sensed her shifting in her seat?

'We might leave Richard here and visit the fabric section? I fear we won't tear him away.'

Richard turned with a turquoise ring in his hand.

'I'll be here when you've finished. I'm having a devil of a job choosing.'

In the fabric bazaar, Isabella was drawn to the row of men making quilts. She stood watching them for several minutes.

'Do you think I could buy some fabric? I'd like to make a cover for my own bed.'

At first she was overwhelmed by the huge variety of silks, and confused by the competing shouts from the vendors.

'Let me help you,' Sir Everard said. 'My family were in the fabric business. I managed their Levant office before I entered diplomatic service.'

The silk felt cool and slippery beneath her fingers. He showed Isabella how to gauge the fabric quality by weight and touch. Finally she selected bright silks in burgundy, gold, and ultramarine, which the stallholder unwound from massive bolts of cloth.

'Thank you for your patience, Sir Everard. A patchwork eiderdown will give me something useful to do.'

Isabella was reluctant to leave the bazaar but her uncle complained of sore feet. When they emerged, blinking in the sunshine, Sir Everard took out his pocket watch.

'You must both be hungry, we've been here nearly four hours. I swear time stops in that place. Let's catch the boat, then I'll take you to a café on the Pera side.'

Isabella took a seat in the dhow's stern to catch the cooling breeze. The boatman untied the mooring then pushed the rudder with his bare foot. The sail filled with wind, curving a scimitar shape against the azure sky. It had been the most extraordinary day, a world away from the grey grimy streets of London. Uncle Richard was listening to Sir Everard describe his former career trading with the Levant Company. Uncle Richard's expression caught her attention, he was genuinely interested, she'd never seen him so relaxed. Might they become friends? On the surface it was an unlikely match.

She didn't know if Uncle Richard had any friends in London, he certainly never brought any to the house. His policy of keeping himself to himself had the knock on effect that she had no friends either. She arrived in Panton Street with her Russell Square accent and Richard wouldn't let her play outside. The local children thought her a snob and shunned her. When she met wealthy young ladies at church in London, they knew where she lived and laughed at her behind their fans.

Would they stay long enough for Sir Everard to introduce her to friends here? Even if not, she hoped they'd see more of him. Every time they met she learned something new about her parents.

'Thank you again for today,' Uncle Richard said when they disembarked. 'I'm so delighted with the items I've bought and I wager they'd have cost twice as much in your absence.'

'Now that I've made the introduction you'll get the same service the next time.'

'I fear I'll empty my purse before I run out of finds to take back.'

'Are you still thinking of selling pieces here too? Many wealthy visitors lack the confidence to buy from the bazaar themselves. I could help you with some introductions.'

Please God no, she thought. Could Richard Godfrey be persuaded to charge a fairer price? Might his admiration for Sir Everard curb his cheating inclinations?

'I'm having a reception at the embassy next Saturday. You must both come,' Sir Everard added.

'We'd be delighted. It's good for Isabella to get out, she lacks both company and diversion.'

Sir Everard turned to Isabella and smiled. 'That's not a good thing at all,' he paused, 'and I have an idea that might interest you. There's a Mistress Nichol arrived here lately from Edinburgh. She is a Scottish spinster, with good references. She travelled here to work for the unfortunate Widow MacDonald, who succumbed to cholera before she arrived. The poor woman is distraught to find herself alone and without employment so far from home. I wonder if you might consider taking her on as a companion for Isabella? Mistress Nichol seems a reliable sort, quite the right temperament for the job.'

'What an excellent idea,' Uncle Richard replied. 'Would you ask her if she'd consider it and perhaps make discreet enquiries about the cost? If we widen our social circle Isabella might get invitations and I confess I've neither time nor interest in drawing room chatter.'

'I'll find out for you,' Sir Everard answered.

When they got home, Isabella was glad to get out of her veil and black robe. It had become uncomfortable as the day got hotter. Uncle Richard frowned, seeing her cotton dress.

'You went out in that?'

She shrugged. 'What difference does it make? No one could see.'

He hung his black frock coat and tricorn hat on the coat stand.

'This Mistress Nichol is a stroke of luck,' he said.

'Surely we can't afford it? And I really don't want a chaperone.'

'I think it's a necessary investment, ladies can't go out alone here. Sir Everard is a route into polite society; mark my words, you'll soon be inundated with invitations.'

'You don't care if I make any friends. You only want more customers.'

He frowned. 'You know our mission here. If you make friends of quality you can meet again in London, I'd be more than delighted. Society contacts open doors.'

Isabella sighed. Uncle Richard had been proven right. A Miss Robinson had been employed to give Isabella genteel lessons since she was twelve. He'd struggled to get access to wealthy customers since he had to close her father's shop and he'd schemed that Isabella would be his gateway back into that world. Too many people knew him in London, so he devised their tour through Europe to test the premise. Turning up in the right hotels and wearing the right clothes, no one had questioned their status. She was more confident in the act now but wished it wasn't necessary.

Richard drew a handful of red velvet pouches from his pocket. He looked at her with one eyebrow raised. 'If you're not interested in doing business here, I suppose you don't want to see what I bought?'

They both laughed. Whatever reservations she had about her uncle's business practices, their shared passion for jewellery brought them together.

She followed him into his study, where he closed the door and opened the French windows. She could smell that the outdoor oven was already lit.

'Shall we make some beautiful things?'

She smiled at him. 'It's been too long,' she replied.

He emptied the pouches onto his desk with a flourish.

'Oh, marvellous,' she said, scooping up the gold brooch set with rubies. This was the piece she would have chosen.

'Such delicate filigree.'

Her uncle nodded. 'I have some small garnets. We could create silver copies.'

'Do you think I could manage? It's very intricate,' she replied.

'We don't want exact replicas. Design something similar that we have the material to create.'

He opened the large wooden cupboard behind him and took out the silver-making equipment. He put two soft leather pouches on the desk, Isabella loved the feel of hers. She rolled it open to reveal the array of small tools. Uncle Richard took a silver disc outside to soften it. He always did the main body of the piece, leaving her to decorate. She could hear him muttering to himself. Judging the temperature was especially difficult on an unfamiliar heat source. The gold brooch was flower shaped with rubies inset. She drew a simplified version, then measured all its dimensions. They'd brought a quantity of silver wire from London and she selected two sizes, one for the outline and stones' places and the thinnest gauge for twisting into filigree. The wire was fine enough to bend without heating and she had an array of tools to shape wires. The process took considerable skill, Isabella imagined a pianist or cellist would take similar pride in their dexterity. Uncle Richard created the brooch back and hammered it into shape. She began placing the filigree while he made the second brooch. They worked all afternoon, only stopping when the light faded.

'We should get to setting stones tomorrow. Do you have some glass in the right colour?'

'Yes, but I might set one with different coloured pastes, yellow in the centre and pink on the petals, just like a real flower.'

They cleaned their tools and put them away. He smiled at her.

'Well done. Your sharp eyes and steady fingers make you

the expert at fine work now, and I have the gift to sell what you create. I believe we'll do well in Constantinople.'

She returned his smile, but felt her usual unease. He argued that people went away happy with their purchases, but his prices were too high.

Chapter Four

On Saturday evening Isabella put on her new blue silk gown for the embassy party. Her mother's jewellery lay on her dressing table. She picked up and cradled an earring in her palm. Her memories of her mother were fading, but this fixed one in her mind. She could see her own chubby hand reaching up to touch it, the weight of the moonstone drop, the candle reflecting on the pearl. She pinned the ruby brooch her uncle had bought to her dress. Their customers often came from someone admiring a piece she was wearing. Isabella glared at her reflection, she disliked her dark looks which were the opposite of an English rose. Today, however, she looked like a prosperous lady, just as her uncle had required.

Hopefully Uncle Richard would find some clients tonight. He'd taken on Mistress Nichol the previous day and all these extra expenses made Isabella anxious. She daren't imagine what his jewellery purchases from the bazaar cost. The thought caused her to acknowledge her own hypocrisy. She lived off the sales she disapproved of, and she had no other source of income. Not only was she complicit, she took satisfaction in attracting new customers. If it was a crime then she was his partner.

Their chaise drove past the huge Sinan Pasha mosque, the waterside position honouring a long dead admiral. The evening sun bathed the high, red-striped stone walls in rosy light. The blue sky faded to gold on the horizon, gilding Hagia Sophia's dome. It was unbelievably beautiful.

Soon they arrived at the embassy and this time they were shown into a grand reception room. Every wall was hung with gorgeous paintings, tapestries and mirrors. There were huge windows and their elevated position gave a breathtaking view of the mosques and palaces of Stamboul. The distant hills of Asia could be seen beyond the Sea of Marmara. The room was crowded, it seemed most of the British community in Constantinople was there. She was introduced to several Levant Company merchants and their wives, a Scots doctor called Mackenzie, and also the chaplain, a Reverend Thomas Payne.

'Shall we see you at the service tomorrow, Miss Godfrey?'

'I'm looking forward to it,' she answered. 'We hadn't found a church, so I was most delighted when Sir Everard explained you take Sunday morning services in the chapel here.'

'I look forward to meeting your uncle too.'

'He plans to come tomorrow and I'll also bring my new chaperone, Mistress Nichol.'

'You will all be most welcome.'

She daren't look in Uncle Richard's direction in case she might laugh. The Reverend might find her uncle elusive. He wasn't religiously inclined and rarely attended services. In London, Issy always went with her teacher, Miss Robinson, and then not because he worried about her soul, but simply that it was part of her education. She assumed she would most often worship with Mistress Nichol after tomorrow.

A gong was rung for dinner and her heart sank when she was shown to the top of the table, just to the right of the ambassador's chair. Her uncle was opposite and they all stood, waiting for Sir Everard's entrance. The table was set with a dizzying array of glasses and cutlery. Would she remember Miss Robinson's lessons?

'His Excellency, the British Ambassador, Sir Everard Fawkener.'

The ambassador introduced them to their neighbours. He explained that they too were relative newcomers to Constantinople. She was seated beside Viscount Southard, who was an extraordinarily thin young man with a prominent nose. His sister Lady Amelia sat on his other side. The gentleman sitting beside her uncle was Sir John Brady. She quickly learned that the three knew each other, having travelled here on the same ship. The ambassador was talking to Uncle Richard, and when one minute of silence extended to two, she deduced the young man next to her might be shy. She would have to initiate a conversation or spend the whole meal in silence.

'What's your first impression of Constantinople, Viscount Southard. Don't you find it beautiful?'

He turned to her with a start and blinked rapidly, before nodding. She tried a different tack.

'I couldn't help but notice your resemblance to your sister, are you twins perhaps?'

This time he shook his head and she was struggling for a question which might require a longer answer, when Lady Amelia leaned across her brother. 'I am the elder by one year, but I dare say our resemblance is enhanced by our closeness, and our shared tastes in everything.'

The word 'everything' was said with such emphasis that Isabella flinched. The woman proceeded to interrogate Issy so vigorously that her brother could hardly reach his food. He grabbed a small pigeon pie before his plate was cleared, then his sister leaned in again.

'Before our own dear mother passed away, she had me promise to make my brother's well-being my life work. It gives me much comfort to know that she would have been proud of my selfless devotion.'

'I envy you, I wish I had siblings,' Issy replied.

Lady Amelia then asked her about her accomplishments. Dear Lord, Issy thought, she's assessing my suitability as a sister-in-law. Could she get away with coming across as hopeless enough to dissuade this lady? In theory the world considered her old enough but Isabella was in no hurry to marry. Her experience with Edward Collins had strengthened her resolve. She was hazy about the details but the idea of married intimacy seemed repugnant. She mumbled affirmatives to sampler sewing and singing but regretted she didn't play the piano. The truth was they'd no room for a piano, even if they'd had the money.

Throughout the questions Viscount Southard spoke not one word, and it was easy to guess why this titled young man was still unmarried. An excellent cherry pie finally drew the lady's full attention. Isabella had to twist out her neck, to dislodge the rightwards crick. Sir John, who was listening to the ambassador, gave her a brief smile that seemed to signal sympathy. When Sir Everard stopped talking, Sir John addressed her. 'I overheard that we share the only child status, Miss Godfrey.'

She smiled at him. 'I had a younger brother but he died when he was a baby, Sir John.'

'Sibling responsibilities can be a trial though, Miss Godfrey,' Lady Amelia said with a smirk. 'I've found this whole tour exhausting. However do you cope with the heat here? And as for the smell, well...' She grimaced, pressed her napkin to her lips, then resumed. 'But perhaps your mother has European family? Your colouring is much better suited to this climate.'

Considering several possible curt replies, she caught the warning in her uncle's raised eyebrows.

'My late mama was from Scotland, and so fair skinned that I fear if she'd come here, she would have shared your dislike of the sun.'

There was a pause as the dessert plates were cleared, and the men's wine glasses replenished. Lady Amelia was whispering to her brother, then they both stood up.

'My poor brother has a headache, so we must ask you to excuse us.'

The couple said their thanks and goodbyes. Isabella guessed that she was the latest in a long line of girls that Lady Amelia had found unsuitable. Thank goodness. Viscount Southard dipped his head at her as he turned to leave, and she thought he looked sad.

When they'd gone, the ambassador spoke. 'May I suggest we take a moment to visit my gallery before we take brandy, gentlemen? I'm hosting a small exhibition for a painter friend of mine and I believe the ladies might find it interesting.'

The ambassador led the way while Isabella took her uncle's arm. 'I'm sorry I scared off Viscount Southard before you could do any business. His sister is a dragon.'

'On the contrary, I spoke to them before dinner and your dragon lady was most interested in Turkish jewellery. I made an arrangement to visit them at their hotel.'

They followed Sir Everard into another room, where the walls were completely covered in beautiful paintings. He led them to the far corner and it was clear all the pieces in this section were by one artist.

'I've become good friends with this Swiss artist, his name is Jeanne-Etienne Liotard. My friend Viscount Duncannon brought him here from Rome four years ago, and he found so much inspiration in Constantinople that he chose to stay on. I swear he's painted every ambassador in Pera.'

There was a small chalk drawing of Sir Everard himself. He wore a richly patterned robe in the Turkish style, which looked like nothing more than his dressing gown. Isabella found it impossible not to smile.

'My outfit amuses you, Isabella?'

She glanced at him to see if he was offended, but he smiled.

'Look at this, Issy, you feel like you might be able to stroke the fur,' Uncle Richard said.

Issy gazed up at the large oil portrait of a bearded man dressed in a full length brown fur-trimmed robe over a bright blue kaftan.

'This artist is amazing. Is the subject some local man?' she asked.

'Not at all,' Sir Everard replied. 'That's my British friend Richard Pococke. He posed for Liotard when he visited, but the portrait wasn't finished before he left. I'm having it shipped to him.'

Uncle Richard walked round all the portraits again, peering at the details. 'This painter has something very special,' he said.

'Viscount Duncannon believed this from the beginning. He tells me that his own portrait is causing quite a stir in London. He's wearing Turkish garb too, he swears it will start a fashion.'

The other guests started to drift away, leaving Isabella and her uncle alone with Sir Everard.

'I'm so pleased you like his work. Why don't you have a painting of Isabella done? Liotard has promised to travel to Moldavia soon to paint the Prince's court. I happen to know that he's anxious to paint an English lady before he leaves Constantinople, I believe he'd give you a good price.'

'A portrait of me? Oh, I don't think so.' The very idea of some strange man staring at her for hours, made Isabella cringe.

'Why not? If you were in London you could be entering your first season, an event often commemorated by a portrait,' said Sir Everard.

She smiled. Girls from her London neighbourhood did not *enter the season*.

'The artist would be disappointed in me if he wants an English beauty to paint.'

'Nonsense,' Sir Everard replied.

Uncle Richard was engrossed in a small painting of a girl wearing a turban and a highly embroidered coat. He looked up. 'Isabella underestimates herself, but I'm afraid the cost would be beyond our means.'

'Then I wonder if I might commission it?' Sir Everard asked.

Isabella shook her head.

'Please allow me,' he said, looking first to her then her uncle. 'Think of all the birthday gifts I've missed over the years.'

She knew from Uncle Richard's expression that he was thinking about the value of such a painting.

'Please, Isabella, I consider it a debt to your parents,' Sir Everard added. 'Your father so loved the portrait of your mother, I feel certain he would have wanted one of you.'

Uncle Richard had sold off all the house contents to cover their debts. Issy often wished she still had that portrait. She glanced at Liotard's spectacular paintings again, before nodding her assent. She would make very sure Richard didn't sell this one.

'Excellent,' Sir Everard said.

'We are both extremely grateful,' Uncle Richard added.

Chapter Five

July 1742

It was too hot to breathe. Isabella imagined she could feel her heart reverberating, beating against the humid air, like the taut surface of a drum. She raised her eyebrows and blinked, struggling to keep her eyes open. The painter expressed his ill temper in the motion of his brush, jabbing at the canvas as if he were in some sort of battle. This was the second sitting for her portrait and she had drifted off once before, his rebuke wakening her abruptly. Monsieur Liotard's appearance was alarming, even when he was not in a bad mood. His long and curly grey beard rested on a full length Turkish robe that swished on the tiled floor. Why he would choose such a heavy garment, when he might wear whatever he liked, was baffling. Perhaps he wore no undergarments? This inappropriate thought made her snort out loud.

The painter looked up and glared. Isabella disowning the unladylike noise, maintained her neutral gaze into the middle distance. When he looked back at the canvas, she risked a glance towards Vittorio, the artist's Italian assistant. The urge to laugh twitched at the corner of her mouth. His amused response flashed in his eyes for a second, before he returned to his work, head bent over, mixing paint colours on a small table.

The temperature was unbearable, and she longed to be out of her stays. A trickle of sweat crept down the curve of the whalebone; she could imagine the red weal she would find there later. Mistress Nichol, her newly appointed companion, was quite asleep on the divan below the window. She expelled a small snore and Isabella saw the painter look over in repugnance. He thought he'd identified the source of the snort, and the Italian boy returned Isabella's brief and secret smile.

Mistress Nichol woke with a groan. Having only recently arrived from Scotland, and unsuitably clad in dark wool, she was never finished moaning about the heat and humidity. She flicked open her black lace fan, and began to beat the air in front of her red and sweaty face.

'Madam, kindly seek the breeze on the terrace, I cannot paint when you are making this noise.'

She glanced at Isabella for permission. Isabella nodded. She could hardly see the point of a chaperone here, cooped up in this small room, but at least it got her out of the house. Mistress Nichol pushed herself up with both arms from the low seat; the movement of her dress sent a whiff of sweat through the room. Isabella saw the boy wrinkle his small nose up in disgust and the painter uttered an 'oof', under his breath. The room was immediately fresher, and Isabella sighed to be rid of the woman. She spent a lot of time alone in London. This woman's constant presence was hard to get used to.

The next twenty minutes settled into the same hot boredom. A fat bluebottle hurling itself against the shutters disturbed the quiet. The boy crossed the room to the window. He caught the fly in his cupped hands and released it through the gap to the courtyard outside. Isabella was surprised by the tenderness of the gesture; she had thought he would kill it.

An angry shout made him spin round.

'Pah! C'est impossible! Vittorio, trouvez une autre robe!'

Liotard flung his paintbrush to the floor; the soft sable hairs spread a splatter of bright blue across one ochre tile. Then he threw off his cap and left the room.

'He doesn't like my dress?'

The nerve of the man, creativity was no excuse for rudeness.

Vittorio smiled at her. 'I think he means only it make you stiff here,' he placed his palms over his ribs. 'Also, he prefer the style Levantine. Come, look.'

He led Isabella towards a beaded screen in the corner of the room, behind it was a wooden trunk. He opened the lid and a tumble of gorgeous colours erupted out of the box within a cloud of cedar scent. He gathered an armful of garments and laid them on the divan. There were cotton chemise, silk pantaloons, and four beautiful embroidered silk dresses. Her hand was drawn to touch the raised flowers made of the tiniest stitches. She picked up a heavy embellished belt.

'I recognise this from the painting of a girl in the British Embassy.'

One cream dress stood out from the others, embroidered with an array of small flowers, their stems the colour of spring grass and flared petals like the orange of a Constantinople sunset. Isabella stroked the skirt. She suddenly understood that the feather light silk belonged in this room, as surely as her stiff gown belonged in Europe.

'Good choice,' he said, 'Monsieur Liotard prefer this one.' Vittorio handed her a cotton petticoat, fine and translucent. 'You need this.'

'I can't possibly wear such a dress.'

'Bella, don't worry, you can, will be beautiful. But you need to take off...'

He tapped his breastbone at the point where her own was crushed by her stays. Then he swept up the dress and draped it over her outstretched arms. She inhaled the smell of an Oriental perfume. Who had worn it before? The desire to wear this dress washed over her like deep hunger. She shook her head.

'It's not proper for an English girl. Mistress Nichol won't allow it.'

Vittorio's mischievous smile caused the green flecks in his pale brown eyes to flash. He moved to the window and beckoned her. 'Look.'

He held open the shutter, revealing a view to the terrace, Mistress Nichol was in a large wicker chair, fast asleep with her mouth open.

Dare she risk it?

'You afraid, little girl?' he teased.

She glared at him and strode towards the partitioned area. He took the dress and petticoat from her and hung them over the screen, then he placed a cream cotton chemise and a pair of silk pantaloons beside them.

'Breeches?' she asked.

'You want show your legs?'

He was laughing at her again. She'd show him. She waved him away with a dismissive flick of her wrist.

Isabella kicked off her shoes and struggled out of her dress, then tried to undo her stays. Mistress Nichol had laced them so tightly she couldn't untie the knot at the back. She pushed her breasts together with her elbows and wriggled to try to ease the tension. Seconds ticked by, and she got hotter than ever as she struggled. Then, she stood suddenly still, registering the sensation of cool fingers at the top of her spine. He tapped on a vertebra, perhaps asking permission, but she couldn't speak. Then she felt his hands move to the knot, he tugged the lace loose and she had to raise her forearms over her breasts to prevent the stays falling. Isabella held her breath and listened to his footsteps walk away. His impudence had caught her unawares. She imagined she could still feel his touch.

Isabella allowed the stays to fall to the floor with a clatter. Now she was dressed only in her stockings and shift and since she couldn't do up the stay laces alone, there was no going back. It occurred to her she wasn't confident that the beaded screen shielded her from view. She peered through, Vittorio had his back to her gathering up the other dresses. However, the painter might return at any minute. She slipped the cotton chemise over her head and stepped into the pantaloons. The light layers of the Turkish outfit were a revelation; beautiful, exotic and blissfully comfortable. She pushed her arms into the dress sleeves, and looked down to fasten the tiny buttons in the blue brocade trim over her waist. Her nostrils flared to receive the gloriously heady perfume. She had to stop buttoning just below her bosom, she daren't tear the dress fabric, and anyway there was no way it would fasten. Was she too fat? Surely the dress was overly ornate to be made for a child?

'Perfect, the top buttons stay open.'

Vittorio was standing close beside her holding out the belt, the heavy metal clasp was formed of two large ovals encrusted with lapis lazuli and tiny pearls. She wondered if they could copy it? She took it from him without a word, and when she struggled to clip it together, he placed his hands over hers as if it were an entirely natural thing to do. Now he'd touched her twice, crossed a line that she doubted she could redraw.

The painter re-entered the room. 'Is she ready?'

Apparently, he was unsurprised to find his assistant on the

wrong side of the screen. Vittorio smiled at her, took her hand and led her into the room. '*Voila*.'

The artist smiled and nodded his approval. 'Over there, mademoiselle, on the window seat, the light is better and you will be more relaxed.'

There was no mirror to reflect her appearance, but she'd seen Vittorio's expression. She'd been repulsed by the lustful gaze of the men she'd met on their journey. Why was it nothing about this boy's open admiration upset her and his proximity sent an unfamiliar shiver through her body? Isabella raised her chin and enjoyed the touch of ornate lace at her wrists and the whisper of the silk fabric. The freedom from corsetry and skirt hoops, allowed her to move in a wholly different way. The silk pantaloons caressed her skin, each step caused them to swish across her hips, beneath the heavier brocade of the embroidered dress. They reached the couch and Vittorio's fingers held hers for three extra seconds, before releasing them.

He moved around her, placing a pillow behind her back and arranging the dress folds to catch the light. He raised her heel to ease on a soft, gold embroidered Turkish shoe. She caught herself anticipating the pleasure of his touch with the second slipper. The Master selected a fresh canvas and began painting straight away. Vittorio returned to his desk and Isabella sank into a happy daze, enjoying the comfort of the divan and the breeze from the open window on her neck.

She didn't see Mistress Nichol enter the room, but she sensed her presence just before she screamed.

'Monsieur, oh, monsieur, what have you done. Poor, poor Isabella, why did you agree to this wickedness?' The woman grabbed her wrist. 'You must change immediately. Whatever will your uncle say?'

Isabella first resisted her, she'd felt as if she was under a beautiful spell, she didn't want it broken. Then Mistress

Nichol began to cry. 'Your reputation will be ruined. They'll say it was my fault.'

Isabella noticed that English vowels had been replaced by her native Scots accent. She felt a stab of guilt, the woman was obviously not faking her distress.

The painter rubbed his paintbrush on a rag, and his irritated expression had returned. 'Get dressed, Mademoiselle Godfrey. I'll talk to your uncle.'

He signalled Vittorio to follow him out of the room. Isabella had expected to see the boy laughing at her, but instead his expression was sympathetic. She heard his master say:

'We must go to Sir Everard, Vittorio. Please ask him if he will afford me a few minutes of his time?'

Mistress Nichol helped her change and Isabella felt the rebuke in the extra tug on her stays' lace. Her chaperone kept up the noisy lament all the way to their carriage. 'I'll be dismissed and how will I find my way home from here? I should have listened to my sister, coming amongst the heathens was bound to end in disaster.'

They arrived home and walked rapidly across the courtyard. Disturbed doves flew from the purple bougainvillea on the walls. Once inside, Isabella escaped up the stairs. Mistress Nichol went to find her uncle, declaring herself determined that she should explain the scandalous events, before he heard it from anyone else.

This wooden house had belonged to a rich Turkish merchant and Isabella's room was in what had been the women's quarters. She loved everything about it. Her bedroom in London was tiny and windowless, whereas this room had a view over the beautiful garden. The first floor also had interesting acoustics. There was a balcony in the corridor outside her door. It had an ornately carved wooden screen, designed to shield the Turkish ladies from male eyes. This gave her clear sight of the reception room below without being observed, and she could also hear what was said. Mistress Nichol was complaining to her uncle about Liotard. Advising that the portrait should be abandoned. Uncle Richard made listening noises, but Isabella couldn't see his face. Finally, he said: 'Thank you for informing me, Mistress Nichol.'

Her chaperone bustled off and Isabella held her breath. She expected him to shout for her, but just then Sir Everard arrived.

Her uncle rose to his feet. 'Your Excellency, what a pleasant surprise.'

'Sit, sit, Richard. I hear Monsieur Liotard has been upsetting the redoubtable Mistress Nichol.'

'She claims he had Isabella dressed up like some concubine from the Sultan's harem.'

'I know. He visited and asked me to intercede on his behalf.'

'What's your opinion? I loved his Turkish styled portraits but is it acceptable for Isabella? Surely a coming out portrait is destined for the walls of an English gentleman's home? Any hint of the Turkish whore will not do at all.'

Isabella felt the blood rush to her cheeks; the portrait was an advertisement to find her a husband. She rested her forehead against the wooden screen, her eyes screwed up and her hands balled into fists. She fought the urge to scream; she needed to hear the rest of the conversation.

'It's my fault, I should have anticipated this,' Sir Everard said. 'The Ottoman costume has become his signature style. I might have realised he longed to use it again.'

'With respect, Sir Everard, surely it's a different thing for a young lady?'

'Well, it's up to you. If you insist on her English dress I'll support you. But I believe it's his use of Turkish robes that makes his paintings extraordinary and I suspect you'll find that Mistress Nichol is exaggerating the scandalous nature of the dress.'

Her uncle was quiet for a moment, he stood up and moved to the fireplace where Isabella could see his face.

'I recognised Isabella's earrings the other night,' Sir Everard continued, 'her mother always wore them. If Isabella were posed reading a suitable book and wearing her mother's jewellery, then her rank would be clear. I admit it's unconventional but Duncannon is influential, if he says he's setting a trend then I'm sure he's right. I believe I could persuade him to host a viewing for the portrait in London.'

Isabella knew that would sway the argument. Uncle Richard might agree to almost anything to get into a viscount's circle. She could tell from his face that he was trying to hide his delight. Was it possible that he'd hoped for this from the beginning?

'I'm no expert on polite society, so I must be guided by your opinion. And of course, what with Isabella's unusually dark colouring...' Uncle Richard paused, 'well, it might work to her advantage.'

Isabella's anger exploded in her ears. Well, they could both forget the portrait. She wasn't going back.

She got Jamila to help her out of her clothes and asked her to inform Meryem the cook that she was tired and required no supper. Once she was alone she raged. She was not some breeding mare, she wouldn't co-operate. But as she paced the small room, a mocking voice in her ear grew louder. Why hadn't she expected this? Uncle Richard had always made it clear that she was a financial burden. Playing the lady this year brought them trade, but the costs were higher too. Suddenly it was clear as day to her. They'd travelled all this way to get Sir Everard to introduce them to wealthy suitors, not customers. Marriage to a rich man could lift them out of poverty forever. She was the jewel he meant to sell.

She lay on her bed and buried her face in the shoulder of her nightgown, it was old and faded, but it had belonged to her mama and she liked to imagine she could still smell her scent. The dim memory of her mother's voice, and the pure joy of her loving touch flooded back. Loneliness overwhelmed her and she cried angry tears into her pillow.

Later, when she woke in darkness, she felt calmer. She'd dreamt of Vittorio. He'd come as a gentle, loving salve, cooling her rage. She recalled the soft Italian inflection in his pronunciation of 'Bella' and the sensation of his fingers on her skin. They could all go to hell, but the Turkish dress made her feel free, and if it put off boring, straight-laced English aristocrats, even better. She'd seen the painter's work, surely the portrait itself would be a beautiful thing. She knew she was colluding with her own auction, but she had to see Vittorio again.

Chapter Six

Mistress Nichol was still sulking when they returned to the painter's studio. Uncle Richard had emphasised that Sir Everard supported the Turkish dress and it was his commission, but Isabella knew she was unconvinced.

The painter met them with a courteous bow, and immediately asked to see her jewellery. He nodded thoughtfully, as he lifted out the bracelet and earrings. Only when he held up the pearl strings he frowned. 'These are lovely, mademoiselle, but they are... well, very English,' he shrugged. 'Get changed *s'il vous plaît.*'

The Turkish clothes were laid out on the divan. There was no sign of Vittorio and Isabella walked behind the screen with the reluctant Mistress Nichol. The corner, which had shimmered with daring and excitement, was now dusty and ordinary. The studio door opened, her instinctive smile on recognising Vittorio's voice was quickly banished by her chaperone's frown. Nothing got past this woman.

Once she was dressed, they emerged to find both men

bent over Vittorio's desk. It was Vittorio who was sketching and Liotard watched him intently.

So he was an artist too. She should have guessed, there was something so sensitive about him. He was lucky to learn his craft from such an expert. Wouldn't he be surprised to know that she was an apprentice too.

Liotard suddenly thumped the desk with his hand. '*Bravo, bonne idée.*'

The apprentice grinned at her as he brushed past them to get to the trunk. 'I have the very pretty hat for you, Bella.'

'Don't you think Miss Godfrey's outfit is ridiculous enough?' Mistress Nichol said, with a pronounced emphasis on her proper name.

Nobody had ever called her Bella before, and she loved both its informality and double meaning. No doubt the same reason Mistress Nichol particularly objected. Her chaperone put her broad back between Isabella and Vittorio to make the adjustments to her dress. It took huge effort not to laugh at Vittorio, grimacing behind Mistress Nichol's shoulder. His face instantly rearranged when she turned around.

'*Merci beaucoup*, madam. Just one more thing.' He held up a brown cap in his hand, then pushed past Mistress Nichol without waiting for permission. He had the leather jewellery box in his other hand. 'Permit me... Miss Godfrey?'

Somehow he pronounced it in a way that inferred the same intimacy as Bella. He took the bracelet and the earrings from the box. 'The bracelet on the left wrist please, and one earring in the right ear.'

Isabella felt for the hole to thread through the gold wire. She saw a silent exchange between Vittorio and her chaperone, it said 'look I didn't touch her'. Mistress Nichol nodded her approval, before turning to go to her seat. He smiled at Isabella.

'The pearls are most beautiful, but perhaps too formal for the painting composition. I have the suggestion.'

Isabella eyed the small cap in his hand, it looked distinctly unglamorous, made of some simple cloth and surely meant for a boy.

'Trust me,' he said softly under his breath.

He fetched a blue scarf from the trunk and turned to Mistress Nichol.

'Madam, I want pin on the cap.'

She looked sceptical but nodded.

Vittorio's knee was against Isabella's leg; she could feel his body heat through the silk. She struggled to steady her breathing. He took some pins from his waistcoat and placed them in his mouth, and then used both hands to fold and secure the scarf onto the hat. His face was so close that she could have kissed him. As if reading her thoughts, he dipped his gaze and winked at her. Lastly, he took the pearls and hooked the second earring through the catch, attaching this to the cap, then looping the pearls up and over her hair. He stepped back to admire his work. Mistress Nichol didn't share his opinion.

'Are you trying to make Miss Godfrey look like the grinder's monkey, boy?'

He smiled at her. 'Of course not, madam, come closer, I explain you both.'

He went back to the table, returning with a hand mirror and a feather. He poked the feather into Isabella's cap, and then held up the mirror for her to see, whilst addressing Mistress Nichol. 'Monsieur Liotard's skill, his fame, is for capturing light and texture. Isabella's beauty need nothing extra, but this tableau,' he waved his upturned hand along the length of Isabella's body, 'makes most of the light. When you see the finished painting, I promise, Mistress Nichol, the embroidered dress, the shine on the pearls and every detail of the feather take away your breath.'

Isabella could tell Mistress Nichol was flattered by his personal explanation. She nodded, took the Book of Common Prayer out of her bag for Isabella, then returned to her seat. Vittorio leant in again, draping one string of pearls around her neck and adjusting the double string in her hair. The briefest brush of his fingers over the top of her ear was like a caress. Her desire to feel his touch again was shockingly intense. She closed her eyes and allowed this delicious sensation to rush through her. It set her skin tingling, and felt like new life, a promise of something exciting. She tried to hang onto the feeling, but it faded. She could hear the long minutes stretch in the tick of an unseen clock, and the muffled street sounds reducing as the temperature outside rose. The suffocating heat in the room and the rhythmic sound of the Master's brushstrokes made her drowsy. Her eyelids and chin drooped, snapping back to consciousness when she heard Liotard's voice.

'I am so sorry, mademoiselle. I need thirty more minutes of your patience. Vittorio, please talk to Miss Godfrey.'

'What shall we talk about, mademoiselle?'

Isabella began to turn, and then remembered she wasn't allowed to move. 'Tell me about your childhood, where are you from?'

'I was born in Bologna, but I grew up in the Palazzo del Re in Rome. My father was a valet in the court of King James Stuart.'

Mistress Nichol's small gasp revealed her reaction. Issy already knew she was a Catholic, she'd seen her silver crucifix when she snuck into her room to search for playing cards.

'You grew up as part of a royal court? How exciting,' Isabella said.

'Did you think I learned the French and English in a shep-herd's hut, Isabella?'

She frowned at his teasing. 'I'm sure I gave no thought to your upbringing at all, Signor...'

'Also no my name? It is Bassi, I was born Vittorio Bassi in 1725, son of the late Giuseppe Bassi, and young playmate to the Stuart Princes.' He paused, head cocked to one side, smiling at her. 'No that you're interested.'

'Of course, it's interesting, signor, please do tell us more. Is the prince as handsome as they say?' Mistress Nichol asked, she actually sounded breathless.

At the same time Isabella said over her, 'You lost your father, I'm so sorry. I lost my papa seven years ago.'

She turned to look at him. They exchanged sympathetic smiles. She felt their bond heightened by shared bereave-ment. The Master's cough reminded her of her pose.

'My father died since five years,' he said, then turned towards Mistress Nichol. 'You mean Prince Charles, madam? Yes, he is handsome. But I can't claim to know him very well. I am same age with Prince Henry. He was my very good friend when I was young. Our temperaments were well matched. Prince Charles thought us the dull sorts I think, but that is oft the way with elder brothers.'

'Are you in contact with them still?'

Issy smiled at Mistress Nichol's girlish excitement, it was so unlike her usual dourness.

'Well, you know boys are not much for the letter writing, Mistress Nichol, but I am most thankful to the family. Prince Henry help arrange my apprenticeship to Monsieur Liotard, when my father's death made paid employment necessary.'

'Quiet now, Vittorio, I want to add some touches to Miss Godfrey's face, and I need her to regain her former thoughtful expression.'

Silence reigned for the rest of the session. Isabella got

changed and they went to leave. Mistress Nichol's whole demeanour was altered.

'*Au revoir, messieurs*,' she said, 'and we look forward to more of your story next time, Vittorio.'

Isabella exchanged an amused smile with him behind her back.

When they got home, she noticed the oven was lit in the courtyard and Uncle Richard stood at the open French doors. Mistress Nichol walked indoors first. Her uncle beckoned to her.

'It's too hot to do anything, Mistress Nichol, I'll rest, you might do the same,' she said, when they reached the first floor.

Her chaperone didn't have to be told twice. Isabella put a work apron over her dress, then tiptoed out of her room and down to her uncle's study. Her own tools were already laid on the bench. He'd made an elaborate gold brooch.

'This is exquisite. Which stones do you want?' she asked.

'You choose.'

'Lapis lazuli then. Like the belt in my costume.'

She took his place at the bench. Once she'd selected the best stones she took them one by one in her smallest tweezers to place them in their settings. Her uncle checked the prongs were closed tight.

'Excellent. We'll make two silver copies, let's set one with turquoise to complement the lapis, then another with pastes.'

'Are you sure? I haven't many left.'

Isabella had been making these diamantes using the famous Monsieur Strass's method. It was by no means easy, requiring careful cutting, polishing of the glass and backing with silver, but the sparkle of the end result looked like real gems. She'd brought some from London, but hadn't the equipment to make more on the road.

'I sold the one you did for me in Vienna and I want one in this Turkish style.'

They worked in silence for some minutes and when he spoke it was casually done, as if not planned. 'We are to host a dinner on Friday. Sir Everard will honour us with his presence and Sir John Brady is coming to pick up his purchases.' He nodded to two items on the corner of the table, an inlaid snuffbox and an engraved watch fob, both in solid gold.

'Sir John has taste, those are good pieces,' she said.

'He was keen to buy something for a certain young lady but I dissuaded him. I knew you'd think it presumptuous.'

So, she thought, this odious marriage business has begun. A mixture of anger and fear caused an almost imperceptible tremor at the end of her tweezers. She put them down.

'He wanted to buy me jewellery after two meetings and only a handful of words? He's both presumptuous and idiotic.'

'I found nothing idiotic about him, quite the contrary, and he has no dragon as a sister. What is it you object to?'

Sir John Brady was very wealthy. She imagined Richard Godfrey counting his guineas.

'I simply refuse to be paraded as if for sale. I shan't come down to dinner.'

Her uncle laid down his magnifying glass and shook his head.

'Sir Everard's presence in our house is an honour and I trust you wouldn't be that rude.'

She pushed her tools away, she understood now she'd been lured here for this conversation. 'I heard you both talking about the portrait being destined for the wall of some gentleman, I won't be treated as if I'm an item of stock.'

'Keep you voice down, Issy, or you'll rouse Mistress Nichol,' he sat back and crossed his arms. 'Why are you pretending to be so shocked? How do you propose to support yourself without a good marriage?'

'I hope in time I might meet someone I actually like. You surely care for me enough not to auction me off to the first old man who comes along?'

'He's not yet forty and how do you know you can't like him if you won't meet him?'

'I'm not ready for marriage.'

'No one is forcing you into marriage. Just be polite to him for a few hours. He's a good customer.'

'All right,' she muttered.

He waved the file he had in his hand.

'But, please bear in mind that we might never be in this situation again. The ambassador's interest lends you status here. Since Sir John gained a dowry from his first wife to augment his fortune, he is free to follow his fancy and I cannot supply you with a dowry.'

Isabella clenched her jaw and replaced all her tools in their leather case.

'I'll go and talk to Meryem about the menu.' She turned back with her hand on the door. 'But I'll not be bullied into marrying that fat fool.'

Her uncle didn't look up but she saw that he smiled.

Chapter Seven

The following Sunday, Isabella and Mistress Nichol attended the service in the British Embassy. Afterwards, their route took them past the Catholic Church on Grand Avenue. Isabella noticed her companion glance over.

'Mistress Nichol, if you'd prefer to come here next week I can easily go to Reverend Payne's service on my own. I need no chaperone for church.'

Mistress Nichol looked startled and flustered her reply. 'How did you...' She restarted, 'I wouldn't want to cause any embarrassment.'

'My own mama was a Catholic. She converted and I was brought up in the Protestant faith.'

Mistress Nichol looked thoughtful. 'It's a kind offer, Isabella, but I'm happy to worship in your family church. I'm quite sure my Lord understands the necessity of my compromise. I might, however, arrange to attend confession. I have no great sins to relate, but I haven't been in months.' She paused. 'Also, I notice Sir John wears a Masonic ring, I believe your uncle would advise against telling him about your mother's religion.'

Isabella nodded and sighed at the mention of Sir John. The dinner hadn't been as bad as she feared, but although she'd done nothing to encourage him, Sir John had arranged to visit them again.

The following week after a few hours in the studio, Liotard called a break to allow a section of the painting to dry. He took himself off to his private quarters. Vittorio laid down the paint grinding materials. Mistress Nichol smiled at him. There had been a shift in her chaperone's attitude to Vittorio since the revelation of his connection to the Stuart royal family in exile, and he was especially in favour today. He'd taken Mistress Nichol to his priest to hear her confession. Her tone of voice when describing his kindness was so warm, that Isabella understood she was not the only person completely charmed by Vittorio Bassi.

Isabella rose from the couch and stretched her back. She walked over to Vittorio's desk, where he'd been mixing a gloriously bright orange paint.

'The Master use this for the flowers on your dress,' he explained.

'I wish I could see the painting,' Isabella replied.

'He never shares painting not finished,' Vittorio answered, 'but I show you his chalk drawing.'

He took up the portfolio from the corner of his desk, it contained dozens of small sketches, nearly all drawings of her.

'So many!' she said.

Vittorio looked embarrassed. 'He did only one, others are my poor attempts.'

He placed Liotard's sketch on the table and went to put away the other drawings. Isabella put her hand on his arm.

'May I see your sketches?'

'Please understand I still have much to learn.' He spread the sheaf of drawings.

Stooping to see better, she breathed in his delicious closeness, a very faint smell of sweat suggesting fastidiousness, plus a mixture of paint and linseed oil. 'Oh, they're marvellous, Vittorio, you should be so proud of these. Why do you both use red chalk?'

'It's cheap, and coloured chalk is needed on white paper. Liotard say the red colour work best here in Turkey. It captures the mood, the roofs, the colour of the earth, the sunsets.'

Isabella nodded. 'Do you turn your drawings into full scale paintings?'

'Almost never, canvas and brushes are too expensive. Sometime, Monsieur Liotard give me the canvas he doesn't want. I got the blue dress one he started with you,' he hesitated, 'but I didn't want to paint it over.'

Isabella daren't look at him. He'd done all these drawings and kept her painting safe. Dare she hope her growing attachment was returned?

'He teaching me the pastels also, I love the effect.'

Vittorio unrolled a piece of cloth to reveal a dozen small coloured nubs. Then he went to Liotard's desk and came back with a single, full-length tube of vivid red, solid like a piece of chalk. He carried it as if cradling an egg.

'This is new one, those,' he gestured to the stubs, 'he gave me, because they now too small for his fingers.'

Vittorio offered her the red pastel. Their fingertips grazed when she took it from him, and she felt her senses soar. His scent, the pastel colours, everything in the room seemed magnified. The texture of the pastel was unusual, smooth but with an underlying graininess. She rolled it between her fingers, where it left a pink stain. She imagined absorbing the colour through her skin and up her veins, to her heart.

'Will he use pastels on my portrait?' she asked.

'No. Sir Everard ask for oil and he doesn't mix this with pastel, but he plans to use them more. There's no need to grind paint, and it may take him time to find new assistant in Moldavia.'

'You're staying in Constantinople?' Hope rushed through her, Issy filled her lungs and held her breath.

Vittorio's sad expression gave her the answer. 'No. I return to Rome when he leaves.'

She let her chest deflate and her heart crush.

Mistress Nichol's voice rang out from her corner. 'Will you return to King James's court?'

'I'm not sure, madam,' he answered. 'My apprenticeship is over, so I go back to my mother house, but I must find some work. Perhaps I will teach children. I doubt I can earn enough money as the painter.'

'Surely you're happy to go home to your mother?' Isabella said.

'Of course, and I know she's glad, but I wish I have longer with Liotard.'

'How long have you worked with him?' Isabella asked.

'Over four years, the arrangement was three, but he agree I stay until he leaves Constantinople.'

'You can't go with him?'

'No,' he said, shaking his head sadly. 'I always know that this dream must come to the end.'

Like mine, she thought. Vittorio was already moving away, alert to the sound of footsteps in the corridor. He replaced the pastel in its box, and Isabella returned to her pose on the couch. When he bent over her to rearrange her dress, she pressed the back of her hand against his fingers. She smiled and hoped he understood she was trying to comfort him.

53

Inside, her heart sank. He was definitely leaving, her brief hope made the knowledge harder to bear.

Isabella's low spirits made her a poor match for Sir John's exuberant chatter at dinner that night. He and her uncle had become friends and he came to dine frequently. They usually chatted about the jewellery business and he seemed genuinely interested. Tonight Sir Everard joined them too and Isabella was barely listening when Sir John sprung a question on her. 'I'd like to explore Constantinople, Miss Godfrey. Are there sights you would recommend?'

'I'm afraid I'm no expert, I've barely been out of Pera, but Sir Everard is an authority.'

'He already told me that you enjoyed going to the Stamboul side and that he's finally got your permissions to enter Hagia Sophia. Might I join you on the excursion?'

The ambassador had the grace to look guilty.

'I did say I'd like to go but it's much too hot now. In any case my days are fully busy sitting for Monsieur Liotard,' she replied.

Sir John sat forward in his seat, reacting as if she had suggested a second helping of pudding. 'You're being painted by Liotard? I so admired the Turkish portrait of Pococke.'

Her uncle replied before she could close the conversation down.

'Sir Everard predicts Isabella's portrait will start a trend, Sir John.'

'It's my friend Viscount Duncannon who predicts fame for Liotard in London. I've seen Liotard's chalk sketch of Isabella in Turkish costume, it's going to be quite stunning,' the ambassador added.

'In Turkish dress? Oh, I'm sure it will be delightful,' Sir

John agreed, his eyebrows raised over eyes shining with enthusiasm. Something about his gaze made Issy feel queasy.

'I must visit the studio, I have in my mind to commission him myself.'

'Unfortunately, Liotard has no time to paint another portrait in Constantinople,' Sir Everard informed him. 'He's been contracted by Prince Constantine to travel to Moldavia next month.'

The reminder of Vittorio leaving brought a fresh pang of sharp disappointment, but if Issy's face betrayed her distress, Sir John seemed not to notice.

'So, if it's too hot for Hagia Sophia, we might walk in the cooler evening when your sittings are over. What about the English cemetery? I hear that it's a popular walk. Perhaps you'd like to join us, Richard?'

'I'm afraid my workload prohibits it. I'm sure Mistress Nichol, will be happy to come with you,' Uncle Richard said.

She opened her mouth to voice an excuse but her uncle flashed her a warning look. Her mood was too low to argue. 'Excuse me, it's been a tiring day.'

At the top of the stairs she found Mistress Nichol lingering in the corridor. 'Apparently that gentleman is very determined.'

Isabella grimaced and Mistress Nichol squeezed her hand. Her sympathetic touch took Issy by surprise. They parted and Isabella got ready for bed. Just before she blew out the candle, there was a soft tap at her door. Issy let Mistress Nichol in, she looked completely different in her nightgown and cap, somehow smaller and softer. Her hair hung down her back in a long braid. Issy had only seen the grey hair at the edge of her bonnet, but her braid still blazed like the leaves of a copper-beech tree in autumn.

'Sit down, Mistress Nichol,' Isabella said, motioning to the chair.

Her chaperone seemed reluctant to speak. The silence became awkward. Mistress Nichol clasped her hands in her wide lap. 'It's maybe not my place, Miss Godfrey,' she hesitated again, 'but I feel for you because I also lost my own mother too young. I will happily come with you regardless of the heat, but,' she faltered again, 'I'd urge you to resist being pushed into early marriage. It's not a decision to take lightly.'

There was real feeling in her voice. Mistress Nichol's understanding, brought a lump to Issy's throat.

'Thank you for your advice, Mistress Nichol, believe me I mean to take great care.'

'I'm sure you can rely on your uncle's protection,' she replied.

Then with an encouraging smile and a nod of her head, she rose and left.

'I wish that were the case,' Isabella said quietly, after her chaperone had gone. She had the sinking feeling that something terrible had been set in motion.

Chapter Eight

Their carriage exited the city walls near the round Galata Tower and arrived at the English graveyard just after five. Sir John took her arm and Mistress Nichol walked a few steps behind them. When they stopped at a marble bench, she walked onto the next one. The cemetery was situated high on the hill above Pera and gave them a panoramic view. Minarets from Stamboul's many mosques pierced the skyline.

'Sir Everard is organising the permissions for me to enter Hagia Sophia,' Sir John said. 'I'm sorry I couldn't tempt you,' he laughed, adding, 'I would have loved to see you in the outfit.'

Isabella had to smile. 'I didn't mind the veil, it's interesting to walk without being observed, but I think Mistress Nichol would hate it. Anyway, it's much too hot in the summer.'

Isabella glanced at her chaperone. She couldn't be persuaded out of her heavy dress. The sun was now low in the sky, but it was still warm and Mistress Nichol had turned an alarming shade of puce.

'I appreciate you both humouring my request,' Sir John said. 'I so miss the comfort of female company, since the death of my wife.'

'I'm sorry for your loss,' Isabella said. Should she have been more sympathetic towards this man?

'It's more than two years and this tour has helped to mend my spirits.'

'Still, you must miss her dreadfully.'

Sir John sighed, he took a few seconds to answer.

'I'd hoped for a long and happy marriage. I thought Anne would make a perfect mistress for the estate. Her own father had a country seat with twenty thousand hectares. She'd been involved in running his house for years.'

'You chose her because you thought she'd be good at running your house?' Isabella stared at him in disbelief, her opinion swinging against him again. He looked abashed.

'Of course not and we got on rather well at first, but you're quite right in surmising that I didn't give the enterprise enough thought.' He stretched out his legs and leaned back with his hands clasped on his belly. 'Anne was an excellent housekeeper, but she had a very reserved temperament and I had no notion of the physical demands of childbirth. I know now I need someone healthy and spirited, who is able for my exuberant nature.'

The conversation had taken an alarming turn, Isabella sensed he was looking at her, she continued to stare straight ahead. 'You had children?'

'Sadly, no. Anne conceived, but the first two were lost early and both she and the baby died trying to birth the last.'

'I'm so sorry,' she said.

He gave a heavy sigh. 'I think poor Anne was born to be a spinster. She was narrow as a whippet. Pregnancy didn't suit her and bedding didn't please her.'

Isabella could only say 'Oh,' to this extraordinary

pronouncement. She got to her feet. 'It'll be dark soon, I should get home.'

Sir John stood too, he made a small bow. 'I've shocked you and I'm most sorry. I've been a bachelor too long and forgotten how to speak around a lady.'

She managed a nod. He deserved no reply.

When they arrived home Sir John came in to call on her uncle. She was unsurprised when he shouted for her, just after Sir John had left.

'Are you sulking?' he asked. 'Sir John fears he's offended you.'

'He was offensive,' she replied, meeting his questioning look with a glare.

Uncle Richard sighed, 'Isabella, you seem to have forgotten that this ladylike charade is simply that. I've heard you deal with the barrow boys of Covent Garden and you're trying to convince me that you were offended by one His Majesty's peers?'

'He lists his late wife's deficiencies as if discussing a dog or a horse.'

He threw up his hands, his voice took on an exasperated tone. 'For God's sake, Isabella, make up your mind. You're never done complaining that people talk down to you because you're a girl, then when a man uses direct language you complain about that too.'

She gripped the table, her knuckles whitened. 'I will not be treated as breeding stock.'

He leaned on the other side of the table, his head brought in level with hers. 'And I'll have you remember you have a role to play. And as for suitors, well, Sir John is a good man and if you're determined not to like him, remember you might be faced with fewer choices later.'

Isabella left the room, banging the door behind her.

Mistress Nichol loved to hear Vittorio's stories of Stuart court life, so Issy had no difficulty in persuading her to change their previous schedule. They'd got into the habit of arriving at the artist's studio early, giving them time to talk before Liotard arrived. This morning Mistress Nichol got in first with a question. 'Do you still expect to return to Rome, Signor Bassi?'

'Alas, I have no better plan,' Vittorio replied.

'I'd like to visit Rome,' she said, 'your stories of the young princes and their court life have quite entranced me. Also, there's a Roman convent I'd love to visit.'

'Then, I hope one day to welcome you there. Perhaps you might all travel through Rome on your way back to England?'

He looked at Issy so hopefully, but her heart sank.

'Mr Godfrey was very clear that my contract was for the short duration of his stay in Constantinople,' Mistress Nichol replied. 'I'm very grateful to have found this job, but now I must look for another.'

'Then surely you should consider Rome,' Vittorio said. 'It's quite teeming with the rich British travellers and they complain about the shortage English speaking staff.'

The idea that Mistress Nichol might travel to Rome and visit Vittorio made Issy want to scream at the unfairness of it all.

'Is there no chance you might travel through Rome, Mademoiselle Godfrey?' Vittorio asked.

'The choice is not mine to make but I fear...' she struggled to control the catch in her voice, 'I fear we may go back the way we came, through the route from the north.'

The front door slamming broke the high tension in the room. They all turned in surprise towards the sound of heavy footsteps in the corridor. Sir John burst through the door. 'Oh, my dear, look at you,' he said, striding across the room and grabbing Isabella's hand. She snatched it back but he continued: 'You are positively ravishing in that dress.'

'Sir John, really,' Mistress Nichol protested, getting to her feet.

Liotard came in and Sir John turned towards the startled artist. 'You must be Monsieur Liotard. I'm a huge fan, sir. And look how you have transformed young Isabella.'

He beamed at her, there was proprietorial gleam in his eye that made Isabella feel sick.

'May I see the painting?'

He strode towards the portrait which was turned to the wall. Isabella jumped up but the artist blocked his way. 'I regret not. I never share an unfinished work.'

'No matter.' Sir John turned and nodded to Isabella, 'I can already see what you've captured, I don't doubt it will be delightful.'

Liotard inclined his head. 'Now I must return to my work, Monsieur...'

'Sir John Brady, Monsieur Liotard, and I can't leave until I obtain your promise to come to London and paint my own portrait. It's my fervent hope it will grace my walls as one of a pair.'

He bowed to Isabella who was speechless at his arrogance. 'Forgive me, Isabella, I won't keep your artist for long. I shall look forward to seeing you at dinner tomorrow.'

'Excuse us, ladies. I'll be back in a few minutes.' Liotard stretched out his hand to invite Sir John to step outside.

'The outrageous cheek of the man,' Mistress Nichol said.

Isabella sat heavily on the couch. She looked at Vittorio, his pained expression cut right through her. 'I didn't know you had a beau, Bella.'

'He's not my beau,' she protested.

61

'But such a man of wealth and title could give you a good life.' Vittorio shook his head. 'Excuse me, I see if Liotard needs me.'

Vittorio didn't return and Liotard cut the session short. 'Your expression is all wrong today. I fear that English gentleman overestimated his welcome. I'll see you tomorrow, Mademoiselle Godfrey.'

Mistress Nichol made sympathetic noises as Isabella complained throughout the coach journey home. Issy marched into the house and found Uncle Richard at his desk. 'That awful man has gone too far.'

She clenched her hands to stop them shaking. Uncle Richard looked up. 'What's wrong now, Isabella?'

'Sir John turned up at the studio uninvited. His rudeness is astonishing.'

'He came here too and I never find him rude.'

'He tried to get to see my portrait and demanded one of his own. He had no right. He spoiled the session and Monsieur Liotard was upset.'

'So, did Monsieur Liotard turn him away?'

'No, but...'

'Of course he didn't. I'm sure Liotard was very pleased to have the promise of future business. Your artist has benefitted from the ambassador's patronage as have we, and that will be over soon enough. He too must look to future commissions.'

'But he talked to Liotard as if we have some sort of romantic arrangement. He even described his own portrait as one of a pair.'

Richard Godfrey sighed and sat back in his chair. 'So that's why you're angry, because the man is being honest again. Don't play the innocent, Isabella, you've seen how he looks at you.'

'I know how he looked at me today and I found it disgusting.'

'Don't be so over dramatic. He bought that lapis gold brooch today without haggling the price, and I believe he intends it as a gift for you.'

Issy replied in the most sarcastic tone she could muster: 'Then you must be delighted to have the income but don't expect it back in the cabinet any time soon. I shan't accept his gift.'

Richard made an exasperated noise. 'It is income you depend on too, kindly don't forget that point.'

'Why does he persist? I've done nothing to encourage him.'

Her uncle shrugged. 'For some reason he finds your spirit amusing. Perhaps there would be no sport in courting someone who agreed too quickly?'

'I am not a hind to be hunted down,' she shouted.

Her uncle stood up. 'There's no need to yell, Isabella. Now, I'm going for a nap. I hope you'll have regained your temper by this evening.'

Jamila followed her up to her bedroom. Isabella sat on her bed, she ran her fingers over the brightly coloured eiderdown. For a few brief weeks she'd been happy in this lovely room. Now everything was falling apart. The memory of Vittorio's wounded expression and the argument she'd had with her uncle, made her burst into angry tears.

'No cry, madam,' Jamila said, reaching out to touch her shoulder.

The girl's sympathy made her cry even more. Eventually, Isabella sniffed and shook her head. 'I'm sorry, everything has gone wrong this morning. Help me get undressed, I'm not going back downstairs today.'

Issy talked to Jamila a lot. It made her feel less lonely and her presence was comforting. They had an understanding that was beyond words. Once she was undressed, Jamila motioned her to sit in her small chair. Issy closed her eyes and felt the comfort of the girl brushing out her hair. Jamila couldn't have known that the soothing rhythm of the strokes reminded Isabella of her mama.

'Isabella, are you all right?'

It was Mistress Nichol's voice outside the door.

'Yes, come in.'

She squeezed her maid's hand. 'Thank you so much, Jamila. You may go now.'

'Oh, you've been crying. I heard your argument with your uncle. Try not to let them upset you.'

Isabella just shook her head. She moved to the bed to offer Mistress Nichol the chair. The woman took a deep breath and sighed. 'I believe there's more to your tears than just Sir John Brady and I think we need to talk about it. Isabella, I'm sure you consider me an old woman, but being in love isn't something you forget. I see how you look at Vittorio and I remember that feeling.'

'Oh, no, it's...' Isabella started.

Mistress Nichol didn't look at her, but kept talking: 'When I was your age I went into service. There was a young man in the house. He was funny and kind, and his parents were often away from home. He would seek out my company and I hadn't the sense to keep away. The first kiss, the secret embraces on the back stairs, it was thrilling and he made me feel so special. He told me he loved me and I believe perhaps he did. We thought we were discreet, but just like you can't hide the way you look at Vittorio, we couldn't behave like strangers. The housekeeper told the mistress her suspicions, and the secret was out. I heard the master shouting at Simon, and whatever he replied was the wrong answer, it got him a thrashing.' After a pause, she continued. 'The family made immediate plans to send him to boarding school. He came to my room to say goodbye. What happened next felt natural and right, perhaps neither of us knew the danger. A few months later it became obvious I was with child and I was dismissed. I don't know if Simon ever knew.'

'How terrible for you, what happened to the baby?'

'Such situations are not unusual, and there are places for women who fall. The baby was a boy; they took him from me. I went home to Scotland, but my father wouldn't have me in the house.'

Mistress Nichol's voice broke with emotion. Isabella leaned over and touched her knee. 'I'm so sorry. How did you manage?'

She shook her head. 'It involved terribly hard times, and some considerable deception to get work again. But, Isabella, I came from extreme poverty, I don't think you'd find that an easy path. Women have a precarious place in this world and I want you to take care. You are not free to follow your heart, and I don't believe Vittorio is trying to persuade you.'

Issy nodded, there was no point in arguing.

'I'll leave you now. I'm most sorry to see you put in this position and I'll help you all I can.'

She left and Isabella stared at the door. She'd never have guessed that Mistress Nichol's straight-laced exterior hid a once passionate woman with a broken heart. It was a very dispiriting realisation. She might argue that she'd no more money than Vittorio. Unfortunately the stark truth of that was it gave them both less freedom.

Chapter Nine

Later that week Isabella and Mistress Nichol found Vittorio in the studio, with his breakfast of bread and cheese still on his desk. He smiled at them. Over the days since Sir John's intrusion, the atmosphere had lightened.

Mistress Nichol placed her gift on Vittorio's plate, wrapped in her own cotton handkerchief. Four plump purple figs, bursting with seeds, tumbled out.

'The tree in our courtyard is so heavy with fruit, that the household and even the garden birds cannot eat them all,' she said.

Vittorio's broad smile made Isabella's insides twist with ridiculous jealousy. They made an unlikely couple, but the friendship between Mistress Nichol and Vittorio grew stronger by the day.

'Thank you, madam,' he said. 'I wrote to my mother about your circumstances. She work in Ville des Londres, which is the popular hostelry with European travellers. I believe, if someone need an English companion, then she will hear it.'

'I am so grateful, signor. What's your mother's connection with this hotel?'

Vittorio flushed. 'Our circumstances are much altered since my father died. My mother must earn a living now. She is the manager there.'

Mistress Nichol straightened herself and frowned. 'That is a position of both difficulty and importance, Vittorio. There is no shame in a woman seeking and maintaining virtuous employment.'

He inclined his head. 'You are right, madam, and of course I no mean offend you. It's just a great way from my childhood, when she was respected from my father's position in Palazzo del Re.'

'Palace of the King,' she sighed. 'I would love to see it.'

'It's the simple building from the outside, and I'm told bears no comparison to his French court in the Palace Saint-Germain. But there are some very beautiful rooms inside. This convent you wish to visit, you know the name?'

She frowned in concentration. 'I'm not sure, but I remember that it was dedicated to Saint Cecilia. My mistress in Edinburgh went on a pilgrimage to Rome, and described it as the most beautiful and spiritual place on earth.'

Vittorio smiled. 'Santa Cecilia in Trastevere. In fact, Prince Henry's mother lived with the nuns there for few years. He said me he visited her when he was very young. I went back to see the church with him, it is most beautiful.'

'The young princes' mother. Yes, that's exactly what she told me.' Mistress Nichol's excitement sent her voice up several octaves. She clasped her hands together, then shook her head. 'To go there would be a dream come true.'

Vittorio crossed the room and took Mistress Nichol's hand. 'I cannot promise I find you employment in Rome. But, if you visit Italy, it would be honour to guide you Santa Cecilia.'

She grasped his hand with both of hers and Isabella could see she was close to tears. Just then, the Master could be heard approaching the studio, so Vittorio returned to his desk.

Uncle Richard had insisted Issy must join them for supper with Sir John, so she was glad that Sir Everard was coming too. She'd just come downstairs from her bedroom, when she heard a clatter of hooves. She opened the front door to see Sir Everard enter the gate. He always travelled with his official contingent of janissaries. These splendidly dressed Turkish soldiers were quite a spectacle. Mounted on beautiful Arab horses, they had white feathers in their high turbans and long vicious looking scimitars hanging at their sides. He spoke to them in Turkish, presumably dismissing them for the rest of the evening because all but two of them turned and left. The ambassador kissed her cheek when she took his jacket, then took off his wig and left it on the hook. He rubbed both sets of fingers over his bald head with a comfortable sigh, then he unfolded a Turkish silk cap from his pocket.

'You've no idea how much I'm going to miss your family suppers, Issy. Having a few hours to relax here has been a life saver for me these last months.'

The sound of the ambassador's voice had brought Uncle Richard out of the dining room and he looked at him quizzically. The ambassador grimaced in apology. 'I still can't say too much about it, but it seems I must soon go back to London.'

'My thoughts have turned that way too. Anyway, let's eat, Sir John is here already,' Uncle Richard replied.

Sir Everard gave Isabella his arm and they walked to the table.

'What's your route back to England, Sir John?' Sir Everard asked.

'I must go via Rome, I left some antiquities there.'

'If you plan to sail through the Dardanelles you shouldn't leave it too late. The risk of storms increases into the autumn.'

'Useful advice, Sir Everard,' Uncle Richard remarked. 'We must make plans too.'

'Perhaps it would be jolly to travel together?' Sir John suggested, looking between her uncle and Sir Everard.

'Sadly I must pass through Vienna. But I'd recommend seeing Rome if you have the chance, Richard.'

Isabella's brain whirred, weeks on a boat with Sir John sounded like the worst torture. But a chance to see Vittorio in Rome might make it worthwhile. She looked to see her uncle's reaction. Quite a dilemma for him: stick with the suitor or the benefactor?

'I can see advantages of passing through new cities.'

'Yes, quite the education for Isabella,' Sir Everard agreed.

Issy knew perfectly well her uncle thought only of money. He'd try to persuade her to accept Sir John on the journey, and Rome might offer new customers to cheat.

'I'll give it some thought. Let me know your plans, Sir John. Do you know when you'll leave, Sir Everard?'

'I've no idea, but before the snows arrive,' he answered.

After dinner the men took their brandies to Richard's study. Twenty minutes later, she heard Sir Everard say goodbye to them. He came back to where Isabella sat by the fire in the dining room. 'I've come to say goodnight and to thank for your hospitality. I'll look forward to visiting you in London, Isabella.'

She smiled, but given their dingy living conditions her uncle would avoid that at all costs.

'Richard says you gave up the house in Russell Square?'

Issy hesitated, was she still supposed to be hiding the extent of their poverty? 'Uncle Richard does no entertaining and we'd no need for such a large place. We moved somewhere more convenient for the workshop.'

'That's a shame. I clearly remember your mother coming down that beautiful curved staircase. She had such grace.'

Isabella leaned forward, resting her elbows on her knees, her chin in her hands. 'What else do you remember? What was she like?'

Sir Everard smiled and sat down opposite her. 'A girl who lit up a room with her laughter and she so loved to sing. When she sang you really heard her soft Scottish lilt.'

'Of course, I'd forgotten her accent was Scottish. It's so sad that her family rejected her.'

'Rejected? What made you think that?'

'Uncle Richard said they threw her out when she married a Protestant.'

Sir Everard frowned. 'She moved to London, it was a long way from her family and I think they had a Scottish marriage planned for her. It's true her mother tried to dissuade her from converting, I believe religion was very important to your grandmother. That's what I remember, but not thrown out and rejected. That's much too strong.'

Isabella sat back. Was her picture of her childhood inaccurate?

'Why would Uncle Richard have the wrong story?'

Sir Everard went to the coat stand to retrieve his wig. 'Just a misunderstanding I should think. He wasn't around when they married and I'm certain your uncle wasn't living with you when I used to visit.' He smiled at her. 'Don't stay up too late, Isabella, you look tired.'

. . .

Later that week, Liotard laid down his paint brush after only one hour. '*Bon*,' he said. 'You can leave early today, Mademoiselle Godfrey. I've advised Sir Everard that he may come to view the portrait tomorrow and he requests that you invite your uncle. I have a few tiny highlights to add, but I'll be ready for them at eleven.'

Isabella thought her heart might stop. She'd hoped it would take at least another week. She glanced over at Vittorio. He didn't look up but seemed to be trying to grind his paint through the table.

Mistress Nichol caught her eye with a look of sympathy. 'I'm sad it's over. We've so enjoyed your company,' she said.

Liotard raised his eyebrows. He spoke rarely but Issy guessed he'd noticed them both grow fond of Vittorio over the weeks. 'I will see you for the final touches in the morning, *mesdames*,' he said, then left the room.

'When will you go to Rome, signor?' Mistress Nichol asked.

Vittorio laid down his tools and sighed. 'I look for a berth. This week I think.'

Mistress Nichol's voice wavered when she said: 'We'll miss you.' She looked at Isabella.

'I feel the same,' he said.

Isabella now sensed his gaze, but she was so close to breaking down, she daren't turn.

'What about your plans, Mistress Nichol?' he asked.

'I'm not sure. Mr Godfrey advises me that he plans to leave Constantinople soon. I'm tempted to risk travelling home via Rome, in the hope that I might find work there. However, if I tarry too long in Italy the weather will prevent the journey and I daren't use up all my savings in Rome.'

Issy's distress that Mistress Nichol found herself in such a

71

situation was another strand in her mounting despair. She'd so far failed in trying to persuade her uncle to extend her employment.

'Mistress Nichol, I do my utmost to help you stay in Rome,' Vittorio answered. 'It is all I can do,' he added.

Issy thought the tremor in his voice would make her heart dissolve.

'When I arrive Rome, I look work for you.'

'Thank you so much, signor.'

Mistress Nichol then rose from her seat. 'I need some air, I shall enjoy the terrace until our carriage arrives.'

She closed the door behind her and Isabella's breathing went into a galloping panic. They were being left alone. Vittorio rose immediately and came over to sit beside her on the couch. He looked at her with wide, anxious eyes. 'I didn't dare hope this,' he hesitated. 'Isabella, there is something I must say.'

He took her hand. His slim fingers were soft, on one he wore a gold ring with a red garnet, Isabella could feel a callous beneath the band. 'We have little time left. I so wish things were different.' He put his hand to her temple, and tucked a stray strand of hair behind her ear. His expression was very serious. 'If I were a rich man I'd make you mine forever.'

This was the declaration she had longed for, but it destroyed the hope that had fluttered to the surface. She felt sick, he was saying goodbye. She grabbed both his hands. 'No. Truly, I'm not what I seem. I'm not a rich at all, it's all an act. Take me with you, we can work it out. I don't care about money.'

He shook his head and pulled his hands free. 'Isabella, it break my heart that I cannot be the man to have you forever, but I promise I never forget you.'

She couldn't prevent the hot tears spilling down her face. 'Nor me you.'

'Don't cry, lovely Bella. I want you remember how happy we were for these few short weeks.'

He leaned towards her, and she thought he might kiss her. Instead he placed his fingertips on her cheeks and tenderly wiped away the tears with his thumbs. She saw her own feelings mirrored in his eyes. 'I have something help you remember,' he said. He took a silver locket from his pocket. Then, with a click, he opened the catch to reveal a very small painting. 'Monsieur Liotard has been teaching me the miniaturist's skill, we think it may be the best plan for me doing a living from my art. I want you have my first one.' Then he raised her hand to his mouth and placed a soft kiss in the centre of her palm, his lips lingered on her skin. A violent erotic charge flooded down through her body. He placed the locket on her kissed hand, it contained a tiny version of her own face.

A sob escaped her throat. 'Vittorio, please...' She pulled him towards her, he didn't resist and when their lips met, his mouth was soft and sweet and willing. She could feel his tears mix with hers. He pulled away, she could see he wanted her. They kissed again, urgently, and desperately. His embrace tightened and he took her lower lip softly between his teeth, she groaned with pleasure. The sound of Mistress Nichol approaching forced them to part.

'Isabella, the carriage is here,' she called.

'I'm so sorry,' Vittorio said. Then in a whisper: 'I love you.' He stood and rushed past Mistress Nichol.

Isabella was reduced to shuddering sobs. Mistress Nichol shook her head, her voice full of sympathy. 'I'll ask the driver to give us a moment, you need to compose yourself, child.'

Chapter Ten

Mistress Nichol excused Isabella from dinner and tactfully left her to grieve. The next morning, she came into her bedroom before Jamila arrived to dress her. She carried a plate of chopped figs, bread and honey.

'I know you're not hungry, Isabella, but you need to get dressed and you must eat. Your uncle advises me that both Sir John and Sir Everard will come to the studio to see the painting. There is no avoiding today.'

'Not him, not today,' she groaned. 'Mistress Nichol, I cannot face them, and how can I possibly look at Vittorio?'

'You can and you shall, your uncle expects it and Sir Everard deserves no slight.'

When Jamila came in, her brown eyes softened at the sight of Isabella's face.

Mistress Nichol put a piece of sweet, sticky fig in Isabella's mouth. Then added: 'Get dressed quickly, Issy, I'll get some cold cloths for your eyes.'

Isabella allowed Jamila to help her wash and dress. Then

Mistress Nichol returned. 'Lie down. This will reduce the swelling.'

Isabella found the cold towel on her eyes was soothing. Mistress Nichol stroked her face. The tenderness of the gesture made her cry again.

'Enough weeping now, Isabella, I know you have the strength to get through this.'

When they entered the artist's studio Vittorio wasn't there. She hadn't known how she would face the pain of seeing him, but it turned out missing him was worse.

Mistress Nichol arranged her dress.

'Well done, madam, just one tiny adjustment, I think.' The painter came over and stretched to move the position of her left hand on the back of the divan. Then, to Isabella's surprise, he slipped a narrow ring onto her smallest finger. The ring had a single stone, a deep red garnet, she recognised it immediately.

Liotard patted her hand. 'Perfect fit, just as he said it would.'

Isabella sat through the morning with her eyes lowered; her thoughts were filled with sadness and also love. The ring told her she wasn't forgotten. She would wear it always, and never forget him.

After an hour, Liotard shook out a rag with a flourish and began to wipe his paintbrush. '*Voilà*, it's finished. Come, ladies, you should see it first.'

Isabella swung her feet to the floor, and then she faltered. Did she care about the painting now?

Mistress Nichol had begun towards the artist, then seeing her hesitation, she stopped. She frowned and signalled with her eyes that Isabella should move. 'I am so excited, but come along, Isabella, you must see it first.'

Isabella didn't want to offend the painter. Liotard stood to the side with a smile as she stepped in front of the portrait. Mistress Nichol gasped at her shoulder. It was the most beautiful painting. The colours were so rich, the details perfect. Each single one of the flowers on her dress looked as if it was the original embroidery. Then she saw the finishing touch. Liotard had painted in the ring, the red jewel sat on her finger at the very centre of the painting. For the rest of her life, whatever trials she must face, this symbol of Vittorio's love would always be there to remind her. She turned to Liotard. 'Thank you, monsieur. Thank you for everything.'

The door banging followed by Sir John's loud voice over the others, signalled their arrival. If only she could stop time, to keep her painting for her eyes only.

The studio doors were flung open, she kept her gaze fixed on the portrait as the three men walked in behind her. She felt a warm hand on her shoulder, it was Sir Everard. 'It is utterly beautiful, Isabella, your parents would have been so proud.'

She placed her fingers over his. 'Thank you, Sir Everard.'

Uncle Richard shook the painter's hand. 'You have excelled yourself, monsieur. Isabella will be the talk of London.'

Sir John appeared, beaming at his side. 'Bravo, bravo, monsieur. You really must come to England to paint my portrait as soon as possible.'

He advanced on Isabella, for a horrible moment she thought he might kiss her. She stepped back and he laughed. 'Forgive my enthusiasm, but I couldn't wait any longer to see the painting. It's just as I imagined, you are like a rosebud on the point of bloom. I adore this costume, Liotard. Godfrey, you should surely buy it. The lucky beggar who snags Isabella is certain to want to recreate the look.'

Isabella cringed and Liotard shook his head. 'I am afraid that's out of the question. This dress is like my muse. It transforms the wearer and I shall need it again.' He nodded towards Isabella. 'Although, I fear I may search long to find another model who suits it quite so well as Miss Godfrey.'

'Well that's a shame but it gives me an idea. Everard, I want to create a room in my London home to site my painting. I'll furnish it in the Turkish style. I'll need rugs and lamps, then of course I must buy an outfit for my own portrait.'

'I'll take you to the bazaar, John. And I know the shop where Pococke got his cloak.'

Sir John turned to Isabella, 'Sadly though the most important element to complete the happy room remains beyond my reach.' He took her hand and kissed the back. 'I hope one day soon my dream will be complete.' He bowed, then he and Sir Everard left.

Uncle Richard examined the painting closely. 'Sir, you are a master. I hope we can find a way to repay your diligence and honour your talent. Isabella and I could not be more pleased.'

They turned towards her and she realised her utter despair must be visible. The artist might imagine she didn't like the painting. She forced a smile. 'Sir, I'm humbled. I shall be forever in your debt to have this beautiful portrait in my life. Thank you.'

Her uncle started to talk to Liotard about his painting technique.

'Uncle Richard, I'm very tired, would you mind if Mistress Nichol and I took the carriage and sent it back for you?'

'No, that's fine. I want to talk to Monsieur Liotard about appropriate plans to show your painting.'

As they got ready to leave, she turned to Monsieur Liotard. 'I never got the chance to thank Signor Bassi for his support and friendship, monsieur. Do you know when he'll leave Constantinople?'

The artist's expression told her he understood the feeling behind her question. He shook his head slowly. 'I'm sorry, Mademoiselle Godfrey. Vittorio discovered a ship in port bound for Rome. He left early this morning.'

Chapter Eleven

The knowledge that Vittorio had gone was like a vice squeezing her heart. When they got home Isabella went straight to her bed. She couldn't imagine wanting to get up again. Day after day, Jamila brought her food on trays, then took them away again untouched. She cried herself out and now felt weighed down by a suffocating lethargy. Her interest in life had gone. She'd offered herself, no strings attached, she'd have followed him in an instant. He'd turned her down.

After a whole week of hiding herself away, Mistress Nichol came in one morning and sat on her bed. 'Isabella, do you feel well enough to admit your uncle? He wants to discuss your passage home.'

Isabella nodded. 'Yes, tell him to come up. It's time I roused myself.'

The issue of Mistress Nichol's passage had to be resolved, if she couldn't persuade Uncle Richard she'd have to ask Sir Everard for help. Just then Jamila arrived and Isabella asked for her robe. When her uncle knocked and came in, Jamila moved to the closet and began selecting fresh clothes. Uncle

Richard was dressed to go out, the formality of his black coat and the shine on his buckled shoes made him look too large for her little room. It was like a visitation from a raven.

'So are you over your mystery sickness? Mistress Nichol was incapable of giving me a straight answer about the nature of your illness.'

His tone was brusque. He glanced at Jamila when she slammed the cupboard door. 'You may go, Jamila.' He waited until Jamila had left, then added: 'We need to discuss our route home, Sir John is keen for us to accompany him.'

Isabella groaned. 'That will mean being in a ship with him for weeks before we even begin crossing Europe. I really can't face it.'

He barked a laugh. 'Listen to you! You've quite lost touch with reality, Isabella. The world does not revolve around your sensitive feelings. I believe you sat for too long lounging on that artist's couch.'

Anger cleared her head. 'The portrait was your scheme. Please don't twist the facts. And if you've already decided to accompany him, then why are you asking my opinion?'

Richard Godfrey leaned back against the wall and steepled his hands over his long nose. He took a deep breath. 'We need to decide how to make best use of the contacts we've made here. We have some nice pieces to sell in London but no solid plan for reaching the right customers.'

'I thought you meant to waltz into Viscount Duncannon's drawing room with my portrait under your arm?'

He glared at her. 'Sir Everard has given me a letter of introduction, but that doesn't mean I'll be able to waltz in, as you put it. Of course, if you were Sir John's fiancée we would be welcome in every society drawing room.'

'No.' Her reply was loud and clear.

'You've decided against him?'

'I've decided I'm not ready to marry anyone.'

'Then it seems you'll continue working with me?' He phrased it as a question but they both knew the answer. She nodded. 'Then I've a proposal, consider it an extension to our European scheme. We travel to Rome with Sir John, and you agree to receive his suit on the journey.'

Isabella opened her mouth to protest, but he raised his hand. 'Let me finish. I hope you'll come to your senses and accept him but if you decide not, we'll travel independently from Rome.'

Isabella grimaced. 'Is it worth it? How much jewellery can you expect him to buy?'

'It's a much bigger enterprise than that. He'll pay our passages to Rome and he wants to discuss becoming a full partner in the business. He's genuinely interested and if you marry, we will both be secure.'

Isabella put her face in her hands for a second. He was boxing her in. 'That's too much pressure. You raise his expectations when I really doubt I'll change my mind. Then I'll end up saying no and upsetting everyone.'

He shrugged and went to leave. 'I'd judge that a foolish decision, but provided you are tactful we'll have saved the cost of the journey and lost nothing. Either way, we must decide soon, Sir John's passage is booked for next week.'

'What about Mistress Nichol?' Isabella asked.

'He'll pay for her passage too,' he replied with a smug smile. He left and closed the door behind him.

Isabella sat for a long time. Her brain was numbed by Vittorio's rejection, followed by so many hours on her own. She'd told herself to forget him but found she couldn't. If she agreed to this odious plan she'd have to endure Sir John but it would get both her and Mistress Nichol to Rome. She'd find Vittorio and persuade him. She'd seen the love in his eyes. He didn't know her circumstances and he underestimated her resilience. Surely they could find a way to be together?

. . .

Sir John beamed when he entered the dining room that evening and found her there. 'Are you feeling better? I must say you still look a little pale.'

She saw her uncle's theatrical glance to the ceiling.

'Thank you, yes. I feel sorry to have lost so many days when I find we must leave Turkey soon.'

He frowned. 'I hope you're not angry to be leaving early on my account.'

'No, and I must thank you for securing me Mistress Nichol's company.'

'My wife would never travel without some female companion. I never yet understood all the hairpins and laces but I do realise they're a great deal of bother. I do have one favour to ask. Sir Everard has helped me scour Constantinople for the items I want for my Turkish sitting room. I went with him to a rug shop in Pera yesterday but I couldn't make the final choice. Would you come and give me your opinion?'

She hesitated, the thought of going was daunting, but she owed him such a small request. 'Of course, if we avoid the hottest hours. I love Turkish carpets. Mistress Nichol would have to come of course.'

'The more female eyes the better. My late wife told me that I have no eye for colour. I'll pick you both up tomorrow evening.'

The small carpet shop was in one of the narrow alleys off Grand Avenue. Inside the whole place was packed with rugs, laid in high piles all around the walls of the shop, which had a distinctive smell of wool and ancient dust. The owner obviously remembered Sir John and had his boys peeling rugs off the pile of large carpets, until they uncovered the ones he'd chosen. They dragged them to a sunlit patch of floor at the front of the shop, unfurling them with flourish.

'What beautiful carpets,' Mistress Nichol said.

'I can see why you couldn't choose,' Isabella added, 'they're all gorgeous.'

The rugs were similar in basic design but with different shades and patterns. Red was the dominant colour but there were flashes of blue, green, gold and turquoise, evoking thoughts of rich gems. She had an urge to sink on her knees to feel the wool, but her skirt hoops made such a manoeuvre impossible.

When would she stop missing her beautiful Turkish outfit? Her portrait was already a lie, that happy girl had gone forever. She stroked the small rug atop the stack at her elbow, looking for comfort in the softness. She'd thought herself destroyed by sadness but found the beauty and skill in these carpets lit a tiny spark. This would be her saviour, so long as she could create beautiful things she had something to cling to.

After some deliberation she helped Sir John select a red and gold rug.

'Now, shall we go to a café?' said Sir John, once he'd paid. 'I know a good one on Grand Avenue, Sir Everard says it does the best pastries in Pera.'

Mistress Nichol ordered sherbet, whilst she and Sir John had the sweet cardamom coffee. It perfectly complemented the sticky baklava filled with honey and nuts. Isabella sat back and looked around the room. In one corner, some old men were hunched over their sticks playing backgammon. A family sat at another table nearby and the lady was fully veiled, she managed to drink and eat using a discreet dipping motion. Isabella doubted she could manage that without getting honey everywhere. She returned Sir John's smile. She had to admit it had been a pleasant evening. Maybe the journey wouldn't be as bad as she feared?

'That was interesting and your rug is beautiful.'

'Would you think me very forward if I said I'm still hoping it might be our rug? I can't tell you how happy I am that we'll travel together.'

She sighed 'I really don't think I'm ready to marry.'

'Then I'll take that as softer than a firm no. It gives me hope.' He touched the back of her hand. 'I know you don't want to be rushed, Isabella, but I'm quite certain the young bachelors of London will have no scruples about bowling you over with flattery, when they see your painting on Viscount Duncannon's walls. You can't blame me for pressing my current advantage.'

'Ugh. I would hate such flattery and the whole notion of being on public display is disgusting.'

'Surely your uncle won't allow it if you tell him it makes you unhappy?'

Isabella stared at her hands clasped on the table. The voyage would be more bearable if there was less deception. How much dare she tell this man? She looked him straight in the eye. 'Our financial circumstances would make that a foolish stance. My life in London is very different to the affluent image we present here.'

'I knew from your uncle that business has been difficult since your father died and that he had to give up the shop.'

'The shop, our house, a whole way of life. I don't mix in polite society in London. My mother and father did, but it has not been my life.'

He shook his head. 'Then that is a great shame. Does it not make you sad to go back?'

She searched his face for a reaction. 'I'm sad to leave here for lots of reasons. But are you not shocked to know my lowly status?'

He shrugged, 'I'm lucky to find you as an undiscovered jewel. It makes you more precious and I admire your honesty.'

He took a small box from his pocket. Isabella recognised it, so knew to expect the gold lapis brooch. 'Would you wear it as a token of my affection?' he asked her. 'As soon as I saw it, I knew I had to have it for you.'

When she didn't take it from him, he laid it on the table.

'I'll wear it if you accept the truth about it,' she answered.

He raised an eyebrow in question. Isabella ran her fingertip over the cluster of lapis in the centre of the flower design.

'You must know that I'm no idle lady. I placed these stones, and our business relies on my labour. I'm an artisan, a common tradesperson,' she looked up and saw Mistress Nichol's astonished expression. Sir John's was hard to read.

'You made this brooch?'

She shook her head, 'I'm not yet skilled enough. My uncle made the brooch, but I created a silver filigree copy and decorated it with diamanté, the use of imitation gems is my specialty.'

He sat back in his chair and laughed. 'You're even more extraordinary than I thought, Isabella.'

'You're not upset? That you've been courting a commoner, someone who earns money with her own hands?'

He put the brooch in her hand and closed her fingers around it. 'There is nothing common about you and you're not the first gentlewoman to fall onto hard times.'

Isabella nodded and pinned the brooch on her bodice. 'Thank you,' she said. 'And I'd be grateful if you kept my confession to yourself. But, I couldn't even begin considering a suitor without honesty between us.'

He signalled for the bill and helped her to her feet. 'I'm so happy that you confided in me, I might dismiss the carriage and sail down the hill on a cloud.'

Mistress Nichol grimaced behind his back.

'Please be clear that I've made you no promise, Sir John, and I believe Mistress Nichol might prefer four wheels,' she replied.

Her chaperone rolled her eyes.

Chapter Twelve

Two days before they were due to sail, Isabella went into her uncle's room and found him rushing around looking frantic. He was moving some of his clothes from a large trunk to a smaller one, checking things off a list and talking to himself.

'What are you doing?' she asked, immediately suspicious.

Sure enough, he looked up as if caught in the wrong. 'Nothing. I just realised that I'd want a small trunk with everyday things for the cabin.'

She nodded, 'Yes, I've done the same.'

He went back to his re-packing. 'Sir John is moving in today,' he said without looking up.

'Really? Why?'

'His landlord let him down. Apparently the maid resigned without giving notice and he isn't offering a replacement.'

'I see,' Isabella said. Her heart sank at the thought.

'I put your tools over there,' he gestured towards her tool pouch on his chest of drawers. A small leather purse sat beside it.

'What's this?' she asked, feeling the weight of coins in her hand.

'Part of the funds for our journey, I thought it might be safer if you kept some.'

She eyed him distrustfully, he'd never taken such a precaution before.

'Jeyhan!' he shouted. When the boy came running in, he kicked the trunk, 'in coach,' he said, then put on his hat.

'Where are you going?'

'North,' he said.

'Where north? And why now? We leave the day after tomorrow.'

Mistress Nichol walked in, Isabella saw from her expression that she also thought his plan was unwise.

'To visit the French ambassador in his country home. He's asked to see some pieces.'

'How long will you be gone? Are you not afraid of missing the boat?'

'That's why I'm sending my trunks to the ship now and I'll keep this small one with me. I've instructed that all your luggage should go today too, the ship berthed last night.'

She still frowned at him, it made no sense. He laid a reassuring hand on her arm.

'I aim to be back, don't worry and Sir John will stand in until I return.'

As if summoned, the gate banged and Sir John's familiar voice rang out from the courtyard: 'Hello,' then he appeared in the doorway. She heard Mistress Nichol sigh.

'Good man, you got my note then,' Uncle Richard said.

'Yes, I'm delighted to assist,' he put a proprietorial hand on her shoulder and she had to subdue the urge to slap his fingers. 'I can't have this precious girl unprotected,' he added.

'I've been perfectly looked after by Jeyhan when Uncle has travelled before,' she grumbled. Both men ignored her.

'I really appreciate it, and I'll just get you those papers I mentioned,' Uncle Richard replied.

'What papers?' Isabella asked.

'Just formalities for the journey,' Uncle Richard answered.

Sir John followed him into his study. They returned within minutes.

'I expect I'll see you both tomorrow, or the day after at the very latest,' he said, then he strode out the front door and towards the waiting chaise.

When the gate closed behind him, Sir John clapped his hands and rubbed them together. 'Right, ladies, time for a proper breakfast.'

Isabella ate little. Sir John's ebullient mood made him talkative, he chattered on about his plans for his Turkish sitting room. Her thoughts were with Vittorio and she wasn't really listening.

'Isabella, what do you think? Isabella?' He had to say her name twice to get her attention.

'Yes, Sir John?'

'About my Turkish costume,' then he laughed loudly. 'Everard took me to the Turkish tailor and I have the whole outfit. A striped robe and a rather dashing fur edged cloak. I thought one of us might expire from laughing, trying to learn how to tie the turban. I hope Liotard knows how to do it, because it's devilish difficult.' He smiled at her, then stretched over to pat her hand. 'Since I still hope you'll be sitting in this Turkish room with me, I had your seamstress run up a copy of Liotard's Turkish robes. Both outfits will be delivered today.'

She stared at him. What need would she have for Turkish robes in London? Had he taken leave of his senses?

'I can just picture us both lounging in front of the fire in our Turkish clothes; the painting has whetted my appetite for a bit of Eastern masquerade. What do you say, my little Turkish maiden?'

The lustful look on his face made her feel sick. Was she imagining a difference in his demeanour in her uncle's absence?

'I say you're being presumptuous,' Isabella replied.

Mistress Nichol coughed and glared at him, and he laughed again. Once he'd eaten enough for four men, he declared he had to go out to oversee the transfer of his luggage to the ship. 'I'll be back before dark. Why not a romantic supper *à deux*?' He looked for Mistress Nichol's reaction.

'Mr Godfrey employed me as a chaperone, Sir John, and for as long as Isabella is in my charge I intend to fulfil my duties. Cook will provide supper *à trois*.' And with that she pushed back her chair. 'Come along, Isabella, there is still a great deal of packing to do.'

Isabella inclined her head and said: 'Good day, Sir John,' and followed Mistress Nichol out of the room.

The rebuff seemed not to damage his good humour. She heard him mutter: 'Damnable difficult race, the Scotch,' and laugh uproariously.

After dinner, Mistress Nichol got Jeyhan to carry their trunks downstairs. Then she motioned that she wanted the massive linen-press outside Isabella's room, moved to sit in the middle of the corridor. Isabella looked on in astonishment, as both Jamila and Mistress Nichol lent their weight to the problem, until, with a great deal of difficulty, the huge cupboard stood blocking the passage.

'Surely you don't really think this is necessary?' Isabella asked.

'I hope not, but I'm a heavy sleeper. I'll lie awake all night, if I fear a certain gentleman might attempt a night-time excursion.'

She made sure that both Isabella and Jamila could squeeze through the narrow gap, before confirming that her broader frame wouldn't pass. Jamila laughed and nodded her approval. Isabella wondered why her maid shared Mistress Nichol's distrust.

Sir John arrived back late, so they didn't finish eating until after ten. He consumed a great deal of her uncle's claret and actually fell asleep at the table. His head was slumped onto his chest, and he slept right through the plates being cleared.

Isabella gave him a shake. 'Sir John, I'm going to bed now. It's time to retire.'

'What? Oh, right. Sorry, my dear. You're going to bed so soon?'

'I always wake early in this hot weather, I prefer not to be too late in bed.'

Mistress Nichol went to get fresh candles for their chambersticks. Sir John stood and caught Isabella around her waist. 'I think, sweet Isabella, it's time we were less formal with each other. Please call me John.'

'Goodnight, John,' she said, squirming free.

He kissed her on her cheek. She felt his hand cup her breast. She slapped his hand away just before Mistress Nichol walked back in. She glared at him but he smiled.

'Good night, Isabella. Sleep well.'

Isabella was too angry to sleep. How dare he make her uncomfortable in her own home. She wouldn't let him spoil these last few days. Issy leaned out of her window to push the shutters open. She'd attract moths to her candle, but it was worth it for the cooler air and tonight there was a full moon. The moonlight turned the night into soft gloom. A smell of night-blooming jasmine rose from the courtyard. The familiar noise of Jeyhan shifting from one foot to the other at the gate, gave her comfort. Someone walked into the courtyard, and she knew from the light steps that it was Jamila. The girl crossed the cobbles, crooning the name of the kitten she'd adopted. Then, there was a tiny answering meow. Issy knew from the encouraging murmurs, that she was feeding the cat. Jamila returned to the terrace, before closing and bolting the front door.

Isabella lay awake in the dark and soon Mistress Nichol began to snore. Then, just as her chaperone predicted, came a creaking noise on the wooden stairs. Isabella sat bolt upright; she had assumed that Mistress Nichol was being over cautious. She held her breath, and listened. The footsteps stopped in front of Mistress Nichol's room, then advanced again. Each foot was placed slowly, she could even hear his fingers on the wall. There were no windows in the corridor, he must be inching his way in total darkness. The hairs on her arms rose and she tried to subdue the noise of her own ragged breathing, even her heartbeat sounded too loud. Then came the bump and curse, which signalled Sir John had walked into the linen-press. There was a scuffling noise and a grunt; Isabella prayed that he'd find the cabinet too heavy to shift, and any attempt would surely wake Mistress Nichol. Nevertheless, she filled her lungs with air, ready to scream for help, but then, she heard him mutter:

'That bloody Scotch bitch.'

And next, the sound of his boots retreating down the stairs.

Chapter Thirteen

When Isabella's breathing returned to normal, her fear changed to anger. How dare he. Mistress Nichol had expected this. Did she sense something about Sir John's character that Isabella had missed? The thought of what was on his mind made her feel sick, was such revulsion an overreaction? Was her repulsion unnatural? Only when the imam had called for dawn prayers, did she finally fall into fitful sleep.

When Jamila came in, she gave her a note for Mistress Nichol and Sir John.

I had a very sleepless Night and I'm exhausted. Please ask Jamila to bring me some Breakfast. I will eat in my Room and try to sleep again.

When she heard Sir John march across the courtyard and bang the outside gate behind him, she squeezed through the gap beside the press. Mistress Nichol was still sitting at the dining table.

'Good morning, my dear. Are you feeling any better?'

Isabella nodded, she'd decided not to tell her. The whole thing made her feel somehow foolish. She'd come to no harm and she hoped her uncle would return today. They both turned at the sound of the gate opening, her expectation of her uncle was dashed when she recognised the voice of Sir Everard. She exchanged a glance with Mistress Nichol. The ambassador never visited during the day. His expression when he entered did nothing to relieve her anxiety.

'Good morning, Sir Everard, you're up and about early. Will you join us for some breakfast?'

'Thank you, but I've already eaten, Isabella.'

She offered him a chair.

'I'm most sorry to disturb you, ladies, but I was hoping to catch Richard,' he nodded towards Sir John's plateful of crumbs, 'but I see I'm too late.'

Isabella exhaled, she'd feared some sort of accident. 'Actually that's Sir John's place, he's moved in. Uncle Richard has gone away on business.'

'Really? What a nuisance. The embassy had a very odd visitor yesterday. I'm sure it's a misunderstanding but I'd hoped to get it cleared up today before you leave.'

'I'm not certain he'll be back today. Is it something I can help with?'

'Maybe. Do you remember meeting a Swedish Count Stenbock in Vienna?'

'I don't think so, but we did meet a large number of people.'

Sir Everard pulled one of Uncle Richard's jewellery boxes from his pocket and flipped it open, sat inside was a silver and pavé-cut diamante brooch. Isabella recognised it as one of hers. Her heart sank.

'The count says he bought a diamond brooch from Richard and that he's been sold a fake.' He held the brooch up to the light, 'I have to say they look like diamonds to me.'

Isabella glanced at Mistress Nichol, who gave a tiny shake of her head.

'Goodness, how terrible. I'm sure it's some sort of misunderstanding. I'll tell Uncle Richard to come and see you as soon as he gets back.'

'Thank you. Where did you say he'd gone?'

'He has some business with the French ambassador in his country retreat.'

Sir Everard looked confused. 'But the Compte de Castellane is in Pera, I had supper with him yesterday.'

The horrible implications of that made Isabella's stomach shift. 'Perhaps I misheard,' she replied, hoping that the feeling of colour draining from her face wasn't visible.

The ambassador stood up and smiled. 'Well, tell Richard I'll be at home for the rest of today. I doubt he'll risk returning on his departure day. In any case I shall see you both tomorrow morning, I plan to call in to say goodbye.'

After he left, Isabella stared at the door, she tried in vain to think of an innocent explanation. 'Mistress Nichol, I think I might be in terrible trouble.'

Her chaperone moved to sit beside her. 'Whatever it is, I'll do my best to help you, Isabella.' She squeezed Issy's hand. After a few moments she ventured: 'Is the brooch a fake?'

'It's most certainly set with pastes not diamonds.'

'Pastes?'

'It means the stones are made from special glass, cut and polished to look like gems.'

'Are you sure?'

'I'm sure because I prepared and set those diamanté myself. That's why I believe I'm in trouble.'

'Nonsense, if your uncle sold them as diamonds that is

nothing to do with you,' she hesitated. 'Could there not be some mistake?'

'A brooch set with diamonds is worth infinitely more than one set with pastes. How could that be a mistake?'

Mistress Nichol's shocked face confirmed her own assessment of the situation. 'Where do you think he's gone?'

'I've no idea, and since I think there is no honest explanation, how can Sir Everard allow us to leave? Richard will face prison, his name and the company name will be ruined. We could lose everything.'

Mistress Nichol frowned. 'Surely he won't leave you to deal with this alone?'

'You would hope not.'

'We have to think fast, Isabella. Consider all the implications of the different scenarios. Shall I ask Jamila for more tea?'

She stood with the bell in her hand.

'Coffee for me, and perhaps some biscuits, I want to tell you everything.'

'Then I might try some of that coffee too, I'm told it makes you feel more alert,' Mistress Nichol replied.

Isabella asked Jamila to bring their coffee to the terrace. The sight of Sir John's breakfast plate was distracting. He was one of the many things troubling her and she must focus on this new and immediate danger.

She described her life story from the beginning. How her happy childhood ended when her mother died. Then how her circumstances changed dramatically after the death of her father.

'That's terrible, but how did things go wrong so quickly?'

'Richard said my grandfather lost money in the South Sea Bubble. They hoped Father would marry well but he fell in love with my mother. Then my mother and baby brother's illnesses were costly, my father's illness and death wiped out the last of the money.'

'Your father made no provision for you at all?'

She shrugged. 'It was never talked about, I suppose I was too young to understand. The shop went first, then the house and Uncle Richard confesses he was less good at the selling side than my father. When his own eyesight became worse he feared we might starve. My involvement became a necessity. If he hadn't had the idea of training me up I believe we would have ended up in the workhouse.'

'You poor girl. I was surprised enough when you told Sir John that you worked in the business, but I never imagined you labouring over a workbench as a child.'

Isabella groaned. 'I've just remembered I told Sir John I was an expert in using imitation gems.'

Mistress Nichol grimaced. 'I approved of your instinct towards honesty, but I hope you won't regret your openness. Will you tell him about Sir Everard's visit?'

Isabella shook her head. 'But when my uncle resolves the problem with the count, I'll urge him to tell Sir John. It's the kind of scandal that could emerge later.'

'What do you think your uncle can do?'

'I suppose he'll claim it a mistake and offer him the money back.'

'And you expect him back today?'

Isabella shook her head. 'He didn't promise.'

'Surely this problem can't be left until tomorrow. Perhaps we might ask Sir Everard to find out the amount the man paid? Do you have the funds to repay him?'

'I don't know. Uncle Richard left me with some money and there's value in our jewellery stock. Maybe the Swedish gentleman will accept some replacement?'

Isabella fetched the purse from her bedroom, then she

and Mistress Nichol went to her uncle's study. She opened the heavy cupboard with the keys he kept concealed in his desk. Almost everything was gone, including all her uncle's tools. He normally kept the strong box key on his person, so her dread increased when she saw it in the lock. Inside she found the box contained only her mother's jewels, the silver brooches set with pastes, the amethyst rivière gold necklace and two gold rings.

Isabella exhaled, her worst fears were confirmed. 'He's taken nearly all the valuable items.'

'The rogue,' Mistress Nichol replied.

'Wait, there's one more place.' Isabella took out the removable tray to expose the compartment where he usually stored loose stones. Beside the small bag of stones, sat a silver and diamond brooch. One he told her he'd sold in Vienna.

Chapter Fourteen

Isabella daren't wallow in her heartbreak any longer, this was an emergency. She sent a note to Sir Everard, advising him that her uncle still hadn't returned. Issy asked him to find out how much the count paid for the silver brooch and whether he would accept a replacement. Within an hour, a messenger brought his reply.

Dear Isabella

It pains me to involve you in this unfortunate Business. The Count refuses anything other than a full Refund and even then I've had to involve my Friend, Baron von Höpken to persuade him to drop the Matter. Please find enclosed a Copy of his Receipt. If Richard doesn't come here tonight, I will come to your House first Thing in the Morning.

Yours, Sir Everard

·   ·   ·

The amount was another blow, even more than she'd feared. She hadn't the funds to cover it. She showed the note to Mistress Nichol.

'What will you do? Might you ask Sir John? I'm sure he can afford it.'

'I don't want to be beholden to him,' Issy replied.

'And will we sail with Sir John tomorrow if your uncle doesn't come back?'

'I imagine that's what he expects me to do. Maybe he means to meet us in Rome, or perhaps on the way? The ship will stop in Smyrna, I suppose he might have gone ahead?'

Mistress Nichol made an exasperated noise. 'How could he leave you in such a pickle?'

Isabella shook her head. 'Perhaps he feared for his life? It seems this Swedish gentleman is very angry.' Her words concealed the sense of abandonment twisting her insides.

'Talking about gentlemen, where has Sir John got to? Meryem says the supper is spoiling.'

'Goodness knows. Ask her to serve, we can't wait any longer.'

Jamila brought the soup, then they heard the gate. The sound of singing confirmed it was Sir John. He stumbled into the dining room with his wig askew; it was clear he was drunk. 'Sorry, Ishabella,' he slurred, 'had to say goodbye to some people.' He came over and tried to kiss her, she pulled away from the smell of his breath, then realised she could also smell perfume.

'Aw, don't be like that, 'twas just a few drinks.' He shuffled over to his seat. 'Jameela!' he shouted. When she came in he held up his empty glass.

'Don't you think you've had enough, sir?' Mistress Nichol said.

He glared at her. 'I don't think servants should be at the supper table.'

'You are hours late, would you have Isabella eat alone?'

He didn't answer. When Jamila poured his wine he was blatantly trying to look down her dress. She immediately straightened but when Jamila stepped back she yelped, he'd obviously pinched her bottom.

Isabella stood and pushed back her chair. 'I find I've lost my appetite, I'm going to have an early night, I suggest you do the same, Sir John.'

'Good idea, Isabella. I'll fetch our candles,' said Mistress Nichol.

She made to follow Mistress Nichol out, but Sir John stood and caught her hand. 'Don't be like that, Issy. I came away from my companions to be with you. We should celebrate our last night in Constantinople.'

He loomed over her, then in an instant he was kissing her neck, working rapidly downwards towards her bosom. Isabella struggled. His hand grasped at her skirts and her mind flashed back to the incident with Edward Collins.

'No. Please stop,' she shouted.

'Shoosh, shoosh,' he said, his voice gruff with desire.

Just then, the door flew open. Mistress Nichol stood in the doorway. 'Sir John!' she bellowed.

He stood up, and turned to face her, a stupid grin on his face.

'Just a little kiss, Mistress Nichol, what's the harm in that?'

Isabella pushed him away, her face blazed with embarrassment and disgust.

'Go to bed, sir,' Mistress Nichol said, handing Isabella her chamberstick.

Once they were upstairs, she followed Mistress Nichol into her room. Issy closed the door and sat down on the bed. 'I don't think I can face travelling with that man.'

'What happened? Did the brute hurt you?'

'No, but he terrifies me. He's like an animal. And you were right about moving the cupboard, I heard him trying to come to my room last night.'

'Oh Isabella! Confound the man. I'm sure he would have left when you told him to go, and now he's drunk. It's the most outrageous behaviour, no wonder you're frightened.'

'I don't trust him, and the idea of being stuck in a ship with him for weeks appals me. Do you think there's something wrong with me, Mistress Nichol? Just the thought of facing my wedding night is terrifying.'

Mistress Nichol sat and put her arm around Isabella's shoulder. 'It's quite natural for you to be nervous. When you meet the right man your fears will disappear.'

Isabella nodded but she wasn't convinced. Were her feelings towards Vittorio just a childish romantic dream, the stuff of poetry? Was the reality of marriage something she had to endure?

'You should rest now, my dear, we'll talk about the journey in the morning,' Mistress Nichol said.

Isabella squeezed past the cupboard on her way to her bedroom. She paused when she heard Sir John walk into the parlour below. He shouted again: 'Jameela, bring brandy!'

Isabella knelt beside the screen to watch him. Jamila entered, the girl made a big circle around Sir John, before wordlessly depositing the whole bottle at his elbow. Sir John turned his head to watch her leave, but he didn't move. Isabella sat motionless in her hiding place, watching him drink. Eventually, she saw his head bob then droop. She decided that with no one to wake him, and so little left in the brandy bottle, he might stay there until morning.

Back in her room, Isabella stood at her window and watched Jamila cross the moonlit courtyard to the fig tree at the far

102

side of the garden. She summoned the kitten with a soft, high-pitched call. Issy leaned on the window frame. The familiar thrum of cicadas was comforting, the sound of Constantinople. Their rhythm seemed to sing out a description of the heat and the humid smell of greenery. It felt inconceivable that this was her last night in this house. How could she delay? She doubted her uncle would turn up now and she feared Sir John's behaviour on the long voyage. Surely she might persuade Sir Everard that she must sort out the business with the Swedish count first? Perhaps she could wait and travel back to London with him?

Jamila hummed a tune under her breath, as she walked back towards the house. Sadness rose as a hard lump in Isabella's throat. She was going to miss Jamila; even if she managed to delay, it wouldn't be long until she left Constantinople forever.

Then, as Jamila stepped onto the terrace, her singing stopped abruptly; there was a muffled sound and scuffling. Next, heavier footsteps walked inside and the front door closed.

An intruder! Someone had got into the garden and grabbed Jamila. An instinctive surge of energy propelled her out of the room, past the press and down the dark corridor. Her feet were bare, and she ran down the wooden steps without a sound. The hall was empty. She glanced at the closed parlour door; Sir John would be no help. After so much brandy, she doubted if he could even stand. She'd fetch Jeyhan. She opened the heavy front door, but then, heard sounds of a struggle from the kitchen. No time, someone was harming Jamila. Isabella lifted a heavy poker from the hearth. She hesitated at the kitchen door. She was no match for a robber, she must be careful. Cautiously and silently she unlatched the door.

Moonlight from the window illuminated Jamila on her

back on the kitchen table and a man standing in front of her. Isabella's fingers curled in horror, and her nails dug into her palms. He held Jamila down and gagged her with one large hand, while Jamila kicked and bucked. Then he raised his other hand to strike her. The sound of the slap rang out. 'Keep still, girl, keep still and I won't hurt you,' he hissed.

Recognition came in a wave of shock that buckled her knees. She grabbed the doorknob to stay upright. Jamila looked over, and their eyes locked.

Then, Sir John yelped with pain, and snatched back the hand that had covered Jamila's mouth. 'Bitch.' He put his forefinger in his mouth, she'd bitten him.

When he raised his hand to hit her again, Isabella shouted: 'No!'

He twisted towards her. She met his gaze for a second, saw shock but not guilt. Then, Jamila kicked out at him, and he doubled over with a groan. Jamila took her chance to escape, and as she passed, she grabbed Isabella's hand, and dragged her into the hallway. They almost ran into Mistress Nichol standing in the shadows. 'Come with me,' she said.

They all three fled up the stairs. Mistress Nichol gestured them to go into her room. 'I should have had them place that cupboard against his bedroom door,' she muttered.

The girls sat on the bed. Isabella held Jamila in her arms, her dress was torn and her headscarf had been ripped from her hair, Isabella could feel she was crying. 'Are you all right?' she asked.

Jamila raised her head. Her face was streaked with tears but her eyes blazed in the moonlight. She let out a stream of angry Turkish.

'Don't move, girls, lock the door and I'll be back in two ticks. I need Meryem to translate,' Mistress Nichol said. Then under her breath: 'I'd better find out how much he's damaged this poor lassie.'

Isabella turned the key in the door, they heard the door to the servants' quarters close behind her. Almost immediately another door opened. They looked at each other in horror at the noise of heavy male footsteps in the hallway, but he didn't come near the stairs, instead he went out the front door. They ran to the window. Sir John was carrying his own bag and went straight to the gate. Jeyhan opened it and Sir John barged past without acknowledging him, or looking back.

'He's the Devil,' Isabella said.

'*Sheitan*,' Jamila agreed.

They unlocked the door and Mistress Nichol arrived back, accompanied by the cook. 'Isabella, I'm going to ask Jamila some very personal questions. You may wait in your bedroom if you prefer.'

'No, I want to hear,' she answered.

'Please tell Jamila not to be frightened, but I need her to describe exactly what happened. I must know if he defiled her?' Mistress Nichol asked Meryem.

Meryem looked horrified, her stream of Turkish lament was like a wail. Jamila put her face in her hands.

'Ask her please,' she repeated.

Isabella put her hand on Jamila's back, while Meryem translated Mistress Nichol's question. Jamila's reply was angry; she acted out the hand across her mouth, and then her legs kicking.

'She say Jamila too strong, she kicked and bit him, then Miss Isabella rescued her.'

Jamila wept again and Isabella hugged her closer.

'Thank God,' said Mistress Nichol.

After a few minutes, Jamila stopped crying. 'Please, I want go home,' she said.

Mistress Nichol instructed Meryem to ask Jeyhan to help them move the linen press, then lock them in while he saw Jamila safely home.

Before she left, Jamila took Isabella by the shoulders, she shook her gently once, then delivered some serious instruction. Isabella understood not one word, except the last: '*Sheitan*.'

'I will never forgive him for what he did to you. There is no question of a marriage. I hope I never see that devil again.'

They nodded to each other, and the promise was understood.

'Meryem, tell Jamila to stay home. We'll send for her when Sir John leaves town,' Isabella said.

Once the press was moved and Jamila had gone, Mistress Nichol put Isabella in her bed and pulled the sheet up to her chin. 'Sleep now. I've instructed Jeyhan not to admit him, but I'm certain we won't see him again. We'll get our luggage back from the ship in the morning. You cannot travel with that man.'

Chapter Fifteen

I sabella got out of bed at dawn, after another sleepless night. Her whole world had unravelled, but she had important things to do. She must get her luggage off the ship as soon as possible and she hoped never to see Sir John Brady again. She began to dress, then walked barefoot to Mistress Nichol's room. She was glad to find her awake. 'Can you help me with my stays? I'll send a note to Sir Everard asking him to come as soon as possible this morning. I must explain why I cannot sail with Sir John.'

It was after nine when Sir Everard arrived. 'I'm sorry I couldn't be here sooner, Isabella. Sir John turned up at the embassy just when I was about to leave. He explained there had been some misunderstanding between you.'

Mistress Nichol breathed in sharply.

Isabella clenched her hands, trying to keep her temper. 'There was no misunderstanding, Sir Everard. He attempted to rape my maid.'

He looked shocked. 'Rape? Surely not, he described some sort of skirmish.'

'A skirmish that had her held down on her back with his hand over her mouth?'

Sir Everard closed his eyes for a few seconds. 'Could you be wrong, Isabella? Sir John said it was dark, and that in your innocence you misunderstood.'

'There was a full moon, Sir Everard, and I can confirm Isabella's report,' Mistress Nichol added, her Scottish consonants even more clipped than usual. Isabella smiled at her gratefully.

The ambassador rubbed his eyes. 'You seem to be surrounded by trouble this week, Isabella. I so wish your uncle was here. Especially when your betrothal now puts you in a difficult legal situation.'

Isabella stared at him. 'Is that what he told you? There is no betrothal.'

The ambassador's pained expression turned to shock. 'Sir John showed me the document, Isabella. Your uncle signed it this week.'

'No!' Isabella said.

'Outrageous!' Mistress Nichol's outburst came over her own and they both jumped to their feet.

Isabella took deep breaths to quell her panic. Fear crawled up her back. She had to think quickly. 'Surely in the circumstances you must see I cannot travel with him and I certainly won't marry him. Please, Sir Everard, I need your help, think what my parents would say.'

He sighed. 'The betrothal specifically names Sir John as your guardian in your uncle's absence.'

Abandoned and betrayed, how could he do that to her? She gritted her teeth. She couldn't let them win. 'I can only imagine Uncle Richard thought to protect me if I had to travel without him, but the circumstances have changed. I'm not sailing,' Isabella said.

'You should know that Sir John insists you must.'

Isabella shook her head vigorously. 'He knows what I saw, whatever he told you. I cannot believe he would even consider marriage. There would never be any affection between us.'

'The man is a complete blackguard,' Mistress Nichol said.

'A blackguard and a fool to force the issue. He surely doesn't care for me at all,' Isabella added.

The ambassador frowned, he looked very uncomfortable. 'He blames too much to drink causing him to behave out of character, and claims to have done the maid no real harm.'

'My counterclaim would be that we have only one character and I cannot live with that man.'

Sir Everard stood and put his hat on. 'This conversation should properly be had with your uncle, but I can certainly understand your objections. Leave it to me to reason with Sir John. It's obvious that sailing with him now would be intolerable to you. I'll explain there are some business matters that cannot be resolved today, and that is the truth.'

Isabella exhaled the breath she'd been holding. She'd escaped, at least for now.

'So do you expect Richard will go to Rome?' he asked.

'I cannot say, but since he loaded his luggage on the ship, that does seem the most likely thing.' She hesitated but decided to say what was on her mind. 'Might I perhaps travel with you to London, Sir Everard? I'm sure Uncle Richard would approve of that line of action.'

He shook his head, his expression was pained. 'I wish I could help but I might not leave for many weeks and I expect to go north through Buda and Vienna, with no exact plan for London arrival. If you assume Richard has gone to Rome you should go there. He can break your engagement. It's not my place to interfere and in truth I have no legal right to do so.'

He turned to Mistress Nichol. 'I'm correct that you planned to go to Rome, Mistress Nichol?'

'I did, although I imagine Sir John will withdraw his promise to pay my passage if we don't travel with him.'

'Well I'm glad that at least I can help with something. I'll cover the cost. Now I must sort out your luggage and look into alternative berths for you both. I'm sorry to raise it, but have you considered what you want to do about Count Stenbock?'

'Unfortunately, I don't have enough money to pay him. I need to sell some jewellery to raise the funds,' Issy answered.

'I'm most sorry for that and it's a large amount. Can I help? I have some cash to hand and could borrow the balance,' Sir Everard said.

'No. You're already too kind covering our passage. It's stock not personal jewellery and I believe it should raise enough.'

'Then I'll talk to my jeweller friend about the pieces you wish to sell.'

'I would be very grateful.'

Isabella brought in the strongbox and handed over all the valuable pieces except the diamond brooch.

'I'll see what I can do and return this evening. Send Jeyhan to the port to bring back the luggage.'

He made to leave, then turned back. 'How is your maid, Isabella?'

'Thank you for asking. Jamila was very upset and I'm sure bruised from where he struck her. I've sent her home. Thank God I interrupted him before he could do more serious damage.'

He nodded and left.

'At least there's one decent man left,' Isabella said.

'I cannot believe your uncle had you betrothed without your agreement,' Mistress Nichol said.

'Since it happened this week, I assume it coincides with his need to go into hiding. If there hadn't been an incident I might never have known. I could have sleepwalked into a trap.' Isabella shuddered.

Mistress Nichol shook her head. 'It doesn't excuse it, he knew your reservations.'

'Well I'm not co-operating. They might make a contract but they won't force me to marry.'

'We're lucky to have Sir Everard's backing, you might be surprised what women can be forced to do. But why did you not give him the diamond brooch to sell, Isabella? Surely that would yield the amount you need?'

'That's why I kept it back. I prefer Sir Everard doesn't learn the difference in the true worth of such a brooch and the amount Uncle Richard actually charged the Swedish man.'

Mistress Nichol voiced her disapproval with her particularly Scottish 'tsk' sound. 'Your uncle doesn't deserve your protection, Isabella. You must now learn to put your own interests first.'

Jamila walked through the gate in the afternoon, just as Jeyhan arrived with a cart full of their luggage. He gave them both a broad smile. 'Sheitan gone,' he said, swishing his hand through the air, to indicate the ship sailing.

Jamila hugged her.

'That is the best news in days. Thank you, Jeyhan.'

The thought of what might have happened on the ship made Issy's stomach clench.

When all the trunks were lined up in the hallway she realised her uncle's largest trunk was missing. She flung open all the lids and found none of his jewellery tools or equipment.

'He's taken with him those things that would allow him to set up business again. What if I arrive in Rome and he's not there to meet me? What if he's gone for good?'

Mistress Nichol's expression did nothing to calm her panic.

'That's been on my mind all day. We have no way of knowing what happened to him, we can't even be certain there's been no accident. If you have no protector in Rome you're very vulnerable to Sir John.'

'I still cannot believe he'd want to marry if I'm unwilling.'

'In my experience, there are some men who glory in having everything they want. Opposition can make them more determined.'

'What can I do? There's no way to know how long I'll have to wait for Uncle Richard in Rome, then what if Sir John spins the same yarn to him? It never occurred to me that he'd deny it, and he and Uncle Richard have become friends.'

'That's a possibility we should prepare for.'

Mistress Nichol's determined tone bolstered her resolve.

'We'll begin by solving the issue with Count Stenbock today. Then at least I'll know my situation over funds.'

Sir Everard sent a note saying he'd return at six and Isabella had Meryem set another place for supper. When he came, she knew from his face that he had some happier news. He kissed her cheek and placed a purse of coins in her hand.

'Your pieces yielded enough to settle with the count and a little over. He heads north tomorrow and I hope you won't hear of this again.'

'Thank you. This will pay for Rome lodgings. I'll wait for Uncle Richard there.'

The ambassador's concern passed like a shadow over his face. 'And I pray he'll be there. I've good news about the passage. There are few passenger ships on this route but there's a navy frigate in port and I know the captain. He's agreed to take you as a favour to me.'

'Thank you. Do you know when we'll sail?'

'Tomorrow, providing the weather is good.'

'And the ship's bound for Rome?'

'Ultimately they'll go to Portsmouth but he's scheduled to call into Naples and you'll easily get a carriage from there.'

Jamila brought up a platter piled high with *lahmacun*. This flatbread covered in spicy minced lamb was one of Meryem's specialities. It was a popular snack on the streets of Constantinople and not at all the kind of thing the British Embassy kitchens would prepare, Isabella knew that Sir Everard loved it.

'Your cook is a genius, Isabella. I need to make sure your landlord lets this house to someone I can visit.'

Isabella shook her head and sighed. 'I wish I could leave more money for all the staff. I hate to abandon them without work.'

'Write some references before you go and I'll recommend them. There's a new Levant Company factory manager coming soon. I've an inkling he'll take the house and the staff.'

They finished eating and Jamila brought them coffee.

'Isabella, did you find a copy of this marriage contract Richard had drawn up?'

Isabella shook her head. 'I knew nothing of it until you told me.'

Sir Everard's frown made her nervous. 'Is there no property associated with the business?' he asked. 'The workshop premises perhaps?'

'No, the workshop and our rooms are rented.'

'So he kept nothing back for you after your father's death? Any money associated with your portion of the business will go to your husband.'

Isabella sat forward in her chair. 'So when I marry I lose even the little I have?'

The ambassador shifted in his seat. 'Sir John is so wealthy it would hardly have mattered, but I'm surprised your father's lawyer didn't advise keeping some of your money tied up in property. That can be set up as a trust, but all other possessions go with you into a marriage.'

Isabella caught Mistress Nichol's look of alarm.

'Another reason not to marry anyone I cannot trust.'

Jeyhan brought in the basket of smouldering charcoal for Sir Everard's *nargile*. He liked to smoke the Turkish water pipe and it was something he couldn't do when on official duties. Sir Everard inhaled and blew out a stream of cool smoke. The room was filled with the smell of the apple tobacco and the soothing gurgling noise.

'This always reminds me of your father. We smoked sheesha together in Aleppo.'

'That makes me love the smell even more,' Isabella replied.

'I wish I could travel with you, Isabella. Unfortunately, there's no British representative in Naples or Rome, but my dear friend Horace Mann is the diplomatic representative in Florence. His banker in Rome acts as a point of contact for him regarding British citizens. I'll give you that address and you may use this office as a way of sending me news via Horace Mann. I will use the same method to write to you.'

'Thank you.'

'I pray Richard joins you in Rome and that your current difficulties are swiftly resolved.' He paused then added: 'Aside from the problem with Sir John, who would be your legal guardian if Richard died? I hate to raise such a subject but it's sensible to plan for every eventuality.'

'I think there is no plan. I'm not aware of any other relative.'

'No one in Scotland on your mother's side?'

'Not that I know of.'

He shook his head. 'That's really not good enough. You don't reach majority for another six years. I'm going to write to my lawyer in London and ask him to look into your legal affairs. If you decide not to marry then you should have a back-up plan.'

'Would it be too much to ask for you to take on that role?' Isabella said.

He smiled and squeezed her hand. 'I hope this whole thing with Richard and Sir John is a series of misunderstandings. Nevertheless you have a right to the security of good guardianship and I would be honoured.'

Chapter Sixteen

She'd let Jamila go home, so Mistress Nichol came to help her get ready for bed.

'I feel foolish for allowing myself to be so exposed,' Isabella said.

'Your father trusted your uncle but I do wonder if he was the best person to manage your affairs,' Mistress Nichol replied.

'What if we have to face Sir John in Rome?'

Marrying Vittorio was a secret hope, burning like charcoal embers in her heart, but she daren't rely on that. Mistress Nichol helped her into her nightdress, then sat heavily on the edge of her bed.

'I've been wracking my brain for a plan and I can only think of one option...' Mistress Nichol hesitated, 'but you might reject it.'

'I'm determined not to marry him. I have no interest in being married at all. We'll run away,' Isabella said.

Mistress Nichol shook her head. 'No, we need to be clever about this. I have hardly the funds to support myself and you've no income to survive on. We must protect you from

Sir John until we can get you out of the betrothal.' Mistress Nichol took a deep breath, apparently reluctant to voice her idea. 'In my faith, when a young woman determines not to marry, she may seek sanctuary in a convent. It's a safe and honourable alternative for those who reject marriage. But, of course, you might find the idea repugnant.'

Isabella turned the idea around in her head for a few seconds.

'Not repugnant, not next to the alternative. But surely it's not open to me as a Protestant?'

'It's not unheard of for young women to convert. Most difficult in England of course, but there are many English girls who have sought the safety of convents in France and the Low Countries, and some of them travelled from Protestant homes. Would you consider converting to your mother's faith? You'd need to be baptised.'

For the first time in days, Isabella experienced a flicker of hope. 'I'd consider anything; wait, there's something I must show you.'

She ran to her bedroom and returned with a small leather book in her hand. She passed it to Mistress Nichol, who read the inscription aloud.

'*For my darling Isabella, from her adoring Mama. I pray God will guide you throughout your Life.*'

'The next line is in another hand,' Mistress Nichol held the small faint writing nearer her candle.

'*For Isabella Charlotte Gordon Godfrey, on the day of her Baptism, Father Francis Graham, Stobhall Chapel, Perthshire.*'

Mistress Nichol looked up. 'You were baptised in a Catholic Church in Scotland? But how?'

Isabella smiled. 'It's a secret, although I suspect my father knew. My mother went to visit my grandmother in Scotland and she was horrified that I had no Catholic baptism. I believe she considered me bound for hell. My mother was in favour of it too, so they had me baptised in the same church where Mama had been blessed as an infant.'

Mistress Nichol laid the Bible in her lap. 'Isabella, I believe that God and your dear departed mother are looking over you. This makes the plan easier.' She smiled. 'I should have guessed from your brave and determined nature, that you had Scottish ancestors.'

'Do you think we could get to France undetected?' Isabella asked.

'Maybe, but that would be a huge risk. I'm wondering about the convent at Santa Cecilia in Rome? It took in the princes' saintly mother, with her English lady-in-waiting. They lived there for several years. If they would offer you sanctuary, we might get you there without raising suspicion.'

Mistress Nichol handed Isabella back her Bible. She held it to her breast and inhaled deeply. 'If Uncle Richard isn't in Rome I'll go there.'

'I'm not sure that I see you as a nun. The best situation would be if the sisters will offer you some sanctuary until your present danger has passed. I think that's not an easy request, we should have it in our prayers on the voyage.'

Isabella spent the morning considering her plight. It was obvious she had to take control of her own destiny. Her uncle had shown himself to be a swindler. The more she thought about it, the more she feared he'd want her to marry Sir John. If she got out of it, he'd be searching for someone else. A profitable marriage had obviously been the real purpose of her expensive education. Would the convent offer her sanctuary? Perhaps if she stayed until she was twenty-one she'd be free to make her own decisions? And then, what about Vittorio? Maybe his mother hoped he would marry someone with money? He'd been emphatic about being unable to marry her.

Was that because of his family or his artistic ambitions? She couldn't count on persuading him and maybe it was unfair of her to try. Her head was in turmoil but it was clear she must act. She picked up her Bible and knelt to pray for guidance. After a few minutes, Isabella sat back on her heels. She looked up at the ceiling and sent one last prayer to her parents.

'Papa, I need your protection and, Mama, I want your courage,' she said aloud.

In the courtyard the servants stood ready to see them off. Meryem and Jamila were in tears. Jeyhan was silent and serious. Isabella pressed a silver coin into each hand.

'No Sheitan,' Jamila said.

Isabella looked her straight in the eye. 'I promise,' she replied.

Issy turned to look back at the gate. Leaving Jamila felt like losing a friend, something she'd never experienced before.

'Come along, Isabella,' Mistress Nichol said. 'Don't worry about Jamila, she has her family, she'll be fine.'

They exchanged one last smile and Jamila waved goodbye.

When they arrived at the quayside, Sir Everard went off to deal with their papers. When he returned, he put a purse in Isabella's hand. 'I want you to have more funds in case you have to continue your journey to London.'

She tried to give it back to him. 'That is so kind but I can't accept your money.'

'Please. Your father would have expected me to help, I only wish I could do more. If Richard isn't in Rome, please get in touch with Horace Mann for advice. He can help you with your onward journey.'

He drew her into a hug. 'Good luck, Issy. Your papa would be proud of your bravery.'

Sir Everard came on board and stayed until the last minute. Mistress Nichol stood by her side and they watched him alight. Unfurling sails cracked above them, and men worked to loosen the ropes, then the boat slipped into the pull of the water.

'I'm going to investigate the accommodation,' said Mistress Nichol.

Isabella soon lost sight of Constantinople's sloping streets and the tight-packed wooden houses. She stood until the last minaret became blurred, and the city was just a speck on the horizon. She'd hoped to find happiness in Constantinople and it had ended in disaster. Now she was sailing into uncertainty. Her stomach churned with fear but also excitement. For the first time in her whole life she was responsible for herself.

* * *

Bessie watched her from the ship's stern. The sight of Isabella standing there alone with her shoulders set in rigid determination, brought back memories of her own trials. At that age she'd had no one to protect her, but she was resolved to fight for this girl.

Chapter Seventeen

Bessie made the cabin as comfortable as possible. When Isabella came downstairs she looked completely exhausted.

'I'm sure you've hardly slept this week. You need to rest now.'

Bessie opened the window. The salt-laced air eased the cabin's heat. She stayed beside Isabella until the rocking motion lulled her to sleep.

With hair strewn over the pillow and her brow free of worries, Isabella looked like a child. Bessie was struck by that protective urge again, it wasn't her place to mother the girl but she couldn't help feeling it. To take on such a responsibility was risky, she'd maybe not be able to keep her from harm and that would break her own heart. She sighed. But what was the point of life if you never took risks? Her heart had that many cracks it could surely survive another.

Up on deck Bessie found a quiet spot where she could watch the crew without being in their way. This was the most splendid vessel, a world away from the grimy boat she'd taken from Edinburgh to Rotterdam. Three tall masts and a row of gun places declared its military pedigree. A horde of barefoot boys scrubbed the decks and tended the sails, under the watchful eyes of a handsome, whiskered man with a straight back. Bessie admired the sense of order.

Isabella was very quiet as their journey continued, Bessie understood that her world had been turned on its head and she needed time to recover. On the second evening they let down the ship's anchor at the edge of the Sea of Marmara. Bessie asked a red-haired boy why they'd stopped.

'Dardanelles are dangerous, mistress. Capt'n waits for safer passage on the dawn tide.'

The boy leaned on his brush at her side, and took little persuasion to chat for a while. Bessie liked his company, his colouring made her think of home. The next morning she was wakened early by noise on deck. When she got there, she found they'd entered a narrow strait. Steep rocky slopes were on both banks and a squat town with a round fort lay to their right. She smiled to see Isabella appear from below. The girl hesitated, as if unsure of her footing on the deck. The red-haired sailor rushed to help her walk over.

'Thank you, Freddy,' Bessie said, 'you're a good lad.'

She pointed towards the town. 'What's the name of this place?'

'Gallipoli, mistress,' he replied. 'We'll be in this passage all day, we should reach the Aegean in the evening.'

'The Hellespont,' Isabella murmured, 'where Hero watched for drowned Leander. This strait feels like Turkey's last embrace. I prayed my life might change here. I certainly got that wish.'

'Try not to worry. It seems very likely your uncle will find us in Rome.'

'I think so too. His eyesight gets worse every year and he hasn't a steady enough hand for setting stones anymore.'

'I hope you can rely on him coming to his senses regarding his family duties, rather than just such mercenary concerns,' Bessie remarked.

Isabella shrugged. 'He's all the family I have and I'm the same for him.'

'Just like me and my sister Agnes,' Bessie replied.

'You've never talked about your sister.'

'My sister keeps very poor health and she is forced to rely on me. Such situations are difficult.'

Bessie stood and brushed down her skirts, deciding to change the subject. 'Might I tempt you with some eggs, Isabella? You should eat while we're in calm waters.'

Getting a nodded agreement, Bessie set off towards the galley. Later, she was pleased to see her eat them all.

'Do you know the captain actually has a few chickens on board. This ship is quite the palace compared to my voyage from Scotland.'

'How did you cross? Uncle Richard and I came in a small vessel to Calais, then overland through France to Vienna, and Buda.'

'I sailed from Edinburgh. They sent me on a terrible rat-infested mail packet to Rotterdam. I endured it for two whole days in a storm. I considered turning back, but then the Dutch section of the journey was so clean and organised. Their canals are a wonder.'

'Who sent you?' Isabella asked.

'Mistress Jackson, my former employer and sister to the Mistress MacDonald who was left a widow in Pera. They heard news that she was too weak to travel back to Scotland, so they sent me to help her home. I don't believe they had any notion of the journey's length, never mind the discomfort and danger. The road after Vienna was weeks of rutted tracks and dirty inns. I heard wolves more than once.'

'Why did you not refuse to go?' Isabella asked.

'Money,' she replied with a shrug. 'My sister cannot work and we could barely afford our rent on my Scottish wages. Agnes got the bonus Mistress Jackson gave me before I left, and they offered me a good salary to accompany her sister home safely. She was to her word and paid half to my sister throughout the many weeks of my outward journey. And then of course, I arrived too late. If I'd known she was ill with cholera, I'd have realised it was a fool's errand.'

'Poor lady, and her poor sister being so bereaved.'

'Mistress Jackson was not so grief stricken that she forgot to stop paying my monies when she heard of her sister's death,' Bessie said drily.

'How awful!' Isabella exclaimed. 'How does you sister manage?'

'You uncle's employment saved us. I have sent money home already and Agnes has enough to manage for a while.'

'Sir Everard gave me a generous purse. We can send her more with the captain. This ship is bound for England after we disembark in Naples.'

'That's kind of you, Isabella, but I fancy I'll be travelling home once you're safely delivered to the convent or to your uncle.'

Isabella looked appalled. 'I was hoping you might remain in Rome, don't you mean to find work there?'

Bessie smiled at her. 'Let's deal with one step at a time. I shall go nowhere until I'm certain you're safe from Sir John. I'd like to stay on in Rome if I can find employment. It seems a great distance to travel only to return after a few short months.'

'Vittorio promised he'd find work for you,' Isabella said.

'He promised he would try.'

Bessie gave her a knowing look. She'd seen the ring on Isabella's finger of course. Did it represent some sort of pact?

. . .

They sat companionably on deck, watching the banks glide past them. Freddy sidled up. He gave Isabella three tiny apricots.

'Oh, how kind of you! Jamila used to bring me apricots from the market, I love them.'

The boy smiled shyly and ran off.

'Thank you, Freddy,' Bessie called after him.

'I talked to that lad quite a bit when you were sleeping. I doubt he's much more than ten years old, much too young to be so far from home.'

'Why is he here?' Issy asked.

'He ran away to sea on a whim, I'm sure he regrets it but is too proud to say. His poor mother must be frantic.'

They sat in silence watching the boy work.

'I don't wish to distress you, Mistress Nichol, but what happened to your son?'

It wasn't an interruption to her thoughts, she was surprised that Isabella had sensed them so accurately.

'When my father died and I'd earned money, I went to the orphanage. I hoped I might find him and take him up to Scotland.' It was difficult to go on, Isabella grasped her hand. 'Of course he'd gone and they wouldn't tell me anything. But one of the nurses came running after me. She said she thought it cruel to have me spend my life looking for a face in the crowd. There'd been a measles epidemic in the orphanage. My wee boy died when he was only three weeks old.' She had to stop speaking, gulping air until she recovered herself. 'It broke my heart completely. That's why I wear black.'

'I'm so very sorry. To lose the boy you loved and then your baby too.'

Bessie blinked back her tears. 'Simon and I had so few months of happiness, and it may have been no more than a boyish notion for him.'

She knew what was on the Isabella's mind.

'First love is a fierce thing, and I know you imagine you'll never get over it. But it will fade to a lovely memory in time.' Then under her breath she added: 'But loss of a child, that's something you never get over.'

Chapter Eighteen

Three days later, Isabella stood with Mistress Nichol at the ship's bow. They were approaching Smyrna. This ancient place was built on a bay surrounded by hills and a sizeable fort was visible high on an escarpment behind it. The town's status as a trading port was clear from the many large sailing ships moored offshore.

The captain came and stood beside them. It was the first time they'd spoken since she was introduced by Sir Everard in Constantinople. Isabella had been avoiding him and was aware she may have caused offence. She dropped a curtsey in response to his small bow.

'I'm delighted to see you on deck, Miss Godfrey. I was beginning to fear for your health.'

'Thank you for your kindness, Captain Jones. I feel a little better today.'

'I'm sorry our time in Smyrna will be brief. I'm anxious to cross the Aegean whilst this weather holds. We'll anchor here for only one night, then continue our journey.'

'I quite understand, Captain.'

'Will you go ashore? I'd be happy to walk with you.'

'Thank you, we'd be delighted.'

They fetched their parasols and prepared to disembark. At the last minute Captain Jones came rushing up. 'I'm sorry, ladies, I've had a message advising me that the British Consul will visit the ship. Can I give you one of my sailors to come with you instead?'

'May we take Freddy?' Mistress Nichol asked him.

They looked over in Freddy's direction. The boy was sat on a coil of ropes with his chin in his hands.

'Ah yes, good idea, let me ask Bosun Grimes if he can be spared. That boy spends too much time alone.'

'Freddy needs cheering up,' Mistress Nichol said. 'He's been told he has to take a position on the rigging. One of the other boys had a fall and broke his arm.'

'He doesn't want to work in the sails?' Isabella asked.

'He's afraid of heights and hasn't admitted it yet. I did point out he might have considered that before he signed up as ship's crew.'

Captain Jones brought the boy over. 'I have an onshore duty for you, Freddy. These ladies have a mind to visit the market and they need someone to walk with them and carry their parcels.'

'Aye, aye, Captain,' Freddy said, standing extra straight, his face flushed with pride.

'Make sure you allow no harassment from the stallholders,' Captain Jones instructed. The boy nodded his agreement.

They were rowed ashore and walking down the quay Freddy visibly relaxed. His excited gait caused his red curls to bob up and down.

They stopped in the fruit market to buy bags of grapes, peaches and figs to last their journey but didn't linger. The sweet fruit attracted swarms of flies and many wasps. Next they stopped at a stall selling cotton, where Issy bought a blue shawl to protect her from the evening chills. Mistress Nichol nudged her to point out that Freddy was looking at some plain beige boys' shirts. She nodded.

'Can I get you a couple of new shirts as a thank you for your help this afternoon?' Isabella asked.

He looked down at the shirt he had on, which was torn and grubby. 'Thank you kindly, mistress. My only spare shirt fell to pieces last week and I've no talent for stitching.'

'Neither stitching nor climbing? I'm not sure you made the right career choice, young Freddy,' Mistress Nichol said.

They all laughed. His youthful face under his curls gave him an impish look.

Isabella handed him the string-tied parcel and he smiled broadly. 'I'm most grateful, Mistress Godfrey.'

A European looking man who was walking past, stopped dead in this tracks. He stared at her, then quickly walked on. His grim expression caused a shiver of apprehension to cross her shoulders. They all turned to watch him walk down the quay.

'Whatever got into him?' said Mistress Nichol.

He hailed a small boat, which crossed the harbour towards their own ship.

'I've a sinking feeling we're about to find out,' Isabella replied.

Freddy helped them down into their rowing boat. 'Thank you for the outing and the shirts, Mistress Godfrey.' He held his shirts against his chest as if they were precious objects. Isabella wondered if he'd ever had a present before.

'Best you roll them up and not tell the other boys they were a gift,' Mistress Nichol advised.

He nodded, composing a serious face. Once back on the ship they watched him disappear below deck.

'My heart goes out to the laddie. He's a target for bullying amongst some of the crew. He has no knack for hiding his feelings and they revel in making him cry,' Mistress Nichol said.

'Poor boy,' agreed Isabella.

Isabella looked around for the man from the market. She spied him talking to Captain Jones and they were both staring in their direction.

'Whatever next,' Mistress Nichol said.

'Let's get it over with,' Isabella replied.

As they got closer she took a deep breath. She was determined not to be intimidated.

'I hope your shopping was successful, ladies,' said Captain Jones.

'Thank you, it was,' she replied.

'Allow me to introduce Mr Samuel Crawley, British Consul in Smyrna.'

'Pleased to meet you, Mr Crawley. Sir Everard recommended I should call on you in Smyrna if I had time.' She curtsied and gave him her sweetest smile. 'It's most fortuitous you came on board.'

Isabella saw that this surprised the consul.

'You're acquainted with the British ambassador?' he asked.

'He knew my late father,' Isabella told him.

'Your father is dead?' he looked confused.

'Perhaps we could discuss this in my cabin,' Captain Jones suggested.

Isabella followed the two men down the narrow wooden steps, an awkward descent in her wide skirts. They all sat down. Isabella clasped her hands tightly in her lap to hide her nerves. She smiled and looked directly at the consul, although she was aware of the captain's curious gaze.

Mr Crawley cleared his throat. His previous stern look had been replaced by a nervous expression. 'I'm most sorry to bother you with this matter, Miss Godfrey, and I'm quite sure it's only a coincidence over names. But last week I received a letter from a Swedish gentleman, a Baron von Höpken. He introduced himself as a diplomat and long-time resident in Constantinople and he bade me be on the lookout for an Englishman called Mr Godfrey.' Isabella merely smiled at him, forcing him to carry on to fill the silence.

'In fact he asked me to search all ships with British passengers. It appears this man has swindled a Swedish count out of a large sum of money.'

The consul sat back in his seat and blinked. She had the impression that he wished he'd never come looking for her. For a second or two she hesitated, before deciding to be as honest as she dared. 'I am Miss Godfrey and I believe I know the reason for this request.' The consul's eyes widened. 'I never met this Swedish count and I'm afraid I'm unable to explain the exact circumstances of the misunderstanding. Richard Godfrey is my uncle and guardian and he was called away on business before this complaint came to light. However, I can assure you that the matter was resolved in Constantinople before I left. Sir Everard liaised with the Swedish gentleman on my behalf and Count Stenbock has been given a full refund. He withdrew his complaint and the matter is now closed.'

The consul's shoulders relaxed. 'I'm delighted to hear that, Miss Godfrey. Please accept my deepest apologies and I hope you're not offended?'

'Not at all, Mr Crawley, you are merely doing your duty. I'm sorry to have used up your precious time.'

They all went on deck and watched the consul be rowed away.

'I'm most sorry to hear that you've had to deal with such a distressing situation,' Captain Jones said. 'I must say you handled that conversation very well.'

She inclined her head in response, then she and Mistress Nichol went down to her own cabin.

'Well done, Isabella,' Mistress Nichol said, 'you chose just the right tone with that man.'

Issy put her fingers to her temple, where her head throbbed.

'Do you think that's how it's going to be in every port? Will I spend all my time defending Uncle Richard?'

Isabella woke the next morning to find the ship already under sail. She went next door but found Mistress Nichol not in her cabin. Once on deck she knew from her chaperone's face that something was wrong.

'What happened?' she asked.

'Freddy got stuck in the rigging, he only managed a few feet off the ground and then froze. He had to be brought down and another boy was sent up in his place. I fear this will make him the target for more bullying. Freddy was sitting on the edge of the deck with his head bowed and several boys stood above him jeering and laughing.

Just then Grimes appeared, the bullies scattered under his glare but he managed to land a slap around the ear of one. 'Get to work!' he shouted, then in a more kindly tone: 'Up you get, Freddy, back to your cleaning. We'll talk about the sail problem later.'

He walked over to join them.

'What will happen to Freddy?' Isabella asked.

'I might try him again in calmer conditions, but I don't want anyone new up there right now, we're in for some bad weather and I can't afford to have another fall.'

'Bad weather?' Isabella replied.

The sky above was blue as usual. But when she followed the man's gaze, she saw a dark strip of clouds hanging in the distance.

. . .

The storm made Isabella horribly seasick. When she finally struggled back to her cabin, she was unable to leave.

'How can you stand it?' Isabella asked Mistress Nichol, during a lull.

'Maybe it's in my blood? My mother's family were fishing folk from Arbroath. The North Sea crossing was my first time afloat, yet I was the only passenger not sick on that journey.'

Mistress Nichol never left her side all night, although Isabella knew that the cabin smelled horrible. She stroked her back and made crooning, sympathetic noises, as if dealing with a sick child. In fact, Isabella was as helpless as a baby, and felt huge comfort from the older woman's presence.

In the morning, when the waves subsided, Isabella was overwhelmingly weary. 'Thank you so much for staying with me,' she said. 'I believe I'll sleep now. You should go and get some rest.'

'You sleep, child. I'm happy right here.'

She reached out for Mistress Nichol's hand. 'Would you mind if I used your given name? I'm sure I behaved like a spoiled baby when we met, and I'm sorry for that. But now... well I owe you so much and I'd be honoured to call you a friend.'

'You owe me nothing, Isabella,' and after a pause added: 'My given name is Elisabeth, but my friends call me Bessie.'

'Bessie, what a lovely name,' Isabella murmured, just before she drifted off to sleep.

When Isabella woke next, she was alone. The storm had passed. She pulled her skirt over her petticoat but couldn't find the matching green jacket. Then she remembered the disgusting back-spray at the ship's rail. She chose a blue waist-coat from her trunk. It didn't fit as well as the green coat, but it would have to do. She pulled on some buttoned boots. The deck might still be wet and these were the nearest to sensible shoes she owned. Mistress Nichol came in.

'Ah good, you found something to wear, I sent your coat to be laundered.'

'Thank you, Mistress Nichol.'

The older woman glanced up. A hurt look passed across her face.

'Sorry, it's just a habit, Bessie,' Isabella said, and hugged her. 'I can't tell you how lucky I feel to have you by my side. And I'm Issy in the same way that you're Bessie. Isabella's a terrible mouthful.'

Bessie smiled and nodded. 'I'm very glad you're feeling better, Issy. Come upstairs, the weather is much improved.'

On deck they found Mr Grimes watching the sailors work. Freddy ran past, smiling and holding his mop aloft in greeting.

'The boy did well,' Mr Grimes said. 'This is the first really bad storm since we took the new crew aboard in Portsmouth, and many of the younger boys were ill. Not Freddy though and he has worked tirelessly to cover for all those too sick to contribute.'

'I believe he very much regrets disappointing you, Mr Grimes,' Bessie said.

Issy heard both warmth and pride in Bessie's tone. She was convinced that Freddy made Bessie feel maternal. She couldn't imagine how Bessie lived with her loss every day. It had so disabled her own mother.

'I can find plenty of work for willing hands on this ship. I cannot abide shirkers but this boy means well,' Bosun Grimes replied.

As if to demonstrate the truth of this opinion, Freddy dropped to his knees and began energetically scrubbing the salt from the deck.

'Shall I go and find us something to eat, Issy?'

'Thank you, Bessie.'

The bosun smiled and nodded his approval at the change of greeting. When Bessie went off towards the galley he said: 'You're lucky to have that good woman with you.'

'You have no idea how much I'm certain that's true,' Issy replied.

'We're heading for a safe anchorage off the island of Ipsera,' he said, 'we need to check the ship for storm damage before heading to Malta.'

'I'm sure we'll all be grateful for a few hours of stillness after the storm,' she replied.

Chapter Nineteen

The next morning, the sunny weather lifted Isabella's spirits. Richard's fall from grace was no huge surprise, she'd long suspected he was capable of dishonesty. It might be better if he wasn't waiting for her in Rome. So long as she managed to escape marrying Sir John, she'd work out her next move with Bessie's support. Of course her dream was that her next move would involve Vittorio.

They watched two sailors row a small boat towards shore.

'The captain has sent ashore for some Ipsera lobsters,' Bessie remarked.

They heard the sound of a familiar voice from below the ship's rail. They looked down to find Freddy and another young sailor standing on a plank, high above the water. They were applying a black substance to the hull with large brushes.

'Be careful down there, Freddy,' Bessie called.

'Don't like the look of your girlfriend, Fred,' the other boy said with a laugh.

'Very funny, Bob,' Freddy replied and flicked his brush in

the direction of his workmate, then the boy launched at him with his fist. Freddy swayed out of the way and the boy overbalanced. He fell over fifteen feet into the water below. 'Watch out for the big fishes!' Freddy shouted, with a laugh.

The boy surfaced, spluttering, he thrashed at the water, then went under again.

Someone further down the ship shouted: 'Man overboard!'

Freddy didn't hesitate. He flung down his brush and took off from the platform in a graceful arcing dive.

'Freddy!' Isabella and Bessie shouted in unison.

The bosun ran to their side.

'A boy fell in and it seems he cannot swim, Mr Grimes,' Isabella said.

Freddy surfaced. He looked frantically, first one way, then the other, and took a deep breath, before duck-diving under the water again. Seconds later he surfaced, this time he dragged the other boy's head clear of the sea. They heard the lad gasp for air.

'Don't fight me, Bob, I got you.' Freddy flipped on his back, dragging the spluttering boy to the anchor chain.

Mr Grimes shouted, 'Hang on, lads, we're coming for you.'

The rowing boat had already turned towards them. Isabella's heart pounded inside her tight waistcoat.

'Why would you have a sailor aboard who cannot swim, Mr Grimes?'

'Most sailors prefer not to swim, miss. If Freddy had gone in after that boy when the ship was moving, we wouldn't have been able to get back to them in time. Sailors tell each other that drowning is a fast death and it's better to give in quickly.'

They watched the rowing boat pull the boys aboard. The rowers clapped Freddy on the shoulders and the many sailors who had been leaning over the rails cheered.

Just before sunset, Mr Grimes brought Freddy over.

'Congratulations, Freddy. You're a hero,' Isabella said.

The boy reddened under his freckles. 'I'm no climber, miss, but my big brother taught me to swim.'

'Well done, Freddy, I'm very proud of you,' Bessie added.

'I've just told Freddy that I propose a reward for his actions,' Mr Grimes said. 'I've asked the gunner to take him into his team. This is a serving fighting vessel and we need brave boys like Freddy, learning the cannon craft.'

'Fighting?' Isabella asked, horrified.

'Oh, yes, miss,' Freddy said in an excited voice, 'powder monkey is the job that all the boys want. I hope the ship will see action soon.'

'Well, Freddy, I'm pleased you're happy, but I earnestly hope you don't attain your violent ambitions,' Bessie said.

Freddy ran off down the deck.

'What's the voyage plan now, Mr Grimes?' Isabella asked.

'We lost some time, Miss Godfrey,' he replied. 'But weather permitting, we should be in Malta in three more days.'

The weather held but they battled with currents, so they only stopped off in Malta overnight. The captain apologised that they had no chance to go ashore, and Valetta did look very impressive. Nevertheless, Isabella's chief concern was speed. If news of their arrival reached Sir John, their plans were for nothing.

* * *

On the morning of thirtieth of September, fifteen days after leaving Turkey, Bessie and Isabella stood on deck, ready to disembark in the Kingdom of Naples.

Bessie sought out Freddy to wish him luck. She pressed two coins into his hand. 'For all your help, laddie,' she said.

He smiled, then ran back to his duties. Bessie watched him go, too emotional to speak. Mr Grimes moved to her side.

'Don't you worry I'll look out for him, mistress. And when we get to Portsmouth, I'll make sure he visits his family.'

'Thank you,' she answered.

The Bay of Naples lay in front of them, with the famous Vesuvius volcano towering to one side. Bessie saw that Isabella was nervous. She squeezed her hand.

'Will you stay in Naples, or travel directly to Rome, ladies?' Grimes asked.

'I would have loved to enjoy the sights of Naples, but sadly we must find a coach to take us to Rome as soon as possible,' Isabella replied.

'Then I'd be honoured if you'd allow me to come ashore with you and secure you a chaise. I'll make sure you get a good driver.'

'Thank you, we would be very grateful,' Bessie replied. She heard the catch in her voice give away her reluctance to say goodbye.

Suddenly, Isabella grabbed her arm. 'Bessie, hide, it's him.'

'Damn and blast the brute,' Bessie replied, stepping behind Mr Grimes.

'Miss Godfrey, are you ill?'

Bessie gripped his arm. 'There's someone ashore we wish to avoid.'

The three walked quickly towards the ship's stern.

'Mr Grimes, this is going to sound very strange, but that man is Sir John Brady. He intends to take Miss Godfrey off in his carriage and force her to marry when she does not wish it. Will you help us?' Bessie said.

Mr Grimes looked first astonished, and then thoughtful. 'If Miss Godfrey does not want to marry that gentleman, then I'm sure she has good reason. We need a diversion. Let's you and I go ashore, Mistress Nichol. We'll distract him long enough to allow Miss Godfrey to escape. I'll task Bob and young Freddy to land you further down the dock, Miss Godfrey. Bob knows the way to a coaching inn I use. Wait for us there.'

'Thank you, Mr Grimes, I'm sorry to drag you into our troubles. There are few enough ships coming from Turkey, I should have asked the captain to set us ashore at some other place.'

'I'm more than happy to help you, but if this Sir John is a man of influence, it's better that the captain can report he knew nothing.'

Bessie had all their luggage loaded into the rowing boat, then Mr Grimes climbed down beside her. 'I hope you're a good actress, Mistress Nichol,' he said.

'Please call me Bessie, and you might be surprised what I can do if I have a mind to, Bosun Grimes,' she replied.

'I don't doubt it and I'd be honoured to hear you call me Joseph.'

Joseph helped Bessie up the harbour ladder, then they waited for the boys to bring up the trunks. She found herself unsteady after the motion of the ship, and more than a little anxious. She was very glad when Joseph took her arm.

She saw Sir John recognise her, then scowl.

'That'll be the gentleman then, steady as we go, Bessie.'

Sir John stood beside a large Berlin carriage with two horses. They walked straight towards him, whilst the sailors brought the trunks loaded on a trolley.

'Where is she?' Sir John said.

'Good morning, sir,' Joseph said with a small bow. His extreme politeness, a sharp contrast to the man's rude tone.

'Poor Miss Godfrey has had the most difficult journey,

suffering with terrible seasickness. I advised Mistress Nichol to let her take a little extra sleep this morning. I'm sure she'll join us presently.'

'Who are you to be giving instructions?' he asked, glaring at Joseph.

'Bosun Joseph Grimes, His Majesty's Navy, happy to be of service, Sir John,' he said, with a broad smile, as if oblivious to Sir John's expression.

'Now then, lads, let's get this luggage sorted.'

While he was creating a great commotion with trunks, Bessie saw a small boat with two sailors slip out from the far side of the ship. She joined in to make maximum confusion over the baggage.

'No, the other one first, boys. Steady, carry it carefully,' then, once the trunks were already loaded in the carriage: 'Goodness what was I thinking? Please get that bottom trunk down. I must put Isabella's riding dress in her valise, I believe she'll want it for the journey.'

Bessie made a play about opening the trunk and rummaging around. Eventually Sir John lost patience.

'Enough of this! Go tell your mistress we must leave immediately, she can sleep on the road.'

Bessie smiled and gave a small curtsey. 'Of course, Sir John, I'll go and fetch her.'

He frowned at her. 'No. I don't trust you one inch. I'll go and bring her ashore.'

'As you wish,' she replied.

She watched the small boat passing the lighthouse on the corner of the pier, then it disappeared from view.

'I'll have my lads take you to the ship, I'll keep an eye on the luggage,' Joseph said.

'I shan't be long, we really must leave within the hour.'

He started to walk towards the harbour edge, then

stopped and turned. 'Before I left Constantinople I heard that Richard Godfrey had gone missing. Is there any news?'

Bessie gave him a cool, hard stare. 'Sadly, not yet. We expect him to meet us in Rome.'

He inclined his head, but strode off without comment.

Meanwhile, Joseph took a note from his pocket. He turned to the sailors. 'I've got some business to attend to in Naples. Please row Sir John to the ship and wait for him until he's ready to come back. Make sure you row slowly and with great caution, we wouldn't want such an important gentleman to be splashed. When you've done, I want you to give this note to Captain Jones.' He gave each sailor a coin. 'Can I rely on you?'

The boys smiled widely. 'Yes, Bosun,' they said in unison.

They watched the rowing boat head slowly towards the ship. Joseph led her out of earshot of the carriage driver. 'What's this about Miss Godfrey's uncle?'

'He went missing just before we left Constantinople. Then there was an incident that revealed him to be a complete rogue. Unfortunately in his absence Isabella is vulnerable to Sir John.'

Joseph's eyes widened and he shook his head in disbelief. 'That poor girl. I should go to her now, Bessie. I'll organise a carriage then we'll come back for you.'

Bessie shook her head. 'No, that's too risky. Leave me here. Just make sure she gets away. Tell her I'll meet her at Ville de Londres in Rome. If I don't appear, she should proceed with the plan as we discussed.'

Joseph looked concerned. 'You realise that Sir John is going to be mighty angry when he finds out he's been tricked?'

'Don't worry about me, I can deal with that ignoramus.'

Joseph flung his head back and laughed. 'I declare you're

both brave as lions, I wouldn't want to argue with either of you.'

He doffed his hat. 'You are the most extraordinary woman, Bessie. I'm going to miss you.'

'I'll miss you too, Joseph.'

'My intention is to travel with Miss Godfrey for part of the way. There's a nice inn just off the Rome road, near Gaeta. I'll pause with her there. If you don't catch us up before dawn, I'll make sure her onward journey is secured. I've begged leave of absence overnight with the captain.'

Bessie nodded. 'Thank you and I wish you both God's speed. Take her valise and tell her not to worry and she mustn't wait for me. Now go!'

Chapter Twenty

Isabella stood shivering just inside the stable doorway. Her jacket was damp from the crossing and she was both cold and frightened. She'd decided not to wait inside the inn, if Sir John turned up he'd find her immediately. At least the stable had some dark corners where she might hide.

What was Sir John thinking? The law might allow him to force her to marry but she'd scream the church down if he tried, surely no clergyman would undertake the ceremony in those circumstances? Then she thought of a worse scenario. In her uncle's absence he might force himself on her without any need for marriage. That horrifying idea was in the front of her mind, when the sound of male footsteps approaching caused her whole body to stiffen. Seeing Bosun Grimes, she stepped into the courtyard and he rushed over.

'I am so sorry to hear of your problems, Miss Godfrey.'

Joseph had a ruddy complexion from his outdoor life but despite his very masculine appearance he had expressive eyes. The genuine concern she saw there nearly brought her to tears.

'Thank you for your kindness, and your help in this plan is more than I could have hoped for. But where's Bessie? I daren't delay.'

'She refused to leave the luggage. She means to confuse Sir John further. She's both brave and wise, because if he found her gone he'd pursue your chaise at full speed.'

Isabella shook her head in disbelief. 'I wouldn't have asked her to take such a risk, what if she comes to some harm?'

'I get the impression that Bessie can look after herself. Now, let's see what chaise is available. I'm going to come with you as far as Gaeta. If Bessie can get away, she'll meet us there.'

Once he'd arranged the transport, Grimes beckoned Bob from where he sat with Freddy in the corner of the yard. 'Great job bringing Miss Godfrey here safely. Now I have one last task for you. Mistress Nichol is waiting on the quay. If she escapes that English gentleman I want you to bring her safely here. Tell her that I've reserved a chaise and driver to take her to Gaeta and if necessary to Rome.'

'Aye, aye, Bosun,' Bob replied.

Bessie watched Sir John's rowing boat return. Isabella had been ashore less than forty minutes. Would she have had enough time to escape?

Bob appeared out of the crowd and walked past her as if a stranger, but as he drew level, he gave her an imperceptible nod. Surely that meant Isabella must be on her way. She squared her shoulders as Sir John marched towards her. His expression was thunderous. He came up close and hissed under his breath, 'Where is she? I know you're behind this charade.'

She spoke quietly, and with a smile that faked politeness.

'I have no idea, but I pray that she's out of your reach. Only a monster would expect that innocent child to want to marry. I saw your sin with my own eyes and I hope you burn in hell.'

Sir John turned on his heel. 'Signor, kindly unload Mistress Nichol's trunk,' he barked at the coach driver.

He turned back to her with a look of complete contempt. 'Your employment is over, and be assured, I will find Isabella. Your interference has caused this problem and now I shall have to be firm with her. Richard Godfrey has proved himself an unfit guardian but I shall look after her properly and I mean her to learn who's in charge.' He dropped Bessie's trunk at her feet. 'I've written to Horace Mann in Florence, the minister now has the scandalous news about Richard's dishonesty and I've sent proof of our betrothal. No doubt he will think Isabella lucky that I'll still take her.'

When Sir John had driven off, Bob sidled over to her. 'Bosun Grimes has hired you a chaise, Mistress Nichol. Can I help you with your trunk?'

'Good lad, Bob, but first get you back to the inn. I'm quite sure that gentleman will find his way there. Only when he departs, I'd be obliged if you would come back for me.'

Bessie sat down on her trunk to wait. She imagined she must look a sorry figure abandoned on the dock, and she found that the whole episode had left her knees quite weak.

* * *

After supper in the Gaeta inn, there was nothing to do but wait.

'We'll give her until daybreak, but then you must go,' Grimes said.

Isabella shook her head. 'I won't leave her.'

'Sorry, miss. But I have strict instructions, and Bessie is not a woman to be trifled with.'

It got past midnight. The innkeeper had long gone to bed, but Isabella refused to leave the window. The candle had burned out and Joseph was snoring in the fireside chair, his boots visible in the glow from the fire's embers.

She jumped to her feet at the sound of a horse approaching. Joseph was right behind her, and when the chaise pulled to a halt they rushed outside.

Joseph let out a whoop of joy when he saw Bessie smiling out at them. He gave her his hand to help her out, then picked her up and spun her around. 'Bessie Nichol, you are a wonder!'

The chaise driver yawned and stretched. He'd accepted an extra payment to get fresh horses and be ready to set off immediately. Joseph would take the other carriage back to Naples.

'I can never thank you enough. We couldn't have evaded Sir John on our own,' Isabella said.

'I wish you every luck with your journey. Although I still don't understand why you didn't just stay with us until we reach Portsmouth?'

'You make it sound simple, that I may do as I please. Legally, as a woman I have no such choice.'

He shook his head. 'But who is your guardian with your uncle missing?'

'My uncle signed betrothal papers without my consent. They name Sir John as my fiancé and guardian.'

He looked alarmed and placed his hand on her arm. 'But then you're not safe in Rome, come back with me!'

'And have one of His Majesty's peers charge your captain with kidnapping? No, I'll seek sanctuary with a company of holy sisters in a Rome convent. No man can take me from the Lord's house.'

'A nunnery? Surely not? You have too much life to with-draw from the world, Miss Godfrey.'

'I'll be delighted if they'll have me until the danger is over. I'm sure my uncle will dissolve the marriage agreement when he tracks me down.'

Isabella was completely unsure, but there was no point alarming Bosun Grimes any further.

'Well I hope you find the sanctuary you seek.'

She clasped his hand and thanked him again. Then she told Bessie she'd wait for her in the chaise.

* * *

Bessie was close to tears.

'Joseph, you've been a true friend these last days, and I hate to say goodbye to you.'

'Bessie, I would carry you off this instant, but I know you've a job of work to do here, and would most likely bite me to make your escape.'

Despite her sadness, that made her smile. 'I've never had to resort to such violence yet, but I'll keep it in mind.'

'I wish you every success with your adventure. If it's not too much trouble, could you write to me in Portsmouth? I don't know how long it might take, but a note to the ship, care of the naval dockyard, will reach me.'

'Of course, and I'll let you know where you can write to me. If I can't find work in Rome, I'll go home to Scotland. Sir John has dismissed me, so if we fail in our plan, I won't be able to stay with her.'

At that she broke down, she hadn't yet had the heart to tell Isabella. Joseph put his arms around her. Bessie leaned into his warm chest and felt the strength in his arms. It was the first time in her whole life she'd been held by an adult man. She so wanted to stay there.

'Bessie, you are the most marvellous woman. I wager you two will outwit him.'

She encircled his chest with her arms, closed her eyes and squeezed him for a moment. Then with a sigh she pulled away. 'We're in danger of causing a scandal here, Joseph, and in truth I am not the scandalous type. I pray we'll meet again one day.'

'Joseph Grimes is always at your service, ma'am.'

He swept off his hat with a bow, then raised it to the chaise. 'God's speed and good luck, Miss Godfrey!'

Chapter Twenty-One

'I'm so sorry I lost your trunks, Isabella.'

'If I enter the convent I won't need many clothes, and if our plan fails, then I'll be reunited with my trunks,' Isabella said with a grimace.

They'd been travelling for many hours, stopping only to change horses. The driver managed to make them understand that they would be in Rome late in the evening. But, when the chaise came over the brow of the next hill, Bessie grabbed her arm. 'That carriage stopped ahead is Sir John's.'

Isabella clambered over to look. 'Should we try to get past?'

They exchanged a glance. Isabella tapped the driver, she met his expectant look with a hand signal for speed. He whipped the horse and they took off at a gallop.

'Hang on, Bessie!'

They drew level with Sir John's carriage and he looked into their chaise. Isabella saw recognition on his face as they sped past. The road wasn't good, and they had to cling on to prevent being thrown out of their seats. Isabella looked back as they reached a bend. Sir John's Berlin was much more substantial, with four wheels and two horses. She turned to Bessie, her head drooped in disappointment. 'He's bound to catch us, it's over, Bessie.'

'Then we should say our goodbyes now, Issy. Sir John dismissed me in Naples. I'm so sorry, but if he stops the chaise he'll take you out and leave me behind.'

Isabella's eyes widened. 'No, he can't do that!' She could hear the larger carriage getting closer.

Bessie reached out and gripped her hand. 'Let's fight it. He has no right. If he takes you, I'll accuse him of kidnapping.'

Isabella shook her head in disbelief. Was this really it? Might he listen to reason? What kind of man would coerce her to marry? Then she recalled his aggression with Jamila. Did he actually enjoy using force? His chaise was right behind them. Isabella gritted her teeth. She wouldn't give him the pleasure of seeing her cry. Sir John's carriage began to pull alongside.

'The man's crazy!' Bessie shouted.

Their smaller chaise had the inside track, where only a small ditch separated the road from a rocky bank. A steep cliff fell away at the road's edge. Isabella held her breath. Sir John's carriage was edging ever closer, trying to force them off the road. She must tell their driver to slow, he or Bessie might be injured. Then, they rounded a bend to find an oxen cart in the middle of the road.

'Lord help us!' Bessie cried.

Behind them they heard the neighing of frightened horses, Sir John's driver had slowed. Their driver yelled encouragement to his horse and cracked the whip above his head. They sped through the small gap, close enough to see the terror in the eyes of the cart driver. Isabella looked back and saw Sir John's carriage veer violently towards the rocky bank. One of the horses reared and she heard a crack. The carriage came to halt at an angle, a wheel had gone into the ditch.

Bessie cheered. Within seconds they were round another bend and out of sight of the accident.

'I believe God is on our side, Bessie. He won't catch us now.'

Bessie hugged her. 'Of course he is.'

They sped onwards to Rome.

They came through the city gates in darkness. After descending a long hill with high walls either side, the view opened up. Suddenly ahead was the unmistakeable towering silhouette of the Colosseum.

'Mercy, it's huge,' Bessie said.

Isabella judged it safer to avoid the final chaise station and further tipped the driver to take them directly to Ville de Londres. After twenty more minutes, he halted the carriage beside a fountain in the middle of a large square. Their driver found them a boy to carry in the trunks. Isabella's heart was racing. They'd been so intent on their escape, but ever since they entered Rome's city walls she'd been experiencing full scale butterflies. Vittorio might be right here inside that house. How would he react to seeing her unexpectantly? Surely he'd be pleased?

They'd decided to hide Isabella's identity. At reception, Bessie booked two rooms in her name for herself and her niece, and asked if Signora Bassi was available. The boy went into a back room, then returned to tell them that the signora would be with them in a few minutes.

A small lady with Vittorio's hazel eyes came into reception, she wore a white cotton cap over her greying dark hair, and a white blouse with wide sleeves under a simple brown dress. She extended her arms in greeting. 'Mistress Nichol! How wonderful to finally meet you! And Miss?'

'Isabella,' she supplied, 'and are you Signora Bassi?'

The woman nodded, Isabella thought she saw a flicker of something in her eyes. Her name most certainly didn't get the same warm welcome as Bessie's. Issy's skin prickled with apprehension. The reply came after a tiny, discomforting pause. 'At your service, signorina. Although in Italy, women keep own family name, so I am Signora Sirani, but I be happy if you call me Anna.'

'What a sensible arrangement,' Bessie muttered under her breath.

'Please come through. Are you hungry? I dined, but I get you something.'

They walked down a narrow corridor behind Signora Sirani. Bessie asked the question that was consuming Isabella. 'And is Vittorio at home?'

'Sorry no, Mistress Nichol.'

She didn't turn around, but Isabella could hear tension in her voice. Her heart sank, this was not the joyous welcome she'd dreamt of.

'Vee works long hours in Palazzo del Re, and rarely comes home to eat.'

'He's working at court? How marvellous, you must both be so pleased.'

They'd reached the end of the corridor and she turned to reply to Bessie, her fingers on the door handle.

'Vee is very pleased, madam. However, I worry. The artist's life is very not certain.' Anna shrugged. 'But you know young people, they are not easily persuaded from their dreams.'

She opened a door to reveal a small, neat parlour and invited them to sit down. Next door was a kitchen where the wooden table was still set for supper. Anna called back through the door as she cleared away the dishes.

'You have veal and rice, and perhaps a little wine?'

Vittorio's mother worked quickly, keeping her back to them, but Isabella could see that she was clearing away two sets of bowls and beakers. Suddenly, she understood, it hit her like a blow. He had been here and he didn't want to see her.

Isabella was hungry after the long journey, but the dull pain of disappointment made it difficult to swallow. She could feel that both the older women were watching her, and she knew she should make polite conversation, but she felt like crying and didn't trust herself to speak. Bessie filled the gap.

'It's so kind of you to welcome us into your private quarters, Signora... I mean, Anna. We appreciate it so much after our arduous journey. We were lucky with our driver, but the inns along the way were very simple and we chose to hasten here, rather than linger.'

'The small inns of the Naples road are not the best of Italy, and you were very lucky if you had good calash driver. Most travellers coming from Naples, do less compliment about their journey.'

Bessie smiled. 'Well it was bumpy enough, but the driver was willing to get us to Rome quickly.'

They lapsed into silence again. There were several portraits on the wall, including a well-executed painting of Anna herself. Isabella was about to ask if Vittorio painted it, but stopped herself. She couldn't be certain that Vittorio's mother had worked out who she was. Keeping her identity secret increased their chances of getting safely to the convent.

As if reading her mind Bessie asked: 'I wonder if I might trouble you to give Vittorio a message when he returns? He was kind enough to say he might take me to the Santa Cecilia convent at Trastevere, and well, I was hoping we could go tomorrow morning? Our Rome visit may be very short, so we'd rather avoid delay.'

Anna looked confused. 'Vee has been back very small time and the appointment to the court happened so quick. Maybe I misunderstood what he said me about your plans?'

Isabella saw the two women regard each other. Anna clearly knew there was something going on.

Bessie held her hands apart, as a sort of apology. 'There have been some complications since Vittorio left Constantinople. If you would just let him know that Isabella and I are both anxious to go to Santa Cecilia tomorrow.'

'Vee very often sleeps at Palazzo del Re, but if he comes home tonight, I say your message. If no, I send one of the boys with a note in the morning,' Anna replied.

Just then, there was the sound of an outer door banging beyond the kitchen. Isabella couldn't help looking hopefully towards the noise. She turned away immediately, but she saw that Anna was watching her. She addressed Bessie but kept her gaze on Isabella.

'Vee already said me your interest in the Trastevere Convent, Mistress Nichol. If there are is any problem for him tomorrow, I be happy to take you.'

'You have been so kind, Anna, but please call me Bessie, and thank you again. Now, I think we must retire, it's been a most exhausting day.'

Isabella sat down on the edge of her narrow bed and stared at the floor. She hadn't for one minute imagined that Vittorio wouldn't want to see her. It made no sense. She felt sick.

After a few minutes, Bessie came in carrying fresh candles. 'Now, Issy, you need to get some sleep. Remember you're not safe yet. You must be most convincing tomorrow. We don't know how the sisters will receive you.'

Isabella nodded, she stood and started to unbutton her coat.

'Also, I know quite well why you're so quiet. Firstly, you're jumping to conclusions and Vittorio most likely has no idea you're here. Secondly, he had no notion you would travel home through Rome, and I can imagine him preferring to avoid going through the pain of parting again.'

Isabella managed to smile. Could that be an explanation? 'You're right, of course.'

She stepped out of her skirt. Then, seated at a small dressing table, she let down her hair. 'I wonder how Jamila is doing, I do miss her.' Her eyes filled with tears and Bessie squeezed her shoulders.

'Time to go to bed now, Issy, you're exhausted.

Chapter Twenty Two

Rome, September 1742

Isabella pushed open the shutters to let in the sunlight. She'd considered writing a note to leave for Vittorio but decided she didn't know why he was avoiding her. Might she be wrong about his feelings?

She watched young people streaming off the bottom of the wide steps in the piazza below, she could hear them chatting and laughing. How she wished to be one of those carefree girls. She pulled her shoulders back and stood very straight. She daren't indulge in feeling sorry for herself, things could be a lot worse by evening if she lost her resolve.

There was a gentle tap at the door, she answered to find Bessie there, with a cup of milk and some warm bread. 'I thought it might be quicker for you to breakfast while I help you dress.'

Isabella nodded, although she'd hoped she might find Vittorio downstairs.

'He's not at home,' Bessie said, guessing her thoughts once again. 'Anna will take us to Santa Cecilia. She's a good woman, Isabella. I think we should bring her into our confidence.'

'I'm sure she is, and it would be wrong to deceive her when she's helping us.'

They were all outside the lodging house before eight.

'Come, ladies, I know this driver, we'll take his chaise,' Anna said.

'Might we see some of Rome's famous buildings on our journey?' Issy asked.

'We can easy go past the Pantheon,' Anna replied, looking at her curiously, 'but why you choose Santa Cecilia to visit first? There are many more famous sights.'

'It's a complicated story, I'll explain on the journey,' Issy said.

'Are we very far from Palazzo del Re?' Bessie asked. 'I might walk there tomorrow.'

'Is no far from the Pantheon,' Anna replied. 'Vee knows I no happy he didn't keep his promise to come with you today. Perhaps I can say him to take you, when he goes there tomorrow?'

Isabella had to blink to hold back tears. The idea that Vittorio was avoiding her but might meet Bessie, was too much to bear.

Bessie threaded her arm through Isabella's. 'Could we drive past there too? Isabella will explain why she can't come with me tomorrow.'

'Of course,' Anna replied, and instructed the driver.

'The truth is, that if I get my wish, this trip to Santa Cecilia is one way for me,' Isabella explained, and then went on to tell Anna the whole story.

Anna listened, her eyes growing wider throughout. She gasped in horror, hearing of Jamila's assault, and Sir John's denial. Finally, on learning that her guardian had gone missing

158

and Sir John was attempting to force her to marry, she cried aloud.

'*Oh mio dio*! You poor girl. Can I say Vittorio? He be so shocked. I'm sure he regret no coming.'

Isabella nodded. 'I'm sorry we didn't tell you yesterday, but I feared discovery. I'm certain that Sir John is searching Rome for me, and your establishment is well known amongst English travellers.'

'Well, if he come, he get nothing from me,' Anna replied firmly.

'But where is your luggage?' she asked, looking around the carriage as if it might be hidden somewhere.

'He took it,' Isabella replied. 'We are hoping I can persuade the sisters in Santa Cecilia to give me refuge. If they agree, I'll not need many gowns in the convent.'

'I get my seamstress make you more dresses,' Anna replied. 'Also, I can introduce you to the nuns. I arrived in King James's court after Queen Maria Clementina left Santa Cecilia, but she used to visit. She also trusted me to deliver gifts. There was a nun I come to know, I believe Sister Maria Teresa still there.'

'You're too kind,' Isabella said. 'Look, is that the Pantheon?'

The grand building with its row of huge marble columns stood to one side of a piazza.

'Yes. I say the driver to stop?' Anna asked.

Isabella shook her head. 'It's too risky.'

They drove on through the beautiful city in silence. After ten more minutes, Anna pointed out Palazzo del Re. She asked the driver to pause.

'You might be disappointed? Is beautiful inside, but outside is very plain. Of course, wasn't built for the King.'

'I don't find it disappointing at all,' Bessie replied firmly.

'Just the thought that the King could be looking out of those very windows.'

Bessie leaned out of the carriage to peer upwards. Isabella was doing the same on her side, but she wasn't looking for royalty.

Anna's voice became quiet: 'We had happy years there, when the childrens were small. Of course Vee is too low born to be friends Prince Henry now, but the prince is loyal supporter.'

'A great supporter to have indeed,' Bessie commented. 'Does the prince know him as Vee?'

Anna smiled. 'He use first. When they met, Henry was only four and found Vittorio too difficult to say. It is the child nickname, but I like it.'

Isabella turned the syllable silently in her mouth. She liked it too. Simple and perfect. Please God, let there be a straightforward explanation for Vittorio avoiding her.

Suddenly, Bessie pulled Isabella back inside the chaise.

'Sir John's carriage!'

Isabella shrank back against the seats, furious that she'd been so careless. 'Is he coming? Did he see me?'

'No, I shouldn't think you would be seen, he's on the wrong side.'

Bessie edged back to the window. 'The carriage hasn't moved, the driver is staring at the palace entrance.'

'We should leave,' Isabella said.

'We must pass him,' Anna answered.

Anna moved to be beside the window nearest to Sir John's coach, Bessie and Isabella turned away, their bonnets shielding their faces. They passed the palazzo and turned into a side street.

'Was there anyone in the coach, Anna?'

'No sure,' she replied, then asked, 'The coach driver know you?'

'No. Unless Sir John showed him my painting,' Isabella replied.

Bessie's outburst was angry: 'Of course, that brute has your portrait, I'd forgotten it was in your trunk. I'm so sorry, Isabella.'

Isabella smiled sadly, laying her fingers on the miniature she wore beneath her chemise. 'I cannot imagine he'll want to look at it after today. Perhaps he'll return it?'

'That blackguard? I doubt it,' Bessie said.

'But why he looking for you here?' Anna asked.

'I'm sure it's Vittorio, not me he's watching for. Perhaps he hopes to follow him to my hiding place?' Isabella replied.

'Then he wasting the time. First, he maybe no recognise Vee in court dress. And second, Palazzo del Re have three entrances and Vee always enter from Piazza della Pilotta.'

'I hope he doesn't harass Vittorio,' Isabella murmured.

Bessie squeezed her hand, then turned to Anna. 'What is Vittorio painting?'

'He copy portraits of the King in miniature for Stuart supporters. There are many peoples who must keep their allegiance the secret.'

Bessie made a tutting noise under her breath.

They crossed the river and after a few minutes, Anna announced they'd reached Basilica di Santa Cecilia. 'I think it best you wait in the church, Miss Godfrey. I go find Sister Maria Teresa.'

'We are most grateful, and please call me Isabella.'

They passed through the entrance into a high-walled garden courtyard. In just a few short steps, they left the bustle of Rome and entered an oasis of peace. Small birds made the only sound.

'It's lovely,' Isabella whispered.

Passing through the marble pillared portico, they entered the cool shade of the church itself.

'Incredible, it's everything I hoped,' Bessie said.

The church was heavily decorated, the rows of arches and painted walls edged in gilt. They walked slowly towards the ornately carved central altar. As they got closer Issy saw a white marble statue of Saint Cecilia lying below the altar, as if in her tomb. The life-sized statue portrayed her lying on her side with her face turned away, and the sculptor had managed to make the marble folds of her dress look real.

'She was martyred for her wish to serve God and remain a virgin,' Bessie whispered.

Bessie knelt and Isabella followed her lead. She prayed with all her heart that she might find safety in this place. If the sisters turned her away, she had no alternative plan. She opened her eyes. Thoughts of Vittorio were inappropriate here but she couldn't keep him out of her mind. If she could stay in Rome, surely the mystery would be resolved? Whatever the problem they'd overcome it.

Vittorio's mother returned with an elderly nun, who was even smaller than Anna herself. 'Maria Teresa speak no English. Sit down and I translate what you want say.'

Isabella passed the nun her Bible and explained that she was being forced into a repugnant marriage and wished to seek sanctuary in the convent. The nun took the leather book and asked why she didn't want to marry. Isabella explained that she'd never agreed to the match and she'd discovered some very unpleasant facts about her suitor. Her uncle had signed the betrothal papers without her knowledge and then gone missing, and her fiancé was determined to exploit his absence. She was being held to a marriage pact that she believed her uncle would allow her to break.

The nun shook her head as she began her reply. Panic rose in Isabella's chest.

'Sister Maria Teresa very sorry to your situation, but say the convent is no a place to hide. Novices come because they want dedicate life to God. It is more difficult than marriage.'

Isabella could hear that Bessie shared her dread, her voice trembled. 'Holy Sister, please. I brought young Isabella to you. Your renown as the place of sanctuary for Queen Maria Clementina; God rest her soul; is a famous story amongst all Catholics.'

Anna translated the nun's reply. 'It is true Maria Clementina lived in the convent for few years, but she was complete devoted to the Lord. She would have been well suited to the nun life, if no a queen. Also,' she paused and shrugged, 'her godfather His Holiness Pope Clement.'

The nun looked Isabella full in the face, her skin was very wrinkled, accentuating the vitality in her blue eyes. Isabella sensed that her mind was made up.

'She say is no right to interfere in your family affairs. And you no speak Italian, the idea impossible.'

Isabella's desperate reaction was instinctive. She sank to the ground at the nun's feet, touching the hem of her habit. 'I beg you, sister, in the name of Santa Cecilia. I am an orphaned virgin in terrible peril. I hate to voice the sordid details in this holy place, but I saw my fiancé trying to rape my maid with my own eyes. Since he knows I hate him, surely his pleasure must be in the thought of subjugating me.'

'*Per favore*, Maria Teresa,' Anna whispered.

'I know some Latin and I'd learn Italian quickly,' she pleaded.

The nun looked down, she placed her hand on Isabella's head.

'Please, sister. Let me stay for a few weeks until the present danger has passed.'

'She say get up, child,' Anna translated.

Isabella got to her feet.

'Maria Teresa is no convinced that you have the nun calling. However, in the name of Santa Cecilia, she cannot turn you away. You be expected to take full part in the duties of the convent. If the Mother Superior agrees, you can stay a few weeks or until you find another place for safety.'

Isabella curtseyed and kissed the nun's hand. 'Thank you, sister.'

They'd done it. She was safe. The rush of relief was dizzying. Bessie hugged her and promised to visit soon. She also felt real warmth in Anna's embrace. Her previous wariness seemed to have gone, and Isabella was sure it was her personal plea that had persuaded Sister Maria Teresa. She couldn't guess why Vittorio was hiding from her, but it seemed his mother was not the source of the problem.

Chapter Twenty-Three

Bessie found herself downcast. They'd fought so hard to get Issy entry into the convent but she couldn't help feeling it was a hollow victory. Sir John deserved punishment but it was Isabella who was shut away. She looked for Anna to ask for something useful to do. Then spent the next four hours ironing bedlinen in Anna's kitchen. The rhythm of the iron and the familiar smell had a calming effect. Bessie placed the iron on the stove and picked up a fresh one. She held it close to her cheek, and finding it too hot, waited for it to cool.

'You good at this,' Anna said with a smile.

'I ironed enough bedlinen when I was first in service,' Bessie answered.

'Is how I come to work for Stuarts,' Anna replied. 'The Swiss woman who did the princes' laundry have too much work, so I went help. Henry love it when Vee come with me, and his tutors pretend no see they friends. No in public of course, but they loved to run through the palazzo corridors together. Henry was the different boy to Charles. He ride and

165

hunt with his brother but need quiet time also. He and Vee made good friends as children.'

Bessie finished a bedsheet. Anna took one end, and years of practice made the stretching and folding an easy co-operation that needed no words. Anna passed her another sheet from the basket.

'So you knew Maria Clementina? I would love to have met such a beautiful and saintly lady.'

Anna shrugged. 'I didn't know her well. She very busy in good works.'

Bessie wondered if she caught something in her tone. She ignored it, she wouldn't hear anything said against the late Queen. She'd been brought up to revere the Catholic royal family in exile.

Anna insisted Bessie join her for dinner as a thank you for the ironing. Bessie wondered if Vittorio might appear now Isabella had gone. But he didn't come.

The next morning Bessie asked a maid if Monsieur Vittorio was home. She answered no, but with such a strange expression, Bessie deduced that something was very wrong. She faced a dilemma. Vittorio had seemed so sincere in his promise to help her find work and she hated to rely on Isabella's charity. She was loathe to mention the problem to Anna, who might think she was asking for some reduction in the cost of her board.

At least she had a task to fulfil today, Isabella needed some undergarments. Anna had given her the address of a shop near Palazzo del Re.

Bessie set off after breakfast. The overcast sky promised a cooler day. She walked with a determined air, swinging her heavy parasol, both protection from the weather and handy for shaking at any beggar who might try to detain her. Her confident stride was a front, so when she emerged beside the Stuarts' church, Basilica dei Santi Apostoli, she smiled in triumph. Admittedly she was not on the corner she'd been aiming for.

Dare she go in? The freedom to enter a Catholic church was unfamiliar. There were no Catholic churches open to the public in Scotland and services were held in private houses. Her heart raced when she met no challenge at the entrance. Once inside she was overwhelmed by the opulence, it was even more decorated than Santa Cecilia. The fluted columns were gilded, and a skilled ceiling painter had managed to create the impression that the figures above her head were falling out of heaven itself. Truly a place of worship worthy of a royal family.

She knelt and gave herself over to the pleasure of prayer, asking the Holy Mother to guide her next steps. After some time she rose stiffly and looked around. Anna had told her that King James came often to pray at Maria Clementina's shrine. It wasn't amongst the side chapels, but eventually she found the marble monument hung on a column – a depiction of white angels hovering around a grey marble urn. The bottom angel held a human heart in his hand. Macabre confirmation that Maria Clementina's heart was within. Bessie jumped when she felt a hand on her shoulder. A young priest seemed to be telling her she should move. His level of agitation caused her to turn around. A small party of gentlemen standing at the doors bowed low to the man entering. He wore no crown but Bessie knew his distinguished profile. James Stuart was approaching and she was in his way.

Bessie let out a little squeak of fear and scuttled sideways into the nave's shadows. She was both transfixed by the sight of her idol and mortified that she'd been so wrong-footed. He knelt in front of the shrine, bowing his head into his clasped hands. After some minutes he raised his head, his expression of grief was heart-rending, and tinged with something further. Bessie felt convinced that the true King, God's intended ruler of Scotland looked wracked with remorse. She felt sick. An aide helped King James to his feet and lent him his arm to support him from the church. He looked so vulnerable, so ordinary.

Bessie stood there afraid to move, expecting to be admonished for trespassing on such a private moment. After twenty minutes she crept out, blinking in the sunshine. She walked without plan to the end of the road, only the shop window brought her to her senses. Issy wanted petticoats.

Back at the lodgings Bessie went straight to her room, until Anna sought her out. 'The Berlin is outside, I get you same driver.'

Bessie was sitting on her bed, still in her bonnet.

'You all right? You find the shop?'

Bessie looked up and saw the concern in her face.

She nodded, laying her hand on the parcel beside her. 'Yes, thank you. I found it.'

'And the Basilica? Is beautiful?'

'Yes, the most amazing church,' Bessie replied. 'I saw Maria Clementina's shrine. I found it...' she hesitated, 'most affecting.'

'Terrible tragedy, such a waste,' Anna shook her head. 'She was the very beautiful young woman, you can see it in her portrait. But she was thin and like old when I met her and she ate so little. Such a problem for the boys. Henry missed the mother help he need. Losing her in convent years and when she came back she was so sad.'

Bessie stared at her. Sad. Lonely. Those were the words she might have used to describe James Stuart.

'You look very tired, Bessie. Would you like me deliver the parcel? It is no trouble.'

'Thank you but no. I must see dear Isabella.'

. . .

The nun who answered the convent door motioned that Bessie should wait. She sat on a bench in the courtyard. When Isabella came out Bessie was shocked by her appearance. 'My dear. Did they make you...?'

Isabella smiled. 'No. They did not. But I'm resolved to fit in as best I can. I believe the Mother Superior might not have had me, if Sister Maria Teresa hadn't already agreed.'

The coarse, grey cotton dress was made for a nun in training. Also, Bessie thought, suitable for a peasant. Isabella sat down beside her and Bessie noticed the rough weave of her stockings. 'I brought you some cotton chemise, petticoats and some silk stockings. I would like to think that you are at least comfortable.'

Isabella took and squeezed her hand. 'Thank you, but don't worry. Remember that the fine dresses I wore in Constantinople were a pretence. I wore very simple clothes in the London workshop.'

Isabella went on to describe the convent routine, the early start, the prayers, the work. Bessie had never considered what Isabella would actually do in the convent.

'Don't look so worried. They have the most beautiful walled garden, they grow lavender, oranges and lemons, the smell is divine. They harvest and sell their produce. I've asked to be assigned to this work.'

'You're going to pick fruit?' Bessie looked at Issy's soft white hands. If she'd done manual work in her workshop you'd never have guessed.

Isabella smiled again. 'I'm sure I can learn. I thought I might like to help them making jam.'

'Jam?'

Their eyes met, then they both burst out laughing.

'I know, imagine what Meryem would say!'

'I trust you won't ask me to sample any of your first batch,' Bessie replied, and they laughed again.

It was good to hear Issy laugh.

'Well, I'm glad to hear that you're settling in and keeping your spirits up. I'll see you tomorrow. Anna asked if she should send her dressmaker?'

Issy groaned and pulled a face.

'These simple clothes are much better for working in the convent and I've no wish to be imprisoned in stays again.'

Bessie raised her eyebrows.

'But I suppose I'll need a couple of dresses for when I leave. Ask Anna to send her.'

'You must write to Horace Mann and advise him that you're here. Also so your uncle will know how to find you.'

Isabella's face fell. 'I must write to both Horace Mann and Sir John, I'll do it tonight.'

Bessie nodded. 'I'll take your letters to that banker's office tomorrow. Sir John has told the British Embassy in Florence a parcel of lies, so you need to put them right. Sir Everard will back you up.'

Bessie rose to leave.

'How are things at the lodging house? Did you see...?' Isabella started to ask.

She smiled sadly at her and shook her head. 'No, he didn't come. Issy, I don't know his reasons for staying away but you must put this behind you. Hankering after the impossible will damage your health.'

Isabella nodded. 'I know and you're right.' She was silent for a couple of seconds. 'I won't ask you again. But if you do see him, would you just let me know that he's safe and well?'

'If I see him,' Bessie echoed.

. . .

The next morning, Isabella handed Bessie sealed envelopes, for Horace Mann, Sir Everard and Sir John.

'What did you write?' Bessie asked.

Isabella sighed. 'Writing to Sir John was easier than I feared. I honestly believe what I told him. Our marriage would have been unhappy for him too. He'd have tired of his victory and blamed his prize. He deserves to rot in hell, but the sisters preach forgiveness,' she paused and shook her head. 'I can't manage that yet. I only pray he'll harm no other woman. My letter to Horace Mann, relates the true story of my circumstances, and that I have no intention of marrying Sir John Brady. I've also asked him to send on my letter to Sir Everard. I'm sure he'll be pleased that I'm safe but I fear he'll withdraw his offer to be my second guardian.'

'Why ever do you think that?'

Today they were sitting inside the church to escape a rain shower, Issy gestured towards the altar.

Bessie shook her head. 'What?'

'Sir Everard is closely associated with His Majesty's government. He cannot be associated with a Catholic.' Isabella drooped her head over her clasped hands. 'It's such a disappointment. Now I must depend on Uncle Richard coming back, otherwise I've nowhere to go and no one to turn to.'

'No, Issy, you have God and you have me.'

Isabella turned to her and gripped her hand. 'You're right, and I know I need no other.'

Chapter Twenty-Four

On the way home Bessie stopped to buy writing materials, including several sheets of the finest grade linen paper. The cost was ridiculous and it might not work, but she had to try. Bessie's father hadn't believed in education for girls but her mother had more sense. When a kind nun in their parish had offered to teach Bessie her letters, she'd agreed. Bessie had read everything she could get her hands on in the houses she'd served in. Writing, on the other hand, she'd had less chance for practice, her hand was shaky and progress slow. Finally, she copied the letter onto the fine paper.

Ville de Londres
Piazza di Spagna, Rome
3rd October

Dear Sir Everard,

Forgive the Impertinence of inserting my Note, but this is of the utmost Importance. Miss Godfrey is safe in Santa Cecilia Convent but has given up Hope of retaining your Support. I pray you will see the necessity of pursuing the Guardianship issue.

I know you are a Man who believes in Justice. I confirm my witness to Sir John's disgusting Actions and I implore you to have someone talk to Jamila, the Maid in question. I believe she will convince with her honest Testimony. The Man may be a Peer of the Realm but he believes himself above God's Commandments. He tried and failed to take Isabella by force when we landed in Naples. I struggle to understand his Motivation, but I'm sure this Marriage is not in her Interests.

Miss Godfrey anticipates your Repugnance in her choice of Catholic Refuge, but I'm sure you will acknowledge the Need for drastic Action. She has written to Sir John breaking the Engagement and so far has not heard from her Uncle. She needs your Guardianship now more than ever.

Assuring you of my best Intentions and continuing Support of dear Isabella,

Yours,
Elisabeth Magdalena Nichol

Bessie folded the note to make it as small and thin as possible, she needed this message to travel undetected. The letter was securely closed by the wax, but Bessie had seen a gap in the folds. She gently squeezed the edges of the letter and slid her single folded sheet inside the small opening. When she let go, the letter sprang shut. It looked as before.

She was downstairs fastening her bonnet, when Anna emerged from her quarters.

'I'm taking Isabella's letters to Horace Mann's banker, I'm assured they can organise delivery.'

'Banker will be taking *riposo* now. I cook meatballs, come and eat with me first? Better go at four o'clock.'

Bessie unpinned her bonnet again. 'Of course, I'd forgotten. I'd be delighted to join you, thank you.'

They sat to eat in Anna's kitchen.

'So Vittorio isn't returning for dinner?' Bessie asked.

'He does not come home during day,' Anna replied.

'But for supper?' Bessie added.

Anna met her gaze. 'Sometimes.'

The unasked questions hung in the air. For several minutes they ate in silence.

'Anna, I so enjoy your company, but I cannot in all conscience continue to share your table when I'm sure this prevents you eating with your son.'

Anna blinked and gave a tiny nod.

'This afternoon I must complete this errand, but tomorrow I'll look for humbler lodgings. I doubt that Vittorio's reason for avoiding me can be so very bad, but if he won't face me, we cannot continue in the same house.'

Nothing in Anna's expression suggested disagreement. Bessie continued: 'I've told Isabella to put Vittorio out of her mind. While I'm certain she cannot do that, I expect she'll keep to her resolve not to mention him again. I hate subterfuge, Anna, but if there is some secret I'll not break his trust.'

Anna laid her hand on Bessie's arm. 'Please no leave, Bessie. I have the small room at the top of house, I let you have it for little money. You could help me with ironing?'

Bessie smiled. 'You are beyond kind, Anna, and I'd like to stay in Rome to see Issy settled, but I cannot accept. I refuse to be a barrier to your son feeling comfortable in his own home.'

Anna nodded. 'I talk with Vee.'

Bessie found the banker's office. After a short wait a clerk called her through.

'I've come on behalf of Miss Isabella Godfrey.'

'Miss Godfrey isn't with you? We were told to expect her.'

'She was unable to come herself. I am Mistress Nichol, her chaperone. Should you need to reach her, you'll find in her in the Santa Cecilia Convent in Trastevere.'

The man's expression was as if she'd described Isabella kidnapped by pirates. Bessie ignored him and took the letters from her bag.

'I assume you're able to pass this letter onto Sir John Brady, who is presently visiting Rome?'

His eyes widened, he nodded.

'The other three should go to Horace Mann at the British Embassy in Florence.'

Another frightened nod.

'Isabella has written to Sir Everard Fawkener, the ambassador in Constantinople, and there is a second letter to him from me. Can you can see they're all delivered?'

She was confident that her decoy letter would be rerouted to be discarded by Sir John. It was full of melodramatic complaints about his behaviour towards Isabella, also grievances about her unwarranted dismissal and unpaid wages.

The kind of nonsense Sir John would expect. In case she was wrong about the interception, she had signed this letter Bessie McTavish McIvor MacDonald Nichol. Sir Everard had seen her formal references and would understand her ruse.

Bessie headed home, feeling content that she'd done her best. Pausing on Via della Pilotta, she realised that the two men who'd been behind her had also stopped. Was she being followed? Thieves, or spies for Sir John? Perhaps it wasn't safe to go back to her lodgings. She daren't turn around but could hear their footsteps following. Her heart thudded in her ears. There was no one in the road ahead. Would they attack her? Of course, they'd probably been waiting for her to turn up at the banker's house. How stupid of her not to have expected it.

The footsteps were getting closer and Bessie could barely breathe, she gripped the shaft of her parasol with both hands. Could she fight them off? She was hugely relieved when a carriage approached, they wouldn't harm her in front of a witness. The road was narrow and Bessie had to move beside the wall to let the carriage pass. Suddenly, she was swept up by strong hands under her arms, the coach door opened and the two men flung her inside. She landed heavily on the floor. The Berlin, which had never stopped moving, now set off at a trot. She'd guessed the occupant's identity before she looked up. 'Sir John.'

'You will wish that it wasn't,' he replied.

His cold smile made her blood freeze. She grabbed the seat to haul herself up. Now sitting opposite him, she glared. She hoped her bold stare gave no clue of her fear. She could easily imagine him having those thugs hurt her, but surely he wouldn't do her any harm in his own carriage?

'Now, mistress, the game is up. You will take me to your hiding place.'

Bessie continued to glare. 'Isabella is not with me, and she is safely out of your reach.'

Sir John leaned forwards placing his hands on his knees, his face intimidatingly close to hers. His breath smelt foul and there was an unpleasant odour from his wig. 'You must know, Mistress Nichol, that you are acting outside the law. Richard Godfrey is missing and I have the papers confirming our betrothal. Now, I will ask you one more time. Where is she?'

He hissed out the last words. Despite her resolve, Bessie shrank back in her seat. Then a new wave of anger passed over his face.

'By God, she's with that apprentice boy, isn't she? I know he's been hiding from me. I'll have him flogged if he's deflowered her, and you will pay the price for your part in it.' He banged his hand on the leather seat.

Sir John's accusation against Isabella's virtue made Bessie furious. She replied slowly and deliberately: 'Isabella is as pure as the Virgin herself and is choosing to remain so. You're wasting your time looking for Vittorio, he's not involved.'

He leaned further over and spat his words out in her face. 'Enough of this, take me to her now.'

Bessie turned her face away and wiped the small amount of spittle from her cheek with her glove. 'Isabella has written to you. I left her letter with Horace Mann's agent this afternoon. She has found sanctuary with the nuns in Santa Cecilia. You cannot reach her.'

She smiled in triumph at his appalled expression. Suddenly, he struck her face with the back of his hand. 'You Papist bitch!'

Bessie was flung back by the blow. There was a searing pain at her cheekbone and she could feel blood trickling from her eyebrow. She touched her face and her glove came away stained red. She saw Sir John glance down at the large signet ring on his right hand. His expression when he looked up, was pure hatred. 'Your mistress will rue the day she made a fool out of me, and you will regret meddling in my affairs, madam.'

Then he opened the door of the moving coach and pushed her out.

Chapter Twenty-Five

Isabella hurried to the courtyard, Bessie hadn't come the day before as promised. Her heart lurched when she saw her visitor was Anna. Had something happened to Bessie? Or to Vittorio?

Anna smiled. 'Don't worry, Isabella. Bessie is a little no well today, she asked I come in her place. Also, I translate for my dressmaker Signora Bernini, she will be here in few minutes.'

'Bessie's ill? That's so unlike her. Did she see a doctor?'

Anna was avoiding looking at her. 'Yes, I know the English speaking doctor. He came this morning.'

'Then it's something serious, if you called him in so soon. And she seemed so well earlier in the week. What did he say?'

Anna looked down at her hands, she hesitated before replying. 'That no need to worry.'

Isabella could tell Anna was hiding something. Just then the dressmaker came into the courtyard and Anna made the introductions.

'I'll ask the sisters if there's a room we can use for the measuring,' Isabella said.

The seamstress was efficient and the measuring was quickly over. Isabella was little interested in the dress style and agreed to the two pictures she was shown. When Anna made to leave with Signora Bernini, Isabella put her hand on her shoulder. 'Anna, I can tell you're hiding something from me. If you won't tell me, then I must come with you to check on Bessie.'

'Oh, no, signorina, is no safe. He could be watching the house.'

'Who? Sir John? You've seen him?'

Anna sighed, she shook her head, looking defeated. 'Bessie made me promise no to say you, but I certain she prefer I say than have you leave this safe place. Sir John found her.'

Isabella gasped.

'Don't worry, she be all right. She need doctor for the cut on her face and has bad bruising.'

'He hurt her?' Actual violence was even worse than she'd expected of him.

'He hit the innocent lady and flung her from the coach in moving. Very bad man.'

Isabella stood up. 'Wait for me here. I'll tell the sisters, I must go to her.'

Anna grabbed her wrist. 'No! This exactly what he wants. She is hurt but she be better soon. If that man find you now, her heart is broken.'

'You're right. But Bessie must go to the authorities, he cannot get away with it!'

'I say this also. But Bessie say that she has no witness and her word against the English gentleman no be believed. I am so sorry but I agree.'

Issy clenched her fists in anger. 'It's just not right.'

'No,' Anna agreed. 'Isabella, I look to Bessie. The important thing is Sir John no catch you. You must stay here.'

Isabella reluctantly agreed. Anna got up to leave.

'I come tomorrow.'

'No,' Isabella replied. 'You're busy and Bessie's injuries give you more work. Also, the nuns here receive few visitors, I don't want special treatment.'

'Then, I see you next week, when Signora Bernini is ready for dress fitting.'

Isabella hugged her. 'Thank you. And please look after Bessie and give her my wishes for her recovery. Tell her I'm so, so sorry.'

* * *

Bessie rose from the day bed with some difficulty. Although badly bruised, she'd had a lucky escape. Two women had witnessed her fall from the carriage and had run to her aid. Showing kindness to a foreign lady in distress, they'd found her a chaise to take her back to Ville de Londres. Apart from the pain, Bessie was furious. This man knew there was nothing she could do. Also, her precious parasol had been left behind in the coach.

Anna came in. She'd persuaded Bessie to stay in her quarters overnight. Bessie accepted her argument that she needed help and it wasn't convenient for Anna to run up and down the stairs.

Anna took off her bonnet and shoes.

'You found Isabella in good health?'

'Yes, she is well. But why you stand?'

Bessie went to sit down but grimaced in pain. Anna hurried over and helped her sit and lift her legs onto the day bed.

'Thank you, Anna. I so hate being a burden and I'm sure I'm in the way here. Perhaps I might manage up the stairs tonight?'

'Can I look?'

Anna lifted Bessie's skirts. They'd left off her stockings, and her leg was now an even more alarming colour than this morning.

'No tonight, tomorrow maybe. I get the boys help you up the stairs. I make the attic room for you. I think you find it comfortable.'

Bessie shook her head in frustration. 'I'd hoped to start looking for somewhere else to stay today. I really hate to impose on you any longer.'

Anna smiled and shook her head. 'Bessie, you and I must always manage alone. You right to help Isabella stop this marriage. Allow me help you for her sake.'

'Then I'm most grateful.'

She touched her swollen cheek with her hand. 'When do you think I may go to the convent? Might the swelling be down tomorrow?'

Anna laughed. 'You strong, Bessie, but you cannot go tomorrow. You afraid the nuns.'

'But Isabella will worry.'

Anna sighed. 'Isabella knew our lie easily. I must say her what happened, but say your injuries small.'

'Oh no, I didn't want to worry her.'

'She want come see you. I must say her the truth to stop her take the risk.'

'She mustn't! He'd capture her!'

'*Sì*, I say this and she agree. I visit next week when her dresses are ready. She want like other nuns, no too many visitors.'

Bessie nodded. 'That man hurt me to frighten her. He should be flogged.'

'I afraid this Sir John is the dangerous enemy.'

'I hope he'll give up and leave now he knows she's out of his reach,' Bessie said.

'We pray for that. So, Bessie, no more say leaving. The attic room is always empty. Too small for guests and both the maids live home with their families. When your injuries finished is plenty of ironing.'

Bessie insisted on moving upstairs the next day. It was much more painful than she admitted, but they managed with the help of a serving boy. Anna had given her a new parasol as a gift and its strong wooden handle served as a stick to lean on. The flimsy Italian material would be little use when she got home, but gifts were so outside her experience, that she'd been moved to tears.

'I don't know how I can ever repay your kindness.' Bessie sniffed and dabbed her nose with her handkerchief. 'Also, would you pass this onto the boy who helped me upstairs?' she gave Anna a coin. 'I had thought that Vittorio might have been home to help us?'

Bessie felt guilty as soon as she said it. Anna looked embarrassed.

'I'm sorry. I didn't mean to pry.'

'Vee has explain to make. This go on too long,' Anna replied.

Bessie awoke in the dark, for several seconds she couldn't work out where she was. Then confusion turned to fear. She could smell smoke. Her instinct was to run, but she'd forgotten her injuries and managed to only half rise before tumbling to the floor. Her head pounded and a searing pain shot through her left leg. When she remembered where she was her mouth went dry. The building was surely on fire and she wasn't certain she could move.

Bessie crawled across the floor to pull open the door, her

ribs hurt so much she could barely breathe. Smoke, no doubt about the smell, her eyes smarted and she could hear the sound of crackling. The steep steps plunged down into the darkness, if she fell here she'd break her neck. She heard herself whimper but there was no time for cowardice. The house was full of sleeping travellers and Anna's bedroom was at the back of the building. She leaned across her body to grab the bannister and pull herself up, but found she had to bear all her weight on her right leg. When she reached down with her left foot, pain shot through her body, then she quickly brought down her right leg with a thud. Crab-like she continued down, pain, clump, pain, clump, her head resting on the wall between each step. The smoke became thicker as she descended. Her instinct was to retreat, but that surely meant cowering alone waiting for the fire to find her. She reached a small landing, now she could see the flickering glow of the fire reflecting on the stair wall. Realising she'd reached the guests' corridor. Bessie began to shout.

'Fire! Wake up, the house is on fire!'

A door banged. Bessie kept shouting. A woman's scream, then lots more doors. A man rushed past, almost knocking her over. She clung onto the handrail and resumed her slow descent. A door opened downstairs and she heard a whooshing sound, heat radiated upwards. Bessie clung onto the rail, over and over she whispered: 'Hail Mary, full of Grace. Hail Mary, full of Grace.'

She could hear boots pounding, she'd surely be trampled in the rush. Her bad leg gave way on the next step down and she landed heavily. She could go no further.

Bessie breathed out, then in, accepting the inevitable. She was drifting out of consciousness when she heard Anna's voice in her ear.

'Bessie! How you get here?'

'Leave me, Anna. Save yourself. I can't go any further.'

'No,' Anna said, coughing in the smoke. Then calling to two men coming down, '*Signors*, help here please.'

For the second time in a week, Bessie was lifted off her feet. Pain in her ribs caused her to close her eyes. 'But the fire?' she whispered.

'Vee get the drivers bring in buckets of water from the fountain. The fire nearly out.'

The ground floor stank of smoke. Looking down the hall, Bessie could see the street through the open door. A boy with a soot-streaked face rushed in and threw a bucket of water on the blackened cupboard, steam billowed up in a hissing cloud. The two tables that had flanked the front door were reduced to piles of charred embers.

Outside she heard a familiar voice: '*Grazie a tutti, il fuoco è spento.*'

A cheer went up, the fire was out.

Then two figures appeared, their silhouettes framed in the doorway. Vittorio's secret was out.

Chapter Twenty-Six

Isabella took the steps two at a time. Sister Caterina had said her visitor was a man, her Italian was improving fast. Now, meeting the nun at the foot of the stairs, she registered the girl's disapproving expression. Issy slowed to a dignified walk, she knew her unspoken prayer for the visitor to be Vittorio fulfilled what the nun suspected. But when she opened the door to the courtyard, Isabella found a complete stranger standing there.

'Miss Godfrey?' he said.

His English accent surprised her.

'My name is Thomas Carter. I've come from Florence on behalf of Mr Horace Mann.'

Isabella nodded and swallowed, she feared an official visitor from the British representative in Florence must mean bad news. 'Is something wrong?'

'Luckily no, but the whole incident could have had very serious consequences.'

'You mean Mistress Nichol's accident?' she asked. Surprised, since Anna had said Bessie wouldn't report it.

'I do not, although you are right about that too. Mr Mann

regrets that Mistress Nichol thought she wouldn't be believed.' He frowned, 'Of course, perhaps you don't know about the fire in Ville de Londres?'

'No! What fire?' Isabella's hands flew to her face in shock.

The man raised both hands in a calming gesture. 'Everyone is fine and the building was saved. I'm most sorry to worry you, I should have realised you wouldn't have heard.'

'What happened?'

'I should start at the beginning. Mr Mann apologises that he cannot visit a convent but asked me to reassure you that he knows you're resident here and urges you to stay.'

Issy nodded but she didn't really understand.

'You were the subject of two messages Mr Mann received recently. One from a Sir John Brady, accusing you of being complicit in swindling a Count Stenbock in Vienna...'

'That rogue!' Isabella interrupted. 'I wrote honestly to Mr Mann explaining that although I made the paste brooch, I had no knowledge of its sale and the Count has accepted a refund.'

'Exactly, obviously Sir John didn't know that and it seems he wished to discredit you. Then, only last week the Vatican sent an intermediary to advise Mr Mann that they believe Sir John culpable for a fire at Ville de Londres.'

Isabella shook her head, still confused. 'I don't understand.'

'There was an arson attack at Ville de Londres a few days ago. Your friend Mistress Nichol is quite the heroine for raising the alarm.'

'They think the fire was started deliberately by Sir John? Surely not?'

'It seems hardly credible but apparently there's evidence that his driver was involved and Mr Mann is advising Sir John that he should leave Rome. Mr Mann strongly encourages you to stay here until that happens.' He held up a purse. 'In fact he has sent me with a small donation for the Mother Superior's charity fund, as a token of thanks for their protection.'

Three days later, Sister Caterina brought her a letter addressed to Signorina Bella Godfrey, Isabella knew the hand-writing. 'When was he here?' she blurted out, then instantly regretted acknowledging she knew it from a man.

'I didn't see who delivered it,' Sister Caterina answered, in a disapproving tone. 'Is he some relative?'

Isabella had no defence, so left the question answered.

'Thank you, Sister Caterina,' she said, and waited for the sister to close the door behind her. Caterina was a gossip and she was going to have to do something to reverse the damage to her reputation.

Issy's hands shook opening the letter. Joy at hearing from Vittorio was tinged with fear of what he might say.

30th October 1742
Dear Bella

I hope this Letter not make you angry, after such long Neglect. There are no good excuses for my Rudeness. I went through so many Emotions when I hear you are in Rome. But I failed you as a Friend and I am very sorry.

Mama tells me that you're happily settled in Santa Cecilia. I have no right to an Opinion, but I am also very happy you did not marry that Man. I feel this from the Beginning and his dreadful Behaviour confirms my low Estimation. Being accused of Arson is no small Matter. He misjudges his Situation here, and he will soon face Conse-quences.

As it turns out, he has done our Family a Favour. The young Princes were furious to hear an English Aristocrat endangered the Life of a Family loyal to their Cause. They trying to have him expelled from Rome. They also sent generous Monies to pay for the Repairs. Mama is delighted, although after the Years of her Loyalty, it is no more than she deserves.

I do hope Sir John leave Rome soon. In a fairer World you and I could live our Lives freely. As it is, we must both make the best of Things.

While it is of no practical Use to either of us, you are always in my Thoughts.

Yours, Vee

Always in his thoughts. That was what she'd longed to hear. Not a declaration of love, but surely enough encouragement that she could cling to her hopes? Issy smoothed the paper and folded it again. She would keep it safe on her person always. Someone reading it would find nothing scandalous, but she knew the truth of the way it made her feel.

* * *

A week later, Bessie found Anna and Vee waiting for her in the kitchen.

'Sit down, Bessie, we have the idea,' Vee said.

Anna's eyes seemed to plead for whatever she was going to say. 'We have the business plan to say you.'

Vee took over the explanation: 'There is the small, top-floor flat for sale next door. The landlord who owns both buildings, offered sell it at low price to Mama. He wants capital and his idea is she would make it an apartment for those visitor who wish the private arrangement. This man is old friend of my father and he try help us. If we can find deposit we pay him the balance through guest income. Sadly, although we have saved diligently, we had no enough. However, the gift from the Stuarts come just in time. It more than covers the repainting after fire. Destroyed furniture belonged to Mama and we don't need to buy again.'

Anna interrupted again. 'Owning this small place give me income once landlord debt is paid and I maybe live there when I am old lady,' she added, her eyes gleaming with enthusiasm. 'Maybe good for us both? I hope you accept the housekeeper position managing this new business? Wealthy visitors can be very difficult, but I think,' she hesitated, 'you and I can work good together and it allow you stay in Rome.'

Bessie nodded. For a few seconds she was too overcome to speak. 'Thank you, Anna,' she whispered. 'I can think of nothing I would like more than to work here with you.'

But there was a problem. 'What about Isabella? I'm not convinced the threat from Sir John has gone.'

'Isabella is safe in the convent.'

'She is, but it was only ever a short term solution and she has no firm plan for what happens next.'

'Maybe Isabella live Rome too? Please stay?' Anna asked. She looked so disappointed.

Then Bessie's reserve broke down, she got to her feet and embraced Anna. 'I'd love to work with you.'

Isabella flung open the convent door and rushed towards her. Bessie managed to disguise her shock at Issy's appearance, before the tight embrace was over.

She reached up to touch Isabella's grey cotton veil. 'Have you decided to become a permanent member of the sisterhood?'

She was surprised at her own uncomfortable reaction. Isabella shook her head and twisted the veil edge between her fingers.

'No. But it's a way to show my commitment to the sisters and their work here,' she said with a shrug. 'Anyway, what about you? Are you fully recovered? I've been frantic with worry and I want to hear the whole story about this awful fire.'

'Anna has been a most diligent nurse,' Bessie replied. She went on to describe the arson attack.

'I can't believe Sir John actually put lives in danger. I didn't think I could loathe him more,' Isabella said.

'Vee took the report of both assaults to Prince Henry and he's taking it up with the Vatican,' Bessie said.

'I know. I had a visit from a friend of Horace Mann's and then Vittorio wrote to me,' Isabella replied with a broad smile.

In the silent second's pause, Bessie could feel that her mouth was open.

'Here. You can read it.' Isabella handed Bessie the folded letter.

'Vittorio writes to me as a friend, and I'm so pleased,' Isabella said.

Bessie read the letter. When she handed it back, Isabella folded it with utmost care and placed it in her pocket. Her contented smile said the letter pleased her, but Bessie was less happy. Vee hadn't been honest about the true barrier to their relationship. But at least they were in contact, it made her more comfortable about her own news.

'The money sent by the Stuarts is allowing Anna to start her own business. She'll buy the apartment next door and run it as part of Ville de Londres.'

'How satisfying that Sir John's worst efforts might end up being a good thing for Anna.'

'It might be a good thing for me too. She's asked me to manage the new venture.'

'How wonderful, so will you take it on?'

Bessie hesitated, searching Issy's face for her reaction. 'It's a job I'd like to do, but I'm nervous about committing when you don't know what you'll do next.'

Isabella jumped up and hugged her, crushing Bessie's sore ribs for the second time in five minutes. 'Of course you must take it, it's what you wanted from the beginning.'

'Anna asked if you might stay too?'

Isabella sighed, 'I certainly need to come up with some sort of plan. It's becoming more obvious that I can't stay here indefinitely. One of the nuns complained I have contact with men. I believe it was Mr Mann's donation that helped smooth Mother Superior's irritation, and perhaps my request to wear the veil helped. I'm ready to leave, they're very good women but of course they're not saints.'

A few weeks later Vee came home shaking with laughter. 'He's gone. Not a finger lifted but he fled in fear!'

'What you mean?' Anna asked.

'Sir John. They took him on one side and 'persuaded' him of the mistake in his ways. He left this morning.'

'Who persuaded him? The Stuarts? The Vatican?' Bessie asked. She was surprised by her own squeamishness. She wanted him gone. Why did she care how?

Vee shrugged. 'It the same thing. The Vatican funds the Stuarts.'

Bessie shook her head to dislodge a creeping discomfort. The Stuart family were chosen by God Himself, above reproach. This drama had drawn them into tawdry human squabbles. 'What did they do to him?' her voice wavered, she needed but didn't want to know.

'That is best bit. They didn't need do anything. Henry say that masked men took him from the street and put hood on him. He straight way soiled himself. That man who beat you and mean to burn us in beds, pissed himself like baby.' Vee laughed some more.

'What did they say to make him so afraid?' Bessie knew her reaction illogical.

'A perfect threat. They say Sir John that if he not gone the very next day, they give the English the proof that he is the Jacobite spy.'

Vee's laughter halted the story for several seconds. 'The English distrust those who travel here. Sir John betrothed himself to girl who turns out to be the Catholic and then joins a nunnery. He is completely afraid.'

Bessie allowed herself a smile. It was a most poetic justice.

She went the next day to give Isabella the good news. That her idols were tarnished she kept to herself.

* * *

Isabella found she had mixed feelings about Bessie's story of Sir John's departure. Delight at being rid of him was tinged with anxiety about leaving the convent. Bessie's expression when she read Vee's letter had made her reread it more carefully. The uncomfortable truth was that said he hadn't said he wanted to see her and it alluded to some lack of freedom. Had he found someone else? The idea was unbearable. To add to her worries she'd received a letter from Sir Everard. She hadn't yet summoned the courage to open it.

'So will you leave the convent now Sir John's gone?' Bessie asked.

'Yes, but I don't know where I'll go next. In any case this letter might help me decide.' She drew the note from her pocket. 'It's from Sir Everard. Another letter from a gentleman; Sister Caterina nearly had a fit.'

Bessie nodded, her expression said she shared her nerves about the content.

'He's reached Vienna,' she said, then scanned through the letter. She looked up at Bessie. 'You wrote to him on my behalf?'

'Yes. Is he angry?' Bessie asked.

'Not at all, and he spoke to Jamila, he calls her a good honest girl.'

Isabella read on in silence. When she finished, she nodded and smiled.

'He still agrees to being my guardian,' she said, and handed the letter to Bessie.

Bessie squinted and held the paper at arm's length to read.

The gist of the letter was that an embassy dragoman had helped him translate Jamila's account. This then led to reports of bad behaviour from some of the embassy maids. Finally, he'd discovered an assault at Sir John's lodgings had led a maid to leave her job. Sir Everard was full of apologies to Isabella, for his role in encouraging her in the engagement.

'I hope you'll tell him the depth of violence the scoundrel sank to in Rome,' Bessie said.

'I expect he will have had a report from Horace Mann by now,' Issy replied.

Bessie read aloud the last paragraphs. '*I expect to be in Vienna for some Weeks before returning to London. It might be best if you see out the Winter in Italy. If you prefer to leave Rome I'm sure Horace Mann would find you some Accommodation in Florence.*

Please send me any change of Address to my Wandsworth Address above. I wish my Plans were more settled so I might commit to inviting you to London now. However I think I will know in the New Year. Please be assured that I'll have the legal Guardianship papers drawn up as soon as I go back. I'm sure my Lawyer can word something for you to sign to cope with Richard's continued Absence.

Very best Wishes

Your loving Guardian, Everard.'

'Excellent news,' Bessie said and returned the letter. 'What happens now?' she asked.

'I'll ask Mother Superior to allow me to stay another few weeks to sort out a plan. I so long to see Vittorio, but I'm nervous too.'

Bessie met her gaze but said nothing.

'I know I said I wouldn't ask, but am I right that you've spoken to him now?'

'Yes,' Bessie said.

'Is he married?' Isabella whispered.

Bessie shook her head in annoyance. 'No, but I won't be drawn on the subject. It's up to Vee to resolve.'

'So you think it could be resolved?'

'I think it possible,' Bessie said and rose to leave.

Issy sat for a long time after Bessie had gone. He wasn't married, that was surely great news. But if he rejected her again she wasn't sure she could bear it.

Chapter Twenty-Seven

January 1743

I sabella was pleased to see Bessie's reaction to her new dress. After months of simple clothes she was glad to wear colour and its beauty gave her the confidence to face the world again.

'Oh, Issy, it's gorgeous. Spin around and let me see the back.'

The skirt flared as she turned. It was made of dove grey silk, inset with a rose pink stomacher sewn with tiny pearls. Pink ribbons tying off the sleeves at the elbows completed the effect.

'It's perfect and those pearls just set the whole thing off, but wasn't it very expensive?'

'No,' she replied, 'these faux pearls are so clever.'

Just then Signora Bernini arrived with her pin box. Issy had asked her to take in the dress, she'd lost weight working in the convent garden. Issy put her habit back on and handed over the dress to be altered. Before leaving, Signora Bernini handed Isabella a single pearl. She thanked her and held it up between her thumb and forefinger. 'Look at this, Bessie. I asked the signora to bring me a larger example, I've an idea that I might use these to make jewellery. I'll try to visit the factory when I leave.'

'So do you think you might stay on in Rome?'

'Maybe. I have to assume Uncle Richard isn't coming back now. I do wonder if he came to some harm.'

Bessie shook her head. 'Don't waste your thoughts on that rogue. He abandoned you and I'd wager he's holed up safe somewhere.'

'I expect you're right, but Sir John did prove himself capable of violence. Might he have decided to get Richard out of the way?'

'There's another rogue not worth your time. He's the kind to strike a defenceless woman, but I doubt he'd challenge your uncle.'

'Anyway, I'll use the time until the Alpine thaw to consider my options.'

Issy assumed Bessie realised that the outcome of the meeting with Vee would be the deciding factor. Anna had insisted she come to Ville de Londres, but she felt very nervous about her welcome. Mother Superior had agreed she could stay through December, but the time for action had come.

'What's the idea with the pearls?' Bessie asked.

'I might make earrings with them. Uncle Richard took all the jeweller's equipment for making bigger pieces.'

Bessie made her signature 'tsk' noise. 'Surely some of those things were yours? Did your father leave no will?'

'Not that I'm aware of and Richard always maintained that there was no money in the business.'

'Well if you ever see that rascal again you must be clearer about your finances. He took all that jewellery and left you with a pittance.'

'I've asked Sir Everard to help me understand my legal and financial situation with Richard missing.'

'Have you no other family at all?'

'No one on my father's side. There might be relatives in Scotland, but I'm not sure. We lost contact when my grandmother died.'

'You're not sure? You must take control of this, Isabella.'

Isabella shrugged in annoyance. 'I know and I so wish I could just take charge of things myself.'

Bessie made a dismissive noise. 'I control my own finances, as meagre as they are. My sister and I handle our affairs between us. The law in Scotland is different, many women have their own money.'

'Really? That's interesting. Anyway, you're right and that's why I've asked Sir Everard to look into my affairs.'

'Your uncle's absence poses problems but it also gives you a chance to ask questions about the business and you must know if there is any male relative.'

Isabella frowned. She might have avoided Sir John, only to find herself beholden to some stranger managing her life. It was so unfair.

* * *

Bessie pinned on her bonnet and picked up a shawl for Isabella. The January weather varied but it had been cold this week. Issy would leave the convent today. Anna looked up and gave Bessie a strained smile. Anna and Vee had argued. Anna was furious that Vee had left the confession to the last possible moment.

Bessie's Italian was now good enough to eavesdrop.

'We will make poor Isabella welcome, I cannot leave her without a home. You must deal with this today, Vee,' she'd heard Anna say.

Anna hugged Bessie and promised to have supper ready for Isabella's return. Vee spoke: 'Can we delay eating for a couple of hours, Mama? Bring Isabella to Palazzo del Re, Bessie. I'll tell her there.'

Anna and Bessie exchanged a look of surprise, then Bessie set off.

* * *

Isabella was sad to say goodbye to all the nuns, even Sister Caterina had come to wish her luck. She didn't feel a calling to the convent but she admired their way of life and owed them a great deal. Mother Superior placed her palm on Isabella's head and murmured her blessing. Sister Maria Teresa's health had waned over the winter, but she'd insisted on being helped outside to say goodbye. Isabella crouched before the elderly nun and took her hands.

'My time here has taught me so much, sister. I pray I can live up to your saintly example.'

'The Lord has chosen your path, Isabella. The world will benefit from your goodness.'

The sun was setting as Isabella and Bessie crossed Ponte Sisto and the coach made quick progress through the narrow cobbled streets. After twenty minutes the coachman reined in his horses, bringing the chaise to a halt. Isabella frowned and looked out. 'Why have we stopped here?'

Then she saw Vittorio standing in front of Palazzo del Re. He held out his hand towards her. Her happy smile faded when she turned to Bessie, who looked so very stern. 'Isabella, you need to be brave. Vee has a confession to make. Go now, child. I'll take your valise back to the house and see you there.'

Isabella couldn't help the eruption of joy when Vittorio took her hand. Bessie's warning made her expect something terrible. She'd wondered if he might have had smallpox or some disfiguring accident. But Vee looked as handsome as ever. Then almost certainly she must expect that he'd given his heart to another. Bessie said he wasn't married, but maybe he was engaged? But why had he brought her here?'

Vittorio held up the lantern. The familiar look he shot her under his lashes, the twinkle in his eye, the small shy smile. Isabella felt her heart might explode.

'I want show you my work. They're all out at the opera. Let's begin your first night back in the world with small trespassing.'

Isabella laughed. Vittorio took off at a run, dragging her through the arch and into a courtyard. She stopped abruptly when she saw the grim looking guard in their path. Vittorio held the lamp up near Isabella's face.

'*La mia amica*,' he said, explaining she was a friend.

Presumably she didn't look like a thief or a spy, the guard raised his eyebrows at them, but nodded his assent.

They tumbled through a door and ran up a double flight of marble steps, halting at the top, out of breath and in fits of laughter. Vittorio squeezed her hand. 'I missed you, Bella.'

Isabella was so happy she could barely speak. 'Me too.'

He led her through a series of rooms into a long gallery with an ornately painted ceiling. Rows of royal paintings hung three deep were revealed as the lantern light crept along the walls. At the end of the gallery stood a small desk, chair and easel. The smell of paint hung in the air.

'This is what I copy now,' Vittorio said. He held the lamp up to the easel, revealing a portrait of James Stuart in full court regalia and a long wig. 'Many peoples want miniatures, and I must work day and night. Good that my small portraits can be lit by a few candles.'

He lit a taper from the lantern and set it to the three half burnt candles on the desk. Isabella leaned in closer to see the tiny painting, almost complete and a perfect copy. Vittorio's nearness made her skin tingle.

'Almost as nice as mine,' she said, pulling her locket from inside her dress. This was the first time she'd been able to wear it in months and she'd been very conscious of it nestled between her breasts all evening. She drew the chain over her head, opened the locket and laid it on the desk beside the King's miniature.

Vittorio gave her the warmest smile. 'It is the treasonous thing to say, but James Stuart is less handsome.'

They stared at each other for several seconds, Isabella saw his cheeks were flushed.

'These pieces go to Jacobite supporters all over Europe. This one is the snuffbox. Look.' Vittorio closed the snuffbox lid. When he opened it again, the Pretender's face was replaced with that of a long-nosed young man. 'Rich patrons like trick of revealing their loyalty with the pinch of snuff.'

Then, with an almost imperceptible click, he opened a second lid under the top painting, once more revealing the painting of James Stuart.

'A secret button,' Isabella said. Then: 'Goodness, does mine...?'

She picked up her miniature and went to press the knob on the top. She felt it give under her thumb. Vittorio placed his hand over hers, shutting the mechanism again. Isabella saw his eyes glistened with tears. Sensing some confession was coming, she felt her exposed heart snap closed like her locket.

Vittorio whispered: 'Dearest Bella. I know you hate me from now, but please believe, I didn't set out to trick you. My hopeless devotion never mean to cause you pain.'

He turned his face to the shadows and took his hand away, the release of pressure made the mechanism open. A hidden painting was revealed behind her portrait. Not the Stuart king, but a beautiful girl. Vittorio's face but with long waves of lustrous dark hair. A sister?

Isabella looked up in confusion, to see Vittorio sweep off his burgundy silk cap, allowing those dark tresses to fall around his shoulders.

She could only manage, 'Oh!'

Her legs gave way, and Vittorio caught her arm to guide her back to the chair. She heard her miniature fall to the ground. The girl she called Vittorio picked it up and pressed it into her hand. Conflicting emotions spun in Isabella's head. He wasn't married. He didn't love anyone else. The relief of that was joyful. Jealous fear had burrowed into her soul. But now everything had changed. She gazed at this girl. She didn't feel any different. Surely that was very wrong?

'I thought you maybe find the secret painting. I should have told you, but I knew you be angry and shocked.' Vee hesitated. 'My disguise was necessary to allow my apprenticeship. But kissing you... forgive me...' She shook her head, her brunette waves shone in the candlelight.

She made to let go of her hand, but Isabella grasped it back and rose to her feet. She stretched out trembling fingers to touch the girl's hair. 'It was I who kissed you,' she whispered.

Issy replaced the miniature on its chain back around her neck and took a deep breath before she looked up again. 'What's your real name?'

'Vittoria,' she said with a smile, 'or Vee.'

They stood looking at each other properly for the very first time. Then, as if drawn by an irresistible force, Isabella moved one step closer.

Suddenly, the door at the other end of the room was thrown open with a crash, and a young man strode in. He was dressed in an embroidered silk frock coat and silk breeches in the same duck egg blue, and he held a small wig in his hand.

'Vee, are you still here? I hear you've been creeping about in boy's hose again.'

Isabella and Vee sprang apart. For a second they both stared at the young man. He bore a striking resemblance to his royal father. Isabella dropped into a deep curtsey, to hide her embarrassment.

She heard the man's approach and she stood up, his eyes were sparkling with amusement.

'Well, this must be the lovely Bella,' Prince Henry said.

Chapter Twenty-Eight

February 1743

Bessie wasn't sure what to make of Isabella's mood this week. She and Anna had expected tears and drama when Vittorio brought Isabella home from Palazzo del Re. Instead they came in subdued, but quickly dissolved into fits of laughter, describing Isabella being caught trespassing by Prince Henry. Anna had told Vee off, pointing out that James Stuart might not have been so forgiving about her bringing a stranger into the palace, but Bessie could tell she shared her relief. Still, Isabella appeared to be dealing with the situation, when she had expected her to be heartbroken. Perhaps she underestimated Issy's resilience.

Today she'd gone with Signora Bernini to visit her faux pearl supplier in Trastevere. When they arrived back the signora was making a such commotion with apologies, Bessie surmised there had been a problem. Isabella had to repeat her assurances that she was neither upset nor offended several times, before the lady eventually left.

'Did they not admit you?' Bessie asked.

Isabella removed her bonnet and threw her gloves on the hall table. Her expression said she was annoyed. 'They were most welcoming at the beginning and I learned what I wanted to know. The problem came from my question at the end, and it was entirely my fault.'

Bessie waited for Isabella to explain.

'The beads are made from a soft stone called alabaster, which men slice into sections, then create a round bead with a hole. The rest of the work is done be women, who smooth each bead then coat it in wax and fish scales.'

'Fish scales?'

Isabella smiled, 'Yes the whole place smells horribly of fish, Signora Bernini was most embarrassed.'

'Is that why she apologised?'

Isabella shook her head, 'No, it's because the man laughed in my face.'

'The scoundrel. Why?'

'I had an idea that I could purchase the rock beads and learn the finishing skills myself. So I asked him how much it would cost to buy an apprenticeship. He wanted to meet the girl I intended to send and it took several minutes to get him to understand that I wanted to learn myself. That's when he laughed at me.'

'Oh Issy, could you really see yourself sitting in puddles of fish scales?'

She shrugged. 'Why not? Anyway, once he stopped laughing he told me that his workers would get no work done for staring at the English lady. It was the same problem in London, I'm a worker who looks and sounds like a lady. Too grand looking for a worker and too poor to be grand.'

'So have you given up the idea of using these pearls for jewellery?'

'I'll go and visit the other workshop. Apparently there's a French company making pearls from wax filled glass.' She stood up.

'Where are you going now?'

'Vee promised that she'd come home for supper tonight. I'll go and meet her, I feel like a walk.'

'You shouldn't be walking about Rome on your own,' Bessie called to her as she disappeared through the door.

'I'll take a chair to Palazzo del Re and we'll walk back together,' Isabella shouted back.

* * *

Isabella waited in the shade of Basilica Santi Apostoli's arches. Her heart did the usual flip when she saw Vittoria walking towards her.

'Do I smell fishy?' she asked, kissing her friend on both cheeks.

'No,' Vee replied with a laugh and threaded her arm through hers. 'Why? You been fishing?'

'Pearl fishing,' she replied, and described the events of the afternoon. 'I need to buy some simple dresses like those you use at work. When I go to the next workshop I won't make the mistake of looking as if I'm going to have tea with a duchess.'

'Explain me again about the fishes. How they get fish to stick to stone?'

'They boil up thousands of tiny fish just to make a small amount of this substance, they call it *l'essence d'Oriente* and it's as expensive as it's pungent. They put it on the stone dipped in wax then polish it up. That was the part of the process I wanted to learn.' She shook her head in annoyance. 'I'll dress more appropriately next time.'

Vee smiled. 'You are beautiful foreigner, Bella, you cannot hide that.'

She pecked Isabella on her cheek and Issy put her hand around her waist, breathing in Vee's glorious smell. 'Have you been putting linseed oil in your hair?'

'No on purpose but I put paintbrush behind my ear,' she replied.

Isabella pulled away and looked around to see if they were observed. She hoped that their level of affection was acceptable for two young friends. No one, least of all Vee, could tell how she ached with longing for her touch.

They walked the next few streets in silence.

'You know you are my first ever friend,' she said quietly.

Vee looked at her with raised eyebrows.

'I spent my days bent over a workbench, like dozens of other apprentices in the area, but my accent was always wrong and Uncle Richard insisted I dressed like a lady outside the house. The local children used to call me names. When I started to attend church with my teacher, the young ladies we met there shunned me too. What he created is a misfit, I don't belong in either world.'

'I misfit too. We belong together,' Vee's smile and the squeeze on her arm, set her heart off soaring.

They were almost back in Piazza de Spagna when Vittoria spoke again. 'So does this plan mean you stay in Rome, Bella?'

'If it allows me to support myself. I like Rome and I'd like to be near Bessie.'

'And me?' Vee asked.

Issy answered while still looking straight ahead. 'Most especially you.'

Vee laced her fingers through Issy's and squeezed her hand before opening the heavy door to Ville de Londres.

That night in her small room in the eaves, Issy knelt to pray for God's guidance, then for Bessie, Anna and Vee. She prayed for Richard Godfrey too, she found she didn't wish him dead. Finally she made herself say the words she could share with no one else:

'Dear Lord, forgive me for the wicked and sinful feelings I have for Vittoria. Show me how to turn away from them.'

She rose after ten minutes, she couldn't even convince herself. It was futile to pretend, and praying for something she didn't truly want intensified the sin. She couldn't separate Vittoria from Vittorio in her heart.

The following week Isabella and Bessie visited the other workshop. She'd insisted that if Issy was even considering doing some sort of business with these people, she must come. This factory was situated on their side of the river, a little beyond Palazzo del Re. The distinctive smell of fish met them before they entered. Bessie put her handkerchief to her nose. Issy glared at her until she pushed it back in her sleeve.

A woman looked up from a desk where she was using a grooved wooden tray to grade pearls into sizes. Issy explained she had an appointment to meet a Monsieur Topart. When he arrived she switched to speaking French. 'Monsieur, my name is Isabella Godfrey, I'm an English jeweller visiting Rome and I'm fascinated to know more about your excellent pearls.'

The man bowed. 'You are welcome, mademoiselle. I was trained in Paris by Monsieur Jacquin himself and I'm very proud of the small operation we've established here. You realise of course that the method of making *l'essence d'Oriente* is secret.'

'I understand entirely.'

'Monsieur Jacquin's chief business is in making *chapelets de perles*, and there is a huge demand for rosaries here in Rome.'

He took them to watch some men create and cut thin tubes of glass, then to see the girls smooth and polish the glass into beads. At another bench girls used pipettes to blow a single drop of the precious essence into each bead, before filling them with wax. Lastly they came back to the girl who graded the sizes. She dropped one pearl into a small basket at her elbow.

'May I?' Isabella said, picking it up.

'This one is being discarded?' she asked.

'*Oui*,' Monsieur Topart answered, 'because not perfect.'

'Might you sell them?' she asked.

He gave her a gallic shrug. '*Peut-être.*'

Isabella made to return the pearl but he shook his head, 'Keep it.'

She gave Monsieur Topart a small velvet pouch and he shook a pair of delicate silver earrings into his palm.

'These are very beautiful. You made them?'

Isabella nodded, noticing new respect in his eyes and tone. 'Yes, and as you see they have freshwater pearls, I'd like to experiment with your glass pearls. Can you make teardrop pearls too?'

He nodded. Isabella looked up at the large skylight above them, then walked to the window overlooking the river. 'You have very good light here, monsieur. I wonder if you'd consider renting me this small space for my workbench? I'd also need access to your glass forge for melting small amounts of silver.'

'*Peut-être*,' he said again, his head thoughtfully to one side.

'Good,' Isabella shook his hand and thanked him again. 'It's been a pleasure meeting you, and I hope you'll consider my proposal. You can reach me at Ville de Londres in Piazza de Spagna. Do you know it?'

'Of course,' he replied.

Back on the street Bessie turned to her.

'Are you planning to steal Monsieur Topart's secrets?'

Isabella laughed. 'You're confusing me with my uncle. But it could be a suitable place for me. Nearly all the workers are women and the light is perfect. I've an idea to specialise in pearl earrings, and I could handpick the glass beads.'

'Have you the money to rent the space?'

'Not yet, but I have a plan.'

Monsieur Topart's proposal arrived three days later. Isabella took her mother's pearl necklace from its box. She pooled the pearl strands into her palm for the last time and a pang of sadness spread across her collarbone. She put them back in their box with quick determination. It was a necessary sacrifice. Issy muttered a prayer. 'Forgive me, Mama. I have no need of pearls to wear but I can use them to buy myself a living.'

She made her way to the jewellery shop. When Issy decided to leave the convent, Anna had sold the diamond brooch there on her behalf. Isabella had told Anna she wanted to visit the shop, not admitting she was now selling her mother's pearls. As instructed, she told the man she was a friend of Signora Sirani. The man took the pearls and walked to the window to examine them, then offered her enough for three months' rent and funds to buy a workbench. She was about to leave when something caught her eye. 'May I see that silver brooch?'

He put it in her hand, the mark was unfamiliar.

'Do you happen to know who made this?' she asked.

'It came from a local supplier but they have many workers.'

She completed the transaction and left the shop. The answer to her growing sense of unease came immediately. There he was, crossing the road towards her. 'Isabella,' he said.

She struck Richard Godfrey hard across the face.

Chapter Twenty-Nine

Today the carriages in Piazza de Spagna were abandoned by the fountain. All the drivers had come down the alley to watch Isabella's carpenter. She'd borrowed use of a shady stable to allow him to complete the work on the table he'd just delivered.

'They all think you are the lunatic,' Vee said. She was standing in her bonnet and cloak ready to go to work, but instead she leaned against the wall with her arms folded.

'You're going to be late,' Issy replied.

'This I cannot miss and anyway it good story to tell Prince Henry. The day the mad English girl turned the perfectly good table into the joke.'

Isabella was aware of the group of smirking drivers but she was delighted with the carpenter's work. She ran her hand over the smooth curve he'd cut out of the table front. She handed over the large piece of soft calf leather she'd bought, and showed him how she wanted it gathered to form a pocket within the curve. He nodded and commenced attaching it with shining brass tacks. Isabella also asked the carpenter to saw half an inch off both front legs. This sent a ripple of murmurs through her audience.

'They think you want it tilted for writing and that maybe the pouch is for your bonbon,' Vee said, nodding towards the drivers.

Once the carpenter had finished, Issy sat at a stool in front of the desk. She put the solitary faux pearl at the top of the table and watched it roll down, landing in the leather pouch with a satisfying plop. She heard the murmur of comprehension spread through the crowd. She nodded her approval to the carpenter and stood to fetch her purse, then came a voice at her shoulder.

'Such a desk would accommodate a very fat silversmith.'

'Or a lady jeweller with wide skirts,' Isabella replied. 'Did you bring the vice, Uncle Richard?'

He nodded and produced it from the large sack on his shoulder. Issy took it to the carpenter and showed him where to clamp it to the desk. Then Richard opened the box he'd brought, it contained one of the two globe magnifiers they'd brought from England. Isabella stroked the glass, this was the one thing she'd been missing. Part of her bargain in taking him back.

'What in the world is that? A lamp with no candle?' Vee asked.

'Uncle Richard, you remember Monsieur Liotard's apprentice,' Issy said.

'Of course, although I find him somewhat altered,' Richard replied.

He bowed and Vee curtsied. Issy placed the globe on the flat ledge the carpenter had made at the back of her desk. It focused a bright shaft of sunlight onto her worksurface.

'Ah, I see,' Vee said.

'You need good light for jeweller's work,' Issy explained.

She turned to her uncle. 'I'm busy setting up my workshop today, but I'll visit you tomorrow afternoon. Then Anna insists you join us for supper.' Her tone was deliberately cool and business like.

Richard nodded, 'I'll see you tomorrow then, Issy. Good day, Miss Bassi,' he said and turned to leave.

They watched him disappear round the corner.

'Why you talk to that man?' Vee asked.

Issy shrugged, 'I'm still angry with him but he's all the family I've got. In any case, he has something I want.'

'More jeweller equipment?'

'No, more knowledge. I realised he only taught me the finishing touches. I haven't the skill to produce anything but the simplest pieces alone. I want to make small hammered items: powder pots; jewel boxes; buckles maybe,' and lockets, she thought but didn't say.

'So you work with pearls in the morning and he teach you in afternoons?'

'Richard Godfrey never did anything for nothing. His eyesight is worse, he needs me to finish his pieces and in exchange he'll teach me to wield a silver hammer.'

'And so he'll come into our home.'

'I refuse to keep house for him anymore but working together requires us to be civil. It's good of your mother to ask him to supper. I just hope I can prevent Bessie from finishing off the beating I started.'

Isabella waved Vee off to work, then she caught sight of her uncle leaving a coffee shop on the other side of the piazza. He'd pleaded her to help him, saying that he'd used up his funds journeying overland through Greece. He claimed to have been beaten up and robbed of all the jewellery on the way. That he would waste money in an expensive coffee shop confirmed her suspicions about that story. Nevertheless it was obvious that his sight continued to fail. She'd visited his workplace and found him working outside, only able to see in the strong sunlight. The speed of his decline did not bode well, but she still didn't trust him and his bad behaviour absolved her of any need to feel responsible for him.

* * *

'I cannot believe the rogue had the nerve to come back after all this time,' Bessie said.

They were waiting for Richard Godfrey to arrive for supper at Ville de Londres.

'He claims he watched me and surmised I was safe.'

'And has he any words about swindling the Swede?'

'He says the count picked up the brooch and offered him a price. He never said they were diamonds and he thought the man might never discover he was overcharged.'

'I think you forgave him too easily.'

'I haven't forgiven him but his situation is bad. He lost a trunk of possessions to Sir John and claims to have been robbed of all his jewellery. Also his eyesight is worse, he manages simple work in the strong sunlight of Italy, but I doubt he'll ever work in London again.'

'So we're stuck with him here.'

'I need more skills and I'll make sure he keeps his side of the bargain. There's to be no swindling and no more talk of marriage suitors,' Issy replied.

'Will you tell Richard about Sir Everard's offer of guardianship?' Bessie asked.

'I don't see he needs to know,' Issy replied.

Bessie clenched her jaw and glared across the supper table at Richard Godfrey who affected not to notice.

'Do you have any contact with Sir Everard?' he asked Issy when they'd barely started eating.

She heard the girl hesitate while forming her reply. 'I only recently heard that he's in London. It seems he won't return to Turkey.'

'You must tell him that John Brady made off with your portrait. The rogue might try to sell it in London.'

'Kettle calling pot black,' Bessie muttered under her breath.

'Sir John Brady tried to kill you twice, I hope you don't compare him to me, Mistress Nichol?'

'You really feel no guilt?' she demanded.

Richard laid down his spoon and sighed. 'I am most sorry about everything that happened. Although my absence emboldened Sir John to reveal his character.'

'That is true and I'm most grateful for that,' Isabella lifted her glass. 'Let's toast to our joint successes in Rome and put the past behind us.' She raised her eyebrows at Bessie, who extended her own glass in reluctant agreement.

Chapter Thirty

Two Years Later – March 1745

Isabella and Vee linked arms on their customary morning walk via Palazzo del Re. Issy had been working between her uncle and her own workshop for two years. She made steady business from selling faux pearl earrings and Richard gave her a fair percentage on the brooches and necklaces she finished for him.

Today she had a present in her pocket for Vittoria. It marked a turning point in her journey as a silversmith. She'd planned to give Vee her gift yesterday, but she'd hung back because of her friend's evident bad temper.

'You're still very quiet. Are you going to tell me what's wrong?'

Vee kicked a pebble across the marble kerbstone. 'Everything is pointless. I bored with copying the paintings of others and the miniaturist's work is never known. I am invisible.' She glared at Isabella. 'You are too, your earrings are just baubles and the silver pieces don't even bear Richard's mark.'

Issy swallowed back the urge to make an angry retort, although the accusation stung. 'Workers may have their marks stamped over by the retailer in London too and at least

I have my own money now. I'm proud of the earrings you call baubles. Grand ladies buy them only as day wear and keep their real pearls for formal events, but I love that many are bought by ordinary girls. Why should they not enjoy the glint of pearl at their ear?'

Vee looked guilty. 'Sorry,' she said.

They'd reached their usual parting place at the arches of Santi dei Apostoli. Issy lowered her voice to a whisper, 'Don't be cross, Vee. I'm more content with my life now than ever before. Bessie and Anna are like mothers to me and your friendship means everything.' She took the silver locket from her pocket and gave it to Vittoria. Vee touched the intricate engraving on the heart-shaped locket, then clicked it open to reveal the single pearl inside.

'That one isn't faux,' Issy said.

'You made this?' Vee asked, and Isabella nodded.

'I've been practising so hard. I have decent boxes and buckles too, all without Richard's help.'

'It's incredible, Bella. We're both so skilled and yet no one knows us. One day, I swear we'll find success in this world.' Vee put on her locket and hugged her goodbye.

Issy watched her walk into the Palazzo del Re courtyard. Glancing up she saw Prince Henry's face at one of the windows.

In the afternoon she found Richard Godfrey was in a bad temper too.

'Can you call in to the shop? They have some commission for me and I couldn't understand what the fellow said.'

'Why don't you go back to your Italian teacher? If you mean to stay here you have to learn.'

He shook his head, 'I'm too old to be learning languages now. I've been thinking we might do better in the Americas,

Issy. They have a sunny climate but speak English. What do you think?'

Isabella snatched up her bonnet and gloves. 'I'll go to the shop for you,' she turned at the door, 'and the answer is no.'

The next morning Bessie came up to Issy's room. 'There's finally a letter from Sir Everard,' Bessie said.

Issy tore open the note, anxious for news. Over the last year he'd stopped writing altogether and her letters went unanswered.

'What does it say?' Bessie asked.

'It seems that letters have gone missing,' Issy answered, 'Sir Everard's and mine too.' She read on. 'He got my last letter and was surprised when I mentioned Uncle Richard, apparently all my letters explaining his return didn't reach London.'

'And does he share my opinion that you shouldn't have taken him back?' Bessie said.

'You know very well my reasons for working with my uncle and he's still my legal guardian.'

Issy sighed and put the letter in her lap. 'Sir Everard tries to convince me to return to England. He wants to secure my future and fears war with France might soon make the journey across Europe too risky.'

'And will you go back?' Bessie asked.

'No, I like it here. Uncle Richard was pushing me to consider America today. As soon as I get happy, men are intent on uprooting me.'

'Ignore them,' Bessie replied.

. . .

The following week a note came from Horace Mann himself. It said he'd travelled to Rome to speak to her on Sir Everard's behalf and asked her to meet him in the banker's office.

'What do you think he wants?' Bessie asked.

'Something important if he's come all this way. Could you ask a boy to take this note to my uncle's lodging? It explains my absence this afternoon.'

Horace Mann was a respected diplomat and the English King's senior representative in the region. Isabella had changed into her grey and pink silk dress and silk shoes. She travelled in a sedan chair and the bumping motion from the men's gait was echoed by her nervous heartbeat. Sir Everard wouldn't have received her note declining to follow his advice, so she feared bad news. She was shown into a room where Horace Mann rose to greet her. He wore an elegant silver grey, silk frock coat embroidered with gold thread, heavily powdered wig and very serious expression. Her apprehension increased. Had something happened to Sir Everard?

'Please sit down, Miss Godfrey, Sir Everard has asked me to bring some very grave news in person.'

So it wasn't Sir Everard but what then? She was glad to sit down. He took a deep breath: 'I'm sorry to tell you, Miss Godfrey, that the man you know as Richard Godfrey is a fraudster and he has been swindling you out of your inheritance for years.'

Isabella gripped the chair's arms. 'He isn't my uncle?'

'Sir Everard is still investigating his true identity. He is most certainly not your uncle. Your father had no brother.'

Isabella slumped back against the leather upholstery of Horace Mann's carriage. His aides had returned from their search of Richard's lodgings to say they'd found him gone. How would she have felt if he'd been dragged back under guard? As it was, they'd found the room empty apart from her own silver hammer. There was a note wrapped around the handle.

Sorry.

He had neither addressed nor signed it. Ten years they'd been together and that was the best he could come up with. She was furious and ought to want to chase after him. Instead the sense of abandonment and betrayal overwhelmed anger, and settled in her chest like a hard, dark rock. Mr Mann had insisted she take his carriage but she couldn't face home, so had the driver drop her at the deserted pearl factory. All the other workers had gone for the day. Isabella cleaned the silver hammer and returned it to her tool pouch. She opened the strong box she'd brought from Constantinople. It was filled with her own silver pieces and the lower compartment held over a hundred pairs of earrings. She clenched her jaw in grim determination, she would survive on her own. Apparently she'd always been on her own. The empty factory echoed with her wails of angry despair.

Eventually, the thought of Bessie waiting anxiously made her dry her eyes and lock up the workshop. Vee would be home now too. Her spirits climbed a notch. She'd made her own family. Maybe in her heart she'd always known she must.

* * *

Bessie sat with Anna and Vittoria, opposite Issy at the kitchen supper table.

'No, Issy, surely not? What did Horace Mann say exactly? Are they certain Richard's fled?' Bessie said.

'They found his lodgings empty. Apparently he'd presented himself as my guardian to Horace Mann's bankers.

He's been claiming Sir Everard's letters and destroying mine. I suppose when I wrote him that Horace Mann had summoned me, he knew he'd been exposed.'

'Where could he go?'

'He tried to persuade me to go with him to America, perhaps he's gone there?'

'Tell them to search in Leghorn and in Naples. They'll surely catch him boarding ship like a rat.' Bessie shook with anger at the thought.

Issy shrugged, the sad droop of her shoulders cut Bessie to the core. 'Let him run,' she said. 'It's been a sham from the beginning. He kept me for gain all along.'

Bessie changed her seat to put her arms around Issy.

'Don't waste a single tear on him. I should have insisted you send him packing.'

'I feel so sad. I can't face the thought of travelling to England.'

'You have us, Issy, and you shouldn't be forced into leaving.'

'Horace Mann advises I must. Sir Everard says Richard spent Father's money on gambling debts and fears he hasn't lost that habit. Sir Everard found there is a little money to salvage and says I should go back to claim it. I'm waiting for his final instructions but Mr Mann urges I must be ready to leave.' Isabella turned towards Vittoria. 'He also told me that the British Government knows about Charles Stuart being in France.'

King James's eldest son had gone in secret to France the previous year, he was trying to persuade the French to raise an invasion force.

Vittoria looked almost as white as Isabella. Bessie hugged Issy tighter.

'Then surely I must go with you,' Bessie said and looked to Anna, who gave her a determined nod.

Isabella pulled away and shook her head. 'You most certainly will not. Your life is here. I'll go for only long enough to put my affairs in order, then I'll come back.'

* * *

Isabella had decided she would travel to Scotland after visiting London. She assumed Sir Everard would be able to dissolve her link to Richard but the possibility of a male relative still worried her. She'd go home to finalise her financial and family affairs for good. No one was going to exploit her again. However the thought of leaving Vee made her ache. What if war prevented her returning? It was a terrifying idea.

It was after midnight and Issy was in bed when she heard Vee come home. Her heart surged at the sound of her running up the stairs. Vee burst through the door and came to hug her.

'You're lovely and warm, Bella. Move over, I have something to say you.'

Vee wriggled out of her clothes until she was down to her petticoats and climbed in beside her. Her hair was damp against Issy's arm and cold radiated from her leg through the layers of cotton. Isabella struggled not to tremble at her closeness. 'You're freezing,' she said.

'Not for long,' Vee replied, rubbing her cold foot against Issy's warm calf, and making her shriek.

'Monster! Keep your cold toes to your own side!'

'Shush,' Vee said with a grin, 'you wake everyone.'

'What is it you've got to tell?' Isabella asked.

Vee gave her a strange look, both excited and apprehensive.

'A dangerous secret,' she replied.

'Fun or horrible dangerous?' Isabella asked.

Vee looked more serious. 'Both.'

Vittoria drew up her knees and rested her chin there for a moment, then turned to Isabella again.

'I don't know what say to Mama. Prince Henry asks your approval for me come with you on the journey into France.'

Isabella flung her arms around Vittoria. The wave of happiness was dizzying. 'Yes, yes, and of course that's a fun secret!'

'No, but listen,' Vee replied, pulling out of the hug, 'dangerous too.'

Isabella nodded, her heart thumped.

'Prince Charles asks for more miniatures, Prince Henry suggest I take them and stay on in France to paint him more.'

'A perfect idea,' Isabella agreed.

'But the journey no safe, Bella, there are many English spies. Prince Henry had the idea that we are like enough to travel as cousins, and two young ladies travel together looks no so suspicious.'

'I think it's a wonderful idea. I've heard from Horace Mann that he's found a family called Crouchley I might travel with soon. We can travel together.'

Vee shook her head. 'I think we should no involve others.'

'Then we'll travel alone. I shan't be afraid with you at my side,' Isabella said.

'You need to give more thought, Bella. Prince Henry will pay all your costs as the reward for your help, and...' Vee took a deep breath. 'He say no tell you this, but I want we have no more secrets. He want to have his own eyes and ears in France, to know the truth about the invasion plans.'

'He wants you to spy on the French?' Isabella's question took her voice up in pitch and down in volume, as she finally understood. Vittoria put her finger to her lips and nodded.

'Spy no the word he used and I say we don't use it again, but that is what he want.'

'Oh, Vee,' was all Isabella could think of to reply.

'I do understand if you don't want, Bella. It really is so much to ask.'

'But why? Does he not get the news from his brother?'

'That is the problem. Charles will not give up his hope to claim the crown for his father. But he has no kingdom, no way to raise money for army. He depends completely on the French. Henry say his letters are full of certainty, but he has been there over one year and there are different stories from others.'

'So we go to France under the guise of cousins. You bring Prince Charles the miniatures he needs and get Prince Henry some reassurance. Let's do it!' Isabella said.

Vee took her hands, excitement danced in her eyes. 'I'm so happy you feel it. We visit Paris and we go there together!'

Her smile faded. 'The problem is, how tell Mama?'

'Oh yes, of course,' Isabella replied.

'She is already worry that Prince Henry will go France, how can I tell her that I want go?'

Chapter Thirty-One

essie found Anna crying in the kitchen. Vittoria was
standing with her back against the range and her
head down.

'Whatever is the matter, Anna?'

'Vee want go to France. Prince Henry tell her take the
miniatures to Prince Charles. A dangerous journey more
dangerous plan.'

Bessie looked from one to the other and decided she
should keep out of this family dispute. 'Excuse me, I'll go and
see if Isabella is awake.'

She took some of the newly baked bread Vittoria had
brought in and made to leave the room.

'There's note for Isabella,' Anna said, nodding towards the
red sealed letter on the table.

She met Isabella already on her way down the stairs. 'I
wouldn't go in there right now, Isabella. Anna is very upset.'

'Oh,' Isabella replied, 'Vee told her.'

Bessie handed Issy the letter. She wondered why Vee
would share something with Isabella, before her own mother.
'I got you some breakfast. Let's go in here,' Bessie suggested.

It was still not seven in the morning and the guest dining room was empty.

Isabella pulled apart her bread. 'Lovely, thank you, Bessie,' she said, her mouth full as she broke the seal on the letter.

'Good, that makes things easier,' she said, laying down the note.

'What makes which things easier?' Bessie asked.

'Horace Mann informs me that Lady Crouchley has a fever and they've delayed their departure for the foreseeable future.'

Bessie stared at the girl in confusion. 'Why is that good news? How will you travel?'

Isabella flushed. 'Vee and I will travel together. We need no chaperone.'

Bessie's eye's widened. Why would the Crouchleys have made the journey more difficult? 'What's going on, Isabella? None of this story makes sense. There are any number of ways of delivering a few tiny paintings to France. What are you two up to?'

Isabella didn't look at her, when she asked: 'What did Vee say to Anna?'

'Clearly not the whole story, I would say.'

Just then, the front door bell jangled on its wire.

'I'll just go and get my bonnet,' Issy said, heading up the stairs.

Bessie opened the front door. She could have sworn her heart actually stalled.

'Joseph Grimes!'

'At your service, ma'am,' he said, with a small bow. When he stood up, he held his head to one side in mock dismay. 'Are you not pleased to see me, Mistress Nichol?'

Her heart's lurching reaction had made her quite forget her manners. 'Of course I am. But what in all earth are you doing here?'

'This is my last trip to these parts. The navy are redeploying the ship. I took a few days leave to come up and see thee, Bessie.'

Bessie processed the information. The pang of sadness was very distinct. Also, the feeling of pride that he would want to see her. Just then Isabella and Vee arrived at the front door.

'Isabella, you're on the loose!'

'I am, Joseph,' she replied, with a small curtsey. Then she reached out to take both his hands. 'How perfectly lovely to see you again.'

'I'm surely happy that someone thinks so,' he said. His smiling glance told Bessie he was teasing. 'Well I'd say we should prescribe Rome to all the young ladies of England. You are looking remarkably well.'

Isabella smiled, and lifted her upturned hand to the cloudless blue sky. 'Who would not benefit from the Italian climate? To what do we owe this honour, sir?' Isabella asked.

'I had a few days leave before the ship sails, so I thought I'd look into the rumour of Bessie being a successful business lady these days.' Then turning to Vittoria: 'And this young lady is some relative, Isabella?'

'Oh, excuse my rudeness, sir, I forgot you hadn't met. This is Signorina Bassi. Not a relative, but my very good friend.'

Vittoria curtseyed. 'Please to meet you, Mr Grimes, I hear such good things about you.'

Bessie almost laughed out loud at the questioning look on Joseph's face. He was able to lift the extremities of his extraordinarily bushy eyebrows, in a most comical manner.

'Excuse us, Joseph, we are in a rush this morning. Will I see you later?' Issy said.

'I certainly hope so.'

'It seems I have some catching up to do,' Joseph said to

Bessie, once the girls had left. 'And her terrible fiancé has been despatched?'

'Oh yes, did you not get that letter? The post to England has been so erratic.'

'Shall we find an eating house open around here this early?' he asked.

Bessie nodded. 'I know of somewhere we can get breakfast. I would invite you in, but the house is in uproar today, I'll be back in a moment, once I've told Anna that I'm stepping out.'

They sat together eating small *cantuccini*, watching the people of Rome make their way to work. Bessie told Joseph about Issy's time in the convent and Sir John's crimes.

'What a blackguard. He had better hope we don't meet again. What are her plans now?' Joseph asked.

Bessie explained about Isabella's business, the discovery of Vee being a girl, and then Richard Godfrey's unmasking and recent desertion.

'Gracious that girl has terrible luck. Whatever will she do now?'

'Sir Everard Fawkener who was ambassador in Constantinople has taken over her guardianship and has salvaged some of her monies. However, he's just written to advise he's been appointed to work for the Duke of Cumberland and must travel overseas. Isabella's new plan is to go directly to Scotland. There is a chance she may have relatives there.'

'Well I hope she is luckier with that.'

'On the contrary, Isabella has had nothing but trouble with men trying to run her life. She'd be better off on her own.'

'Of course, I forgot how independent you both are. So how will she go to Scotland?'

Bessie explained this morning's drama. Joseph looked alarmed. 'Those young girls aim to cross Europe alone?' he asked.

Bessie frowned. 'I wanted to go too, but Issy is very stubborn and she refuses to allow it.'

Joseph shook his head. 'I hate to think of you putting yourself in harm's way, Bessie, but you should persist. There are strong rumours of a French invasion. Our own ship has been recalled, and we assume this means preparation for battle. It's a particularly dangerous time to travel.'

'That's what I feared. I'll talk to her again.'

'Perhaps I could get you both a direct passage to Portsmouth on our ship? The captain was mortified when he heard the story of Isabella's narrow escape. I'm sure he'd be keen to help.'

Bessie shook her head. 'I doubt she would agree to that now she's arranged to travel with Vittoria to France, that is if Anna allows Vee to go.'

Joseph laughed. 'Imagine that pretty wench persuading everyone she was a boy. The citizens of Constantinople must be slow-witted.'

Bessie flicked him with her glove.

'Are you calling me stupid, Joseph Grimes? She fooled me too.'

'Why can't she assume her male garb for the journey to France? It would be safer.'

'The same reason she had to quit her disguise and come home. She went with Liotard at fourteen, when her smooth face and high voice were unremarkable. It isn't credible now she's in her twentieth year.'

'Well, the offer to talk to the captain stands if you change your mind. Although heaven knows, travelling with us may be risky too. The ship is in Leghorn right now, readying her guns for battle. What between the Spanish and the French, I fancy we may see some action on the homeward journey.'

Bessie experienced a shiver of fear. 'Oh, Joseph, really? And young Freddy, is he still with you?'

Joseph laughed. 'He is beyond excited at the idea of a fight. You'd hardly recognise him now, he's as tall as me.'

'Well you tell him I send my regards. I need to head back now, Joseph, I've work to do.'

'I'll walk with you.'

When they arrived in Piazza de Spagna, Joseph doffed his hat.

'I might stay in Rome for a week, if you would spare me more time?'

'I'd like that a great deal, Joseph. I have a day off on Sunday. The gardens in Villa Borghese are pleasant, or you might like to see some antiquities? Where are you lodging?'

Joseph gave her his address.

'I'll send you a note about Sunday,' Bessie promised.

Chapter Thirty-Two

That evening, Vittoria came home for supper. Isabella knew she was hoping to get her mother to agree to France. Anna communicated her feelings by slamming pots on the range. They ate in leaden silence, eventually Vee pushed away her unfinished plate. 'Mama, I will stay here if you cannot bear me going.'

'Finish your supper. I work all afternoon preparing.'

Vittoria picked up her fork, but only glared at her plate. Anna snatched the plate away and banged it in the sink.

'I said I won't go!' Vittoria shouted, pushing her chair back to stand up.

'If the prince wishes it you have no choice!' Anna shouted back in Italian, with her hands on her hips and her chest heaving with emotion.

Bessie rose and gently got Anna to sit down.

'Surely Prince Henry will not make Vittoria go?'

Anna just shook her head, her expression now one of resignation.

Vee answered: 'We have been friends for the long time and of course he allow me refuse, but it would damage our relationship and I depend on him completely. That dependency is one of the reasons I wish go.'

She sat next to her mother. 'Mama, I am not so foolish as you think. My work is good, the King praises my miniatures as the best they ever have. But here in Rome I have no hope of bigger audience. I want one day to make large paintings to be seen by many, no hidden at the bottom of someone's pocket. In France I can meet clients face-to-face. I might find commissions for other works and no relying only on Stuarts.'

Anna raised her head. 'You want stay in France?'

Vee took her mother's hands. 'I go with no set plan. Only to use the journey as a chance of getting my work seen by others. Please, Mama, I need this opportunity.'

Anna shook her head in resignation. Isabella felt a pang of guilt, she had set this in motion.

'I know you must go. That is why I so angry. I afraid for you, Vee.'

'We will be very careful,' Vee looked towards Isabella, 'we will look after each other.'

'But two pretty girls, you'll find the bad attention of every scoundrel on the journey,' Anna said.

Bessie spoke up. 'Could you spare me for a few months, Anna? I believe my presence might deter those malicious individuals.'

Anna looked at Bessie in surprise. 'You want take on such difficult journey? It hotter every day now.'

'Bessie, we don't want you to give up your life here, it's too much to ask,' Isabella said.

'I shan't give it up, only take a break, if Anna can allow it. I'll visit Scotland to see my sister one last time, and make plans to move back here for good.'

Anna hugged her. 'Thank you, Bessie. It would make me feel much less worry.'

'Then it's settled. Joseph will be relieved, he shared your apprehension and urged me to go.' Bessie turned towards Isabella. 'In fact, he suggested that you sail back to England with them, but I told him you are resolved to travel through France with Vee.'

'Oh goodness no. We couldn't involve Captain Jones in a Jacobite venture!' Isabella said with a laugh.

Anna narrowed her eyes at Vee. 'Is this Jacobite venture? Only some small paintings?'

Vittoria gave Isabella an exasperated look. 'Prince Henry needs your help with one extra thing, Mama.'

'What thing? I swear the Stuarts think they own us.'

'Henry worries about the French commitment. He only asks me send a few words of honest report in a letter to you, then you can pass them on to him. He finds Charles's accounts, well, not without bias.'

'Heaven above, you spy on King James's heir and include such words in the letter to me? You want your poor mother go jail?'

Vittoria smiled. 'Of course not. We agree on some code, I would never put you in danger.'

Anna's snort implied her cynicism. 'Anyway, good that Henry not jumping into this war without think. The French let down the Stuarts before.'

She got up from her seat and fetched a large cake from where it was cooling by the window. 'Now, girls, take some cake and leave me and Bessie in peace. I want hear all about Bosun Grimes.'

* * *

Later that week Vittoria arrived back with an invitation.

'There will be *musica* in the King's chambers. Prince Henry wants you come, to say thank you for your help.'

'Meet the King? Oh, Vittoria, I'd be too nervous,' Issy replied.

'Why be nervous when I going with you?' Vee replied. 'Anyway, you can't refuse the royal invitation.'

The next evening Isabella took a chaise to Palazzo del Re. There she found the palace walls illuminated with flaming torches and sparkling candlelit chandeliers visible through all the windows.

Isabella's carriage stopped inside the palace courtyard and Vee came out of the stairwell to meet her. She took her hand and they climbed the stairs together.

'Tonight is the aria from famous Florentine opera singer.'

Sounds of conversation and laughter drifted down from above. From the top of the stairs they walked through a series of adjoining chambers. Unlike Issy's previous visit, every room glowed with candlelight, bouncing off huge mirrors and revealing the glory of rich tapestries and paintings. Eventually, Isabella found herself standing at the back of a room full of people. Recognising the paintings on the wall she realised she was back in the Grand Gallery where Vittoria had revealed herself.

The richly dressed guests were seated in rows of chairs facing a gold-painted harpsichord. Issy saw Prince Henry standing to one side, talking to an older gentleman. Issy knew from Vee's miniatures that this was James Stuart, the Pretender himself. Isabella also became alarmingly aware that many people turned to look at her. She'd hoped to blend in unnoticed, worrying that reports of her presence here might embarrass Sir Everard. Vittoria was chatting to a lady on her left, apparently oblivious to the attention. Then Isabella felt a little finger curl around hers and squeeze it before dropping again.

An excited murmur signalled that the prince had taken his seat at the harpsichord. He played so beautifully, Isabella quite lost herself in the music. He introduced the opera singer with a great show of deference. As soon as the man started singing it was evident that he was one of the famous castrati; his glorious voice reaching incredibly high notes. Isabella looked around, taking in all the royal paintings and richly dressed people. She could hardly believe she was here. The performance finished and after enthusiastic applause, people stood up and began to circulate. Issy saw several ladies heading in their direction.

'Can I see what painting you're working on now?' she asked.

They escaped to far a corner where Vee pointed to a painting of a young man wearing Highland Dress. 'Prince Charles, so stylish he can look good even in the Scottish skirt. They hope for help from Scottish lords, I paint miniatures for them.'

'I wonder if he'll get to Scotland? Perhaps I'll meet him there?'

Isabella turned with a start when she felt a hand on her shoulder. It was Prince Henry. 'No talk of Charles's absence tonight, ladies, my father needs the diversion.'

He addressed Vittoria in Italian: 'Why are you hiding over here, Vee? Are you afraid I'll ensnare your enchanting friend? You are alike but she is more pretty,' he teased.

Isabella answered on an impulse she instantly regretted. 'I don't agree and I lack Vittoria's talent.'

He turned to her in surprise. 'Your Italian is excellent, signorina, and I see you are as outspoken as your friend.'

His eyes glinted with mischief. Isabella, who'd coloured at

her regretted boldness, dropped into a curtsey by way of reply.

'I'm delighted to meet you again, signorina, and most thankful for your assistance in this delicate matter. I wish you a safe journey.'

In the week of their departure, an engraved glass pitcher arrived as a thank you from James Stuart. It came with a note for Anna from Prince Henry:

Please tell your Butcher to present your Bills to the Palazzo for the duration of Vittoria's Absence.

Bessie asked why Vee was laughing.

'Practical Prince Henry know very well that the King's glass is both beautiful and useless. We would never use such an ornate jug for our table, and the Jacobite engraving prevents it being used for guests. Mama relies on a big range of tourists, Ville de Londres no benefit from the association.'

Nevertheless, on their last night they filled the jug with water and placed it in the centre of the table. Vee held her wine glass above it to raise a toast.

'Here's to the success of my mission and to Isabella's safe delivery to Scotland. There she will remember us when she makes her toast in his rightful kingdom. To the King over the Water.'

Vittoria passed her wine glass over the jug. Anna, Bessie and Isabella repeated the gesture and held their glasses aloft.

'To the King over the Water!'

Chapter Thirty-Three

O n a fine May morning, Vittoria, Isabella and Bessie stood on deck, watching Leghorn disappear. The wind filled the ship's sails, and soon the fort and the lighthouse were the only things they could still see. Isabella struggled not to cry. She reminded herself that she'd arrived in desperate circumstances and had found happiness in Italy. Now she must find a way to return with her future settled.

Sir Everard's final letter announced his official appointment as secretary to the King's son, the Duke of Cumberland. Since he expected to travel to Europe he advised her to go directly to Scotland. He'd organised access to her money as an allowance through a bank in Edinburgh and promised a full account of her finances and Richard's story when they met next. He finished by wishing her luck in finding some family. Issy hadn't yet told him she'd no intention of settling with Scottish relatives and that she planned to return to Rome.

Vee took her hand.

'Let's walk to the front, I want to feel the wind on my face,' Isabella said.

Their journey so closely coincided with Captain Jones's planned journey from Leghorn to Genoa, that it would have caused unnecessary offence to refuse. Isabella also sensed Bessie's reluctance to say goodbye to Joseph. The two had spent every free minute together in Rome.

Isabella introduced Vittoria to Captain Jones. 'Delighted to meet any friend of Miss Godfrey and I trust you will all dine with me this evening.'

After supper, Isabella and Vittoria came on deck. A sliver of moon was reflected on the sea's surface and a swathe of tiny stars arced across the sails.

'It's beautiful,' Isabella whispered.

They watched for shooting stars until their necks ached. Then they crept down the stairs and along the narrow corridor. The ship's timber floors creaked at each step, but the sound of Bessie snoring reassured them they hadn't disturbed her.

Isabella realised that she needed to pee. She found the chamber pot under the bed and carefully arranged her skirts over the pot, before squatting. The stream sounded deafening and seemed to go on for ever.

'Sorry,' she mumbled, glad her darkness hid her blushes, 'too much wine.'

When she straightened up, she found Vee already stripped to her petticoat. 'My turn,' she said. Vee flung her petticoat skirts over her forearms and squatted. Issy saw her pale naked bottom in the moonlight. When Vee looked up and smiled, she turned away, embarrassed to be caught looking and at her own prudishness. Issy faced the wall and took off her dress.

Vee climbed on the bed to fling the window open, then scrambled off again to fetch the chamber pot. 'Let's get rid of this,' she said. 'Hold onto my legs, I don't want go overboard.' Vee thrust the chamber pot out the window, followed by her head and shoulders. Isabella was shocked out of her stupor and flung herself onto the bed to grab her legs. When Vittoria started to wriggle backwards, she helped her back in.

'What were you doing, you idiot?' Issy said through her giggles.

'I want make sure the wind don't blow it into Bessie's cabin,' she replied, sending them both into fits of laughter again.

They collapsed onto the bed, and within a few minutes Vee was asleep.

Issy inhaled the cabin's deep nutty smell of wood warmed by the day's sunshine. Turning her head, she caught the scent of Vee's perfume and the wine on her breath. The sensation of Vee's bare leg against her own was so glorious. Deep joy replaced her earlier sadness.

The ship approached Genoa in the afternoon. Prince Henry had advised the girls to buy a chaise and find a driver in Genoa before travelling overland to Turin. They would have to disassemble the carriage to get over the Alpine pass. But they hoped to avoid conversations with strangers and certainly didn't want to share transport.

Genoa was set on a hillside, they could see some noble looking buildings and many gardens.

'*Bella città!*' Vee said, admiring the view. 'Lovely like you,' she added, also in Italian.

The girls had agreed they would converse in Italian in public to obscure Issy's nationality. Of course she wouldn't pass as an Italian cousin but she might avoid being identified as English. Listening to Vittoria speak animated bouncing Italian made Issy realise how tiring it must be for her in English. Now it was she who hesitated and made mistakes.

Within a few minutes of docking, Joseph was loading their trunks into a rowing boat. He was coming into Genoa with them, insisting he would find them a good chaise and driver for the journey. They'd begin their long overland journey at first light.

* * *

The next morning, Joseph took them to meet the driver he'd found. The man was clean and seemed pleasant. He wouldn't take on the whole journey, but promised that he knew several men at the French border who could be trusted to take over. Then he said something in Italian that Bessie didn't catch.

'He bring blankets for the Mont Cenis Pass,' Vittoria translated. 'He say it be very cold at the top and we maybe see snow.'

'Really?' Bessie replied. It seemed impossible to believe, standing here in the hot sun.

'Well, looks like you're all set,' Joseph said. 'I need to be heading back to ship.'

'I'll come and see you off,' Bessie replied, taking his arm. 'How long will it take to reach Portsmouth?'

Joseph shrugged. 'Depends on the weather and meeting no hostilities. We'll stop in Gibraltar and Lisbon, eight weeks perhaps?'

'And then?'

'Shore leave I hope, then wherever His Majesty decides. What about you, Bessie, what will you do once you get to Scotland?'

'I must visit my sister in Edinburgh. But I don't plan to

stay there for long. I hope to make the return journey before the winter sets in.'

Joseph nodded. 'You have a good set-up there in Rome.'

'Yes, Anna's a fine friend,' Bessie replied.

'And she's lucky to have found you, Bessie Nichol.' He squeezed her arm where it has tucked under his.

'Can I write to you at your sister's? And will you promise to send word to Portsmouth of your journey's successful conclusion?'

'Of course,' she replied, 'and please write me your onwards plans.'

'Could be I won't be able to say. A sailor's destiny depends on others in times of war.'

Soon they reached Genoa's busy harbour. It had filled up over the last day and there were dozens of tall ships.

'Goodness, however will you find it?' Bessie asked.

'Just like I'd know you in a crowd of people,' he replied with a smile. 'I arranged to meet the lads just over there, they won't keep me waiting.'

As predicted, they reached the appointed set of ladders to see a rowing boat with two sailors appear out of the throng of ships. Bessie felt a tug of loss at the thought of him going. His embrace brought the tears she'd been fighting.

'Let's not say goodbye, lovely Bess. If you promise to let me know where you are, I promise you'll see me again.'

Bessie nodded, too full of emotion to say another word. He disappeared out of sight down the ladder. She heard the sound of his feet on the metal rungs, followed by the splash of oars. As the boat pulled away, a boy's voice rang out. 'So, you'll be telling Mistress Grimes about your girlfriend in Italy then, Bosun?' Any reply was drowned out by their laughter.

The sensation was like a cold wave washing down her back and through the soles of her feet. A dull pain of lonely disappointment that settled was an unwelcome but familiar feeling. 'You foolish, foolish old woman,' she said aloud.

Turning to walk away from the harbour, she missed Joseph's final wave and he saw only her back.

Chapter Thirty-Four

Bessie's solemn mood on their journey to Turin cast gloom in the carriage. When they managed to be alone, the girls conjectured that perhaps Bessie was convinced Joseph would be killed on the journey.

Approaching Turin, even Bessie was drawn out of her lethargy to look at the stupendous view. Turin was contained by an impressive crenelated wall, against the backdrop of snow covered mountains.

'God's glory puts all man's efforts in the shade,' muttered Bessie. The most words she'd said in days.

Once in their hotel, Isabella and Vee found their double room was on a different floor to Bessie's.

Vee flopped on the bed. 'I swear if she keeps this up I shake her. The countryside is breath-taking, the birdsong sweet, as if we are in paradise. But she behaves like we are heading for the Inferno.'

Isabella smiled at her friend. Vee's prostrate pose with her hands above her head and her skirts and petticoats in tumbled disarray was heart achingly beautiful. 'It's most unlike her. I'm afraid leaving Bosun Grimes has broken her heart.'

'At her age she should have more sense,' Vee grumbled.

Isabella put her head to one side. 'Is that what you think? That the heart becomes cold and unfeeling when we get older?'

Vittoria propped herself up on her elbows and met Isabella's gaze. 'I think...' she hesitated, 'that some feelings stay with me forever.'

Isabella blinked under the intensity of her stare.

Vee jumped up and went to their window. 'What we do tomorrow?' she asked.

They were to stay two days in Turin, to give the driver time to organise things for the Alps journey.

'Bessie wants to visit Christ's shroud in the cathedral,' Isabella said.

Vee turned away from the window and wrinkled her nose. 'We no spend the day stuck inside church, Bella. I hear there are many beautiful buildings in Turin and I want take out my sketch book.'

The three women had supper together in the evening and Bessie's mood had clearly improved.

'You found the relic uplifting?' Issy asked.

Bessie pressed her napkin to her lips. They had just eaten some excellent veal in fish sauce. 'Definitely, Isabella. When faced with God's power we realise the insignificance of our own troubles. I'm now ready for this mountain journey. His creation is well expressed in these high places.'

'I have no idea what she talking about,' Vee observed in their bedroom later, 'but I am very glad she happier.'

Vee climbed into bed, then she leaned over to stroke the hair from Isabella's eyes and kiss her cheek. 'Sleep well lovely, Bella,' she said and turned to face towards the window.

'Night, Vee,' Isabella whispered.

Much later, in the darkest hour of night, Isabella was woken by the bed creaking as Vee turned. Her senses were immediately on full alert. The sensation of Vee's breath on the back of her neck made the tiny hairs stand on end. Nothing happened for the longest time and Isabella thought she'd gone back to sleep. Then, she felt Vittoria's fingers on her own hip. That lightest of touches had her fall asleep smiling.

The road became noticeably steeper as they reached the lower slopes of the mountains, and Isabella could hear their horse breathing heavily. Their driver stopped the carriage. He explained the horse would manage the climb but not pulling the chaise, so he'd hired two chairs, one for Bessie on her own and one for her and Vee to share. Their chaise was disassembled astonishingly quickly and the parts were strapped to three mules. The horse, who'd be led over the pass by the driver, carried some smaller pieces and two trunks. The day was fine and the coolness of the mountain air was refreshing.

'Why don't we walk, Vee?' Issy suggested.

'Good idea, I'll tell the driver.'

The driver met Vittoria's words with a sceptical look. 'He afraid we too slow to complete the journey before dark,' Vee said.

'Tell him we'll get in the litter if we start to fall behind,' Issy replied.

Finally the bearers hoisted Bessie's litter into the air.

'Heaven preserve us!' they heard her exclaim.

Issy and Vee laughed then linked arms. Vee whispered in her ear: 'France here we come!'

They strode up the mountain path, determined not to fall behind. It was easy in the beginning but the air seemed to get thinner as they climbed. Their early chattering ceased and Vee admitted that she was getting a blister. Issy was secretly glad when the whole party stopped at the summit to let the litter bearers rest. At first, clouds obscured the view, then suddenly the sun broke through. Isabella had imagined the Alps in a line, like a natural wall. Instead, she found they were surrounded by mountains on all sides and stretching far into the distance. Soon the driver said it was time to go.

'Please get into the litter now, girls, you're making me anxious,' Bessie said. 'It's easy to slip going downhill.'

They didn't argue and tucked the offered blanket over their cold legs. Vee's fingers slid over Issy's thigh under the rug and took her hand.

They had to stop to clear some fallen rocks which lost them an hour. Then they plodded on into darkening evening until the ground started to level out. Suddenly the man holding the front of their litter grunted and Issy heard gravel move beneath his feet. Their litter lurched to one side. She braced against the post, and for a second it seemed safe, then the man behind stumbled too. Vee shouted and stretched out her hand. Their fingers touched, before gravity took Isabella out of reach. Cold air rushed past her face as she fell backwards into the void. And then, nothing.

Chapter Thirty-Five

The next thing Isabella knew was the sound of Vee's voice.

'Her eyes moved. She wake up.'

'Maybe, but the sleeping may move their eyes,' Bessie replied.

'Go and rest, Bessie. You look so tired, I stay here.'

'I'll just be next door. Be sure and wake me if there is any sign of improvement.'

Isabella felt like she was weighed down underwater. She willed her eyes to open, instructed her arms to move, nothing. Was she paralysed? Blinded? Deep panic started to swell up in her chest. Then she felt calming fingers stroke her cheek and Vee's voice, soft in her ear. 'Wake up, Issy, try open your eyes.' Then in a more urgent tone: 'No leave me, my Bella. I swear I fight for us. I never let you go.'

Then came the glorious sensation of Vee's lips on her cheek. A sudden red hot certainty of love shot through her. As if the tethers binding her beneath the waves were cut, Isabella felt herself rushing towards consciousness.

Turning to Vee took no effort at all. As their lips met,

Isabella opened her eyes. The briefest kiss, dry-lipped, tenta-
tive, then warmer, more insistent.

'Vittoria,' Isabella murmured.

The sound of a door alerted them to Bessie's approach.

'I thought I heard her voice?' Bessie asked. 'Did she
wake?'

Isabella tried to sit up. The sharpest pain from her arm
made her cry out and fall back.

'Goodness, Isabella, don't move. The doctor thinks your
arm may be broken.'

Bessie laid her warm, plump hand on Isabella's face. 'I'm
so glad to see you awake. How do you feel? You look a little
flushed.' She felt Issy's forehead. 'No fever, that's good. The
doctor will be pleased.'

Isabella touched her lips where she imagined they
throbbed from the kiss.

'Did you bite your tongue? Let me see.' Bessie pressed
strong fingers either side of Issy's mouth to open it. 'I can't
see any damage. The doctor will do a proper examination,
now you've come round.'

'What happened?' Isabella could hear her words sounded
slurred.

'You bang your head. You were unconscious for only the
moment, but you spoke nonsense when you woke,' Vittoria
answered.

Bessie interrupted. 'We were so fortunate that there was a
French doctor in a party behind us. He tended to you and
declared the confusion was caused by the bump on your head.
He gave you a draught to make you sleep.'

Isabella's mouth felt strange, as if her tongue was swollen.
'Can I have a drink?' she asked.

Bessie cradled her head to allow her to take a sip of ale.

'How long did I sleep?'

'Since yesterday. We worry,' Vee replied. 'You slept

through the whole carriage journey and had to be carried up here.'

'Where's here?' Isabella asked.

'A village called Aiguebelle, still in Savoy. The doctor advised against going on to the French border until you recover,' Bessie replied.

'Hmmm,' Issy heard her own voice, as if far away, her eyelids drooped.

'Go and rest again, Bessie,' Vee said. 'I'll watch her.'

Issy forced her eyes to stay open until they were alone.

'Sleep, my Bella,' Vee whispered and kissed her.

'My love,' Issy managed to mumble, before she drifted off.

When she woke next, a strange man in the room explained in French that he was Doctor Geraud. 'You took longer than I expected to wake up,' he said.

'Because the fall?' Vee asked.

'Seeing Miss Godfrey in daylight, I find her more slight than I calculated, perhaps the laudanum dose was too high. How do you feel, mademoiselle?'

Isabella moved her head cautiously. 'Much better.'

'*Bon*,' he said. 'I would like to examine you.'

They helped Isabella to stand. The doctor looked into her eyes. 'Dizzy?' he asked.

Issy nodded. 'At first, but it's settled now.'

'*Très bien*,' he said. 'Mesdames, I'll step out, please remove her skirt and jacket.'

Bessie undid Issy's skirts, while Vittoria's deft fingers flew through the buttons on the front of the riding habit Issy wore for travelling. Vee shot Isabella a heart-stopping smile when she straightened. Issy flinched when the weight of the garment came over her right wrist.

'I'm so sorry! Did I hurt you?' Vee said.

'Just a twinge, don't worry,' Issy replied.

Bessie turned to readmit the doctor. Vee lifted her hand and landed a kiss in her palm. Just as she had that first time in Constantinople.

The doctor found no injury in her spine, but when he touched the side of her head, Issy's hand shot up in reaction to the pain.

'I'm sorry,' he said. 'The bump is large but the pain will ease soon.'

He coloured when he requested permission to examine her ankles. Observing she could move both feet in circles and checking she reported no leg pain, he deduced her lower limbs were fine. 'Finally, mademoiselle, could you unfasten the chemise *ici*,' he asked, pointing to Issy's right wrist.

Vee's fingers stroked Issy's pulse point as she undid the blouse ties. But then she gasped at the sight of the huge greenish blue bruise on Issy's lower arm.

The doctor peered closely at the skin, then looked up at Isabella. 'I'm sorry but I must feel the bones, to know if we have a break.'

Isabella nodded. She gritted her teeth, gripping hard on Bessie's hand and gave a small moan when pain shot up her arm.

'Sorry, but I don't think we need the services of a bone setter. I'll bind your arm and you mustn't use it for at least six days.'

He gave Isabella another small dose of laudanum for the pain, then wished them adieu.

'I'll come down with you, Doctor,' Bessie said. 'I'll fetch something from the kitchen for Isabella and settle your bill.'

When they left, Isabella felt overcome with tiredness again. 'I can't keep my eyes open.'

'Then I must distract you until Bessie returns, for you

should eat something before you sleep again.' Vee whispered in her ear, 'I declare you need kissing better.'

Vee took Issy's left hand and kissed the end of each finger, grazing her tongue across her palm, while looking into her eyes. Isabella groaned with pleasure. Her small teeth found Isabella's earlobe. Vee's ragged breathing matched her own.

They both looked towards the door at the sound of Bessie's footsteps on the stair. Turning back to her with the most mischievous look, Vee slipped her hand inside Isabella's chemise and rolled her nipple between her fingers. Issy gasped and Vee quickly withdrew her hand before Bessie came in. 'It seems you will recover,' she said.

Bessie insisted on sleeping beside Isabella.

'Do you feel well enough to travel? I know our driver is anxious to reach Le Pont-de-Beauvoisin and hand over to the Frenchman,' Bessie said in the morning.

'If someone will help me dress, I'm sure I'll be fine.'

Just then Vee came in, dressed only in her petticoats with her hair down. Isabella was stunned with longing to nuzzle her sleep-warm neck.

'I'll help. What you want wear? Your riding jacket needs clean after your fall,' Vee said.

Vee helped her into her blue dress, its stomacher would allow her to keep her stays loose behind it. Issy couldn't face whale bones for today's long coach journey. Bessie was in and out of the room while Vee was dressing her, but she still contrived to stroke her. 'There,' Vittoria said, 'I'll just get your stockings.'

'Good,' Bessie remarked. 'I'll tell the driver that we're ready.'

Issy looked down at her bosom bulging above the stomacher like two overripe melons, and pulled a face. 'I do wish I was slim like you, Vee. My breasts are obscene, I feel like a milking cow.'

'Your breasts,' said Vee, 'are *stupendo*.'

She ran a licked finger across her cleavage and Issy felt the air between them was simmering. Vee took her face in her hands and kissed her full on the mouth, their tongues met, the urgency intensified by the inevitable sound of Bessie returning. Isabella's body raged with frustration and she clenched her fists to prevent herself shouting at poor Bessie to leave them. Vee knelt at her feet. Her fingers stroked her inner leg all the way up as she rolled on the clean stockings, sweeping a few inches further as a flourish at the top. Mounting desire left Issy dizzy.

'Right,' Bessie said. 'Now that you're dressed let's see if you can stand.'

Isabella swayed slightly, causing Bessie to come up close and look questioningly into her eyes. Issy was seized with the illogical fear that she might know her thoughts.

'Are you in pain? The doctor left more laudanum if you need it.'

Isabella coughed and shook her head to clear it. 'I'm fine, Bessie. But I think I prefer to try to manage without it and keep my wits about me.'

Isabella thought Vee gave her a sharp look, but had no opportunity to ask what it meant. Bessie had them all bundled into the chaise.

Chapter Thirty Six

The intensity of those few moments of furtive touching left Isabella physically drained and filled with joy. She knew it was reckless. What they were doing was most certainly both sinful and dangerous, but she clenched her jaw in defiance. She didn't care, they were doing no one any harm. She'd never experienced such passion and she wouldn't give it up. This felt utterly right, like a destiny.

The coach sped through the small town of Chambéry. Bessie shared out their picnic: wizened apples, goat cheese, bread and a flask of wine. Bessie sat beside Isabella, she broke the bread and cheese into pieces for her to eat with her unbandaged hand. Vittoria coldly refused Bessie's offer of food and kept her eyes closed.

Had she done something to offend Vittoria? Isabella's so recently swollen heart, constricted with fear. She was an inexperienced idiot, a naive fool. Had she missed some clue?

This stretch of the road was rutted and her arm hurt with every jolt. She scrunched up her eyes in pain, then opened them wide at a sudden thought. She'd received Vee's touch like an indulged child. Vittoria was two years older, already twenty, an adult, and Isabella had the sense that she'd caressed someone before. She should have touched Vee in return, given her pleasure back. Vee must be angry and disappointed, to discover her a self-centred baby. Issy nursed her throbbing arm in her lap, willing the coach to travel the last miles to their destination. She had to get Vee alone, to show her how much she loved her.

They reached Le Pont-de-Beauvoisin. They were finally in France and should be celebrating, but Vee still avoided her gaze, Issy's heart sped as if she was in mortal danger. When they were shown into a room with three beds, she had a strong urge to cry.

Bessie placed her voluminous nightgown on the middle bed.

'Don't worry, girls, I'll be careful to sleep on my side, I shan't snore at all.'

Issy instinctively looked up, expecting to exchange an amused look with Vee, who still didn't turn towards her. Isabella felt cold and the pain in her arm intensified. What if she'd made an irreparable mistake? She sat down on her own bed.

'Bessie, excuse me, but I don't feel able to go down for supper. Perhaps someone could help me undress?'

She daren't look in Vee's direction. Bessie came over.

'You're as white as a sheet. I do believe we've moved you too soon.'

Bessie unpinned her bodice and released her from her stays. Isabella stepped out of her skirts. Bessie grunted from the effort of bending.

'For goodness' sake, Vittoria, come and help me here with Isabella's stockings.'

Vee didn't move.

'No it's fine, Bessie. Look, I can manage to take them off with one hand.' Isabella said.

Issy undid her hair and climbed underneath the sheet Bessie held up for her. She looked over at Vee, the sadness in her eyes frightened her further.

When they came back some two hours later, Issy pretended to be asleep. She lay awake worrying most of the night. Exhaustion must have overcome her, because when she woke, Bessie and Vittoria were already dressed.

'Do you feel well enough to travel, Isabella?' Bessie asked.

'I think so.'

'Then let me see if I can organise some breakfast, you must eat.'

Bessie left the room and Issy saw Vee was going to follow.

'Vee!' she called. 'Please could you help me here?'

Vittoria stopped in the door, then she turned slowly and walked back. Her head was bowed.

'I am so, so sorry...' Issy started then hesitated. 'I'm such a fool.'

Vee looked up. Issy thought her stricken expression might break her heart.

'I didn't know how, I mean I should have known...'

Vittoria stopped her by raising her hand.

'Please, there no need for you apologise, you are ill, I took advantage. It was unforgivable.'

Their eyes locked.

'What?' Issy replied.

'You must not blame yourself, the laudanum damaged your judgement.'

'Of course I blame myself,' Isabella knew she was speaking too loudly, they both looked to the door, expecting the usual interruption. She dropped her voice to an urgent whisper. 'You made me feel like a queen and I behaved like a spoiled princess.'

Isabella lunged towards Vittoria and kissed her passionately on the mouth. Vee pulled away, she shook her head.

'No, please, you must no feel you have to.'

Issy narrowed her eyes. For the first time it dawned on her they were talking at cross purposes.

'I want for nothing else. I feel like a dunce, but I thought,' she hesitated, 'well I'll learn if you're willing to teach me?'

Vee grabbed her hand. 'You're no angry? No disgusted?'

Isabella laughed out loud. 'Angry? No, I thought you were angry with me for being too slow.'

Vee broke into a smile. 'And I thought you angry for me being too fast.'

This time Vee kissed her back. They parted at the sound of Bessie returning.

'I think she's doing it on purpose,' Issy said.

Bessie stopped in the doorway, she put her hands on her hips. 'Well, I see you two are friends again. No time for dawdling. I hate to remind you of the fact that we're meant to be travelling unobtrusively. I would say that so far we are failing completely.'

The reminder that they were on a serious mission wiped the smile off both their faces.

'Yes, Bessie,' Issy replied.

'You are right,' Vee added.

The coach journey was no longer dull. The closeness of Vee's thigh leant an excitement to the days and her proximity at night with Bessie nearby, was excruciating torture. Issy had to content herself with the sight of Vee's shining, smiling eyes in the moonlight.

Finally, after over two weeks on the road, they reached Lyon in the middle of June. They all agreed they'd experienced enough sleeping on straw and asked their French driver to find them a clean lodging house. The landlady offered that she had one large room big enough for three.

Vittoria spoke up. 'Maybe you have one single and one twin room, Madame Bertin?'

Then she turned to Bessie.

'Isabella still needs help dressing but we all want some sleep. Why you no have a single room, Bessie? It will be, well, more quiet... I mean more comfortable for you.'

'There's no need to mince words, Vittoria. I know very well that I sometimes snore a little,' Bessie said.

In truth, Bessie snored like a drunken soldier. Issy daren't even look at Vee. They saw Bessie to hers first. A very lovely room, with a pretty bed and a large blue and white ceramic washbowl on a stand.

'Oh, girls, one of you should have this room, it's too grand for me.'

'Of course you must have it, Bessie. I'm sure ours will be equally nice,' Isabella replied. She made a small, selfish and inappropriate prayer that their room would not be inferior, in case Bessie should insist on giving hers up.

Luckily their room on the next floor was even prettier. The breeze through the open balcony doors set the muslin drapes fluttering and sunlight spilled over the terracotta tiled floor. Two single beds were made up with embroidered white sheets and a tall washstand stood between them. The lovely smell of lavender came from dried bunches hanging from the rafters.

'Oh, it's simply lovely,' Isabella said.

'I'm sure you ladies will want to wash after your journey. I'll have water brought up after supper,' Madame Bertin said.

'*Merci beaucoup*, madame,' Vee replied.

Anticipation filled Isabella's abdomen with a swooping sensation. She couldn't sit still. 'I'd like to see a little of the city before supper, shall we walk?'

'We all need to stretch our legs after that infernal carriage,' Bessie replied.

'Madame, could you direct us to the river?' Vee asked Mme Bertin.

The riverside path thronged with walkers and men were busy loading and unloading their cargoes from distinctive open boats. Isabella remarked that their shallow design and upturned ends, reminded her of the gondolas she had seen in Venetian paintings.

'I'd love to go to Venice. Have you ever been?' she asked Vittoria.

'Sadly no. Perhaps we go together one day? I long to meet Rosalba Carriera, this Venetian lady proved a woman may be the successful artist,' Vee replied.

Isabella heard Bessie sigh. She realised their high state of happiness might be annoying, especially when Bessie was so obviously sad about Joseph. She dropped Vee's arm and took Bessie's. 'Is there anything you'd like to do in Lyon?'

'I shall enjoy not being jostled about in a chaise all day, and I should like to try a French pastry,' Bessie replied.

'Well we could do that now,' Isabella said, glad to find her enthusiastic about something.

'Madame Bertin expects us for supper and I'm loathe to spoil my appetite. But we might visit a cake shop tomorrow morning.'

Their supper consisted of beef in wine, which Isabella found pleasant, and eels, which she did not.

After supper, Madame Bertin preceded them up the stairs with a large jug of warm water. She took away the one in their room, promising to return with it filled. The light had turned golden and the sky outside their window was full of swooping, screeching swifts. Isabella was breathing too fast, determined to act, but she'd imagined taking the initiative in the dark. She busied herself taking down her hair and unpacking her night shift. She turned back to face Vittoria with her light cotton gown in her hand. 'Which bed do you want, Vee?'

Vittoria kissed her full on the mouth.

'We no need two beds and you no want that.' Vee flung the shift on the bed and nuzzled into her neck. Issy groaned, the softening warmth between her legs came back, melting her shyness and giving her courage. She extricated herself and took Vittoria's hand. 'Wait a bit. I want to attend to you first.'

She led Vittoria over to the washstand. She managed to unloosen Vee's hair with her uninjured hand, then there was a soft tap at their door. The landlady brought in the second jug of water, two linen towels and a small piece of green Savon de Marseille soap.

'*Merci*, Madame Bertin,' Isabella said, as the landlady left the room.

'They have this in Palazzo del Re,' Vittoria said, throwing up the soap and catching it again. 'The French are so clever.'

'I need you to raise your arms.' Isabella's words caught with emotion. Their eyes met as she tugged free the lace fastening Vee's jacket. Then she moved around her, releasing first one arm, then the other. She ran her tongue up Vee's inner arms then walked behind her, leaning in tight against Vee's spine, she released her skirt and slid her hand through the gap in her petticoat to caress her thigh. Vittoria gasped and arched her head back. Issy kissed her delicate collarbone, whilst untying her petticoat and hip pad, which fell to the ground with a thud. The sight of Vittoria's buttocks through her translucent shift made her heart pound. Vee turned and kissed her hungrily.

Issy pulled away with a smile. 'Impatient girl.' She unpinned Vee's stomacher, placing the row of long pins on the washstand. Vee's eyes were wide and her small breasts rose and fell above her cream linen stays. Issy pulled the lace and the stays fell.

'I'm afraid your slip will need two hands,' she said, leaning in to take each nipple in her mouth through the thin cotton.

Vee, sighed, then pulled her slip over her head in one movement.

Isabella's eyes pricked with tears at Vittoria's naked beauty.

'Can I sit down?' Vittoria asked. 'My knees shake.'

'Please put the basin on the floor for me first,' she said.

Madame Bertin had added lavender oil to the warm water. When Issy poured water into the basin, a fresh wave of the scent wafted through the bedroom.

Vee sat on a wooden chair draped with a white linen sheet. Issy rubbed a soaked cloth with soap and began washing her, beginning at her face and ears and working her way down. She kissed each place after every stroke, lingering over her breasts and stomach. As she crept down past the navel, Vee flung her head back with a groan.

Smiling up at her, Issy said, 'Goodness, you still have your stockings.' When the ribbons were loosened, the stockings pooled round Vittoria's ankles and Issy teased them off from the toes.

Isabella soaped and rinsed each foot in turn, darting kisses from ankle to thigh. Then she sat back on her toes and looked at the erotic vision in front of her. She coughed to be able to speak. 'I need fresh water.'

Vee looked down at her with eyes half closed. 'Leave it, I cannot stand.'

'Dirty girl,' Issy said, and shook her head in mock admonition. She rinsed the cloth in the jug, and soaped it before working her way up each leg. She could feel Vittoria trembling when she reached her inner thighs. Isabella knew where she should go next and Vee placed her hand on Issy's shoulder, as if willing her on. With shaking hands, Issy wrapped the damp linen cloth around her forefinger and stroked the bud in the centre. Vee shuddered and cried out.

'Did I hurt you?' she asked, pulling back.

Vittoria started to giggle. 'No, idiot.'

Vee jumped up, spilling water from the basin. She pulled Issy to her feet, then dragged to her to the bed, pushing up her petticoats as she tumbled backwards. Isabella was already so aroused, that her own shuddering explosion came after only a few glorious seconds.

While the sky outside their window turned pink, they dozed intertwined and naked. Issy squealed when Vee washed her with water from the other jug, which was now quite cold. They spent the long warm night exploring each other. Finally, when dark was greying towards day, Vee kissed her again.

'We must sleep now or Bessie will know we gone mad.'

Issy climbed into the other bed. Vee had to wake her the next morning or she would probably have slept until noon.

Chapter Thirty-Seven

Lyon, France, May 1745

The next day they sampled one pastry shop after another, until Bessie begged them to stop attempting to split her dress seams. When they returned to the lodgings, Madame Bertin loaned them a copy of Marivaux's *Marianne*, and they sat reading it on the shaded terrace through the hot afternoon. Isabella's arm itched in the heat and she persuaded Bessie to remove the bandages. Vittoria and Isabella took turns reading aloud and translating it for Bessie. The heat and the sound of bees made Issy drowsy.

'I believe you need to be in bed early, Isabella. Your ordeal on the mountain has exhausted you,' Bessie said.

'I think you're right, Bessie,' Vee added, 'and it's rather difficult to sleep in this warm weather.'

Issy daren't look at her.

A young man came onto the terrace. He had been alone in the dining room for both supper and breakfast. Now he approached them. 'I wonder if I might sit here?' he asked. 'Truth is I'm feeling rather homesick, and hearing a Scottish voice is so pleasant,' he added, smiling in Bessie's direction.

Bessie smiled back.

'Please do join us. My brain aches translating this book,' Isabella said, closing the novel and placing it on the table.

'What part of Scotland are you from?' Bessie asked.

'I was born in Orkney but my family moved to Aberdeen,' he replied, 'although I studied at Scots College in Paris this year. Now I plan to visit Rome before I return home.'

Vittoria sat forward in her chair. Prince Henry had told her to go to Scots College for news of Prince Charles's whereabouts.

'What a coincidence, we've just come from Rome and are heading for Paris,' Isabella replied.

'How fortuitous. Perhaps I can recommend lodgings in Paris and you could suggest somewhere in Rome? Miss...'

'Miss Godfrey, and this is Mistress Nichol and Signorina Bassi. We would appreciate your advice, sir. And as to Rome, we know just the place. Ville de Londres, are excellent lodgings run by Signora Sirani, who is Signorina Bassi's mother, Mr...?'

'Chalmers, Alan Chalmers. I'll give you the address of a most agreeable boarding house off Boulevard Saint-Germain and I'd be very grateful for the details of Ville de Londres,' he replied. 'Perhaps you also have advice on sites to visit?'

'It depend on your interest,' Vittoria said. 'There are many things to see in Rome.'

'I shall most certainly want to visit the antiquities, and I hear there are a great number of beautiful churches.' He inclined his head to Bessie. 'I see we are of the same faith, madam. I'm sure you must share my joy in being able to worship in a church.'

Bessie touched the silver crucifix at her throat. 'The churches of Rome are magnificent. Are you studying for the priesthood?'

'No, my father selected the college as a convivial place for a Catholic boy to round off his education.' He looked at Bessie thoughtfully, as if weighing the risk of his next question. 'Can I ask you, madam. Did you visit the church where the Stuarts worship? I have a burning curiosity to see it. I hear that James can often be found there.'

'Santi Apostoli? Yes, and James Stuart visits his wife's memorial there almost every day. Although if you're interested in the Stuarts, Vittoria and her mother are better placed to answer your questions. Her family worked at court.'

The young man's eyes widened, he looked at Vittoria. 'Really? Would it bore you to talk about them? I would be so fascinated.'

Vee answered all his questions patiently and offered to write to her mother, and try to gain him an introduction into Palazzo del Re.

'Might that be possible? What a tale that would be to take home. A fitting end to my time in Europe.'

'You know Prince Charles is no there?' Vittoria said.

'I know he's in France. In fact he visited Scots College at the beginning of the year. Although I wasn't fortunate enough to meet him.'

'And is he still in Paris?' Isabella said. She knew Vittoria was itching to ask that question.

'No, no. He's been on the coast in Nantes for some weeks. It's rumoured he's trying to raise a force himself, being exasperated with French delays.' He had already lowered his voice, and now leaned forwards in a conspiratorial manner. 'To go to Scotland. Isn't that exciting?'

Isabella adopted an expression that she hoped looked only mildly curious. He'd left Paris! She glanced at Vittoria, who was also managing to hide any reaction. 'Well perhaps we'll see him there. Mistress Nichol and I are destined for Edinburgh.'

'How marvellous, then perhaps we'll meet again? I plan to study there.'

'Well, Bessie means to return to Rome, but if I stay, I'll look out for you, Mr Chalmers.'

He looked thoughtful. 'Do you have many acquaintances in Edinburgh, Miss Godfrey? If not, please allow me to write a note of introduction to my friends Robert Strange and Isabella Lumisden. They are about our age and most delightful company. I've known Robbie since my boyhood in Orkney, and I hope I'll return to find you all fast friends.'

'That's most kind, Mr Chalmers, I'd love to meet them,' Isabella replied, standing up. 'Now, you must excuse us. Will we see you at supper?'

He also stood and bowed. 'I planned to eat out. But I'll have that note to Robbie and Isabella ready for you at breakfast tomorrow. Thank you so much for indulging me with your company.'

'I write my mother tonight,' Vittoria said. 'If you take a letter to her, then I ask her to try introduce you to Palazzo del Re.'

'It would be my pleasure and any possibility of going to court would be thrilling. You have all been too kind.'

They went upstairs together and Bessie came with them to their room. 'What will you do?' she asked Vittoria.

'Go to Nantes, I think.'

It suddenly hit Isabella that the change of plan might mean an early parting. 'Surely, Bessie, we cannot let Vee travel alone?' She could feel her heart thudding.

Bessie was thoughtful for a moment, then her reply brought Issy a rush of relief.

'I believe we must go too. We agreed to see Vittoria to the end of her mission. We might investigate sailing from Nantes.

I confess I've had enough of travelling now. I want to get home.'

When the girls retired after supper, Vittoria sat on the balcony to compose a letter to her mother. She handed it to Isabella. It was in Italian but she now read well.

'Remind me what you agreed with Prince Henry?' Isabella asked.

'A coded message in the postscript, nothing that might annoy the censor. I cannot put Mama danger,' she hesitated, 'or your young beau.'

Isabella tutted, 'He's not my beau. What code?'

'Charles is Carluccio, his family nickname, and the words are opposite of the truth.'

Isabella skimmed through the body of the letter. Vittoria gave lots of news of their journey and finally explained that Mr Chalmers had offered to carry the letter, so asked Anna to persuade Prince Henry to invite him to court. It finished:

We now travel West. I'm accompanying Isabella and Bessie to Nantes on the French Coast, and I'll write again from there.

Much love Vittoria
PS. I hear that Carluccio is so happy and people say his French Friends have been most supportive of his Plans. I'm told he is content to wait in Paris, so I may not be able to I deliver the Items he ordered for some Time.

Isabella nodded and handed the note back to Vittoria.

'Have you sealing wax?' Vee asked.

'Yes, I'll get it for you.'

They both went inside and Issy watched Vittoria prepare the seal.

'Will you visit Chalmers' Edinburgh friends, Issy?' Vee's face betrayed that it was more than an idle question.

'Not if you prefer not.'

Vittoria shrugged. 'It is all right. This something I must live with.'

'What are you talking about?'

'That young man was interested about you. This is why he wants to tie you to his friends, to see you again.'

'I didn't get that impression, in fact I thought he looked rather long at you.'

Vittoria made a dismissive noise. 'He may have looked at me, but I am daughter of a servant. A different category of women.'

Isabella frowned. Vee sat on the bed beside her and took her hand.

'Isabella, you are very naive. When alone together we are equal, but in the real world your guardian is important diplomat and my father was servant. These things matter.'

'You know my upbringing was lowly and anyway why should we care?'

Isabella tried to hug Vee, but she pulled away.

'Sorry, forgive me. It is hard to think of you with someone other.'

'But I'm not interested in Mr Chalmers, I'll never give you cause to be jealous,' Isabella replied, her voice raised in protest.

Vee shook her head sadly. 'But one day you will. I cannot ask you give up the chance to marry, to have children.'

'Goodness, you think I'd leave you for a man!' Issy's voice raised louder and Vee placed her finger on her lips, with a smile.

'Shush, Issy, you make the whole house banging on the door. I do not doubt your love, Bella, but thinking not marry is the big promise.' She hesitated. 'I've known for a long time that I only wanted women. But you... well, you thought I was a man when you first kiss me.'

Issy took Vee's hands and gripped them hard. 'I'm absolutely sure I want to be with you and only you. I could love no one else.'

Isabella saw in her eyes that Vittoria believed her. They moved their conversation to the language of kisses. Forgiveness, understanding, commitment, a whole silent discussion with their mouths, soon turned to passion. They tore off each other's clothes, losing a ribbon in the process. Each tried to outdo the other in giving pleasure, until finally they lay panting as if almost drowned.

Isabella was the first to break the long happy silence.

'When did you do this first?' she asked.

Vittoria drew her into a hug. 'In the Palazzo del Re, before Constantinople. She was lady's maid from the Spanish court. She in Rome only two weeks. But it took away huge worry, I thought I was the only one who didn't want men.'

'Maybe I'm the same? I know I found Sir John disgusting.'

'Sir John is disgusting, Issy. It no prove anything.'

They laughed.

'Anyway, I know I don't want children. The pain of my brother's death left my mother without enough will to live.' Isabella stroked Vittoria's cheek. 'I want to be with you always. I can't bear the thought of leaving you soon.'

Vittoria kissed her. 'Do not think about goodbye.'

'Surely, there must be some way to be together?' Issy asked.

Vee pulled away and looked serious.

'It is no easy, we need be patient and clever. First we must both find the way to make money. Will you sell jewellery in Scotland?'

'I'm hoping I might come back to Rome quickly. But if I stay more than a few weeks, then I definitely want to work. I brought two casks full of faux pearl as well as some silver pieces and my tools of course. Even without a forge I have enough to make a start.'

'Well, maybe I no go back to Rome. If I can make the good reputation in France, I can travel to you after. We will find way to be together.'

'Promise?' Isabella asked.

'Promise,' Vittoria replied.

Chapter Thirty-Eight

After breakfast, Vittoria gave Mr Chalmers her letter and he handed Isabella a note. 'This is the address of Bella Lumisden's family home. Alternatively you might visit the oyster bar in Niddry Street, Bella and Robbie are often there in the evenings.' He then lowered his voice. 'Although perhaps I should warn you that this oyster cellar is a favourite place with Jacobite supporters. Bella and Robbie are most enthusiastic about the Cause.'

They took their leave of Chalmers and Issy resisted the urge to tease Vee about the warmth of her tone to him. Yesterday he was a love rival but today a political ally. For someone hoping to be a spy, her allegiances were too easy to guess.

The journey to the coast was full of vibrant colour. Red geraniums and begonias, winding blue rivers and groves of tall, thin green trees. However, the extremes of the artist's palette came to Issy in her nights with Vee, explosions of crimson and magenta. But there was a growing sad undercurrent to her joy. The unavoidable truth was that every day nearer the coast was one day less with Vittoria and Isabella clung to every shared minute. Her sensitivity to Vee's moods was also heightened. She didn't doubt her love but she sensed Vee's thoughts were often elsewhere. Issy dreaded meeting Prince Charles for the first time. He and the Jacobite Cause were in Vittoria's heart too, and it was a chamber from which she was excluded.

Just outside Nantes, a sailor travelling home gave them bad news. Charles had already sailed. He said the prince was heading to meet the *Elisabeth*, a troop ship out of Brest. They rerouted and got to Brest within a day, but when Vittoria tracked down the harbourmaster, the news was worse. She returned to the chaise looking crestfallen.

'The harbourmaster say the *Elisabeth* sailed two days past and surely already rendezvoused with Prince Charles's ship.'

They looked at each other in shock. They were too late, the invasion party was bound for Scotland.

'He had other Jacobite story. He hear that a Sir Hector Munro sailed from Boulogne to Leith, and that this Scottish lord now in Edinburgh Castle jail.'

'Why did they jail him?' Isabella asked.

'He planned to find troops for Charles in the Scottish Islands.'

'Munro is a laird from Mull and his face is well known,' Bessie added. 'He was a fool to think a ship from France would attract no suspicion. Isabella, I think we must seek another route home. Spies may be watching us too.'

They took rooms in a boarding house. Later, Bessie went back to search for a passage from Brest to a port further north.

Vittoria was completely deflated.

'What will you do?' Isabella asked.

'I don't want go home with no good news and no progress for my ambitions.' Vittoria shook her head and sighed. 'After you leave, I go to Paris. I leave the miniatures at Scots College and maybe get some information to send for Henry.'

Bessie came back settled on a plan. 'The harbourmaster thinks he can get us a passage to Rotterdam in a few days. I travelled there from Edinburgh last time. There were many ships plying trade between there and the Forth Estuary, two female passengers travelling from the Low Countries will raise no suspicion.'

A few days later, Isabella and Vittoria went down to the quay to seek news of the passage to Rotterdam. They were talking to the harbourmaster, when a horrified look came across his face; they spun around and looked to sea. A ship coming into harbour seemed barely afloat, its sails in tatters and the deck smouldering. The ship sat very low in the water, as if it might sink at any minute. The harbourmaster shouted for help and several men joined him to run to their boats. Only when they were already heading towards the stricken ship did he call up to them:

'C'est l'Elisabeth!'

Vittoria and Isabella hung onto each other watching the drama unfold. Once the ship was towed in, soldiers and crew began to disembark. They brought off the wounded first, some of them strapped to stretchers. The sound of groaning men drifted towards them. Also the smell of death.

'Where's the other ship?' Isabella said quietly.

Vittoria only shook her head, she was ghostly pale. After the wounded and the few remaining crew disembarked, they brought the corpses wrapped in sailcloth. Finally a few naval officers, their heads down, many of them nursing injuries.

'I must find out what happened,' Vittoria said, 'but better you no involved. Go back to Bessie. I meet you there.'

Isabella explained the events to Bessie. When she admitted that they feared the prince's ship was lost, Bessie broke down in tears. After almost an hour, Vee finally returned.

'Is he dead?' Bessie blurted out.

'No,' Vee replied, but her expression was grave. 'There was the battle with the British, ships on both sides were badly damaged and the captain of the *Elisabeth* was killed.'

'And what of Prince Charles?' Bessie asked.

'He was in other small ship. They escaped and he went on to Scotland.'

'Thank the Lord,' Bessie said.

Yes, but he have almost no weapons and only seven men.'

'Dear God,' Bessie said, 'that's suicide.'

'I decided,' Vittoria said, 'I go to Scotland with you.'

Isabella smiled and grasped her friend's hand. She had longed to suggest this.

'What! Oh no, Vittoria, I cannot allow that. Anna would never forgive me.' Bessie was close to tears again.

Vittoria put her arm around Bessie's shoulders. 'Dear Bessie, I no go to fight, only to be a friend to Charles and get the news for Henry.'

Bessie shook Vee's arm off and went to her room.

Bessie muttered to herself. How in all earth had she got into such a mess? Last week, she was chasing a band of fools mounting an invasion sufficiently numbered to overcome a Scottish village. And now, the invaders comprised enough fighting men to storm a manse. It was madness, she'd let her love of Isabella get in the way of good sense. She'd even managed to lose her own heart to a worthless sailor along the way. Had she let Isabella's romantic nature infect her? Now she must endure her own disappointment, and find the words to deal with Vee and Issy. You need to get a grip on things, Bessie Nichol, or this will end in disaster.

Chapter Thirty-Nine

Rotterdam, The Netherlands, July 1745

Their boat from Brest to Rotterdam was a merchant vessel with the most basic accommodation. The discomfort was compounded by seasickness, and Vittoria suffered particularly badly.

Bessie was impressed by the girls' bravery, they'd never once complained on the voyage. Glancing at them again, she was glad to see colour coming back to their cheeks. She also noticed they sat much too close to each other. She sighed and directed the chaise to a Rotterdam café just before the hotel.

'Wait here for me. I'll go ahead and check they have vacancies.'

She returned after a few minutes. 'I've reserved us rooms. Let's eat here first. I'm sure you must both be hungry.'

Bessie waited until the waitress was out of earshot. 'I've ordered two rooms, one for me and a large room in the attic for you both. I saw it on my last visit and I'm sure you'll like it.'

Bessie saw their exchanged glance. She closed her eyes for a second, summoning the strength to have the conversation she'd so long avoided.

'Tonight there's cause for celebration. We're on the final leg of the journey and so far luck has been on our side. However...' she took a deep breath, 'you need to take more care, gossip spreads fast in Edinburgh and you could easily find yourselves the subject of scandal.'

'Don't worry, I be careful to hide my connection to the Stuarts.'

'Well, I'm mighty glad to hear that, Vittoria. The Stuart court may have given you a false notion of Scotland's attitude to the Jacobite Cause. There are those like me, who believe it just and true, but there are many who do not. Also an heir who minuets in silk shoes and plays the cello will not be to everyone's taste. Edinburgh folk can be narrow-minded, which brings me to my actual subject.' She hesitated, struggling to find the right words. 'You must learn to be less affectionate towards each other, otherwise strangers may misinterpret the nature of your relationship. There are people, particularly men with sordid minds, who would accuse you of depravity and look to have you punished.'

Vee immediately moved her leg from where it had been touching Isabella's.

'You met in unusual circumstances, it's no surprise you're confused over how to behave around each other. Now, I don't doubt your innocence, but some people are always looking for scandal. I strongly advise that this be your last night sharing a room and you must show a little more reserve around each other.'

They both gave her a small nod.

'Well, girls, forgive my bluntness and I'm sure I won't need to mention it again.' Bessie stood up. 'I'm quite exhausted and I'm going to have an early night. I'll see you tomorrow morning at nine.'

* * *

Bessie left them staring at each other in shock. After a few seconds they dissolved into hysterical laughter. It took them some time to pull themselves together.

'Why are we laughing? It's terrible,' Isabella said.

'We are the fools. Bessie never was.'

'We're going to have to change,' Issy added.

Vittoria's smile vanished. 'Yes.'

Hysterics were now replaced by gloom, they both stared at the tablecloth. Eventually, Vee's fingers stretched across to touch hers.

'Let's go. I believe we were given one last night.'

The landlady gave them a key and they climbed the four flights of stairs. Issy fully expected to emerge in a windowless attic. Instead, they walked into a huge, light-filled space, with two dormer windows and a large bed. Drawn to the windows, they found a view of steep pantiled rooftops and the canal below.

'It's like the top of the world,' Issy said.

They undressed quickly and for a long time simply clung to each other. Their love-making when it came, was slow and gentle. Then they spent the hours afterwards sharing childhood stories, glorying in the intimacy and privacy.

Dawn light woke them early. They washed and dressed back into their many respectable layers; placing pins and tying one another's ribbons with care.

'A pact.' Isabella held out her hand. 'The world is set against us, but we can outwit them if we do it together.'

Vee squeezed her fingers, then stepped back.

'France has been the dream, the kind of happiness I never thought to have and never forget.'

It was as if the air between them had dropped in temperature.

'We cannot behave like this in bedroom and hide it after. We couldn't even convince Bessy. We must stop this, Issy.'

Isabella could hardly say the words. 'You mean it's over?'

'I will always love you but we lose everything if we carry on.'

Her heart sped, desperate panic filled her chest. Surely Vee couldn't mean it?

'I value nothing but you. Why should we care what other people think?'

'Because we must. Your family will reject you if you bring scandal and I am on a mission for the Cause. We have to be above suspicion.'

Of course, the Cause. Issy experienced a twisting pain, Vee was deadly serious.

'But how can I manage without you? How can you even imagine you will?'

'You no without me,' Vee put her hand over her heart, 'nothing change in here.'

'It's impossible, I can't.'

'Not for ever, Bella. When we make money, when I make reputation with my art, we can have the house of our own. Old ladies together.'

'Old?' Issy's voice cracked.

'Maybe not so old. But not yet. In Edinburgh we must to learn to listen and watch without being known for what we are,' Vee said.

Isabella shook her head, she crossed her arms over her breasts. The candle of their love had been snuffed out, her grief was like the red hot core of the wick still smouldering.

Vittoria picked up her valise and reached for Isabella's hand.

'Come on, little Bella, you can do this.'

Isabella took her hand, it felt cool and dry. She saw a new expression in Vee's eyes, sadness but also something else. Like a soldier facing a battle, she was excited. Vee's hand held hers but her hopes had flown elsewhere.

. . .

Bessie had found a cargo ship bound for Leith. The weather was fine and Vittoria sat near her, but those few inches between them felt like miles. Issy stared out to sea, deep in thought. Vee had called her 'little Bella', was she immature? Was Vittoria behaving as the adult and thinking of her safety? She tried to cling to that conviction and block out the doubt that nibbled at her soul. Had the whole thing just been a passing fling for Vee?

They sailed up the Forth Estuary into Leith harbour after two days at sea. An impressive castle stood on a distant hill. Was this her final destination? Isabella had been running since Constantinople. Despite all the risks on the journey, she'd been in charge of her fate. In Scotland there might be yet another man who believed it his right to tell her what she may do. Isabella's heart felt crushed just when she was walking towards danger again. She daren't let heartbreak be the thing that defeated her.

Issy imagined a silver box lined with purple velvet. She pictured that she'd engraved the top with forget-me-nots, and placed inside her precious hopes for a life with Vittoria. She closed the imaginary lid on her overwhelming pain, shook her head and pulled back her shoulders. She must walk with her eyes wide open, any hope of a happy future depended on it. Bessie gave her an arm and an encouraging smile, reminding her she wasn't alone.

. . .

The houses they passed travelling into town reminded Isabella of Rotterdam, similarly tall and thin and with crow-stepped gables. Eventually, their carriage stopped beside an imposing turreted gatehouse. Bessie told them this was the Netherbow Gate, where a fee was required to enter the High Street. They found a boarding house with vacancies just inside the gate. They'd agreed that Bessie needed to go and visit her sister alone, and would introduce them later. She nodded her approval when Vittoria requested two single rooms.

Bessie saw people glance at Vittoria and Isabella walking along the quay and realised the impossibility of bringing them into her sister's home. Isabella had long ago given up treating her as a servant and they'd journeyed in harmony, but they were not equals. Anna and Vittoria were from an ordinary background, but their time around the royal court, set them apart. The girls planned to seek out Alan Chalmers' friends. Any new Edinburgh acquaintance would, by asking Bessie's address, immediately identify her as from the lower classes.

The problem also existed in reverse. Changing her accent had been a necessity and a natural consequence of being around ladies for years. But Bessie knew if she spoke in such tones to her sister, Agnes would be full of scorn. Putting on airs above your station was considered a great crime in her house, an attitude shared by many Scots. Bessie found herself annoyed at not to knowing how to speak in her own city, and furious at herself for being ashamed of her family.

She walked into the close below her family flat as she'd done a thousand times. The grime and smell of God knows what hit her like a blow. It was the stink of too many people crammed together, poor souls too exhausted to fret much about cleanliness or the disposal of human waste. Then rounding the corner she found a new culprit. There, at the foot of their stairwell, was a tethered goat.

Bessie opened the front door, still incensed by the encounter with the goat. Agnes looked up, she was obviously surprised to see her and Bessie thought her sister had aged at least ten years in the three she'd been gone. Bessie stepped forward to embrace Agnes, who struggled to get out of her chair. Bessie could smell she'd been drinking.

'Well here's a shurprise,' Agnes slurred, 'I thought ye'd no be bothered wi' yer auld sister any mair.'

'What nonsense, Agnes, it's lovely to see you. And it seems we've got a new neighbour. A goat! As if the close doesn't stink enough as it is.'

'It's no my goat and Mrs Cunningham downstairs, isnae a woman ye can argue with.'

'You could complain to the City Council surely? You can't have a goat living in the middle of a building.'

'You know fine well that folks aye kept animals on the stairs. Our ain faither had chickens.'

'There's a great deal of difference between a couple of caged hens and a nanny goat!'

'Aye well, Mistress Cunningham shares the milk and I'm right grateful for it.'

'But the close smells, Agnes!'

She glowered at Bessie. 'Are you trying to say that we smell? Don't you come back here wi yer fancy continental ideas and gie me orders, Bessie Nichol. Dae they no shit in Italy then?'

And so it went on, until they exhausted themselves. Bessie managed to claw back some peace, with gifts and a big enough pouch of money to buy a celebratory dinner. Bessie knew she wouldn't mention the goat again, but it settled the matter of bringing Isabella and Vittoria. That simply couldn't happen.

When they'd fed and drunk well, they settled down to sleep. Getting into the pull-out truckle bed proved more difficult than ever. Near eleven, when it finally began to get dark, she couldn't keep the question from the end of her tongue any longer.

'What's Alec doing these days?'

'He's apprenticed tae a cooper, making barrels in Newhaven. He'll be up on Sunday, ye'll see him then.'

Agnes had a son Bessie had adored from the moment she'd held him, and Agnes guarded him from her with a vengeance. When he was a baby, her sister seemed to expect Bessie to steal him from her. Even now he was an adult, Agnes accused Bessie of envy. And she was right. That jealousy was one of the many things that stood between them.

Chapter Forty

Edinburgh, Scotland

I sabella tapped on Vee's door. She answered in her petticoats and Issy longed to kiss her bare shoulders. She helped Vee put up her hair and pin on her bonnet.

Vee rested her hands on her shoulders and kissed her full on the mouth. 'Don't frown at me, Bella. We never manage chastity with no kisses. What do you want to do today?'

'Let's do some exploring,' Issy replied.

They walked up the hill towards the castle. Many people nodded and smiled. This was clearly not a city in which to go unnoticed. They paused to look down one of the many sets of precipitous steps that led off the main street. This one gave a splendid view to the Forth Estuary and the green hills beyond. Bessie had told them that these shady alleys were called closes, and Issy wondered which one was Bessie's.

Edinburgh made Isabella think of a sleeping dragon. The cobbled road was like its knobbly spine and the alleys off both sides like ribs. The castle atop the hill stood where the dragon's head should be, she could imagine it quivering to life and rearing in front of them. They stopped just short of the castle gates. It was a formidable fortress right on the edge of the city walls and steep cliffs fell off to both sides.

'He never take this,' Vee said under her breath.

'Do you think he's in Scotland?' Issy asked.

'If he is, he isn't discovered yet.'

They turned and walked back down the hill. Mr Chalmers had given an address for Isabella Lumisden in Writers' Court but they didn't find it on the walk down. They did locate the steep road leading to where Chambers had said they'd find the oyster cellar.

'What do you think?' Vittoria asked.

'Bessie advises we shouldn't go to the oyster bar alone,' Isabella replied.

'And maybe no wise to go directly to a Jacobite place,' Vee agreed.

'Then let's find Isabella Lumisden's home and leave her a note,' Issy replied.

The very next morning, Miss Lumisden sent a reply, declaring herself excited to meet them. She named an eating house and a time of six thirty.

When they walked in, a lady got to her feet and held out both hands to them. 'I'm so pleased to meet you and Robbie is coming in a few minutes. When he heard he was to be introduced to such well-travelled ladies, he insisted he'd leave work early.'

Issy took the offered hand. 'Isabella Godfrey and this is my friend Vittoria Bassi.'

'Pleased to meet you, Miss Lumisden,' Vittoria added.

'Please call me Bella. Only my parents use my full name and it will cause too much confusion to have two Isabellas.'

Issy daren't look at Vittoria. Her name was common

enough but she dreaded hearing Vittoria using Bella with anyone else.

Bella Lumisden was a dark-haired girl with large almond shaped eyes. She wasn't beautiful, but it seemed to Isabella that she filled the room with her presence. When Robbie came in, she hung onto his arm throughout the introductions. He looked at her with such naked adoration, it made her realise how she might have appeared looking at Vee.

'What do you think, Robbie, not just one lady from Rome but two!'

The girls curtseyed to Robbie Strange.

'I'm also an Isabella, but I'm often called Issy.'

'I am Vittoria Bassi, Vee for short.'

They all sat and Bella immediately bent her head towards them and whispered: 'Did you meet the princes in Rome? Are they as handsome as they say?'

Robbie tutted. 'Bella, for heaven's sake.'

She laughed and kissed his cheek.

'I have met them, and yes they are handsome,' Vee answered.

She clapped her hands in delight. 'I was sure of it. I have so many questions.'

Robbie put his hand on Bella's arm.

'Not here, Bella.'

She wrinkled her nose in frustration. 'Goodness, everybody knows what I think.'

'That is most certainly true,' he said drily, 'but our new friends may like to keep their opinions to themselves.'

Then he turned to the girls and changed the subject.

'Alan's letter said that one of you is an artist?'

'We are both artists, Isabella make beautiful jewellery. Look,' Vittoria held up her locket, setting it spinning on its silver chain.

'Are you a silversmith, Miss Godfrey?' Bella asked.

'In a small way,' Issy replied. 'I mostly make jewellery. But I believe Mr Chalmers meant Vittoria, she is an artist and was apprenticed to Jean-Etienne Liotard,' Issy added.

'You are so fortunate. I've just finished my apprenticeship with an engraver called Cooper, but an apprenticeship to a fine painter, that would be a grand thing,' Robbie answered.

'So girls may be 'prenticed in Italy? I like the sound of the place even more,' Bella interrupted.

'My circumstances were unusual,' Vee replied. 'I travelled to Constantinople with Liotard, this is where I met Issy.'

Isabella took her miniature from her neck to allow Vee to show it to Robbie Strange.

Vee clicked the mechanism to show her own face hidden behind Issy's.

'How charming, may I hold it?' Bella said. 'Oh, Miss Bassi, you must do one for me. I could have Robbie's handsome face inside.'

Then she flashed a mischievous smile.

'And perhaps a certain royal prince? I've heard some Jacobite supporters employ this trick.'

Vee blinked, then just smiled in reply.

'Bella! You're doing it again. Perhaps next time we could meet in the oyster cellar, where your favourite subject is less controversial.'

'Oh, yes, do let's. I'd love you both to meet my brother. He's out of town, but back the day after tomorrow, and we've planned an oyster supper. Will you join us?'

Isabella looked to Vee for her opinion, but she just shrugged.

'Is it a place we may go unchaperoned?'

'Well, that depends on your daring,' Bella replied and tapped Isabella's arm playfully with her fan. 'Do you ladies also have tyrannical fathers who try to curtail your freedom?'

'No. My father died ten years ago. Vee lost hers when she was twelve.'

Bella looked stricken.

'Goodness, I'm so sorry. I do talk too much.'

Vee shook her head and smiled. 'Don't worry, we be no so easy offended.'

'Good,' she said. 'We'll pick you up on Friday evening and walk together.'

After only three days in Edinburgh, Bessie was already wondering how soon she could leave. She and Agnes rubbed each other up the wrong way, but she couldn't move out without causing offence. Furthermore, she now saw that returning to Rome might be difficult. There was no word of Prince Charles in Scotland. He may have turned back or perished on the way. How strange it was, after a lifetime of longing for this, to find herself hoping he didn't come. Vittoria was bound to get caught up with his dangerous endeavours. Bessie might see Issy's affairs settled, only to find herself reluctant to abandon Vee. She could never go back to Anna and admit she'd left Vittoria in danger.

After a tortuous day helping Issy and Vee buy suitable shoes for the weather, Bessie dragged herself home. The letter in familiar handwriting was sitting there in the middle of the kitchen table. Her traitorous heart skipped. She had hoped she was over the whole affair but the pain was still raw. She so regretted giving Joseph her address. The first letter had arrived from Avignon before her but this one was posted in England. She dealt with it as before and was so intent on thrusting the poker through its centre to see the flames destroy it, that she didn't hear Agnes come in.

'That's the second letter ye've burnt. Whit's going on, Bessie?'

Bessie spun around, she felt her cheeks colouring. 'Clearly someone I don't wish to hear from.'

Agnes sat in her chair, her eyes glowing with curiosity. 'A man. I kent it! Must be that bosun ye wrote about. I thocht ye'd be making a fool ae yerself, the way ye talked about him.'

Bessie sank into her own chair. There would be no end to it now. 'Well you'll be pleased to be right then, and I'll not be mentioning it again.'

'Fancy you falling fer a sailor! Aifter all oor mother telt us!'

'And you're one to talk. You married a sailor.'

'Aye, and there was nae good came ae that. He was a mean bastard and he brought me nothing but trouble.'

If it was possible to nag a man to his grave, her sister might have done it.

'He brought you Alec.' It was out before Bessie could stop herself. Agnes knew how to rile her, and expose her weak spots.

'And you were aye jealous. Donald might have been a bastard, but at least he married me, unlike your fancy man.'

Oh, the weariness of reliving all the same old arguments.

'He was just a boy, Agnes. And it's such a long time ago.'

Chapter Forty One

Bella and Robbie arrived at Issy and Vee's lodgings as promised.

'I should warn you this oyster cellar is a coarse place, but it's full of friends,' Bella said.

At the foot of a steep hill off the Canongate, they entered a dark cellar with a vaulted ceiling. The faces of the people hunched over their plates of oysters were dramatically lit by tallow candles. Diners had discarded their shells onto the floor and by the noise level it seemed that many had been drinking for hours.

'Sorry to bring you to such a rough establishment, but I love the excitement of open Jacobite talk here. We have to be so careful in general,' Bella said.

'Is James not widely supported in Scotland?' Isabella asked.

'Supported? Yes. Widely? Well, only in some quarters, mainly Catholics and Episcopalians. My grandfather was an Episcopalian bishop. We feel too long put upon by the Kirk and by the English.' Then she put her hand over her mouth.

'Oh excuse me, I've done it again. I forgot you're English, and probably Church of England too.'

Issy shook her head and smiled. 'Don't worry. Although it's true I was born both. I converted to my Scottish mother's Catholicism three years ago.'

Bella gave Robbie a triumphant look. 'See, I knew it.'

Just then a young man walked in. He scanned the room until he spotted Bella, then raised his hand in greeting.

'That's my brother Andrew back from Perth,' she said.

He pulled a stool up, then placed his palms on the table and looked around the group. 'Are we amongst friends?'

'Great new friends,' Bella replied. 'Miss Godfrey and Miss Bassi, lately arrived from Rome. Vittoria worked at the Stuart court,' she added.

Andrew Lumisden smiled broadly.

'Then I can share the best possible news,' he leaned towards them, 'we've had a message from the Western Isles... he's here!'

News of the prince spread through the cellar like wildfire. Soon raucous toasts drowned out any possibility of speaking. Issy gave Vee's hand a squeeze. He'd made it to Scotland. That fact he'd come with only seven men was either unknown or irrelevant, it didn't dim the excitement around them. Robbie had great difficulty in persuading Bella it was time he took the three of them home.

'All right, Robbie, I'm coming, don't nag.'

Just before they exited from the narrow street, Robbie placed his hand on her shoulder. 'Now remember, Bella. It's meant to be a secret and it needn't fall to you to alert the council and the redcoats.'

'Well they'll know soon enough,' she said more quietly, 'when all the young men join his army.'

Bella took Robbie's arm and looked down to step over the drain. So it happened that only Isabella saw his troubled expression.

Two days later, Issy and Vee climbed a set of spiral stairs in Writers' Court to visit Bella. The stairs were too narrow for their skirts so Issy followed Vee's example in tucking one side of her hoops under an arm, thus tilting them onto the diagonal. Walking behind, Issy could see one of Vee's shapely legs all the way up to her stocking garter.

'That charming view is much too cruel,' Issy spoke Italian, a habit they kept for more privacy in crowded Edinburgh. 'I have the strongest urge to run my fingers up the inside of your lovely thigh, signorina.'

Vee turned and replied, 'For a convent girl you have terrible manners.' Her expression turned to horror and Issy heard a familiar voice in her ear.

'Oh you speak Italian! I do so want to learn.'

Isabella spun around.

'Sorry, I didn't mean to make you jump,' Bella added. 'I went out for some shortbread to go with our tea.'

On Bella's landing, they let her past to open the door. Vee shot Issy a wide-eyed look, Bella must have heard.

Once inside they removed their gloves and placed them with their bonnets on the hall table. Issy clasped her hands together to still her shaking fingers.

'Perhaps you could teach me some Italian?' Bella asked, checking her hair in the hall mirror. 'I'd love to be able to speak to him in his own language.'

No one felt the need to ask who 'he' was. She turned and smiled at them both. Issy couldn't see anything unusual in her expression.

'Of course,' Vittoria replied. 'Do you have some basics already?'

'Not a word. I'm a lazy student, even my French is not that good. But the wish to please him would make me diligent.'

Isabella's sigh of relief came out as a kind of shudder. She'd been careless and very lucky.

'Are you cold, Issy? I'm sorry, the weather has been just terrible this week. Come in and get some tea,' Bella said.

The apartment took up the whole of this fourth floor. It looked over the High Street at the front, but Bella led them to a room at the back. This small parlour was surprisingly quiet and with a northerly view across the loch to the Forth, and Fife beyond. Ten minutes later Robbie arrived chaperoned by Bella's brother. Bella asked to see Issy's locket again. 'I'd love one of these secret lockets,' she said.

'I swear one day I'll have the funds to buy you nice things, Bella,' Robbie said.

Bella took his hands and kissed him tenderly on the cheek. 'The best present you can give me doesn't require funds. If I ask Mama for the locket as a family gift, could you paint me your own portrait?'

He beamed at her.

'If Vittoria can teach me. Mr Cooper says my portraiture skills are adequate, but I've little experience of working with miniatures or enamel.'

Robbie flicked the locket open to Vee's painting. 'What about the second portrait?'

Bella looked to Vittoria. 'I wondered, since you know him, could you do me one of Prince Charles, Vee? I'll have Robbie proudly in the front, and I hope that my Stuart allegiance need not be a secret in days to come.'

Vittoria had told Issy she'd to keep the closeness of her ties to the Stuart court a secret. Vee hoped to get more useful information for Prince Henry by hiding his involvement in her journey.

'I believe I could manage a likeness,' Vee replied. 'I brought some spare copper portrait backs from Rome, and Isabella could make the locket if she had access to the materials.'

'I have another suggestion, but you must feel free to say no,' Andrew said. 'It entails a certain amount of risk.'

Vee nodded.

'It is my opinion that there are many ladies and gentlemen in Scotland who would pay for a trinket with a Jacobite connection, if you feel confident to undertake royal portraits.' He paused. 'Charles is going to need to raise funds. If I promise to do my upmost to keep your identity a secret, might you work on making these to order? We'd have to work with a local silversmith to get his mark and of course you'd be properly paid for your work.'

Vee looked apologetically towards Issy.

'I could make portraits for snuffboxes as well as lockets. But I have no studio and very few materials and I'd need a small oven for firing the enamel.'

'I'm sure we could organise what you need and if Robbie masters miniatures he might work beside you?'

He looked to Robbie.

'If Vittoria will help me learn, I'd love to be involved,' Robbie answered.

'What a splendid idea!' Bella said. She turned to beam at Vee and Issy. 'He's very talented. I'm so proud of him.'

It took little persuasion to get Robbie to open his portfolio. Bella wasn't exaggerating, his engravings were superb and the art he did in his spare time was almost as good as Vee's.

While they flicked through Robbie's work, Andrew picked up Issy's locket. He opened first to Issy's likeness then Vee's. Isabella felt he looked at her curiously.

'Give me a list of the items you need, Miss Bassi,' Lumisden said. 'In terms of the silver, I know a trusted Jacobite silversmith, his name is Oliphant and his family live near Perth. I've been at Gask this week and his cousin the laird is already planning to go and pledge his allegiance to the prince. I might arrange a private meeting there.'

'Isabella has a plan to visit Perth,' Vittoria interjected, 'her mother's family lived near there.'

Lumisden stared at Issy, snapped the locket closed and handed it back. 'That journey might provide a cover for Miss Bassi travelling north.'

Vittoria helped Isabella out of her stays that night.

'This chance to paint for Andrew and his friends could be the good opportunity I've been waiting for, but I am sorry he won't use your silver work.'

'Silversmiths must be recognised by the guild, it's the usual system.' And, she thought, are always men.

'Goodnight, Bella. Sleep well.'

Issy saw the excitement in Vee's eyes. Jealousy added a new layer to her pain.

Chapter Forty Two

They set off for Perth a week later. Bessie had decided to come with them as chaperone.

It was the first time Issy had the chance to admire the beautiful Scottish countryside, but within a few hours rain obscured the view. It got so bad they urged Andrew to tie his horse alongside and come in the coach. Issy slept for several hours but was wakened by Bessie's snores. She wondered how Lumisden could sleep through it. The warmth of Vittoria's leg against hers was delicious. Vee had her cloak hood up against the draught, the coach was gloomy but Issy could make out the curve of her cheek at the place where her long eyelashes rested. Vee's eyes opened, she turned and smiled at her.

'I love you,' Issy mouthed silently.

Vittoria closed her eyes again, still smiling.

Isabella faced forward to find Andrew Lumisden staring directly at her. He held her gaze for a second, then turned towards the window. She swallowed the fear driven flood of saliva in her mouth. Had he seen her?

Bessie stirred and looked out the window. 'We're coming into Stirling now.'

The rain had stopped. Fog hung over the river and grassy plain beyond. Stirling also had a large castle, today it sat on its rocky outcrop, as if floating on the mist.

'Goodness, the Scots build fierce looking castles,' Isabella said. 'They must have faced some dangerous enemies.'

'Aye,' Andrew Lumisden said. 'That would be the English.'

They overnighted in Stirling to rest the horses. Andrew announced he had some business to attend to and would meet them again in the morning. Isabella daren't look at him, but imagined she could sense his gaze. She felt sick.

Vittoria suggested they go up to the castle to take in the view. Bessie declared herself too stiff from the journey for such a climb.

The mist had gone and they could see the whole valley from the castle esplanade. A rainbow arced over the distant, wooded hills.

'We're in trouble,' Issy said.

'Why?' Vee replied.

I think Andrew saw me say 'I love you'. When I faced forwards he was staring at me.

'Most likely he was just admiring your pretty face,' Vee replied and kissed her on the cheek.

'Vee!' Isabella admonished.

'There's no one to see us but birds up here, Bella. Anyway, we are the good friends, to be cold and distant look more suspicious.'

Isabella wasn't reassured. She'd seen distaste in Andrew Lumisden's eyes.

· · ·

The next morning Lumisden joined them for breakfast and Isabella found nothing unusual in his demeanour. They drove out of the town gate and over an arched stone bridge. This was the Forth crossing. It was hard to believe this small river was almost ten miles wide downstream in Leith.

The countryside was heavily wooded. Where the road narrowed the trees made a canopy over them. The sun shining through the branches revealed the astonishing variety of nature's greens. Isabella had expected Scotland to be similar to England but simply colder. In fact there was a different atmosphere, a sense of wildness. Men corralled the forests and fields around London, here mankind seemed to cling to the edges of nature. Passing through a dense, gloomy forest, the wheels crushed pine needles, filling the carriage with a strong scent. Isabella sucked in a breath, clean and fresh. Scotland grew on her more and more.

They reached Perth's Salutation Inn late in the afternoon. Lumisden's friends would join them for supper. Bessie and Isabella planned to search for her family the next day. Bessie had insisted on travelling as Isabella's lady's maid and refused to eat with them.

Lumisden entered the private dining room with a young man. He had the upright stance of a soldier and wore his own brown wavy hair tied back at the nape of his neck.

'Ladies, may I introduce you to Laurence the Younger of Gask. Laurence, this is Miss Vittoria Bassi and her English friend Miss Isabella Godfrey. Miss Bassi is the painter I told you about.'

The man threw his head back and laughed.

'Lumisden, you dog! You omitted to tell me that the miniaturist was a beautiful lady!'

He bowed.

'I'm delighted to meet you both.'

Just then the door opened again.

'Ebenezer, perfect timing, may I introduce Misses Bassi and Godfrey. It turns out the talented Italian painter is a lady! Lumisden thought it amusing not to tell me.'

Ebenezer Oliphant was smaller than his cousin and had a pronounced limp. He bowed. 'I'm pleased to meet you both.' He turned to Vittoria. 'I confess I subjected Lumisden to such a torrent of questions, that I uncovered the truth of your fair sex. If you're as good as he says, it's a wonder I've not heard of you.'

Vittoria curtsied. 'I am very flattered by Mr Lumisden's good opinion. And you know how it is with miniaturists, we copy the artist and stay in his shadow.'

'Tell me, are there many female painters in Rome?' Laurence of Gask asked.

'Not at present, but the King does have portraits by female artists in his collection. Including Rosalba Carriera of course,' Vee replied.

'And do you aspire to be a famous artist like Rosalba, Miss Bassi?' Ebenezer said.

'One day, I hope. Now I am making perfect my miniature skills, this is how Rosalba trained too. I hope my talents might be useful here.'

'Excellent idea,' Ebenezer said. 'I can supply the boxes and lockets, and I agree with Lumisden, there's certainly a market. Requiring upmost discretion of course.'

'Of course,' Lumisden replied, looking directly at Isabella.

Goodness, he doesn't trust me, Isabella thought to herself.

At supper the Oliphant cousins had lots of questions for Vittoria and she was kept talking. Andrew Lumisden sat in long silence beside Isabella. Issy jumped, when he suddenly addressed her.

'Where did you say your family live?' he asked.

'I didn't,' Isabella replied, 'because I don't exactly know. I visited my grandmother only once, when I was four. I believe she died soon after.'

'And that was in Perth?' he asked.

'Stobhall Castle near Perth. My grandmother was a distant cousin and lady-in-waiting to Lady Jane Gordon, Duchess of Perth.'

For the first time, Isabella saw a flicker of approval from Andrew Lumisden.

'You're related to the Huntly Gordons?'

'Only loosely.'

'And you think your grandmother has left kin in Perthshire?'

'I honestly don't know, but Stobhall and the Duchess of Perth are my starting points. I thought I'd visit.'

'Well it's some way north of Perth, but on the Tay, so you won't find it difficult to find. The inn will find you a chaise.'

'I'll ask them. Is the duchess still alive?'

'Very much alive and a powerful lady in Jacobite circles. But you won't find her at Stobhall. She owns it, but lives at Drummond Castle with her sons.'

'Oh,' she replied. Isabella hadn't considered the idea of multiple castles. 'Well, someone on the staff might know.'

'Perhaps,' he replied.

Chapter Forty-Three

Andrew Lumisden had lots of questions for Isabella at breakfast. Where was she born? How did she come to be in Constantinople? She was vague about Constantinople and avoided all detail about her family, except saying that her father had been a jeweller in London. She also said nothing about Everard Fawkener. The Edinburgh newspapers had recently described Sir Everard as one of the Duke of Cumberland's close cohort. She felt awkward about his association with the King's son and she was certain Lumisden would be appalled.

Vittoria and Lumisden set off to visit the Oliphants at House of Gask and she and Bessie went north.

'This may be a pointless journey, Andrew Lumisden told me the duchess doesn't live at Stobhall,' Issy said, then lowered her voice. 'Anyway, I'm glad to be away from Lumisden, I sense he distrusts me.'

'There are many Scots who distrust the English as a starting position.' Bessie shook her head ruefully. 'Damned cheek, considering the personal risk you've been taking for his precious Cause.'

Isabella didn't admit fearing Lumisden's distrust was based on more than her nationality. Bessie had specifically warned them and she was embarrassed by her carelessness.

'This is a beautiful area,' Bessie said. 'What do you remember of when you came before?'

'Hardly anything,' Isabella replied. 'I had no idea it was this far out of Perth.'

'Well, in the country everyone knows everyone else. If you have family near here, people will know.'

Their driver turned onto a long tree-lined drive. He pulled up beside a group of handsome, grey stone buildings.

'That's it! That's Stobhall, I remember the church now, and the little tower.'

'What a bonnie place,' Bessie said.

They walked to where the River Tay tumbled over rocks in the gorge below.

'I'll go round to the kitchen. If there's anyone home we'll find them there,' Bessie said.

Issy found herself drawn down past the side of the house to the garden. She remembered she'd thought it a magical place. She now knew the formal beds, with dark green trees, clipped into geometric shapes was called topiary.

'Can I help you, young lady?'

Issy turned to face an older woman with an upright stance and authoritative voice. Bessie came bustling around the corner.

'Isabella, you're in luck, the cook says the duchess is... Oh.' Bessie dropped into a curtsey. Remembering her manners, Isabella did the same.

'Yes,' the woman said. 'The Duchess of Perth is here. And who might I ask are you, and why are you in my garden?' The words were challenging, but Lady Jane Gordon's tone was kind. 'You don't look like a burglar or poacher,' she added.

'I'm so sorry, forgive me. But when I saw the house it all

came back to me. I've been here before as a little girl. My grandmother was your lady-in-waiting, Mary Gordon. My mother brought me back here to be baptised.'

Realisation dawned on the Duchess of Perth's face.

'Are you Charlotte's daughter? Is that possible? Why it seems only yesterday that she was your age. How is the dear girl?'

'I'm sorry, she...' Issy hesitated, unable to say the words.

Lady Gordon's face fell. 'No. How awful. But please come inside...'

'Isabella. My name is Isabella Godfrey. And this is Elisabeth Nichol, my...'

'Her lady's maid, Your Ladyship,' Bessie replied, with another curtsey.

'Isabella! That was Mary's mother's name. How charming, and you look just like her too, a proper Huntly Gordon.'

At that she turned and headed towards the house. Issy stared at her back. 'I look like my great-grandmother?'

The duchess seemed not to hear her. They followed her to the house.

Lady Gordon's wet boots left damp footprints. She sat on a bench beside the door to remove them and smiled in response at their perplexed expressions.

'I have a party arriving for dinner and my ghillie catches the best salmon in Scotland at Stobhall. Once I'm beside the river, I cannot resist trying a few casts. Not very ladylike I know, but my dear father taught me and I like to keep my hand in.' She looked down at her wet woollen stockings. 'Clearly out of practice though, I'd not intended to soak my feet.' Then she laughed loudly and walked into the house.

Bessie and Isabella spent an hour with Lady Gordon. They learned that Isabella's grandmother had been an only child and that she didn't know of any living relatives in that branch of the Gordon clan.

'I knew dear Mary and her mother Isabella only slightly when Isabella asked me to take Mary into service. Mary's husband had died and they'd fallen onto hard times. Little Charlotte, your mother, she was a lovely child.' She shook her head. 'I can't believe it. How did she...?'

'Consumption,' Isabella replied.

Lady Gordon's expression was full of sympathy. 'I'm so sorry. That would have broken poor Mary's heart entirely, good she never knew.' She paused deep in thought. 'Tell me, Isabella, was your mother's life happy? She took such a risk marrying your father against everyone's advice. And having to give up her faith too.' She shook her head sadly.

Isabella smiled. 'I'm told my parents had a very happy marriage. Sadly, Mama died not long after my baby brother and my father was heartbroken. He died too, when I was eight.' Isabella looked around the room. 'I know Mama wished to bring Edward here to be baptised, but she daren't risk the journey, he was born early and never strong.'

'I'm sorry to hear that,' the Duchess replied. 'I remember your baptism day, it so pleased your grandmother. Excuse me, I'm sure you think us Catholics superstitious.'

'My baptism was a godsend. It helped me gain sanctuary in a Rome convent for a short time.'

Lady Gordon looked at her incredulously. 'Did you convert?'

Isabella nodded.

'You seem to have faced a great deal of sorrow for one so young. But your conversion is excellent news. Your grandmother will be smiling down on us now.' Then she stood up. 'I wish I could spend longer with you, but as I said, I'm expecting guests. Would you like to visit the chapel before you go?'

'Thank you. I'd love to.'

The small chapel with a crow-stepped gable was built in

the same grey stone as the house. Inside the door Issy knew to look up. She heard Bessie sigh in admiration of the painted ceiling. Sun streamed colour onto the white-clothed altar table through the stained glass window behind. They all knelt in front of the altar. Issy prayed for her mother and grandmother.

The duchess murmured: 'And finally, Lord, we ask you to guide our rightful heir and give your people freedom to worship again.' The Duchess looked towards Issy as she rose to her feet and Issy nodded. 'I'm so glad to know you're with us, Isabella,' she said, grasping her hand. 'Now I really must go, but do please come and see me at Drummond Castle. All my time is spent on Drummond family business since James died. I expected to be resident here in the Dower House long ago, but my sons show no sign of marrying. Now that Charles Stuart is on his way,' she shrugged, 'well the boys need good counsel.' She smiled. 'In the meantime, do let me know if you need anything, you are a Gordon, even if our kinship is distant. I'd hate to think of you with no one. That is so very hard.'

'Thank you, Lady Gordon...' Isabella said and hesitated. 'I have one last question. You said I resembled my great-grandmother. My mother was so fair. I'd always believed I was like my father's side.'

'Oh no. You're a Huntly Gordon, no mistaking it. Your grandfather was fair and dear Charlotte looked like him. Mary's mother was dark haired and well built. Made of strong stuff. Just like me.' She laughed, then walked towards the door. 'Please call me Lady Jean, I prefer the Scots version of my name.'

Bessie and Isabella went back to their carriage and the duchess waved them off.

'I must say, Isabella. You have a habit of mixing with the high and mighty. First the Stuart Prince and now the Duchess of Perth. Wait till I tell my sister,' Bessie said. Then under her breath: 'Or perhaps not. I'd never hear the end of it, she thinks me above myself as it is.'

Isabella closed her eyes. Everything had fallen into place, she'd been right to come. No family to care about her but no man to interfere. The news that she resembled her maternal great-grandmother pleased her enormously. A Huntly Gordon, a strong line of women. For the first time as an adult, she felt completely comfortable in her own skin.

That evening Vittoria didn't return to the inn. The receptionist said someone had come from Gask for her bag and cancelled her room. Bessie didn't seem worried but Isabella felt a shiver of apprehension. Why would Vee go without leaving a message?

Chapter Forty-Four

Isabella was waiting for Lumisden in reception. He'd met them at breakfast and informed them that Vittoria was staying on at Gask. He said the Oliphants had offered to get an oven for her enamels and a place to paint with no distractions. That word stayed in Issy's head, 'distraction'. Was she the distraction?

She'd voiced her concern to Bessie.

'It may be that you're right but you needn't take it as meaning much. The Cause is their obsession. They've seized on Vittoria as being useful. You are not.'

Just then, Andrew Lumisden came down the stairs. 'Are you ready to go?'

'Yes,' Isabella replied.

'I'll go and settle my bill, then we'll be off,' he said.

Isabella and Vee hadn't been apart for months, the thought of leaving her made Issy feel physically ill.

Then, a small chaise stopped outside and Vittoria swept into reception like a brightly coloured bird in flight. She grabbed Issy's hand and dragged her into the snug.

'I'm so glad to see you! Will you really not come with us?'

Vittoria's smile disappeared. 'I wrote you the note, but I see that Lumisden forget it last night, so I came to catch you. Forgive me, my Bella, I have much work to do here. I promise I'll work hard and be back in Edinburgh soon.'

'I'll miss you,' Issy said.

'Me too. But, Bella, they take me seriously, talk to me like a painter even in my skirts. I think I maybe do good from this venture.'

Vee's face shone with excitement. Was she really sad to stay?

Vittoria produced a note from her dress folds. 'I nearly forget. Ask Bessie to write my mother and add this post-script.' Issy nodded. As Vee pushed the note through into the gap in Issy's skirts into her pocket, she rubbed Issy's petticoat fabric against her moist skin, making Isabella gasp.

'Look after this treasure, stroke her often.'

At the sound of approaching footsteps, Vittoria went to the door. Andrew Lumisden nearly knocked her over. 'Miss Bassi, I didn't expect you here.'

'I came to town for art materials and see the carriage still here. Have the good journey,' she called back with a cheerful wave, as she strode out of the building.

'She walks in an unusually brisk manner for a girl,' Andrew Lumisden said.

'She does,' Isabella replied.

Vee hadn't even asked what had happened at Stobhall.

The coach sped through Perthshire. It had rained overnight. Issy inhaled the smell of wet leaves and damp earth, a quintessentially Scottish scent. This was a country where things took root and grew. She was struck by an unexpected sensation of belonging. Might this be a place to call home?

'What's your plan now, Issy?' Bessie asked. 'Will you go back to Rome?'

'I was thinking I might stay here longer. It seems women might live here without interference from men.'

Bessie grimaced. 'I'm not sure many Scottish women would say that's their experience, Issy. It's a country run by men, just like England.'

'Well I like the feel of Scotland and it seems Vee will stay longer. I might look into making and selling jewellery here.'

Issy pondered it for the rest of the journey. Going back to Rome wouldn't work if she wanted to live with Vee. She loved Anna and Bessie but they'd never manage to be relaxed under their constant scrutiny. Issy would have to be patient and allow Vee's adventure to run its course. If Vittoria's art was appreciated here, she might decide to stay. Why not explore whether she could find her own success in Scotland?

* * *

Bessie trudged up the hill. She was exhausted from the journey and ready to sleep, but she'd have to endure Agnes's sharp tongue first. She loved her sister but they both loathed their mutual dependency. Perhaps if they had been three, things would have been different. Agnes's twin sister was still-born. Agnes herself had survived, but with a bad chest and a disabling deformation of the spine. Her mother had used all her energy to keep Agnes alive, and the childhood notion that she'd favoured Agnes had festered inside Bessie. It was not a Christian thought and Bessie was ashamed of it. Agnes had every right to be jealous of her straight back and her freedom to be out in the world. When Agnes's husband's death had precluded his likely desertion, Bessie had resolved to provide for her. It's what her mother would have wanted and poor Agnes had nothing. Except of course, Alec.

Bessie mounted the worn stone steps to their home. She took a deep breath before she turned the handle, then another when she found a lovely surprise inside. 'Alec!'

'Auntie Bessie!' He enveloped her in a hug. That spindly red-haired boy, who was all elbows and knees, had grown into a giant of a man.

She heard herself laugh and knew it sounded too joyous. She caught Agnes's glower as he set her down.

'I thought to see you Sunday past?'

'Aye well, I usually visit Sundays, but there was overtime late in to Saturday. I came today when I heard you were hame.'

'You're lucky to catch me. I've been up Perth way for the last few days.'

'So I just heard. I've some money on me, let's go to Mrs Clark's tavern for supper. I'll buy the ale and you can tell us all aboot it.'

'I'll just bide here, ye'll no want an auld cripple spoiling yer party.'

Alec laughed, he always treated his mother's sourness as if it were an act. 'Ye'll do no such thing, I'll gie ye a piggy-back doon the stairs if I have tae.'

And so of course Agnes found she could manage the stairs and the three of them walked down the Fleshmarket Close steps to the tavern.

After supper Alec fired dozens of questions at Bessie about Constantinople and Rome. She sensed her sister's eyes on her when she admitted she'd seen both James and Henry Stuart.

'Was there any more news in Perth? I hear they expect him to go there first,' Alec asked.

'Nothing definite,' Bessie replied. 'But Vittoria, the artist girl I told you about, is with the Oliphants at Gask and the laird there is sure to be in the thick of things.'

'I'd love tae meet your Rome ladies. But maybe we're no awfy suitable company fer such like them?'

Alec said it in a joking manner, but Bessie felt a blush reach her ears.

'They'd like to meet you too. Are you off Sunday coming?'

'Aye,' he answered.

'Then I'll ask them to meet us all here to sup.'

'Ashamed tae have them in the hoose are ye?' Agnes said with a glare.

'Would you like me to invite them to the house?' Bessie replied.

'No.'

'Well then. Anyway, it might just be Isabella, I'm not sure when Vittoria will return.'

'Well,' Alec said, setting down his empty tankard. 'If you like them then I'm sure they're nice lassies. I'll need tae be heading back tae Newhaven. Dae ye need a hand up the stairs, Mam?'

'No, you get off. I'll manage if Bessie lends me her airm.'

Agnes smiled at him. That boy has a countenance that could un-curdle milk, Bessie thought to herself.

Back at their flat it was beginning to get dark, Bessie lit the lantern with a taper from the range, then noticed the letter lying on the table. She spun around to face Agnes.

'You opened my letter!'

Agnes shrugged. 'You would've flung it in the fire and there's precious little interesting mail comes tae this hoose. What difference does it make? I left it fer ye.'

Bessie was speechless at her cheek. She held the letter near the lantern, to know what Agnes had read.

6ᵗʰ August 1745
Portsmouth

Dear Bessie

I'm beside myself with Worry, getting no Reply to my last Letters.

I should have carried you bodily onboard the Ship. Although it didn't turn out to be a safe Haven either. I cannot bear to think you came to some Harm on your Travels.

The Ship sails next Week, so if you get this Letter, please reply by Return.

Yours
Joseph Grimes

What did he mean saying his ship wasn't safe? Today was the thirteenth, even if she replied he'd be gone. From the tone of the letter he obviously didn't know what she'd heard.

'Seems he cares fer ye yet. Why dae ye no want his letters? Maybe all this hob-nobbing wi' gentry has gone tae yer heid. He no good enough fer ye?'

Bessie sighed. 'Agnes, I don't want to talk about it.'

Her sister harrumphed and was quiet for a bit. 'So, see anything interesting in Perth?'

Bessie was about to make a sharp reply, but she'd heard the curiosity in her sister's voice. Poor Agnes spent most of her days in this cramped room, she should be more patient. 'Stobhall Castle, oh, Agnes it was bonnie. Come sit beside me and I'll tell you about it.'

Bessie pulled the two chairs together and put a shawl around Agnes's shoulders. They were tied together in a mesh of old jealousies and resentments but also love. It was a net too complicated to untangle.

Chapter Forty-Five

Bessie stepped out of the close. The cobbles steamed, rain overnight had been replaced with a fine morning. She planned to fetch some bread then go to help Isabella. A familiar face made her stop dead. 'Joseph?'

His expression changed from anxious searching, to a look of joy that made her heart swell. 'Bessie Nichol, you are a sight to gladden an old sailor's eyes.'

'You've come all this way?'

'You had me witless with worry. And also,' he hesitated, 'well I've some bad news.'

Her brain reeled, searching for possibilities. She could only think of one.

'Not Freddy?'

She got the answer from his face and felt herself pitch forwards. Joseph reached out to catch her, both his forearms were red with raised angry scars.

'I'm an old fool to be bringing such news to you on the street. Is there somewhere we can go?'

'Yes, of course,' as they stepped into their close, she covered her mouth to stifle a wail.

'Come now, Bessie, lean on me.'

She stumbled up the stairs.

'Come in, Joseph. This is my sister Agnes. Agnes, this is Joseph Grimes.'

He lowered Bessie into her chair. 'Have ye a bit of brandy in the house, mistress? Poor Bessie's had a terrible shock.'

'Brandy no,' Agnes stuck her hand in the cupboard at her elbow. 'Would a drop ae gin do?'

He nodded.

The rough alcohol made Bessie cough.

'What happened?' Bessie asked, once she'd gathered herself.

'We had some action from the Spanish,' Joseph replied, shaking his head sorrowfully.

'I didn't want to tell you such a tale in a letter. But Bessie, why did you not answer? Did you get none of my notes?'

Bessie glanced at Agnes, who had her mouth open. She suddenly seemed to realise that Joseph still stood. 'Here, sir. Take a seat.' Agnes gestured to her own chair, the only other in the small room. 'I'll away and fetch the bread,' she said, then grabbed her shawl and hobbled out.

Bessie waited until Agnes closed the door.

'I thought it better to put some distance between us, Joseph. But I never thought about you needing to give me such news. What happened?'

Joseph looked perplexed, but answered the question.

'We took enemy fire from the Spanish off Gibraltar. Freddy was at his gun, it took a direct hit, then there was a fire.'

Bessie fell to crying again. 'Burned to death, oh, Joseph.'

He knelt in front of her, wrapping her in his arms. 'No, Bessie, he was killed instantly, he knew nothing of it.'

His strong grip was comforting, she touched his scarred arm. 'You were hurt.'

'Aye, but we put the fire out and saved the ship.'

Bessie was struck by the certain knowledge that the life of this man was important to her.

'Poor Freddy.'

'I went to his mother,' Joseph said. 'I told her he died doing his job well and without any suffering. It is what I always say, but it's not often the truth.'

'And his poor mother.'

'Hush now, Bessie.'

She was aware of Joseph's crooning as he rocked her, and his kisses in her hair where it had escaped from her cap. She pushed him away. 'No, Joseph, this is not right.'

He looked terribly wounded.

'I appreciate you coming to tell me, and all this way too, but well, Mistress Grimes...'

His face broke into a stupid grin. She bristled. How dare he laugh at her! She shook off his arm. 'No, really. I insist, Bosun Grimes.'

'Ah yes. The Portsmouth boys think it's very funny that Mistress Grimes is reputed to wear the trousers in my house.'

Bessie glared at him.

'It's not true, Bessie, but it suits us both for folks to think so. She's had a hard enough life.'

She was outraged by his smile.

'Bessie! You didn't think? I'm such an idiot, of course!'

She was ready to slap the ridiculous grin off his face. Maybe sensing his perilous situation, he grabbed both her hands.

'Nellie Grimes is my sister. She's kept house for me since her fiancé died.'

She stared at him stupidly for a second, she saw he struggled not to smile. They leaned into each other's shoulders, helpless with hysterical laughter. Bessie realised she was still crying. Tears of sorrow and joy too.

Agnes came in with the bread. She looked at them as if they'd lost their minds.

'Excuse us, mistress.' Joseph groaned and clambered to his feet. 'My knees! I'm too old to be kneeling before a lady.'

'Goodness,' Agnes said, starting to turn away.

'No need to go, Agnes,' Bessie said.

Joseph looked suddenly serious.

'I have to catch the stage soon, Bessie, I'm expected back at the ship. I came last night but you weren't home.'

She grasped his hand to rise out of her chair. 'I'm so glad you came, Joseph, you've no idea. I'll walk you down the road.'

He gave Agnes a small bow. 'Nice to have met you, mistress.'

Bessie thought she'd never seen Agnes this speechless. As they were about to leave Bessie stopped. 'Are there any ships in Portsmouth bound for Italy, Joseph? I have a letter ready for Anna and I hear many of the mail packets fall foul of the French.'

'The rumour is we're wanted in British waters, but I'll surely find a frigate bound for Leghorn or Naples.'

Bessie put some wax on the range and fetched her letter. She scanned it to make sure she'd added Vittoria's words accurately:

Edinburgh, 14th August

Dearest Anna

Please excuse my Tardiness in not writing for a few Weeks. Life continues as before, Isabella and Vittoria have been making Friends and Vee has started painting again. We had a Trip North to the Perth Area last Week to visit Isabella's Mother's Birthplace. Isabella has found no close Relatives, but is dealing with the Disappointment well.

Since Vee is lingering here, I know you'll approve of me staying on longer. Both girls have taken some adjusting to the plainer Fare in Scotland. They enjoy our Oysters but I cannot convince them that Oats are for Human consumption!

My Sister is feeling a little better and she returns your good Wishes.

Much love Bessie

P.S. Vee has heard that Carluccio has no Plans to come East. The Reports of only seven Men are nonsense. He is quite inundated with French Friends. Nevertheless it's expected he will give up and go Home.

Bessie flicked her eyes to the ceiling with a prayer that carrying this note would cause Joseph no trouble. She dropped the wax onto the fold. Since she had no seal, she pressed it closed with the end of the wooden porridge spurtle, which had a thistle carved into it. She thought Anna would like the look of it.

Joseph put her letter in his pocket and patted it. They took their leave of Agnes and went down into the street.

'I'll choose a good safe pair of hands and a sturdy vessel

for your letter, Bessie. I venture young Vittoria must be back in Rome by now?'

'No. Actually she decided to carry on with us,' she replied.

'Really? Well that must be a great comfort to Isabella to have you both by her side,' he said and pulled her arm in closer.

She smiled. 'I've missed you, Joseph Grimes. I wish you had longer.'

His smile crinkled his eyes in those places where the sun had left white lines. 'I'm also sorry, but I'm right glad I found you and that we're friends again. Would you welcome me for longer, Mistress Nichol, if our ship stays in these waters?'

'I would, Bosun Grimes.'

She looked up at him, the surge of happiness was dizzying.

'Where does your coach leave from?' she asked.

'John Somerville Stables on the Canon's Gait.'

'Then I'll walk you to the Netherbow,' she replied.

Isabella was waiting for Bessie. They were going to look for new accommodation, somewhere with more light for making earrings. She'd chosen a sober business-like dress but she needed help with the stays which was very frustrating. She wondered how Vittoria was managing in House of Gask. The thought of some pretty maid's fingers lingering on Vee's body, was twisting her heart.

Isabella flung open the window to watch for Bessie. The lovely weather made her anxious to get out. She leaned on the windowsill, watching the huge crowd of people in the street below. Issy recognised Bessie's familiar figure and was astonished to see she was arm-in-arm with a man. He turned to smile at Bessie and she recognised him.

'Well, well, Joseph Grimes,' she said aloud. She was about

to shout out to Bessie when she remembered her state of undress. She would just have to wait.

Twenty minutes later, Bessie arrived with delicious smelling bread and a happy expression Isabella hadn't seen since Genoa.

'I saw you from the window. Was that Bosun Grimes?'

Bessie smiled. 'Yes, he's leaving on a stage within the hour.'

'He came all that way for such a short visit?'

Bessie's happy expression vanished.

'He was here yesterday but we missed each other, he brought bad news. Young Freddy was killed in a skirmish with the Spanish.'

Isabella's hands flew to her face. 'Oh, Bessie, how awful.'

Bessie turned away to get her clothes, Isabella saw she had tears in her eyes. After a few minutes, Issy asked: 'But you and Joseph are friends again?'

'Yes. It was just a stupid misunderstanding.'

'Will he return?'

'He hopes to.'

All this time Bessie was helping her into her clothes, while Isabella nibbled at the bread.

'Sit down with your plate, Issy. You're getting crumbs all over your frock.'

They visited several rooms in the High Street and Canongate, but all were too gloomy.

'Bella's flat has plenty of light but I can't afford that calibre of room,' Issy said.

'If you went a bit further out you might get a flat of your own. Boarding house rooms are usually poky,' Bessie replied.

'Good idea,' Issy agreed.

'You'll need a maid if you're in your own place. She could

help with your dressing too, now that Vee is away so much. Would your budget stretch to that?'

'I've money saved from Rome, quite aside from the allowance coming from London. If I can find a place to work from I might avoid relying on the allowance at all.'

'I'll look into it,' Bessie replied. 'I forgot to say. I saw my nephew last night and he's eager to meet you, as is Agnes of course. Might you be free to sup with us on Sunday? Our house can hardly accommodate four, I thought we might go to a tavern?'

'I'd love that, Bessie. I'll look forward to it.'

Chapter Forty-Six

I sabella's new maid was putting up her hair. Flora had been with her only four days but she'd mastered it already. Her father was a baker in the Canongate and she joked that plaiting loaves was good practice.

'Thank you, Flora, you've done a lovely job. I'm meeting Bessie's nephew for the first time and I'm nervous.'

Flora laughed. 'Mistress, I dinnae think a cooper lad will hae any thoughts on what your hair should look like.'

'I'm sure you're right, but Bessie's sister will be there too. Is the dress too simple? I want to fit in but not look as if I don't care.'

Isabella was well aware that she should not be conversing with her maid, but since she answered to no one she'd decided to suit herself. The girl had an open, friendly nature and she liked her. Issy fixed one of her teardrop pearl earrings in her ear.

'The dress is fine but Fleshmarket Close is no the place tae wear expensive jewellery,' Flora said.

'They're not real pearls, but I think you're right.'

Issy selected red paste studs instead.

Flora picked up one of the pearl earrings.

'These are exactly what my sister dreams of for her wedding next week. You'd never guess they're no real pearls.'

Isabella got the strongbox from her wardrobe, and set it on the dressing table. The small chest was piled to the top with faux pearl earrings.

'Which ones would she like?' she asked

Flora's eyes widened. 'You'd lend her them? But why do you have so many?'

'I'm a jeweller, I made these. They're a gift for her wedding day.'

Issy dropped a set of teardrops in Flora's hand.

'They're beautiful, but I couldnae take them, it's too much.'

'I insist and anyway they're not so very expensive and you'd be doing me a favour. I plan to start selling jewellery in Edinburgh and if others admire them it might bring me custom.'

She recounted the story to Bessie, as they walked to meet Alec and Agnes.

'Do you think there might be a market for my earrings amongst the ordinary women of Edinburgh?'

'Maybe,' she replied, 'if the price is not too high. There are other tradesmen like Flora's father, who are doing nicely out of their captive audience in Edinburgh. But would you not prefer to sell to the gentry?'

'I'd hope to sell to them too, but pretty things shouldn't be only for rich ladies. If I could find a flat on the ground floor I might have a shop.'

'Good idea, but I thought silver had to be marked?' Bessie asked.

'Not small things like earrings,' Issy replied.

They entered the tavern. Bessie made the introductions. Alec's freckled face made him look young, but his wide shoulders and muscled forearms were those of a man. Isabella had been nervous that the conversation would be difficult, but Alec asked lots of questions.

'It's right interesting to hear about faraway places. I'd like to travel one day,' Alec said.

'I think we've quite enough family gallivanting around the world with oor Bessie,' Agnes added.

The boy put his arm around his mother's shoulder.

'Now, Ma. Enough ae that. We've been awfy grateful for Auntie Bessie's help over the years. I wouldnae have got an apprenticeship without it.'

Agnes's sour face didn't alter.

'The smell and noise in here's making my heid nip. Will ye take me hame now, Alec?'

'Surely, Ma, ye should ae said before.'

Just then, the tavern door opened. Isabella was astonished to see Vittoria striding towards them. Love lapped over her heart like a warm wave. She must remind her to stop walking like a boy.

'That's lucky, here comes Vittoria,' Bessie said.

Alec turned to his mother. 'Might ye manage a few more minutes, Ma?'

Agnes nodded.

Bessie introduced them and Isabella was very surprised when Agnes spoke first.

'I hear you've been staying with a Cause family in Perth, miss. Is there any news?' she asked, looking around, to see if anyone was listening.

Vittoria leaned in over the table to reply. Her eyes were shining with excitement.

'That's what I came to tell you all. His march has begun. He's on his way.'

Agnes's delighted smile gave a hint of her younger looks.

'And I hear you've met the prince. What does he look like?'

'He's very elegant. Tall, slim and fine featured, with reddish fair hair and brown eyes.'

'Sounds mair like a lassie,' Alec added with a laugh. His mother slapped his knee. 'Behave yersel,' she said.

'I'm only joking. But we'll be needing a soldier, I've heard he's no the fighting kind.'

'It's said he is the excellent shot and rides good. Also he has been to war with the French, I don't think you'll find him lacking,' Vittoria replied.

Alec banged his fist on the table.

'Well, in that case, if he's needing an army, me and all the lads'll be there.'

Isabella saw Agnes look proudly up at her son, simultaneously, she heard Bessie's gasp.

'Oh, no, Alec. Agnes, tell him not tae think about it.'

Agnes shrugged. 'If the time comes, then all the Catholic boys'll be expected tae do their bit.'

Bessie made a noise, a tiny despairing whimper, so quiet that Isabella thought only she heard.

Alec stood up. 'Well that's right exciting news, but ye'll have tae excuse us now, fer Ma needs her bed.'

'I'll be up once I've walked the girls home,' Bessie added.

As they left, she shook her head sadly.

'Sorry, Bessie,' Vittoria said. 'I no wish to cause you worry.'

Isabella laid her hand over Bessie's.

'He's a fine boy, just like you said.'

'Aye, he is, and it'll be a fine waste to send him for a soldier.'

The three of them walked out into the gathering dusk to the head of the close. Isabella turned around to admire the view. The spectacular red sunset had started to fade. Orange clouds were mixed with grey, and a rim of darkness edged the Fife hills.

'There's something so beautiful and somehow sad about the evening light in Scotland,' she said.

'The gloaming,' Bessie replied. 'And aye, it puts me in mind of sadness too.'

They walked down the street in silence. Isabella had something on her mind.

'Bessie, don't answer me if you'd rather not. But well, does Alec make you think of your own child?'

Bessie sighed. 'From the first moment I held him. The resemblance was uncanny.' Her voice was low with emotion. 'I've never said to Agnes but I'm certain she guesses.'

Isabella touched Bessie's arm. 'I'm so sorry I mentioned it. It must hurt you to talk about him.'

'No, I like to talk about him and I've rarely the chance. I believe Simon's family gave instructions to ensure I didn't turn up on their doorstep with a baby. The midwife was supposed to take him directly when he was born, but I begged. She allowed me to hold him, just the once, and for the shortest time. The feel and the smell of his soft head, the downy red hair against my cheek. I swear, it's the strongest and best memory I have.'

'Then your sister had a red-haired baby. You must have found that so very hard,' Isabella whispered.

'Both hard and wonderful. Alec was born three years later, after I'd come back to Scotland. His colouring is hardly surprising, red hair's in my family. But to me he was like a miracle. Watching him thrive, being part of his life. It's the thing that saved me.'

They'd reached the girls' lodging house.

'How long are you here for, Vittoria?' Bessie asked.

'Only until Monday,' she replied.

'You're leaving so soon?' Isabella could hear the unattractive pleading tone in her own voice.

'The Oliphants are using my miniatures to remind Jacobites of their allegiance and the need to raise money and troops.' She dropped her voice to a whisper. 'They're worried. The support from the Islanders was disappointing. It seems he has only a few hundred with him.'

'Dear God, he'll be taken in the first fight,' Bessie said.

'They hope to raise an army as he marches. He on the mainland very soon, then we see.'

'Joseph took that last letter just this week,' Bessie said.

'Joseph Grimes was here?'

'Yes, I'll let Issy explain,' Bessie answered, then added: 'Should I send another letter?'

'I wait longer, things can happen quickly now,' Vittoria replied.

Bessie went home. As they walked up the stairs Issy told Vee the sad news about Freddy and Bessie's obvious happiness after Joseph's visit. When they reached Vee's floor they paused.

'I have much to tell you too. Can I come up?' Vee asked.

Issy nodded. Once behind closed doors, they exchanged silent kisses and took off their hooped skirts and hip pads, these could be put on quickly in the unlikely event of being disturbed. There was only one chair so they sat on Issy's bed. Vittoria's closeness made her pulse race.

Vee's excitement caused her to talk quickly. She described her paintings and all the gentry she'd met at dinner through the Oliphants' campaigning. What they'd eaten and how they'd admired her work. Isabella began to be sorry she'd asked. It was all 'Andrew say this' and 'Laurence say that' and 'Ebenezer tell'. The repetition of their first names and their mutual obsession with the Cause annoyed her. Finally Vee said: 'And I heard from Bella that you've taken on a maid. I went to their house with Andrew this afternoon.'

Vee's happy expression told Issy that she didn't even feel guilty for not coming to her directly. Issy had to swallow her irritation.

'I've got more news too. I want to begin making and selling my jewellery here, so I've started looking for a suitable place, I'll need light and more room. Ideally I'd like a kiln, perhaps even a small shop.'

'*Bueno* idea. The Oliphants will pay me well for the miniatures, we could afford a little house, maybe even with small art studio?'

Those few words lifted Isabella's spirits. Vee saw their future here together.

'That's exactly what I was thinking,' she replied, 'and Flora will be able to help us look after a bigger place. You'll like her, Vee. She's young but obviously bright, I might teach her to make jewellery too.'

Vee yawned and got off the bed. 'I'm so tired,' she said, whilst pulling on her skirt. 'I'll come up to help dress you in the morning.'

'No need. Flora will be here early.'

'You replaced me already!' Vee said in mock outrage.

'Is some maid not helping you at Gask?' Isabella snapped back at her.

'I'm loaned the old maid who attends Laurence's sisters, she has her own beard.'

Issy wasn't in a laughing mood. Vittoria sat back down on the bed and kissed her cheek. 'Don't be cross, Bella. I'm here for such short time, let's no quarrel.'

'I wish you could stay longer.'

'Yes, I'm sorry and I miss you terribly.'

'How long do you expect to be gone this time?'

'It depend,' Vittoria replied with a shrug. 'If Prince

Charles marches to Edinburgh the Oliphants come with him. But I happy to leave for a few days. The laird has no persuaded many of the estate workers to go with them to rendezvous with Charles. Now it make the bad atmosphere between the Oliphants and the staff.'

'It will be the ordinary men who will fall first if there's fighting,' Isabella replied.

Vittoria glanced at the door before she whispered, 'The estate men are afraid their wives and children starve if the fight is lost. The government took estates away from Jacobite families after the 1715 uprising. I hear whispers that the laird is so angry, he no allow them harvest grain for feed their animals.'

Isabella shook her head. The injustice of the situation made her raise her voice. 'So even if they don't go, they could still lose their livelihood through the laird's actions.'

Vittoria put her hand over Isabella's. 'We have to try, Bella. You see how it is for Catholics here, nowhere to worship, no good jobs. The Jacobites give a chance for better future.' She squeezed her fingers. 'Now I go sleep. See you in the morning. Maybe you show this Flora how to do my hair? No one does it like you.'

Chapter Forty-Seven

Vittoria had asked Isabella to write to Anna with news for Henry of Charles's march, she didn't want to ask Bessie again.

13th September 1745
Dear Anna
I thought I would write and update you on our Lives. Vittoria sends her Love and asks your forgiveness for not writing recently. She is extremely busy with her Painting Project, staying with the Family who have commissioned her. Honestly, I miss her and rather wish they hadn't seen it necessary to kidnap her in this Manner! But this urgent Commission requires all her Attention. I can report she is well, the clean Country Air seems to suit her.

I'm busy searching for more suitable Accommodation, with Light for Vittoria's Painting and suitable Space for a Jewellery Workshop. I'm very excited to begin this new Venture.

We will write with the new Address, as soon as it's confirmed. Bessie sends her regards.

Much love,
Isabella
P.S. The News regarding Carluccio is disappointing. So few support him that he stays where he is. It seems the Scottish People won't follow and we doubt he'll come to Edinburgh.

Jeannie's wedding earrings brought Isabella business. Flora's mother had bought some for herself and more for her many friends. She'd also said she knew of somewhere they might rent. It had housed a baker's family and business so had both an oven and a small shop. Issy was anxious to visit but their moving plans were postponed. Charles's army were now camped very nearby, with the King's troops still far to the north. Edinburgh was poorly defended and an attack was expected.

Vittoria hadn't visited Isabella for weeks, so she was astonished to see Vee walking on the other side of the road. Issy stopped so suddenly the man behind collided with her and swore. Vee was deep in conversation with Andrew and Robbie; Issy could only stare. She sat through hours of growing resentment until Vittoria finally burst into her room. 'What a journey! I had to pack up all my painting materials, then the coach take forever. I was so worried it would be all over before we arrive.'

Vittoria swept her into a hug. She didn't seem to notice her stiff reaction.

'I hear he's still some miles away,' Isabella said, then added: 'What time did your coach get in?'

Would she lie to her?

'Eleven but there was much business to do, I go to Ebenezer's shop with Andrew and Robbie.'

A truthful answer. Vee's expression was both innocent of wrongdoing and certain of her welcome. Was she being unreasonable? Issy kept her distance by the window and let Vittoria take the chair. 'So what tales do you have?' she asked.

Vittoria broke into a huge smile. 'I so excited to say you what happened last week.'

'What?'

'Prince Charles came to House of Gask, to have his breakfast with the laird before the march from Perth.'

'No! Did you meet him?'

'That is best bit,' Vittoria replied. 'Young Laurence introduced me as Miss Bassi, an Edinburgh resident from Rome who is supplying some remarkable miniatures to aid the Cause.'

'And did he speak to you?'

Vittoria couldn't answer for laughing.

'Tell me, for goodness' sake!'

'He said, "*Grazie*, signorina. Thank you so much for your support". But then he said: "You look so familiar. I believe I might know your brother".'

'Did he mistake you for another?'

Vittoria collapsed into giggles again. 'No, he make joke about my time with Liotard. Next he lean in to kiss me both cheeks in Italian way and whispered "Come to see me when I get to Edinburgh",' Vee paused for dramatic effect. '"Come alone".'

Isabella breathed in sharply. 'Does he mean to seduce you?'

'Of course no. Anyway, Henry and Charles know about the Spanish maid, her mistress tell gossip. It will be something for the Cause of course. But this could be very good for my future, Bella.'

'Or most likely very dangerous,' Isabella said quietly. But Vittoria silenced her with a kiss.

Isabella was woken very early by noise outside. She went to the window and saw a carriage, stuck part way through the Netherbow Gate surrounded by a large group of soldiers in Highland dress. She raced to Vittoria's room to wake her. Vee squealed with delight, when she saw what was happening. 'They've done it!'

Vittoria flung open the window and shouted her welcome to the soldiers. The sight of a young lady hanging out her window with her hair down, brought cheers back from the Highlanders. A man with a red tartan plaid pinned across his chest, doffed his hat to her.

'That's Cameron of Lochiel, the clan chief,' Vittoria said. 'I saw him in Perth. They name him 'gentle Lochiel'.'

'Gentle or not, his men look fierce,' Isabella replied. Then she recognised a familiar figure, just before he stepped back into the close. He was one of only a handful of spectators up this early. Isabella was sure it had been Lumisden. 'Vee is that...' But the man had disappeared. It was no great surprise that Andrew Lumisden was there, and Vee's voice could have caused him to look up. But why had he looked so grim?

Lochiel strode back through the gate, leaving behind an armed guard. Edinburgh had been taken without a single shot being fired.

Later in the day Issy and Vee joined the crowd surging through the Netherbow Gate. The prince was said to be approaching Holyrood Palace. Bessie shouted Issy's name. She and Agnes pushed through the crowd and they continued together to Holyrood's entrance.

'We'll get a clearer view in the park,' Bessie suggested.

When the army came around the hill, Prince Charles was easily seen riding at the front. As he got closer the cheers became deafening.

'I do wish Mama was here to see, his father and brother also,' Vittoria said.

The prince cut an impressive figure on his black horse. He wore a short tartan coat with a blue sash over his shoulder. His blue bonnet was in the same shade, adorned with a jaunty white cockade. A silver-hilted sword hanging at his side, glinted in the sunlight. Prince Charles disappeared through St Anne's Yard into Holyrood itself and not one man tried to prevent him.

Chapter Forty-Eight

P rince Charles's army easily overcame the King George's redcoats at Prestonpans. Robbie Strange and Bessie's nephew Alec, fought for the victors. With the exception of the garrisons at Edinburgh Castle and Inverness, Charles Stuart now ruled the whole of Scotland. The prince began to hold court in Holyrood. Soon, Edinburgh's Jacobites were flocking to the palace for nightly entertainment.

Isabella arrived at Bella's with the white fans she'd been asked to buy. Robbie was painting fans with colourful scenes to celebrate the prince's arrival. Bella had taken hers to visit friends and now everyone wanted their own. He was selling the fans as quickly as he could paint them, so Vittoria would paint some too.

Bella hugged her when she entered the flat. 'You'll never guess, there's to be a musical recital tomorrow and then a ball on Friday. I'm to be introduced to the prince!'

Isabella knew about the recital. Vittoria had been invited too. 'How exciting for you.'

Bella took both her hands. 'I do so wish you were coming with us.'

Bella looked to Andrew Lumisden, who was sprawled in a chair. He scowled. 'Bella, I can't tell a prince who to invite. I'm sure there will be other opportunities.'

Vittoria had been wholly unconvincing in declaring she wouldn't go, when the single recital invitation had arrived yesterday.

'He wants to see you. You can't turn the invitation down,' Isabella had replied.

Vee's look of relief was transparent. 'They say Lumisden will be powerful now, I want they include me.'

The thought of Lumisden with power was disquieting. The following evening, Isabella had supper with Bessie then retired to her room. It was warm and she had her window open. She heard the chaise pull up, and Vittoria's voice bidding the others goodnight. The door banged shut and Issy heard her walk to her own room. She must have shed her shoes there, because Vee then ran up the next flight to Isabella's and burst in through the door.

'A good evening I take it?' Isabella said.

Vittoria's hair had begun to come down and she had a big grin on her face. 'Scandalous good. He say he need some Italian conversation, then we walk through Great Gallery arm-in-arm. He show all paintings to me, include his grandfather, James VII of Scotland. The Edinburgh ladies most jealous, especially Bella.'

Isabella smiled. 'I can imagine. What else did you talk about?'

'Italy of course. And also you.'

'Me? Goodness, why?' Isabella replied.

'He ask how I can travel to Edinburgh and I told him I come with you. He is very happy to find me here, so he want to thank you at the ball on Friday, the invitation come tomorrow.'

'But why is he so glad to see you?'

'He want me gather the talk in Edinburgh. Be his ears around the ladies. That is why he ask me visit him.'

'Another spying mission? Oh, Vittoria.'

'He told me something also. I think your last letter did not find Henry. His brother leave for France weeks past and should soon be in Paris. Charles hope Henry lead the French invasion.'

Isabella and Vittoria went to Bella's on Friday evening. She had asked all her friends to come and dress there, and the level of excitement in her bedroom was sky high. The Jacobite painted fans were more than mere decorative objects. There were such a large number of ladies dressing, the room got warmer by the minute and the air trembled with the motion of beating fans. They took turns to sit and have their hair powdered. So although they covered their gowns for the process, the air itself was full of powdered starch and soon every surface was covered in white dust.

Robbie arrived in the doorway. 'Goodness,' he said. Looking around the room, now transformed by a sea of coloured silk gowns worn by a dozen young ladies, all flushed with the heat and general excitement. The noise was tremendous. 'I'll go and organise the transport, Bella,' he said, and made a hasty exit.

Bella came over to Vittoria and took her arm. 'So, you still haven't told us what you and the bonnie prince talked about? Edinburgh's maids are distraught to discover that this most eligible bachelor, might be already snapped up by one from his own country.'

She spoke loudly, and the noisy room was reduced to

sudden quiet. It seemed everyone wanted to know the answer to that question.

Vittoria blushed. 'Nothing important. Truly, he no interested in me, he only want relax talk in Italian.'

'We don't believe you for one minute, signorina,' Bella teased. 'Wait until he sees you in that gorgeous gown. I declare you'll be the prettiest girl in the room, and he'll propose directly.'

Vittoria smiled and shook her head. 'He will be charming to everyone. I sure, like his father, the prince will find a bride from a royal house.'

Bella waved her hand dismissively.

'Well, we Scots ladies will endeavour to change his mind about that. Not me, my happy course is set. But I shall encourage my friends.' She turned to the room and raised her fan aloft. 'So, ladies, shall we find this bonnie prince a Scottish bride?'

They all cheered in reply.

Robbie came back to say that Andrew Lumisden had arrived. He was to lead the party in the front carriage. Andrew was now spending every day at Holyrood and a royal appointment was expected.

Everyone left, each lady making the precarious descent one at a time. Isabella and Vittoria hung back and found themselves in the final chaise with one of Bella's friends.

When they were on their way, the girl leaned forward. 'I heard Bella say that you also paint miniatures. What a most rewarding pastime. I'm lucky to have one painted by Mr Strange, he is so very talented, don't you think?' She opened her locket to show them. It contained a miniature of the prince and it was most certainly one of Vittoria's.

Isabella started to correct her: 'No. Miss Bassi…'

Vittoria touched her arm to silence her. Her lips were tight in annoyance but she shook her head. In any case, the young lady was no longer listening, but intent on staring at the people of Edinburgh, descending from coaches in their finery. They got out and made their way towards the entrance.

'But, Vittoria, it's not fair. You taught Robbie how to paint miniatures and he's getting all the credit,' Isabella whispered. 'I wouldn't mind if your Jacobite painting was a still a secret, but everyone knows.'

'He is a man and well known here. It is expected,' Vittoria replied, but Issy knew she was upset. It occurred to Isabella for the first time, that Vittoria's dedication might not get her the recognition she deserved.

The sound of a bagpipe drifted down the stairs to meet them. They joined the mass of people in the magnificent Great Gallery, where generations of Stuarts looked down from the walls. When the piper stopped playing, an expectant hush fell. Charles Edward Stuart walked into the room like an actor onto a stage. He used his height and graceful poise to full effect, enhanced by his colourful Highland outfit. The simultaneous inhalation of breath from dozens of female admirers hung in the air for a second, followed by a sigh and murmured appreciation. A huge chandelier cast the light from dozens of candles on his silvery white wig, creating an ethereal glow. His expression of supreme confidence spoke of a man certain of his right to rule. Issy observed that all the men, including Andrew Lumisden, shared a look of complete devotion.

The Duchess of Perth asked him if he liked to dance.

Prince Charles smiled and replied in heavily accented English, 'I like dancing and I'm very glad to watch you, but I now have another air to dance, and until that dance is finished I'll dance no other.'

Lady Gordon led the dancing in his place. Isabella discovered that a Scottish reel was exhausting and glorious fun in equal measure. She felt thrillingly alive, basking in Vittoria's touch and happy gaze. One dance called for a threesome and Robbie whirled them around in turn. Isabella was aware that the eyes of the room were on Vittoria, news of her conversation with Charles had spread. When the dance ended, they walked arm in arm to get a drink.

Isabella whispered in Vittoria's ear. 'The room is jealous because they think you belong to the prince. I'm so happy that in truth, you're mine.'

They exchanged such a look, that if Bessie had been around it would have earned them a sound telling off. The fiddles started up again for another reel. Issy was so completely absorbed in watching, that Robbie's voice startled her. 'Prince Charles asked after you, Vittoria. He told me to bring the little Roman painter, and that he wants to meet her friend.'

Isabella's heart raced with nerves.

'There you are, Signorina Bassi. And this must be your friend, I'm charmed to meet you...'

'Miss Isabella Godfrey, Your Highness,' Vittoria said.

Isabella gave a deep curtsey. 'I'm honoured to meet you, Your Highness.'

'And it is my great delight to welcome an English lady to my court. I do hope you are the first of many.'

Issy caught sight of Vittoria's expression. She looked at the prince with that disciple-like expression she'd seen on Lumisden's face. Isabella felt a shiver of fear and the certain knowledge that Vee would follow Charles Stuart's behest.

Chapter Forty Nine

In the following weeks the prince offered entertainment at Holyrood almost every evening. Vee went to the Jacobite gatherings with the Lumisdens but Issy refused. Vee delivered gifts commissioned from Ebenezer's shop. This was her cover to allow her to visit Holyrood and brief the prince on her eavesdropping. Issy worried this was risky.

Vee had spent all morning meeting Jacobite supporters at Bella's home.

'My feet hurt from too long standing,' she said, as she kicked her shoes under Isabella's bed.

'Would you come with me to visit the Calton village house tomorrow?' Issy asked. 'I've sold so many pairs of earrings I need to get a workshop soon.'

Vee stretched out her toes and sighed. 'Ask Bessie to come this time. I cannot understand landlord's accent, he speak too fast. Also, Bella say she meet ladies from Scottish Borders tomorrow. Charles want know their opinion.'

'You realise that even if Andrew had hidden your identity as he promised, your presence in Bella's circle and your frequent visits to Holyrood place you firmly in the Jacobite camp,' Issy warned.

Vittoria shrugged.

That night Vee didn't come home from a Holyrood party. Isabella was certain something terrible must have happened and she barely slept. The next morning she took Bella a faux pearl necklace she'd ordered.

'It must have been a very good evening. Vittoria hadn't come home when I left.'

Isabella hoped she sounded nonchalant and Bella seemed unsurprised.

'Andrew didn't come home either and he said there was some important planning meeting today.'

The day wore on and there was still no message from Vee. Isabella went to Calton with Bessie. The old baker's house was nestled in a valley to the north of the Canongate where the rents were cheaper. Issy walked around it one last time, and after a moment's hesitation, she handed the landlord the money he required for the rent. She was excited to work again, it was her plan and she wouldn't let it be spoiled. Isabella walked through the shop at the front into the nicest room downstairs, with the biggest windows and the view of Calton Hill. It was planned to be Vittoria's studio. Today, standing here alone, Issy felt like a complete fool.

She was eating a lonely supper of cold beef and potatoes, when Vee came in. Her eyes shone with excitement.

'You're home then,' Issy said, trying to burst Vittoria's happy bubble with her tone.

'Yes and I can no wait to tell you what I was doing.'

'Really,' Issy remarked.

Vee stopped and scowled. 'Why you angry with me?'

'I've been sick with worry.'

'You didn't get my message? Andrew say he ask Bella to tell you.'

'No I didn't and nor will I get any message you entrust to Andrew Lumisden, you know he doesn't like me.'

Vittoria sat down and took her hands. 'Sorry, my Bella, but I had no time to come myself. Forgive me.' She kissed her cheek, soft lips brushing her skin. 'Don't you want to hear?'

'It better be good since you forgot me entirely.'

Vee's excited manner took over again.

'I worked with no sleeping since yesterday until now, I painted a completely new miniature for Prince Charles.'

'That's exciting.' Vittoria either missed or ignored the sarcasm.

'The Earl of Wemyss want two paintings to celebrate prince's return. The famous artist Allan Ramsay is asked to do the portrait and the prince ask me do a miniature. It is huge honour, Bella. The portrait will take many weeks so Charles want my miniature so quick, he want show it at supper with the earl tonight.'

'And did you finish it?'

'I did and the prince adore it. I'm so happy.' At that she jumped up. 'Is Flora here? I need change quickly.'

'She's gone home, but I'll help you.'

Vittoria left again within twenty minutes and Isabella sat to nurse her bitterness alone. Had she made a mistake committing to a house that required both their incomes?

Isabella couldn't say what woke her, but she was certain it was very late and that the footsteps she heard were Vittoria's. The house fell silent. Something was wrong. Vee always came to talk to her after an evening out. Issy picked up her tinderbox

341

but her hand shook too much to raise a spark for her candle. She felt her way downstairs in the dark. Entering the bedroom she found Vittoria standing with her back to the door.

'What's wrong?'

Vee shook her head.

'Something is wrong, I can tell.'

'Nothing important. I just very tired.' Vee turned her head, the moonlight revealed her sad expression.

'Come upstairs, Vee, you look like you need a hug.'

'No tonight,' she said.

Vittoria continued to be subdued over the coming days and refused to talk about it. Isabella found her sense of abandonment now tinged with rising anxiety. Vee was hiding something from her.

Andrew Lumisden was appointed as the prince's private secretary, and Bella moved with him into the Holyrood inner circle. Robbie's patience with her frequent absences was rewarded when he was invited to Holyrood to do a new engraving for future miniatures. Vittoria would only comment that they wanted an engraving and this was Robbie's specialty.

Two weeks later, Isabella returned from visiting Bessie. She found Vittoria in her new studio. She was sketching Flora.

'You're back early,' she said.

'The prince busy. An envoy has come from the King of France. This Frenchman brought me a note from Henry also. I put on your bureau to read. I want you check my reply.'

'OK. What are you doing?' Isabella peered over Vee's

shoulder. She was part way through a full size sketch of Flora's profile. 'Oh, that's beautiful.'

Vittoria turned to smile at her, a rare occurrence in recent weeks.

'I love draw something no tiny. I plan make it into a painting, as thank you gift for Flora's mother. She brought you much business.'

'Have you seen it, Flora? It's a great likeness.'

'No yet, mistress. My mam is going to be awfy pleased though. Fancy me being in a painting.' The girl was pink with pride.

Vittoria put down her pencil.

'Enough today, Flora, we make again tomorrow.'

Isabella went upstairs to her room. She picked up Henry's letter first. It was written in Italian of course.

Paris. October 1745

Dear Vittoria

I hear you are in Edinburgh with Brother Charles. Many Congratulations on completing your long Journey. That you were there to witness his Entry into our ancestral Home makes me both happy and sad. Happy at the News and most sad that I'm not there to share this Joy. It seems Charles is too busy to write often, so I implore you to send me any News. Your Mother shared the Stories of your Adventures in Europe and I'd love to hear of your Edinburgh Exploits. I'm not sure how long I'll stay in Paris but if you can spare Time to give him any Reply, Alexandre will find me.
I hope, God willing, to join you in Scotland soon.

Yours, Henry Benedict Stuart

. . .

'Is Alexandre the envoy?' Isabella asked, when Vittoria walked into her bedroom.

'*Sì*. Alexandre Jean Baptiste de Boyer, Marquis d'Eguilles. The French like the long title.'

Isabella picked up Vittoria's reply.

'The French will open the letter. I must answer his questions without annoy them.'

Isabella pulled a face. 'They both expect too much from you.'

10 Calton Row, Calton Village Edinburgh
17th October 1745

Your Royal Highness
Imagine my happy Surprise to hear from you. Both you and your royal Father have been much on my Mind these last Weeks. I feel very blessed to be in Scotland to witness your Brother's triumphant Arrival. The People of Edinburgh have welcomed him with the Honour he deserves and I am very busy, painting commemorative Miniatures. I have become acquainted with many of Edinburgh's Ladies and their level of Jacobite Fervour would delight you, as it does Charles.

Your Brother anxiously awaits your Arrival. He has achieved so much when he arrived with so Few, thanks be to God. I can confirm the Reports of Prince Charles's imminent Intention to march South and restore your Father to his rightful Throne. The expected Arrival of French Troops and Funds is the only Thing awaited to ensure his Success. Knowing your judiciousness, I fully expect to meet you next, in the Company of French Forces.
Your humble Servant
Vittoria Bassi.

Isabella refolded and returned the note.

'How you read it?' Vee asked.

'Things go well in Edinburgh, but his support is greatest amongst the women. If the French don't send troops and money, he shouldn't come because it's too dangerous.'

'Exactly,' Vittoria replied.

'Let's hope Charles does nothing hasty,' Issy added.

'Maybe it over soon. Prince Charles is certain the French send troops when they get news of the Prestonpans victory.'

Vittoria hugged her from behind and nuzzled her neck. It had been so long, Issy's senses soared at her touch. Turning into Vittoria's embrace, she sensed immediately that they would ignore the chastity pledge. They spent all evening making love in her little bed with the view of Calton Hill. Issy blocked out thoughts of past or future, just enjoyed the luxury of their intimacy, staring up at the gorse covered hill and the sky above.

Vittoria propped her head on her hand. 'If Flora's portrait is the success, I would like do more big paintings. Do you think there is the market for portraits amongst those Edinburgh people buying your jewellery?'

Isabella felt a flutter of optimism. Might this be something to replace Vee's obsession with the Jacobite campaign? Might she get her back? 'That's an excellent idea,' she replied.

Vittoria pulled her back into an embrace. 'If I stay in Edinburgh,' she added, 'Charles is set on marching to London.'

Isabella stiffened. 'You really think he'll go without the French?'

'Prince Charles say that God intend the English throne for his father and it is his duty to deliver.'

'Please tell him you won't go with him.'

'I must do my duty also.'

'Vee, that's madness!' Isabella got out of bed and glared

down at her. 'You know full well that Charles's popularity here is no guarantee of nationwide support. Have you made that clear to him?'

'I try but he no want to hear. Come back to bed, Bella.' At that, Vee turned on her side and closed her eyes.

Issy went downstairs. She walked through the quiet house and sat at her new workbench with its leather pouch. Flora's bench was next to hers, she was proving to be an able apprentice. During her Rome years Isabella had mastered fashioning the glass beads, and Flora now helped her fill them with wax. She returned the precious flask of *l'essence d'Oriente* to the cupboard and locked it. Monsieur Topart had given her two, he reasoned that she'd earned it by buying so many pearls and anyway the war with England obstructed French business. She loved her new home. She didn't think she could survive giving them both up. If Vittoria was intent on following her ambition, she'd find a way to pay the rent herself.

Chapter Fifty

Prince Charles led his troops out of Edinburgh on the first of November. Isabella joined the crowd gathered to see them leave. The sight of the bonnie prince walking beside his men with his round Highland battle shield on his back, sent the crowd into a frenzy of cheering. Their small party was silent.

Bella had put on a brave face when she said goodbye to Robbie, pinning on the white cockade she'd made for his bonnet and telling him how proud she was. As they watched him march away, Isabella wondered if she regretted her insistence that he should go.

Bessie stood grim-faced at Isabella's side. Her sister had opted to stay at home. Isabella glimpsed Alec in a large group of soldiers, but lost him in the crowd. Robbie Strange had been assigned to the same battalion, so Isabella had asked him to keep an eye on Alec.

'How shall I know him?'

'His name is Alec Cowan, he's taller than average and has a fine head of red curls.'

'I'll look out for him.'

Vittoria was a few steps behind them. She'd barely spoken since she visited the prince yesterday. Issy suspected she'd hoped for a last minute summons, but none came. Robbie Strange had been told to bring his artist materials with him. It appeared Vittoria's inclusion in the daily life of the court was over. The velvet bonnet he'd given her as a memento, lay discarded on her bed. Issy did her best to hide her happiness in the face of Vittoria's disappointment.

'A stupid hat, as if I just one of those girls,' had been Vee's only comment.

Through the long, cold winter, Isabella and Vittoria stayed away from social gatherings. Their private life was still a compromise, more intimate at home, but Vee's thoughts often seemed elsewhere.

The fortressed troops had stormed out of Edinburgh Castle as soon as the Jacobite army left. They retook Holyrood House and harassed those families who'd visited the prince's court. Isabella was nervous of every knock at the door. Bella's father had enough influence to keep the troops away, but she was under strict instructions to stay at home

Isabella's small shop gained passing trade and business grew steadily. Vee got portrait commissions from two of Issy's customers, so she had less time to brood. Nevertheless, Issy still tiptoed around her. Everyone waited anxiously for news of Charles's army's progress. It was as if all the Jacobites who stayed behind were holding their breath.

Isabella received a letter from Sir Everard.

Flanders October 1745
Dear Isabella
I was pleased to have News of you being happily settled in
Edinburgh.
I remain at the Side of the King's son, so I'm sure you understand I
must be vague about my Movements. However I can confirm that our
Party will return to England very soon and I strongly suspect we will
be in Scotland in the near Future. I look forward to seeing you in
Edinburgh.
Best wishes

Everard Fawkener

She had to sit down.

'What is it?'

She handed Vittoria the note to read. Her alarmed expression told Isabella she interpreted the words the same way. The English expected to bring their fight to Scotland, the full force of the army was heading their way.

Isabella, Vittoria and Bessie ignored the welcoming in of the New Year. In fact the whole town was quiet through Hogmanay. Edinburgh was behaving as if those few wild weeks of celebration had never happened. Jacobites still raised money behind the scenes, but the sure expectation of change had fizzled away. They'd heard that the prince had abandoned his march to London and turned back at Derby. The Duke of Cumberland now led his father's army northwards, hell bent on getting rid of the Jacobites for good.

Bessie came to visit Issy's workshop one day, with the *Caledonian Mercury* newspaper in her hands. 'It says the Jacobites are near Stirling but the redcoat numbers have grown. I can't bear it. Alec might get nearly home and be killed on his own doorstep.'

Isabella put her arm around Bessie's shoulder. 'Try not to worry, Bessie. We might get news of Alec from Robbie soon. Vittoria delivered more miniatures to Ebenezer this week and he seems to expect it will be Robbie who picks them up.'

'Goodness, is Vittoria still painting Jacobite miniatures?'

Isabella shrugged.

'I've asked her to stop but she says she won't give up on the Cause. Although she's been busy with large portraits since Flora's mother showed her painting to all her friends.'

'Well, it's good she's got safer work.' Bessie paused, then asked: 'Do you think she might go back to Rome?'

Isabella was startled into panic. 'Did she say something that made you think she might?' Her sudden fear receded when Bessie shook her head.

'No. But my thoughts have turned that way. I hate to abandon you, but I want to get back. Why don't you both come with me? You'd be safer there.'

Issy took a couple of deep breaths to slow her speeding heart as she reassured Bessie. 'You must go, Bessie, you've already stayed longer than you planned. But my business is going well, and I don't think Vittoria is ready to go home. Don't worry, we'll be fine.'

'I certainly can't stay with Agnes much longer. One of us is sure to kill the other before long.'

Isabella thought about Bessie's question. Vittoria had hoped to gain fame through the Jacobites. Would she want to stay in Edinburgh only painting tradesmen's daughters? She was afraid to ask her.

Chapter Fifty One

They were eating dinner when Bessie arrived with news of the Jacobite victory at Falkirk Muir.

'Good news at last,' Vee said.

'Will you join us to eat, Bessie? I've made some broth,' Isabella said.

Bessie sat to describe the reports of victory. Isabella put a plate of soup in front of Bessie. A loud knock at the door made her jump. When she opened it she was surprised to find Bella Lumisden standing there with Robbie at her side. Bella ought to look overjoyed, something wasn't right.

'Great news from Falkirk, Robbie,' Vittoria said.

'Yes, but we're on the move again. We're heading for the Highlands and we'll need more Jacobite trinkets.'

'I don't have them here, I passed them to Ebenezer,' Vittoria answered.

'Why go north so soon after a victory?' Bessie asked.

The colour drained from Robbie's face. 'Mistress Nichol, I hadn't thought to find you here. I came only to get your address. I...'

He'd no need to finish his sentence, Bessie guessed his

news. She let out a terrible wail. Isabella and Vittoria both rushed to comfort her. Meanwhile, Robbie Strange stood, turning his cap between his hands, looking as if he wished the ground would swallow him.

'What happened?' Isabella asked.

'I found Alec's name on the fatality list. I'm so sorry.'

'How did he die?' Bessie asked through her tears.

'I don't rightly know, Mistress Nichol. I was positioned on the other side of the ravine.'

'Then you can't be sure he's dead.' Bessie's eyes were wild with panic.

'I'm so sorry. He'd already been buried when I found out. But I searched and checked with all his friends. I'm sure he's dead.'

Bessie sat with tears streaming down her face for several minutes. Isabella found her silent grief harder to bear than the wailing. Eventually, she said quietly:

'Anyone I love too much is taken from me.' She stood up. 'I have to go and tell Agnes.'

'I'll go with you,' Isabella said.

'Take our chaise, Issy,' Bella offered. 'We can wait here until you return.' Bella looked to Robbie for his approval.

'Of course,' he said. 'We'll wait here with Vittoria. I'll go to Ebenezer when you come back.'

They reached Bessie's close's entrance and Isabella asked the coachman to wait.

'There's no need to come up, Isabella. Mr Strange will be needing to get off.'

'Let me see you up the stairs, Bessie.'

Isabella hugged Bessie at her flat's door.

'Don't come in. There's nothing you can do.'

'I'll call past tomorrow and see how you are,' she offered.

Isabella heard Agnes's scream from halfway down the stairs.

. . .

She got home to find Vittoria and Robbie still sat at the kitchen table.

'I feel like I've let you down. Alec Cowan was most unlucky, our casualties at Falkirk were light,' Robbie said.

'It's not your fault,' Isabella replied.

'Where's Bella?' she asked.

'She wanted a mirror to check her hair before they call on Ebenezer. I told her yours is the best,' Vittoria answered.

When Bella came down, Robbie apologised again.

'I handled it badly, I wasn't expecting to find Mistress Nichol here.'

'It's impossible news to give,' Isabella answered.

They shook his hand and wished him luck.

'Thank you. I don't know when I'll see you again, but I know the prince is grateful for your support.'

When Isabella went to bed, she realised the note from Sir Everard was on her dressing table. Might Bella have read it? Surely not. She wished she'd told them about Sir Everard from the beginning. She'd done nothing wrong and she hadn't seen him in over three years. When the Duke of Cumberland had led the fighting in the north of England, she'd worried whether Sir Everard was travelling with him. Now the newspapers reported the duke was back in London.

The next day, it took all Isabella's courage to climb Bessie's stairs. When she answered the door, Bessie's face showed the signs of a sleepless night. Behind her in the shuttered gloom, Isabella could make out Agnes lying on the bed facing the wall. Issy gave Bessie a basket. 'I thought you might not feel like shopping.'

'Thank you. Neither of us have braved going out yet. People will ask about Alec. We can't bear it.'

Isabella shook her head miserably. 'Would you come and eat with us tonight?'

'I've no appetite.'

'Then in a few days? It's not good for you both to be cooped up in here.'

'I don't feel like talking or eating, but I think you're right.'

'What about dinner the day after tomorrow? Say at one thirty?'

Bessie hugged her. 'I'll try to persuade Agnes,' she whispered in Isabella's ear.

That night, Isabella and Vittoria were woken by loud knocking. It was nearly midnight and Isabella's heart hammered a fearful echo. She pulled on a shawl to answer the door, then grabbed the frame to steady herself at the sight of a red-coated soldier. He gave her a note. She knew Sir Everard's seal on the back.

30th January 1746, Holyrood Palace
Dear Isabella
Please excuse me for disturbing you at this horrendous Hour. We have ridden non-stop from London, and the Duke will march to Stirling Tomorrow. I would very much like to see you and I don't know when we'll be back in Edinburgh. The Captain has Instructions to wait and bring you to meet me in Holyrood Palace. You'll be perfectly safe and I shan't keep you more than an Hour. I think it best you come alone.
Affectionately
Everard

'Please wait for me while I dress,' Isabella said to the soldier.

Vittoria appeared on the stairs. 'Who was it so late?'

Isabella handed her the letter, Vittoria blanched. 'The duke is in Holyrood. Is it over already?' she said in a whisper.

'It seems something new is just beginning. Have Robbie and the others gone north yet?' Issy asked.

'I no sure, but I think they march tomorrow. Bella, I think don't go.'

Isabella laughed mirthlessly. 'So, will you tell that to the redcoat waiting for me?'

Vee looked shocked. 'Then I come with you.'

Isabella shook her head. 'You read what it says. Anyway, you cannot be seen visiting the Duke of Cumberland's quarters.'

Vittoria's hand trembled where she held the letter. Looking down, Issy saw hers shook too. 'Come on, help me dress.'

Fifteen minutes later they both stood in the kitchen. Vittoria hugged her.

'Don't look so worried. Sir Everard would never let anyone hurt me and I'll be back before you know it. Just go to bed.'

Vittoria shook her head vigorously. 'I no sleep. I wait for you here.'

She took Isabella's face in her hands and kissed her tenderly.

'Be careful,' she said.

Chapter Fifty-Two

The coach sped down the deserted Canongate to Holyrood. Isabella hesitated at the bottom of the stairs. It was less than six months since she'd walked up them with Vittoria. Vee had been ecstatic, so sure that her dreams and ambitions were going to be realised. Now all those hopes had crumbled and Issy found herself looking forward to seeing a man who was a sworn enemy to the Jacobites. Was her loyalty to them both impossible? The valet lighting the dark stairs with his lamp turned and scowled at her until she followed him. Sir Everard rose when she walked into the room; she noticed that he'd aged considerably in the last three years. She had unexpected tears in her eyes. He reached out his hand to her. 'Dear Isabella, are you all right? Come and sit down.'

'I'm fine, it's just been an emotional week.'

Sir Everard turned to the waiting valet. 'Thank you, Carruthers, see if the duke needs anything. I'll serve the tea myself.'

The valet exited through the door that Isabella knew led

to the parlour and bedroom Prince Charles had used. The bed had hardly had time to go cold.

Sir Everard poured them both tea with honey and sat back in his chair. He smiled at her. 'You look very well, Issy. So grown up. I can scarcely believe it.'

'I'm afraid you look tired. And now I'm keeping you awake.'

'The duke is furious about the outcome of Falkirk, and he rode us through the night to be here as quickly as possible. As for keeping me up, let's say you are keeping me company. I have much to organise before we leave. I'll sleep when the soldiering business begins.' His face changed expression. 'Talking about soldiering, Isabella, I want you to go to my home in Wandsworth. There will be a lot of trouble before this Jacobite business is finished. I need to know you're somewhere safer.'

Isabella smiled and shook her head. 'I appreciate your concern, Sir Everard, but my home is here now and I'm not in danger.'

'I disagree.' He took a deep breath. 'Isabella, I'm sure you must be aware that there are King's agents operating in Edinburgh, especially when the Young Pretender was here. I have had access to their intelligence to assist the duke with his correspondence.' He looked at her sternly. 'You have exercised very poor judgement in your choice of companions.'

Spied on here? By whom? she wondered.

'Sir Everard...' she paused to choose the right words, she wasn't sure what he'd heard. 'Mistress Nichol and the nuns at Santa Cecilia saved me. Honestly I feel comfortable in my mother's faith.'

Sir Everard looked embarrassed. 'That I was taken in by both those rogues will be a regret I take to my grave.'

Isabella shrugged. 'They were skilful and heartless liars.'

'I concede you had reasons to convert. But the Jacobites, Isabella! You're associating with traitors. The duke will certainly win and those supporting the imposter will face the consequences. Please, I implore you, go to London, at least until this fight is over.'

Isabella clasped her hands and put her knuckles to her lips. 'I know you have my interests at heart, but I cannot leave.' She looked directly at him, hoping she might see some understanding in his eyes.

He sighed. 'I've seen one of that apprentice's miniatures. I wasn't surprised to learn it was Liotard's protégé, although I hardly expected she'd be a girl I'd met as a boy. This friendship puts you in the path of danger, Isabella.'

'Vittoria was born into the Jacobite Cause. She's my dearest friend and we support each other. I cannot desert her.'

'I applaud your loyalty but I have to say I think it a terrible mistake.'

She maintained her defiant gaze. Sir Everard shook his head and sat back in his chair. 'Tell me more about your jewellery business, I hear you've expanded it here.'

Isabella described her business in faux pearls. She told him that they'd rented a property with a workshop, shop and studio and how Vittoria had begun painting portraits.

'It sounds charming, and I'm glad the young lady feels inclined to paint more laudable subjects. But how do you manage for money?'

'I had savings from Rome and our combined income covers our rent. We're comfortable.'

'Is the bank here not reliable about paying out your allowance?'

'There have been no problems since the castle siege ended but I'm determined to support myself and not to rely on it,' Isabella replied.

He shook his head. 'It's your money, Issy, what's left from the business. It breaks my heart that you're forced to work because that man swindled you. Have you heard any news of him?'

'I enjoy my work, and I hope to never see Richard again,' she replied. 'How did you come to uncover his deceit?'

'I met your father's old shop manager by chance in Bond Street. He told me that Richard was your guardian but not your uncle. He suspected his motives from the beginning.'

'Then why did I call him uncle?'

'Your father took him in and grew to trust him; it was a term of affection. He believed Richard a distant cousin but I doubt that now. Your father's lawyer was your other guardian but he died just after him. I think that's when Richard saw a chance. He sold the shop to escape those who might denounce him, then the house for money. I don't believe the business was ever as bad as he described.'

'I trusted him too,' she whispered. She felt the renewed pang of betrayal at her breastbone.

'I'm so sorry, it seems he had huge gambling debts to repay. But I've come to tell you that as well as the money I managed to salvage, I found there's a small dowry in trust for you. He couldn't get to it while you remained single.'

'I won't need a dowry, Sir Everard. I'm quite resolved not to marry.'

He looked thoughtful. 'I might be able to get it released for you to use? There's enough to buy a small property. Once this Jacobite nonsense is over, I'll look into it. I'll also add something from me to your allowance. Since you're determined not to accept my hospitality, I want to know you're comfortable.'

'That's kind of you but not necessary. If there's enough capital from my father then I'll use it to buy premises, to have a home and a place to carry on the business. I really appreciate your help but I'd like to take control of all my finances, rather than the vagueness of an allowance.'

Sir Everard looked hurt. 'I understand that you've good reason to be distrustful.'

Isabella smiled, she hoped he could see how much he meant to her.

'Of course I trust you and I'm so grateful for your guardianship. So long as I have funds in England I assume I still need it. But I'll be nineteen soon, only two years until I reach majority. I need to feel in control of my future, including my finances.'

He rubbed his eyes wearily.

'You're right, I forget that you've grown up. I shouldn't be surprised that you want to make your own choices. Your mother was the same. I'll talk to the lawyer when I get back to London and ask him to look into moving funds to Scotland.'

Isabella leaned forward and touched the back of his hand. 'I'm so glad I found you and I'm sorry if my life didn't turn out as you hoped. But if you care for me, you must allow me to live as I choose.'

'I wish you all the happiness in the world, Issy.'

Isabella recounted the conversation to Vittoria. When she told her they would have money for a house, she took Issy's hands and whirled her around the kitchen.

'But will you still want to stay in Edinburgh if there's no glamorous job at court?'

Vittoria's expression was suddenly serious. 'I no know how this will end, Bella. But I want be with you.'

That's all Issy needed to hear. Their love-making was now a like dance, two bodies perfectly in time.

· · ·

The next day was a Sunday. They went as usual to the house in the Canongate where everyone met for Mass. Bessie joined them after the service. 'My sister won't be budged. She's turned her face to the wall. I'm having a devil of a job to get her to eat.'

'I'm sorry, what a worry for you,' Isabella said.

'It is, and I cannot wallow in my own grief. Agnes needs my support.'

'Must you rush back?'

'No,' Bessie replied. 'I've asked Mistress Cunningham to sit with Agnes. I told her about Alec yesterday. We won't face any distressing questions now. Mistress Cunningham is the biggest gossip in Edinburgh.'

They had dinner and Isabella served an apple pudding. After one spoonful, Bessie turned to her. 'This is like Meryem's.'

'Yes, I took the recipe from her.'

'I am bad cook because I spoiled by Mama,' Vittoria said.

They all laughed.

'I'll make us some tea. Sir Everard brought me some as a gift.' As Isabella opened the tea caddy, there was a rap on the door. Vittoria answered it.

Isabella heard her exclaim: 'Andrew!'

'Stand aside, Vittoria.'

Four huge soldiers in Highland dress barged in. Two grabbed Vittoria and Bessie, holding down their arms. Isabella screamed, realising the other two men were advancing on her. One bound her hands, while the other tied first a gag, then a blindfold around her head.

She heard Bessie and Vittoria shouting and sounds of a scuffle.

'Vittoria, this woman has tricked you, she is a spy,' Lumisden said.

361

'Let her go!' Vittoria yelled.

'I hardly believed the evidence myself, but events this week confirm it. We knew we had an English spy in our midst. I was loath to believe it a lady, but now I'm sure. I'm sorry.'

The men dragged Isabella out the door and threw her into a carriage. She could hear Vee screaming her name.

* * *

The Highland thug pushed Bessie onto a chair. Vittoria must have bitten her captor hard. He swore, then flung her to the ground. The soldiers left, and they ran to the door to see the carriage speeding away. Traitorous Lumisden rode beside it.

'Isabella!' Vittoria wailed.

He didn't look back.

'Come inside, Vittoria. You must have hit your head, you're bleeding.'

Vee pushed Bessie's hand away. 'I'm fine. But Bessie, what we do?'

'Where might they take her?' Bessie asked.

Vittoria shook her head. 'Maybe Bella know?' Vee picked up her cloak.

'No. Vittoria! Her own brother took Isabella away. You can't trust her.'

'Bella is our friend and this is terrible mistake.'

Seeing there was no stopping her, Bessie took her own shawl and followed her out.

The servant at the Lumisdens' door tried to deny them entry. Vittoria stamped on his foot and pushed past. They found Bella Lumisden in her bedroom; she looked terrified.

'Andrew told me not to admit you, Vittoria. We've both been duped.'

'Stupid nonsense, Bella. How you think for one minute that Isabella is spy?'

Bella flushed red.

'Sit down, I explain,' Vittoria said.

Vittoria described how she came to Scotland to work on behalf of both the Stuart Princes. 'Don't you see? Sir Everard Fawkener is her guardian. Isabella took brave risks for our Cause. Andrew has it all wrong.'

Bella looked confused. 'But Andrew told me he'd seen a letter. That Issy wrote lies about the Cause to Rome.'

Vittoria groaned. 'There was a code agreed with Prince Henry to fool the censors. Every fact was opposite of the truth. I told these words.'

Bella looked stricken. 'I don't know how to stop them.'

'What's their plan?' Bessie asked, dreading the answer.

'There will be a trial. For treason,' Bella said quietly.

'Bella, if they find her guilty they hang her!' Vittoria said.

Tears poured down Bella Lumisden's face. Her words were barely audible. 'It was me who told them of Fawkener's letter. I'm so sorry.'

Vittoria seized her by the shoulders. 'Tell me where they take her.'

Bessie thought the girl might faint.

'The Drummond in Crieff. But you have to hurry!'

Vittoria turned and ran.

'Wait for me, Vee.' At the bottom of the stairs, Bessie grabbed her arm. 'What are you going to do?'

'I keep some breeches from Constantinople, I hire horse and travel as boy, chaise take too long. If I tell my story, they must believe me.'

Bessie nodded. 'I'll tell Agnes, and meet you there. I've

another idea that might help. Go to the White Horse in the Canongate, they will give you a reliable animal and tell them to prepare their fastest chaise for me.'

Chapter Fifty-Three

I sabella was thrown about in the coach, unable to brace herself with her hands tied. After many painful hours and a particularly violent jolt, her blindfold slipped, revealing the silhouette of Stirling Castle in the moonlight. Were they taking her to Perth?

The Highland soldier opposite her said nothing throughout the entire journey. Her gag chafed and she was very thirsty. More bruised by every bump and desperate to pee, she didn't sleep.

When the carriage stopped, Isabella turned her head to understand her surroundings. The building sign said: *The Drummond*. Were they near Lady Gordon's home? Turning gave away that she could see. Someone slapped her hard and the blindfold was retied. No one had ever struck her before. Fear made breathing difficult, faltering in the same quick rhythm as her heart.

Her arms were grabbed roughly on each side. 'Walk,' said a gruff male voice on her left. She stumbled when she met an obstacle. The men then lifted her bodily off her feet. She sensed they were climbing stairs.

Andrew Lumisden's voice came behind her: 'Tell him she's here.'

A door was opened and she was pushed roughly onto a chair. Rope looped around her body and bound wrists, secured her to the chair itself. The rope dug into her flesh, the man grunted and tugged it harder.

'Take off her blindfold and gag. I want to look in her eyes.'

A bearded stranger was hunched down in front of her, with his face close to hers. Stupidly, she smiled at him. A polite reflex. He returned a leering, mockery of a smile, then hit her hard across the face.

'Yer charms willnae work on me, bitch.'

Isabella wet herself. Her cheek burned with pain and also shame. She was going to die right here, with her petticoats soaked in her own urine. Anger kindled. She took a deep breath and pulled herself straight. She'd not show any more weakness.

Andrew Lumisden spoke. 'You are here to face a charge of spying against the rightful Cause of his Royal Highness King James.'

'I'm not a spy,' Isabella replied.

The bearded man hit her again. The impact made the chair teeter, then fall. Her head hit the floor. She tasted blood in her mouth. Would they torture her? The two men righted the chair with a thud.

'First, I have some documents to present.' Lumisden placed a paper on the table beside a timid looking man who was taking notes. 'Item number one is a copy of an intercepted letter to the mother of Vittoria Bassi a painter of miniatures and loyal Jacobite. The accused complains to Miss Bassi's mother that the Oliphant family have kidnapped her daughter, and contains a further paragraph which we believe was a message for Prince Henry Stuart.

He read it aloud: '*The news regarding Carluccio is disappointing. So few support him that he stays where he is. It seems the Scottish people won't follow and we doubt he'll come to Edinburgh.*'

Lumisden looked up, as if addressing an imaginary court. 'For the record, Carluccio is a known nickname for Prince Charles. It is our assertion that Miss Godfrey wrote to discourage Prince Henry from supporting the Rebellion.'

'No!' Isabella shouted. 'Vittoria asked me to write it. The code was agreed in advance, the prince knew to take the opposite meaning.'

The bearded man kicked her leg hard. Isabella cried out in pain. 'Dinnae speak unless yer asked a question, English bitch.'

Andrew Lumisden's contemptuous look frightened Isabella more than the violence. 'For the record, I hold myself responsible for not putting a stop to this sooner. I was made aware that this lady, who had ingratiated herself into my sister's social circle, had a connection to Everard Fawkener, Secretary to the Duke of Cumberland. I made allowances for the vulnerability of the fairer sex, and I fear I grossly underestimated the calculating nature of this particular individual.'

Isabella made a noise, as if to protest. The bearded man held the back of his hand just inches from her face. Isabella closed her eyes. This time he backed off.

'My suspicion of an English girl, who supposedly supported our Cause led me to have some loyal Jacobite servants listen at doors. They heard her try to dissuade Miss Bassi from her support and criticise the Laird of Gask's dealing with his own servants. He looked down at a piece of paper in his hand.

'She said: *"So even if they don't go, they could still lose their livelihood through the Laird's actions".*'

Andrew Lumisden glared at Isabella while the clerk

finished writing. 'I believe that Miss Godfrey was asked to spy for the English and that she hatched the plot in collusion with her guardian, Sir Everard Fawkener. I assert she intended to use Miss Bassi as a way of gaining access to our circles. In a moment, I shall present the sordid conclusion I came to in that regard.'

Isabella's bowels cramped in fear.

'This submission is a copy of a letter obtained from Miss Godfrey's bedroom. It was received only weeks ago from her guardian. It contains these lines: *"I remain at the side of the King's son, so I'm sure you understand I must be vague about my Movements. However I can confirm that our Party will return to England very soon and I strongly suspect we will be in Scotland in the near Future. I look forward to seeing you".'*

He slammed the page down on the desk. Isabella felt a tear snaking down her face. Bella had betrayed her. Andrew Lumisden smirked.

'The final proof came when Sir Everard Fawkener, who was only in Edinburgh for a matter of hours, thought meeting this spy sufficiently important to summon her in the middle of the night.'

Lumisden spat out the word 'spy' with venom. Then he looked at the ceiling, as if addressing God. 'I regret having to recount this final piece of evidence, but it's crucial to understanding how an innocent Italian girl became corrupted by this sinner.'

Isabella closed her eyes.

'Miss Bassi first met Miss Godfrey in Constantinople, when she was apprenticed to a painter called Liotard. It is our assertion that Fawkener had her follow Miss Bassi back to Rome, because of her connection to the Stuart court. I believe she was under instruction to seduce the apprentice.'

He paused for dramatic effect.

'The unusual twist to this story, is that Miss Bassi undertook this apprenticeship disguised as a boy. You would have thought that discovering the apprentice was a girl, would have caused the seduction to be abandoned...'

Isabella made herself open her eyes.

The clerk stared at her slack-mouthed.

'...it did not. Miss Godfrey is a spy of such dedication that she didn't hesitate from sexual depravity.'

The clerk's face and gasps from the soldiers behind her convinced Isabella that they would kill her.

Andrew Lumisden continued, his tone managed to convey both moral outrage and, Isabella felt sure, a degree of fascination.

'I have testimonies from a Miss Effie Henderson from Miss Godfrey's High Street lodgings and a Master Thomas Jackson, a neighbour in Calton Village. They endured the unenviable duty of secretly observing her bedchamber. They both assert in disgusting detail, that this woman had unnatural sexual relations with the miniaturist.'

He placed two more pieces of paper on the table. The clerk's eyes slid over them. Isabella swallowed rising bile, her throat burned and eyes stung with humiliated tears. He'd taken her precious love and turned it into a sordid spectacle.

'That completes my testimony for the record,' Lumisden declared grandly. 'Does the prisoner have any reply in her defence?'

Isabella shook her head. There was no point. They wouldn't believe her. The bearded thug grabbed her hair and made her look at Lumisden.

'Answer the man,' he growled.

'I am not and never was a spy.'

'Dirty lying whore,' the bearded man spat in her face.

'Do you deny that you had sexual relations with Vittoria Bassi?' Lumisden asked.

She took a deep breath, 'I would die rather than deny my love.'

The clerk dropped his quill.

'Prince Charles will tell you I did not corrupt Miss Bassi.'

Lumisden walked up to her, his lip curled in disgust. 'The prince is above listening to such depraved filth.' He turned to the guards. 'Give her some water and re-gag her. And for God's sake bring her a pisspot. She stinks.'

* * *

Bessie rushed home and explained her need to leave. Mistress Cunningham would stay with Agnes, obviously delighted to be involved with such an exciting story. Agnes spoke for the first time in days. 'Go,' she said. 'Hurry!'

Bessie's coach sped through the dark countryside. She reversed her conviction of God having deserted her when she found her ally at home. They were both on their way to Crieff before eight the next morning.

When they arrived at The Drummond, the lady sprung from the carriage like a woman half her age. The startled guards recognised her and stepped back.

'Get me my sons!' she roared, as she stormed into the building.

Bessie was about to follow, when Vittoria rushed to her side. The girl was soaked through. She held her boy's cap in her hand and her hair hung wet down her back.

'Thank God you're here. I mad with worry. They wouldn't admit me.'

Just then the lady ahead noticed Bessie was not beside her.

'Let them through, you imbeciles,' she shouted.

She strode up the stairs and they followed. The familiar

voice brought the Duke of Perth and his brother out of their bedrooms in their nightshirts. Lady Jean Gordon, the Duchess of Perth, yelled at her sons in rapid French. Bessie couldn't understand any of it, but the impact was evident from their faces. She finished her tirade with a stamp of her foot.

'She is related to you, you utter fools. Your own flesh and blood!'

'*Pardon, Maman. Nous...*' John, the younger brother began.

'I don't want your excuses, take me to her now!'

One of the guards gestured upwards with his eyes.

Lady Gordon was first on the stairs. Her sons followed and Bessie and Vittoria came behind.

'Please God, let us be in time,' Bessie whispered.

As they approached a door on the top floor, it was flung open and Andrew Lumisden walked out, his smug expression survived less than two seconds.

'What have you done, you idiot! Isabella's grandmother worked for our family,' Lady Gordon shouted at his suddenly terrified face.

They all rushed into the room, forcing the bearded man who was about to exit, to jump to one side. He looked at Lady Gordon as if he'd seen a ghost.

First sight flooded Bessie with relief, she was alive. But when she saw what they'd done to Isabella, her heart crumpled. She looked barely conscious. She had blood on her face and one eye was already swollen. Blood dribbled from her gagged mouth. Isabella's dress was wet. Bessie groaned when she realised that this was the source of the terrible smell. 'You poor child.'

'Bella, what they done to you?' Vittoria pushed past. Tears ran down her face as she untied the gag. 'What have I done to you?' she whispered.

'Set her free,' Lady Gordon commanded the guard. Then she turned to her sons.

'Get dressed. We're going to the prince.'

'He's at Ferntower, I gave him my rooms,' her son replied.

'Then we go there. *Vite!*'

* * *

The prince marched his army north later that day. Lady Gordon insisted that Isabella stay in The Drummond overnight, to have her own physician visit. Issy was pronounced fit to travel and next morning Lady Gordon came to see them.

'I'm so sorry for your ordeal, Isabella. I hope you can put it behind you. Prince Charles confirms Vittoria's long association with his family and that she corresponds with his brother. He ordered the destruction of the records of this so-called trial. Lumisden admits he told those servants what kind of testimonies he'd pay for. He developed a theory and set out to prove it, as a legal man he should have known better. Andrew has signed a written declaration confirming your innocence on all points and I will have someone give the witnesses an incentive to recant and forget their testimony.'

Lady Gordon placed her hands flat on the table and levelled her gaze, first at Isabella then Vittoria. 'There are elements of this story that I think I do better not to dwell on. The prince was in a hurry to leave so I believe he omitted to consider why Prince Henry received reports from Signorina Bassi.'

Vittoria blinked and said nothing.

'Also, I put his amusement at the accusations of sexual impropriety down to his continental upbringing. Such things are not a laughing matter in our colder climate, which I'm sure you both understand. I'm quite certain I'll never hear such a ridiculous accusation again.'

Both girls nodded. Lady Gordon's stern expression softened and she rose to go. 'I wish you a safe journey home. Now, you must excuse me, I have work to do finding provisions to send up the road to feed our brave boys.'

Chapter Fifty-Four

Vittoria held her hand all the way home. Isabella was bruised all over but more than anything she was worried about Vee, who was deathly pale.

'This my fault, I put you in danger,' Vittoria repeated again.

'You were caught up with it all. Everyone was.'

Bessie helped her into bed, then went home. Issy could hear Vee moving about next door, then she registered the sound of a cupboard door being slammed. She dragged herself into Vittoria's bedroom. Her shelves were empty and her trunk already half filled. This was what Issy had feared.

'What are you doing?'

Vee didn't turn around. 'This my fault and you still in danger. I must leave.'

Isabella gripped the bed frame. 'After everything I've gone through? How could you do that?' she said through sobs.

Vee turned to face her, her eyes full of remorse.

'I want you be safe, Bella. The servants' story can spread and the Church will come after us. The Jacobites no win now, if I'm gone you be spared the King's revenge.'

'Please,' Issy pleaded. 'I don't deserve this.'

Vee ignored her outstretched hand. 'I kept secret from you, I don't deserve you.'

'What secret?' Issy's fearful question came out in a whisper.

Vee's eyes were full of guilt. 'I gave Lumisden reason to come after you.'

'For God's sake, what are you talking about?'

'On the night of Earl Wemyss party Lumisden made me the proposal.'

'Of marriage?' Issy asked.

'Of course no,' Vee's face contorted in disgust, 'this man no marry a Catholic servant's daughter. He proposed I be his mistress. He was so sure I would want him that he pushed me into the dark corner.'

Issy gasped. 'Did he...?'

Vee shook her head. 'No, but, he so very certain of success. He whispered hot in my ear that he know how much I need a man.'

'That's awful! Why didn't you tell me?'

'This the worst thing. I so sorry,' Vee looked down and twisted her skirt in her fingers. 'He saw my disgust and he very angry. I embarrass him, this make him so dangerous. He say I lead him on and I must tell no one, especially not you. He threaten if I tell, then I never find painting work in Scotland again.'

'But Andrew would never have known if you'd told me.'

'You are right. I should leave Edinburgh then and I must leave now.'

Vee turned to go and Isabella lunged to grab her hand. 'Please, Vee, let's wait, see if it all dies down.'

'I deserve lose you.'

She put her hands on Vee's shoulders. 'It's not your choice, I won't be got rid of. I love living here but if you leave

I'll follow you. Don't make me do that.'

Vittoria frowned and shook her head. 'You should be angry.'

'You don't get to tell me how to love.'

Vee met her eyes and Issy kissed her as if her life depended on it.

'Please, stay. We need each other.'

Vee squeezed her fingers and gave a tiny nod. Issy's joyous hug crushed her own painful ribs but set the world right again.

'But two things, no more secrets and no more Jacobites.'

'No more Jacobites and no more royal patrons, I am tired of men and their wish for war,' Vee replied.

'I don't believe you,' Issy said. 'Your work is too good to only grace the houses of bakers and butchers.'

So they waited. Bessie discovered that Effie Henderson had left Edinburgh with a dowry gift to marry a Dundee carpenter and Thomas Jackson was given distant work on the Drummond Estate. Isabella held her breath for months, expecting the scandal to surface.

News of the massacre at Culloden reached Edinburgh at the end of April. For many weeks it seemed there were no survivors and the closes around Bessie's home were full of grieving families. When some poor boys dragged themselves back, many were horribly maimed and all were half starved.

Isabella trudged up the stone stairs to visit Bessie, she could hear a woman sobbing in a neighbouring flat. Bessie opened the door with a sad shake of her head.

'It's like that every day, it makes poor Agnes even worse.

Some of the men came home so damaged. I believe I might be glad that Alec went before Culloden.'

'You look exhausted, Bessie. Can you come out for some fresh air this morning?'

'Yes. I'll just nip downstairs and ask Mrs Cunningham to come up for an hour.'

Isabella looked over at Agnes. She was dressed and out of bed, but she rocked in her chair without looking up. Bessie had abandoned her plan to return to Rome. She said even the worst sister couldn't condemn Agnes to bear her grief alone.

Footsteps on the stairs didn't sound like Bessie. The door opened. The man standing in the doorway, with his arm round the waist of a blonde girl, was unmistakably Alec Cowan.

Agnes made a whimpering sound behind Isabella. Bessie appeared in the doorway and the boy turned around.

'Oh, sweet Lord,' she said.

The girl stepped to one side, as Agnes threw herself out of her chair and at Alec. He caught her in his arms.

Alec grinned sheepishly at Bessie, freeing one arm to pull her towards him. Tears flowed down Bessie's cheeks but she laughed too.

'Well, laddie, you don't feel like a ghost.'

'I'm so sorry,' he mumbled. 'I only heard lately that you thought me dead.'

'Well you better come in, and you'd better introduce this young lady.'

Alec's face transformed from shame to pride. 'This is Gracie, she's fae Falkirk and she's agreed tae be my wife.'

'Heavens lad, are you intent on killing me and your mother with shock?'

Isabella smiled at the happy scene. 'I'll leave you. You've a lot of catching up to do.'

Bessie looked over, she seemed to have forgotten that Issy

Jane Anderson

was standing there. 'Sorry, Isabella. Can I meet you later in the week?' Then she shook her head in happy disbelief.

* * *

Bessie went to visit Issy and Vee , she found them both in Issy's workshop. Vee jumped up to hug her.

'Bessie, I so happy to see you and with this smile on your face. Alec's return is unbelievable good news in the terrible year. You and Agnes must be so happy,' Vee said.

'You've no idea how happy and Agnes is transformed, she's like a different woman,' Bessie replied.

'We're both so pleased for you,' Isabella said and added her hug to Vittoria's.

'But how did Robbie come to think Alec was dead?' Vee asked.

'A mix up, I think,' Bessie replied. 'After the battle a whole gang of them descended on Falkirk. They'd had a long hard winter and were helping themselves to whatever they could find to eat and drink. In the beginning Alec was caught up with their mischief. But things turned nasty and he had to prevent some drunks attacking a girl. His Highland friends were set on going home, they'd had enough of fighting. Gracie, the girl he'd rescued, offered to hide him and so he stayed. When Alec confessed to us he'd deserted, he really thought we'd be angry with him.' Bessie laughed and shook her head at the thought.

'So he's been hiding in Falkirk all this time?' Isabella asked.

'Yes. He'd no idea he'd been reported dead.'

'It's like a miracle,' Vittoria said. 'Agnes think she lose son and she get back Alec, and now a daughter too.'

Bessie smiled, 'And more. Those two were cooped up in a

wee house for months. Gracie is certain she's with child. They'll marry early June, before she starts to show.'

'And is she happy about that? Her parents too?' Issy asked.

'Och, yes,' Bessie answered. 'They're young but so in love. Everyone's delighted.'

Both girls smiled broadly. Bessie detected a glance exchanged, the tiniest eye movement between them. Of course she knew how they felt about each other, but thought it better not to encourage any slip in their respectable façade. Lumisden's attack on Isabella was the kind of incident she prayed they could avoid in future, they daren't be complacent. She coughed to bring her thoughts back to the reason for her visit.

'So I was wondering, Issy, could you make me some jewellery to give Gracie as a wedding present?'

'Of course, I'd love to. What were you thinking?'

'One of your pearl necklaces and some earrings and might you do a silver locket like Vee's?'

Isabella grabbed a scrap of paper and a piece of charcoal. 'I'll design something especially for her, and do you want a pearl inside like Vee's?'

'Bessie, please let me do miniature as a gift!' Vee interrupted. 'I can do portraits of Alec and Gracie. I want paint a man with natural red hair, I've had enough of white wigs.'

Isabella showed Bessie the rough design she'd been sketching while they talked. It was similar to Vee's but with intertwined thistles. Vee had run to her studio for a box of pastels, and she also started to sketch. Watching them sitting side-by-side, fingers flying with creativity, made Bessie so proud of them both.

'That's beautiful, Issy. You should sell lockets in your shop.'

'I already do them to order but don't put them in the

window. My ordinary clients don't care that they're not stamped, but I don't want to annoy the Guild.'

'I doubt they'd be interested but you're right to be cautious,' Bessie replied. 'Now you'll have to excuse me, girls. I'm meeting Alec and Agnes in Newhaven. We're going to search for a home for this new family.'

'How exciting for him. I suppose your flat will be too small when the baby arrives,' Isabella said.

'There are plenty of flats with more people in them on our stair, but it's better if Alec is nearer his work,' Bessie replied. 'Agnes will move in with Alec and Gracie after the wedding and so we'll let the Edinburgh flat go when I return to Rome.'

Bessie looked for any reaction on the girls' faces. She was torn on many levels about her plan to leave and she did worry about them. Issy smiled at her, perhaps reading her expression. 'I'm glad you're able to go back as you always planned.'

'Mama will be so happy,' Vee added.

'So do I take it that you two plan to stay on in Edinburgh?' Bessie asked.

'We hope so,' Isabella answered, 'but we know it's not over yet. I hear the Duke of Cumberland is furious that the redcoats still haven't found Prince Charles's hiding place in the Highlands. Did you know there's a list of Jacobites being prepared? It's said those on it face jail or execution.'

Bessie nodded.

'Well we might both be on the list, I could find myself accused of spying again by the other side.'

Bessie saw Vittoria's rueful grimace. She knew Vee still felt guilty.

'We're hoping Sir Everard's influence will keep us off the list, but we'll not buy here until we're sure,' Isabella added.

'I should think he'll look out for you, Issy, but don't rely on it. First hint of trouble you must leave.'

Bessie kissed them goodbye. As she was leaving, she saw Issy put the locket back round Vee's neck. They exchanged one of those looks that caused Bessie to avert her eyes and close the door.

Chapter Fifty-Five

A lec helped Bessie out of the cart, they'd just returned from signing the lease for a house in Newhaven.

'I'll work hard, Auntie Bessie. I promise ye willnae have tae support us fer ever,' Alec said.

'You'll need to work hard to pay for this baby. I'm glad to be able to give you a head start,' Bessie replied.

Thought of a new baby made Bessie sad that she'd miss the birth, but November was too long to wait. She'd not be able to travel to Rome in the winter and she needed to get out of their way. Agnes's good humour might not last if she sensed Bessie getting too attached to this new baby.

She took her sister's arm to help her up their stairs, but Agnes shook it off. 'Look, oor Bessie, it's yer fancyman!' she shouted and cackled with laughter.

And there he was, standing at the close entrance with his arms folded over his broad chest.

'Joseph!'

'Bessie,' he replied with a huge smile.

'And are you going to tell me you were just passing?' she asked.

'In a manner of speaking,' he replied. 'We've spent the last four weeks searching for an Italian gentleman hiding in the west. We were given some leave on the Clyde, I thought I'd pay you a visit.'

'Well I'm glad to see you, Joseph, and you're lucky to catch me. I'm planning to return to Rome in a few weeks.'

He frowned and held out his elbow for her to take.

'Then take a turn round the town with me, Bessie, while I endeavour to change your mind.'

Agnes was still standing there, openly eavesdropping.

'Away you go in, Agnes. I'll see you later,' Bessie said.

'Or maybe no,' Agnes replied and Bessie heard her laughing as she walked up the stairs.

'Your sister seems to have cheered up,' Joseph remarked.

'Wait till I tell you all about it, Joseph. What a time we've had.'

Bessie told Joseph about Alec's story and Isabella's kidnap and rescue. He shook his head in disbelief.

'That Lumisden sounds like a terrible man. Poor Isabella has had more than her fair share of rogues,' he said.

'She has that. But what about you, Joseph? I want to hear about your adventures too.'

Joseph squeezed her arm in the crook of his own. A gesture now familiar. A comfort she'd hardly dared to dream of.

'Wild weather and wily Highlanders, that's been our story. The west coast has thousands of small coves and mountain hideaways. Some of the rebels have managed to sail away, but they think the Young Pretender's still in Scotland. The duke is said to be furious with the local people. I fear he'll take his temper out on them.'

'They fear that in Edinburgh too. Is it pretty on the west coast, Joseph? I've never been.'

'Real pretty. Some places are so remote they're only accessible by sea, but there's a lovely coastline not far from where we're berthed. Why don't you come back with me, Bessie? I've a full week of leave, let's spend it together.'

Bessie laughed.

'I've told you before I'm not the scandalous sort, Joseph. I can't go gadding about Scotland in the company of a man. What would people say?'

Joseph didn't laugh. He stopped walking and turned to her.

'Then marry me, Bessie. Let's make it our honeymoon.'

She stared in disbelief. 'Marry you?' she repeated stupidly.

His eyes crinkled, but in distress, he looked stricken.

'Sorry. I didn't mean to blurt it out. But the thought of you going so far away, Bessie. I can't bear to lose you again.'

Her heart was beating so fast. 'I'm afraid...'

He groaned and grabbed her arm again, setting off at a march.

'Don't say anymore, Bessie. I'm a fool. I love you so much, it makes an idiot of me. Of course you don't want to marry me.'

Bessie stopped dead in her tracks, forcing him to stop too.

'It's not that, Joseph.' She hesitated, dare she tell him? She dropped her voice to a whisper. 'I love you, Joseph, but I'm afraid. Afraid of losing you.'

A slow smile spread over his face, he took both her hands. Bessie was aware of people stopping to stare. They'd reached the gate to the Canongate Kirk, she loosened one of her hands and pulled him down the side of the church.

'Come in here, we can't have such a conversation on the street.'

The graveyard behind the church was green and quiet.

Issy's little village house was in the valley below and Calton Hill beyond it. Joseph took her hand to his lips and kissed it. Bessie felt she was looking down on herself from above, such a romantic scene couldn't be happening to her.

'Oh, Bessie. You've nothing to fear. You can depend on me. I promise.'

She shook her head. 'But you can't promise. You're at sea, in the way of danger all the time. When we thought we'd lost Alec it nearly killed me.'

His kind smile cut through her, how could love and pain be so tangled up together?

'But Bessie, he wasn't lost and it didn't kill you. Please. Take a risk on us. You'd like Nellie Grimes and my home is simple but honest.'

She shook her head, certain she didn't want that. 'No, Joseph. I can't. Sitting for years with your sister only to hear of your death. I'd end up feeling responsible for her too.'

He cocked his head to one side; she saw he understood. She squeezed his fingers. 'I promised I'd go back to Anna. I love my home and my work in Rome. Don't ask me to choose you over that.'

He sighed. 'I understand, and I'd hate to make you give up what you've worked for.'

He was quiet for a moment, his heavy eyebrows pulled together in thought. 'Would you marry me there, if I could save up enough to quit the sea?'

She hesitated, but only for one skip of her heart: 'I believe I would, Joseph Grimes!'

'Oh Bessie Nichol, I love thee!'

Then he kissed her. She'd never kissed a grown man before but it turned out to be blissful. He held her and kissed her again and again, until they parted on hearing someone's step on the gravel path.

'I'd better be getting back to Agnes, Joseph. Will you come and eat with us?'

'I'd love to.'

They linked arms again and began the climb back home.

'And what about this week, Bessie? Will you really send me back west alone? I want to make you mine. It might take me five years to save enough to quit the sea.'

She took a deep breath, realising at once that she knew the answer.

'In Edinburgh I need to be careful of sharp tongues. But I know no one in the west. Life is too precarious to risk waiting. I'll come with you, Joseph. You maybe need to hear my snoring before you commit.'

He whooped and kissed her once more and she cared not who saw it.

'I love you, Bessie Nichol,' he said.

'Not as much as I love you, Joseph Grimes,' she replied.

Chapter Fifty-Six

June 1746

I sabella was late rising. She'd slept badly and was stiff from dancing at Alec and Gracie's wedding. The wedding breakfast had been simple but Gracie's uncle had hosted it in his tavern and plentiful ale had loosened any strangeness between the families. Today she was expecting Bessie to come in to say goodbye. Bessie had hastened her departure because Captain Jones had given Joseph leave to join her in Portsmouth. Joseph would introduce Bessie to his sister before seeing her safely on a ship bound for Leghorn. If the meeting went well, they were hoping Nellie Grimes might be persuaded to join them in Rome when Joseph retired. Bessie had been tight-lipped about her holiday on the west coast but Agnes's elbowing and sniggering at the wedding threatened to expose Bessie's secret.

'Why don't you just tell people you're engaged, Bessie?' Issy had asked. 'It's the happiest news and everyone will be so pleased to hear it.'

'I'm too old to be engaged and it might be years till we can marry. This month is about celebrating young love, no one's interested in a quiet arrangement between two old fools.'

But her contented expression told Issy that she was as happy as Gracie and Alec.

Now Issy dreaded this last goodbye. She'd promised herself she'd not tell Bessie her current troubles. She was going to have to learn to deal with her own problems from now on. She opened the door hoping to see Vee return, instead she saw Bessie coming around the corner.

'Can I get you a drink of something?' Issy asked, hanging Bessie's cloak on the back of the door.

'No thank you and I'm sorry I can't stop for long. I got delayed up the road and the carriage leaves in thirty minutes.'

Issy shook her head in annoyance. 'I can't believe that Vee's not here. She knew you were coming and promised to be back.'

Bessie took her hand and pulled her to sit beside her.

'What's wrong, Issy?'

Isabella sighed, Bessie knew her too well to hide her feelings.

'I'm worried about Vee, she's being so secretive. She's been working on some painting and won't let me see. She even locks the studio door when she goes out.'

'Well I'm sure there's a good reason, Issy.'

'Vee's had a letter from Liotard. She didn't tell me but I think she left it lying on the table for me to find. He's in Germany and heading for Paris. He invited her to join him there.' Issy tightened her grip on Bessie's hand. 'Don't you see, that's where they'll all end up. Bella says that when the men can leave their hiding places they'll all go to France. I'm afraid Vee's painting something to take to Liotard.'

'I don't think Vittoria will leave you, Issy. Not after everything.'

Issy stood up, too agitated to sit.

'But I don't want her to stay out of a sense of obligation. I'm determined to live here, but I cannot be her captor,' Issy replied.

Bessie nodded. At that moment the kitchen door flew open and Vittoria burst in.

'Bessie! Oh my god, I thought I be late.'

She rushed over to hug Bessie and looked towards Issy. Vittoria's joyful smile made Issy's insides soften. It was a look she hadn't seen in weeks.

'And where have you been to make you so late?' Bessie asked sternly. 'Issy says you've been keeping secrets. You have to look after each other when I've gone, Vittoria. You have to promise me that.'

Vee nodded and came to put her arm around Issy's waist.

'I sorry, my Bella, and I know I promised no more secrets, but I was so afraid it might no work. Come I show you.'

Vee took a key from her pocket and opened her studio door. They both followed her inside. Two paintings stood on easels facing the wall. Vittoria turned them outwards. A grand looking man in a black coat and white cravat was next to a beautiful young woman in a pink silk dress.

'This James Baird and his pretty new bride. He asked Allan Ramsay to do him a painting of his second wife. She is much young and he is very besotted. Anyway, Ramsay no have time and referred the old man to me. Baird adored the painting and so did the pretty Dorothy. She begged him to commission me for his own portrait. He delighted to have no young man around his lovely wife and now is very happy with these results. I take them tomorrow and he pay me handsomely.'

Issy hugged Vee. 'They're marvellous paintings. Congratulations!'

Vittoria smiled and shrugged. 'Honestly he is huge idiot and I prefer to paint the honest baker, but this man is lawyer and Protestant. He invite me to the portrait unveiling in front of his friends tomorrow. I think I make more business from this.'

Vee hugged her again.

'So you won't join Liotard in Paris?' Issy asked.

'Of course no!' Vee sounded outraged. 'My home is here, I never leave you.'

Bessie smiled and stretched out her arms.

'Now I can leave without a heavy heart. Come and hug me both of you.'

Bessie embraced them and when they parted they all had tears in their eyes.

'No crying now, girls, or you'll set me off and I'll frighten the other coach passengers.'

'I sorry you go, Bessie, but happy you will be with Mama. You must tell her how well we do here together and no need worry.'

Despite Bessie's plea, tears ran down Issy's face. The relief of Vee's promise was mixed with her sorrow at the parting.

'You mean everything to me, Bessie. I'm going to miss you so much.'

'Oh you'll be too busy for that,' Bessie said, 'especially as I expect a letter every few days. And, Vee, when that baby arrives I want a painting and you make sure it's a good one.' Bessie stood up. 'I'm off now, girls.'

'Give our regards to Joseph,' Issy called.

Isabella secured the door latch. When she felt Vee's lips on her neck, she smiled and turned the key in the lock.

'Now, my Bella, I say we go upstairs,' Vee whispered in her ear. 'I need to rest, the Scottish dancing make my legs hurt.'

Issy turned into her embrace. 'Best idea you've had in weeks,' she replied.

The gorse blazed yellow on the hill beyond the bedroom window. They'd cut down the tree's highest branches but Issy would take no risks in the outside world. She pulled the curtains and turned smiling back to her reckless love.

Afterword

If you enjoyed this book I would be hugely grateful if you could write a review. Thank you!

https://amzn.to/3rNXCD1

Author's Note

This novel is a work of fiction. Some of the characters, places and events are inspired by historical figures, locations and incidents. Any resemblance to any real persons, living or dead, is purely coincidental.

Those characters who really existed, include the members of the royal Stuart family and some major players amongst the Scottish Jacobites. Sir Everard Fawkener was the British Ambassador to Turkey and he was friends with the Swiss artist Jeanne-Étienne Liotard. I later discovered in one of those literary coincidences, that he did indeed become part of the infamous Duke of Cumberland's entourage after he left Constantinople.

However, while I have tried to weave my tale around the real events and dates of the 1745 Jacobite Rebellion, this story and all its interactions are entirely fabricated.

This novel was inspired by a Jean-Étienne Liotard painting, sometimes called *The Girl with a Book*. You can see the image and discover the story behind the inspiration on my website:https://jane-anderson.co.uk/

Acknowledgments

Writing has consumed my life for years, and the support of my family has been absolutely crucial. Thank you for your patience and love, Mark, Louise, Calum and Helen.

Writing is tough. If you are thinking of taking it up, I would encourage you to join a writing group. You need writer friends who will tell you the truth but also have your back when things go wrong.

Angela Jackson was the first person who told me I could write. I joined her writing group over ten years ago. She remains a mentor and a precious friend. I'm so grateful. So many different writing group colleagues have been part of this journey that I'd be afraid to miss someone out, but I'd like to thank you all.

My current writing group of Alison Belsham, Hannah Kelly and Kristin Pedroja are like my family and I love them.

I'm lucky and grateful to have Sara Sheridan as my historical fiction mentor.

Thank you to The Romantic Novelist Association, particularly those who run the New Writer Scheme. Also, the RNA Facebook Indie Chapter, whose advice has been invaluable this year.

Finally, thanks to Helen Baggott for her eagle-eyed editing and Rachel Lawston for her beautiful cover.

Printed in Great Britain
by Amazon

35994238R00229